SWIFT VENGEANCE

SWIFT VENGEANCE

T. Jefferson Parker

G. P. PUTNAM'S SONS

NEW YORK

PUTNAM

G. P. PUTNAM'S SONS
Publishers Since 1838
An imprint of Penguin Random House LLC
375 Hudson Street
New York, New York 10014

Copyright © 2018 by T. Jefferson Parker

Library of Congress Cataloging-in-Publication Data

Names: Parker, T. Jefferson, author.
Title: Swift vengeance / T. Jefferson Parker.
Description: New York : G. P. Putnam's Sons [2018]
Identifiers: LCCN 2017046163 | ISBN 9780735212695 (hardcover) |
ISBN 9780735212718 (ebook)
Subjects: | GSAFD: Suspense fiction. | Mystery fiction.
Classification: LCC PS3566.A6863 S95 2018 | DDC 813/.54—dc23
LC record available at https://lccn.loc.gov/2017046163

Printed in the United States of America
1   3   5   7   9   10   8   6   4   2

BOOK DESIGN BY LUCIA BERNARD

For Rita

SWIFT VENGEANCE

1

THE FIRST TIME I saw Lindsey Rakes she was burning down the high-stakes room in the Pala Casino north of San Diego. Roulette, and she could do no wrong. Big woman, big attitude. Daughter of a Fort Worth–area Ford dealer—"Hit Your Brakes for Rakes!"—and a high school chemistry teacher, I found out later.

Lindsey had drawn a crowd that night. Not difficult, in her lacy dress and leather ankle boots. And all that sleek, dark hair. She looked like some exotic life form, dropped from above into the chain-smoking slot-jockeys and the glum blackjack casualties. When the wheel stopped on another winner, her throaty roar blasted through the room: *Baby, baby, BABY!* Towers of chips rising from the table in front of her. Mostly hundreds and fifties. Just enough twenties to tip the cocktail waitresses, who kept the drinks coming. I had work to do, so I didn't witness her crash.

Now, almost two and a half years later, Lindsey sat at a long wooden picnic table under a palapa behind my house. She looked not very much like that booze-fueled gambler who had moved onto my property the day after we'd met in the casino. Now she looked defeated and afraid. She wore a faded denim blouse and her hair was lumped into a ponytail that rode side-saddle on her shoulder.

I held the sheet of paper flush against the tabletop, a fingertip at diagonal corners, and read it out loud for a second time.

> *Dear Lt. Rakes,*
>
> *I want to decapitate you with my knife, but I will use anything necessary to cause you death.*
> *Until then, fear everything you see and everything you hear and dream. This terror is personal, as you are beginning to understand. Vengeance is justice. The thunder is coming for you.*
>
> *Sincerely,*
> *Caliphornia*

Caliphornia.

One short moment ago, when I'd first read this note, I'd felt a tingle in the scar above my left eye. I earned that scar in my first and last pro fight. Its moods have become a kind of early-warning system for danger ahead: use caution. Now it tingled again.

The death threat was handwritten in graceful cursive script that looked like a combination of English longhand and Arabic calligraphy. The letters slanted neither forward nor back but stood up straight. A calligraphic pen had been used to vary the thicknesses of line and curve. The loops were large and symmetrical. The lead-ins and tails of each word were thick, straight, and perfectly horizontal, as if traced over invisible guidelines. They began and ended in pointed, up-curved flourishes, like candle flames. The letter had arrived one day ago, on Saturday, December 8, in Lindsey's post office box in Las Vegas.

She set the envelope beside the letter. On the envelope were printed her name and her Las Vegas PO Box number. It was postmarked Wednesday, December 5, in San Diego, California. It had a Batman stamp and a return address that Lindsey had found to be World Pizza in Ocean Beach.

"Lindsey, this letter should be on an FBI light table, not on a PI's picnic table."

"Is it real? Do you believe it?"

"It's real and I believe it. You've got to take this to the FBI. The agents are trained to deal with this kind of thing."

"You know any of them?"

"One. Kind of."

A failed smile. "I'd sure appreciate it if you'd take this letter to them. I can't face law enforcement right now."

I tried to make sense of this request. It was strange and irrational that I was sitting here with a rattled young woman who had been threatened with death by a murderer-terrorist-psychopath-crackpot calling himself/herself Caliphornia, and who was now refusing to talk with the law. Strange and irrational that Lindsey would come to me first.

"Because of your son," I said.

Lindsey pulled off her sunglasses and tried to stare me down. Her temper is rarely distant. "Of course, *my son*. I've filed another request with the court for a custody amendment. You can only do that every eighteen months. I've been living clean as a Girl Scout, Roland. I'm teaching math at a private school, hitting the gym, no booze or dice. But Johnny's growing up without me. He's the whole reason I left here and moved back to Las Vegas. And if the court gets wind of this death threat, my custody petition gets red-flagged. The Bureau would poke around, right, talk to my employers. Investigate *me*. Right? Say good-bye to shared custody."

She was correct on those counts. I wondered about her Girl Scout claim because I'm suspicious by nature and profession.

"You saved me once, Roland, and I'm hoping you can do it again."

She slid her sunglasses back on.

Three years ago, Lindsey Rakes—then Lindsey Goff—had been flying Reaper drones out of Creech Air Force Base north of Las Vegas. She was the sensor operator. Or, as the drone flyers call them, simply a "sensor." Her missions as a sensor were often top secret and CIA-directed. Some were surveillance, some were kill-list strikes. Syria, Iraq, Yemen, Somalia, Sudan. Her flight crew called themselves the Headhunters. *We flagged some bad guys,* she had told me more than once.

Then, at the end of her contract in 2015, she quit the USAF against the wishes of her superiors. Experienced drone operators were in high demand at that time; the Air Force couldn't train them fast enough to keep up.

After six months as a civilian she'd fled to California, landed in the Pala Casino, and ended up renting a place here on my property. Back then, as we began to know and trust each other, she'd told me about her life at Creech: the six-day workweeks, the twelve-hour days, the strange psychosis brought on by sitting in an air-conditioned trailer in the desert and flying combat missions seventy-five hundred miles away. Then heading off-base at sunrise to pick up something for breakfast and maybe some vodka, too, on her way home to her husband, Brandon, and their young son, John. Little John. The light and anchor of her life. But not quite enough of an anchor.

Because some days, Lindsey had confessed, she'd get off work too nerve-shot and sickened to even look at her own son. And Brandon was always angry at her anyway. So instead of going home she'd blast off in her black Mustang GT, a wedding gift from her father, Lewis—"Hit Your Brakes for Rakes"—and race downtown to gamble hard, drink harder, and forget the things she'd seen and done in that cramped little trailer.

Until Brandon took Little John to a new home across town and filed divorce papers and a complaint of child neglect against her.

"How bitter was it?" I asked.

Behind the dark lenses, Lindsey studied me. "Very."

"And how is Brandon Goff's anger level these days, with your new move for joint custody?"

"No," she said. "Brandon wouldn't threaten me like this. He would do it clearly. Not hide behind a cryptic name and a threat."

Lindsey would know her ex well enough to judge his capacity for murder. Or would she? I'd seen enough people fooled by their spouses to always leave a door ajar.

I looked out at the gray December sky, the breeze-burred surface of the pond, the cattails wavering. *Fall,* I thought. The big hush. The time to exhale. Always makes me feel the speed of life. I tried to warm up to the idea of cutting off the head of a living human being with a knife. Thought of videos of fear-blanched men in orange jumpsuits forced to kneel in the dirt. Told myself that Christmas was coming soon, birth of Jesus and forgiveness of sin, peace on earth, joy to the world.

"Roland? I'm afraid. I've been to war but my life was never at stake. Weird, isn't it? But this has gotten to me. I have that Smith nine and know how to use it. I'd feel safe if I could land here for a while. This Caliphornia won't know where I am."

Lindsey and I had shot cans off rocks way out on the property here a few times, against a hillock, so the bullets wouldn't fly. She was pretty good against a can. When the target is human, of course, nerves change everything.

More important, I couldn't be sure that this so-called Caliphornia wouldn't find her here.

"You're in the public record of having lived here once," I said.

"Nobody quoted me."

"But the *Union-Tribune* named you as a tenant."

"One time was all. My name in the paper, *once*. And I never gave out this address when I was living here. Nobody. This was my secret hideout. Where you helped me put myself back together. Sort of back together." She wrung her thick ponytail, looking down at the table.

I remembered that night in the Pala Casino, later, when Lindsey crashed onto the stool next to me in one of those thinly peopled, regret-reeking bars found in casinos around the world. She looked like something the devil would eat for breakfast. Or had eaten.

"Welp," she'd said, curling a long finger at the bartender. "Lost it all."

"Maybe you should have stopped."

She had looked at me, eyes skeptical and held steady by force of will. "I'm Lindsey Rakes. You're obviously Saint Somebody. So the least you could say to someone who's just lost her last dollar is, 'There but for the grace of God go I.' Or 'I go.' Or however you saints say it."

After Lindsey Rakes had finished her drink I paid for it, got up, and offered to get her a casino hotel room, a taxi, or a ride home. House security was circling. She took option C. Out Highway 76 she told me she didn't have a home at *precisely* this minute, except for her Mustang, which, after a night in the backseat, made a woman her size feel like she'd been sawed in half by a bad magician.

"I didn't just lose the money," she had told me. "I've lost my son, my husband, my home, too. I can do without any of it except my son. John. Six years, seven months, and one day old. Not being able to see him is like living in a world where the sun won't rise. What did y'all say your name was?"

I hadn't, so I did.

"And how did you do at the tables tonight, Rolando?"

In fact, I hadn't gambled much at all. I'd come to the casino to observe a man suspected of embezzlement by his friend and business partner. They were a two-partner practice specializing in family law. I came to discover that the man who had hired me was in fact the embezzler, and the friend/partner he had "suspected" of the crime—and who had lost about five thousand dollars that night by my loose count—was an addicted gambler but a reasonably honest law partner.

I wasn't thrilled being stuck with a drunk hard-luck case who had nowhere to go, but I did what I thought was right. I usually do. It's a blessing and a curse.

"I can take you back to the casino hotel or put you up for the night," I had told her. "There's an empty casita on my property and it locks."

"Empty casita?"

"Furnished. I rent them out."

She was leaning back against the door of my pickup truck. The hills around us were dark. In the faint moon-and-dashboard glow I could see the pale shape of her face and the glint in her eyes as she deliberated. "Kinda Norman Batesy."

"Pretty much."

"You're big and not real pretty, but you don't look mean enough to worry about."

"It's the little pretty ones you have to watch."

"Marine?"

"Once upon a time."

"I was Air Force. Lieutenant Lindsey Rakes. I hate being this drunk."

I didn't have anything useful to say about Lieutenant Lindsey Rakes's drunkenness or hatred thereof. As a man who has overdone certain things in his life, I know that the world won't change, but you can. Over the six months she lived in my casita, I saw her battle the booze and the gambling and the Clark County Superior Court, which refused to allow Lindsey to visit her son more than one Saturday per month in a county facility adjacent to the jail. Lindsey had done okay with all that. Just barely okay.

Now, two and a half years since I'd first met her, it felt right but also surreal to be making her the same offer again. You could say full circle, but nothing in life is round. "Your old casita is taken, but three and four are vacant."

"I've missed the Irregulars," she said.

I call my tenants the Irregulars because they tend to be non-regulation human beings. And a changing cast.

"And I remember casita three was always vacant," she said.

"For times like this."

"I can't pay you for protection, Roland. But I can make the rent."

"Don't worry about my time until we put a stop to this."

I set my phone on the table, searched "Caliphornia," got what I expected:

A picture of Governor Jerry Brown, wearing a mocked-up jeweled turban, "declaring himself caliph and establishing Sharia law in California." He was actually signing AB 2845, designed to shield students from bullying in public schools.

And:

Caliphornia, a self-published futuristic suspense novel about an Arab Caliphate and runaway global warming.

"Caliphornia," a song by Box O'Clox.

Barenakedislam.com, a website whose motto is "It isn't Islamaphobia when they really ARE trying to kill you."

Counter-jihad T-shirts with various anti-Muslim messages and images.

Such as Koran-Wipes toilet paper made from 100 percent recycled Korans.

Such as Hillary in a hijab.

Etc.

A fool's parade on the Internet.

Rage and volume turned up high.

Made me wonder how America was going to make it through the next week.

I shook my head, closed it all down. Looked up to find Lindsey watching me. "You still have *Hall Pass Two*?"

"You bet I do." My Cessna 182, to be more accurate. One of the older ones with the Lycoming engine and the bass roar of a beast when you punch it down the runway. I fly it for business and pleasure. There is a story behind it.

"And have you been really busy—privately investigating?"

"Just one open case right now," I said.

"Something exciting?"

"Oxley," I said, pointing to the poster that was stapled to one of the thick palm trunks that support the palapa. The poster featured a color photo of a hefty gray-striped cat. He looked peaceful. The photo was cropped so the cat seemed to sprawl in the middle of the flyer, as if lying on a cushion. LOST CAT was the headline. The surrounding text explained that Oxley was missing from his Fallbrook home as of a week ago, that he was much loved, and that his owner—Tammy Bellamy— was heartbroken. Oxley had "hypnotic green eyes" and weighed twenty-two pounds. Tammy had given me a stack of the posters, all professionally printed on very heavy and expensive card-stock, to aid my search and post on my travels. Cats could go far, she'd explained. By the time I got my wanted posters, there were already scores of them put up in and around Fallbrook—on power poles, roadside oak trees, stop signs and traffic light stanchions, storefronts, shop windows, walls and fences. I'd stapled this one to the palapa so the Irregulars could keep their eyes out.

"Tammy is elderly," I said. "And she can't actually pay me. Except in homemade jam."

"I'll bet the coyotes would help her find that cat," said Lindsey.

I nodded, fearing that the cat had already been killed and eaten. Fallbrook was brimming with coyotes. If they hadn't gotten him, then a car probably had. On the other hand, cats are great survivors, so maybe Oxley had found shelter in one of our many avocado or citrus groves, or on some relatively secure, fenced property. Or maybe someone had taken him in and knew nothing of Tammy Bellamy's emotional plea for help.

I looked at Lindsey's black Mustang, parked up by the main house. The Las Vegas sun had not been kind to it. It still had the child's seat in back. When I'd first heard of Lindsey's child-custody quest, the safety seat had seemed to me more a symbol of a goal than a necessity. But she was closer to that goal now, apparently. I refolded the letter, carefully placed it in its envelope, and set it on the table.

"Lindsey, has anything unusual happened to you lately? Unsolicited visits? Weird phone calls or hang-ups? Anything out of pattern in the people you work or socialize with? Neighbors, even."

She shook her head, but indecisively. So maybe I'd brushed up against something. To me, Lindsey had never been a full-disclosure person. There was always more, something else, another layer.

"Anything, Lindsey," I said. "Even the great PI Roland Ford needs help against a stalker-terrorist with beheading on his mind."

She set her elbows on the rough old table, raised and joined her fingers, nodded. She hadn't needed to think too hard. "Well."

2

"TWO AND A HALF weeks ago I went out with a guy," Lindsey said. "First time. I'd met him a little over a year ago, through work. A widower, like you. He was the father of one of my new fall students. Nice guy, and nice looking. Almost formal, but just enough off-center to make me smile. Well groomed and well off. Gave me his full attention. He reminded me of someone, but I didn't know who. I started getting this funny feeling when we were in the same room. I liked it. He's a landscape architect. Designs golf courses all over the world. Shows horses for fun."

"The downside?"

She watched me through her dark glasses.

"He's Saudi by birth," said Lindsey. "His parents both came here on student visas in '78. Married very young. Rasha Samara. Born in Riyadh after they had graduated and returned home. He went to Saudi schools until he was six, then came here with his parents. Became a naturalized U.S. citizen. His extended family lives in Saudi Arabia. Of course."

I thought about that.

"Roland, I spent almost a year learning how to kill violent jihadists in the Middle East, and another year and a half doing it. So when I met this guy, I didn't know if it was morally desirable—or even possible—for me to have any kind of relationship with him. Muslims aren't Christians and vice versa. But I also know that people of those two faiths can get along fine. On account of something that happened to me and I experienced firsthand."

She took off her sunglasses again and leveled her chocolate-brown eyes on me. "I've never told you this, but my mother is an Indian Muslim. Shia. Dad's a Methodist. They've been married for thirty-eight years and they've never said an unkind word to each other in my presence. Silences, yes. They met at Rice in Houston. Her English was very English from school in Delhi, but she took the time to learn to say 'y'all' perfectly. Practiced it. She became the most Texan Indian you can imagine. Loves her Cowboys. Loves her Longhorns. Loves her dancing and her turquoise and her country music. Loves Dad and his Fords. Still quietly observes the Muslim holy days, too, and she prays and believes and fasts. Observant but not devout. Hasn't worn a headscarf since the day she was engaged, except to mosque a few times a year. Used to tell me Christmas was more fun than Ramadan but Ramadan left her feeling closer to God. So with Rasha I thought, *Okay. You can look back at him.* I saw some of Mom in there. And I thought he might be solid, Roland. So when he asked me if I would like to ride horses I said yes."

I'd always been taken by Lindsey's dark eyes and lustrous hair, her striking facial structure. "So that's where you got your good looks."

"Mom's an Indian goddess with a Texas drawl."

"I'd say I'm happy for you meeting Rasha Samara, Lindsey, but I get the feeling there's more to this story."

"Oh yeah. Isn't there always? He lives outside of Las Vegas, a swanky development called Latigo. Big custom houses, pools and clubhouse, tennis courts, golf course, and landing strip. Stables and livery. And of course equestrian trails so you can ride just about anywhere you want. Guys in quads with trash cans and shovels to keep up with the horse poop. You can take the trails right out to the foothills. He's got Arabians, of course. Mares. Very nimble. I grew up on larger mounts, so I wasn't comfortable at first. Got over that pretty quick. We brought them to a gallop, then gave them a long cool-down. Watered them, then sat on red rocks and had salami and cheese and wine and watched the sunset. It was the Wednesday before Thanksgiving. We talked like you do when you don't know the person but you like them—respectfully and not too deep because you don't know what's there. He seemed honest and gracious and he was very much interested in me and the world around him. Not just himself. And that was about it. The Monday after the holiday he came by my school after class and asked me out again. Another ride. I declined. Two days later I got a nice thank-you card from him, with a pen-and-ink sketch on the front that he'd done. Some nice words inside."

"Why no second date?"

A pause from Lindsey. Then, "I'd thought about him a lot. But I told him I wasn't sure I wanted to take things any further. That I would call him when I was ready. I didn't tell him this, but I liked him and thought that I could go further with him. That thrilled me. Scared me. And I had John to think of, and my petition before the court, and what complications might ensue if Rasha became party to that. He was hurt but . . . still gracious."

Lindsey sighed and worked her sunglasses back on. "But then I was thinking about seeing him again. I turned that idea over and over. Changed my mind every hour or so. Felt like such a schoolgirl."

She brought her purse close and pulled out a small square envelope addressed to her PO Box in Las Vegas. Postmarked Las Vegas, Monday, November 26. It was heavy for its size, and I had to worry the card out a little at a time. When I finally righted it I looked down at a skilled ink drawing of two horses cantering along together, heads high, proud. No ground, no background. Sky horses. Arabians, with their short backs and wedge-shaped heads. They were done in just a few lines and would have seemed casual and dashed off if not for the attitudes that the two animals displayed.

"His thank-you card," she said.

> *Dear Lindsey Rakes,*
>
> *Thank you so much for your time. I've never seen a more beautiful desert sunset and I hope you enjoyed those moments of splendor as much as I. The horses, of course, are insisting that they be taken out again. I understand your reluctance to consider a relationship. I have similar doubts. Not about you, in any way. But about myself. May God bless you in your life.*
>
> *Sincerely,*
> *Rasha*

The note looked computer-printed, a common Roman font, ten-point, maybe.

But *Rasha* was signed by hand and looked a lot like the writing in the death threat. It jumped at me. Not quite the same straight up-and-down posture, but close. Graceful, full-bodied letters. Similar calligraphic flourishes—the varying thickness of line, the graceful lead-ins and tails. I unfolded the death threat and held the thank-you card beside it. Lined up *Rasha* and *Rakes*. A similar marriage of English and Arabic.

Lindsey was watching me closely. "Ten days later, when I got the threat and compared the signatures, I completely freaked out."

"This makes me unhappy," I said.

"I have to tell you something else. When Rasha and I sat up on the big red rocks and had our wine and cheese, he cut that cheese with a sharp-looking folding knife. Very deftly. Then he served the wine in two silver goblets with calligraphic engraving on them. They were in his saddlebag with the food and wine, wrapped in white napkins. They looked old. Maybe passed down through his family. Nice. When I got the threat letter, the writing on those goblets rushed into my mind, and the way he used the knife. And rushed in again when I got this note from Rasha. Roland, I *get* people. I know right from wrong and good from evil. So if Rasha wrote that threat, I'm the most wrong-assed I've ever been about anybody in my life. But still . . ."

I let my vision track back and forth between the two *R*'s. Let the letters blur, then squinted them back into focus. Subtle differences, but my first and persistent reaction was: same writer.

"Have you communicated with him since you got the threat?"

"Hell no. Where are you going to start, Roland?"

"Where you probably should have."

"You know a local FBI agent?" she asked.

"We worked the federal counterterror task force together. Before I went private."

San Diego FBI special agent Joan Taucher would curse me—a former San Diego County sheriff's deputy who should definitely know better—for contaminating the letter and the thank-you card. But Lindsey had beaten me to most of it. The contamination, that is.

More important, Special Agent Taucher would want to interview Lindsey. Lindsey could refuse, up to a point. That's why she'd come to me. And Taucher would briefly tolerate me—as a conduit. But I could run interference between Lindsey and the feds for only so long, and I'd never known Joan Taucher to show much patience.

If I had won any leverage at all with Joan Taucher, it was knowing that she was a woman possessed.

And that Lindsey might be holding a piece of what possessed her.

"Brandon Goff know about Rasha?"

"No. Roland, am I just one giant fuckup?"

"You're not giant at all."

She set her hands over mine and looked out at the spangled pond.

3

SPECIAL AGENT JOAN TAUCHER had an athlete's build, lithe but solid. Short white hair, bangs to her eyebrows. Some years ago, I'd seen an article and pictures of her in an amateur MMA fight. She looked lean, muscle-plated, and lethal. A winning record. She'd filled out some since then. Whether wearing her fighting garb or a trim gray suit like she did today, her facial expression remained constant: humorless and unconvinced.

Her shake was very firm and her hand notably cold, as I remembered. "Nice to see you again, Joan."

"Of course it isn't. That was quite a shootout on your property up in Fallbrook last year. Helicopters and escaped mental patients and everything."

"One helicopter and one patient," I said.

"Made you famous again for another day or two. You do have a way of getting into the news."

More than I like. A long story, that—the helicopter and who was flying it and why—and Taucher of course knew most of it. What she didn't know was how close her own federal government had come to killing innocent people in my very home. No one, except those of us who were there that day, really knows that ugly truth. Sometimes the truth has to step aside so life can go barreling along.

"Do you miss the MMA fighting?" I asked.

"No. Even then I was too old for that nonsense. It was supposed to be fun, anyway. You boxed, right?"

"One pro fight a long time ago."

"One. Well."

"It taught me the value of survival." I'll always remember looking up at that ref and those lights and realizing I could beat the count, get up and keep fighting, and maybe find a way to win. Or I could stay where I was and live to fight another day.

She drummed her fingertips on her desktop. It was glass-covered and pin-neat. Taucher had light brown eyes and went heavy on the makeup. Always heavy on the makeup, I remembered. Just a hint of anger in those eyes now. "So what's this about a death threat against someone you know?"

"These are copies," I said, setting the handwritten threat and the typewritten envelope on her desk. I'd made them in my office just two hours earlier, along with copies of the thank-you card and envelope. I'd also printed out a four-year-old article and picture of Rasha Samara from the *Las Vegas Sun* newspaper.

Taucher's Joint Terrorism Task Force office was a sixth-floor corner in an older downtown building, formerly a bank. Good views west and south—the Embarcadero, cruise ships at dock, the bow of the USS *Midway* jutting into the harbor from behind a row of restaurants.

While she studied the photocopied death threat, I studied her office walls. Every single square inch had a face on it. Floor to ceiling, left to right. Part of the ceiling, too. I figured that was where the new ones went. I could barely spot the doorknob and light switches. The pictures were mostly of Middle Eastern men and a few women, most of them dark, young, and unsmiling. Most in Western clothing, many in varying Middle Eastern attire—Arabian, Persian, Turk. Scores of them. A clear push-pin positioned top-center in each. Curled at the edges. Some wallet-sized, some larger. Some were police booking mugs. Others taken inside homes. Some had been shot outside, with law enforcement vehicles in the backgrounds. Most were stills extracted from video, grainy and vague. Not just scores of them, I thought, turning around to see the back side of Taucher's office door plastered with more. Hundreds.

"Who is Lieutenant Lindsey Rakes and how did you get this?"

"She's a friend and former tenant. She lives in Las Vegas now. She overnighted it to me."

A skeptical consideration. Taucher had no doubt noted the postmark, estimated the day of arrival, and come up with barely enough time for an overnight delivery to me. I skeptically considered her in return.

"Is Rakes law enforcement?" she asked.

"Former lieutenant, U.S. Air Force. She flew drone missions out of Creech. She operated the sensors." Joan Taucher's eyes locked on to mine as if acquiring a target. I told her what years Lindsey had flown, and what little I knew about her missions.

She sat back and stared at me for a long beat. "That makes this threat more than just interesting."

"I thought so, too."

"I take it very seriously," she said. "Even if it runs contrary to the current terror model. No group affiliation. No political message—jihadi or other. In fact, the opposite—he says *personal*. The letter claims no credit and is not intended for the public. It wasn't Tweeted, Facebooked, Snapped, or posted on any social or media network I watch—and I watch them like a hawk. Instead, this threat was sent discreetly to its target. Privately. Almost intimately. Islamic State *has* threatened specific former U.S. military personnel with death. Of course they have. However, this letter was composed by an English speaker—very rare for foreign terrorists. And it was handwritten by someone with knowledge of Arabic-style calligraphy—a relatively unusual skill in the U.S. But if you put those last two elements together, you come up with *Caliphornia*. As in Californian. As in *caliphate*. As in terror. As in our worst nightmare—homegrown actors with outside sponsors. We call them homegrown violent extremists, HVEs."

"He says vengeance."

"Right," said Taucher. "So what did she do to this guy?"

I liked the way Joan Taucher's mind was working. She was an original member of the San Diego FBI's Joint Terrorism Task Force. That meant approximately six federal, six state, and thirty-seven local bureaus, departments, agencies, patrols, authorities, commissions, centers, and offices dedicated to counterterrorism in San Diego. Depending on how you count. And, depending on who you talk to, the combined might of the JTTF is either a security dream team or another expensive, inefficient, self-perpetuating federal bureaucracy. Its finest moments— the JTTF is quick to note—are ones that we citizens never hear about. Which of course makes citizens like me wonder how many and how fine these moments really are.

I'd first met Joan in 2010, when I was an SD sheriff's deputy assigned to the—get this—Law Enforcement Coordination Center (LECC), which, in tandem with the sheriff's Regional Terrorism Threat Assessment Center (RTTAC), comprises the Department of Homeland Security (DHS) "Fusion Center," which is "co-located" with the FBI/JTTF, though subservient to it. It's complicated only if you try to figure out who does what. Or if you wonder how long it must take for a nice fat piece of intel to get from one end of this acronym-gorged python to the other.

Joan and I had worked as part of that team but never closely. My job was to go into the mosques and Muslim centers, poking around for sympathetic eyes and ears. I soon learned that my JTTF supervisor, Taucher, had been a freshman FBI agent here in 2001, when the towers fell. And though that event had left its scar on all Americans, it had—according to law enforcement rumor and legend—cut with particular depth into yearling agent Joan Taucher. Stories and gossip flew, not all of them kind.

"I need to see Lindsey Rakes immediately," she said.

"She doesn't want to be interviewed."

"Would she rather be decapitated?"

"She asked me to assess the threat," I said. "That's your world, so I came to you."

"Where is she?"

"A motel in the Las Vegas area. She didn't tell me which one."

"Tell her I need to see her immediately," said Joan. "If she won't submit to an interview I'll get a subpoena and we'll make her talk. I will not negotiate. I mean, really, Roland—why doesn't she want to talk to us? She's obviously scared or she wouldn't have gone to you. She sure as hell ought to be. Somebody put some time and skill into this threat."

"She's a young mother," I said. "Petitioning the court for shared custody of her son. He's nine. She's had some personal issues and she's resolving them. She's afraid that if the death threat came to light, she would be putting her case in jeopardy."

"Tell Soccer Mom she'll be a better mother with her head attached."

"She's willing to talk to you by phone."

"Do you know the ex?"

"Not yet."

Taucher jotted down his name, then shoved herself away from the desk, hard. Rolled backward all the way to the window, reached over her head without looking, and yanked a dart from the dartboard hanging behind her. She reversed the missile with two fingers and flung it hissing past me, flat as an arrow. I heard it hit.

"I can get a subpoena *and* make enough noise to get her blown right out of that courtroom," she said.

"We all know that, Joan."

I turned. She had skewered a young man with a head of bushy black hair and a two-day growth of beard. When I looked again at Taucher, she had glided back to her desk and was staring at the threat letter.

"I'm asking you a favor, Joan. To keep Lindsey out of this for a few days, if you can."

She glanced up at me, then went back to the letter. I could not see the special agent's wheels turning. But I did know that Joan Taucher carried a very large and heavy cross on behalf of the San Diego FBI, which had failed to question two of the 9/11 hijackers who were living, worshiping, trying to take flying lessons, and visiting strip clubs in San Diego, almost right up until the time they boarded Flight 77 out of Dulles. The CIA was partially to blame. Not only that, but Taucher's bureau had also failed to act on the violent encouragement issued by San Diego imam Anwar al-Waliki, just prior to 9/11, from a mosque not ten miles from where we now sat. Al-Waliki was an American-born radical Muslim who had been spewing anti-American venom for years. As I mentioned, Taucher had been a yearling agent in 2001. Twenty-four years old, assigned to San Diego.

Later, during my year and a half working with the JTTF, I had never gotten to know her well. But I continued to hear things—namely, that

Joan Taucher had gone from dedicated to "obsessive" in her quest to prevent another terrorist from so much as drawing a breath in San Diego. That she played loose with the rules. That she was rude, punitive, and secretive. That MMA fit her aggression and meanness perfectly.

So, yes, I was asking a favor of Joan Taucher, but I had already done one for her.

"Lindsey did some quick fact-checking," I said. "And the return address on the envelope is World Pizza in Ocean Beach. That's why I brought this evidence to you."

"Rather than where?"

"Rather than to Las Vegas, where Lindsey resides."

Instant ice age. "This is mine, kind sir. A San Diego postmark makes it mine. World Pizza makes it mine. It's still Nine-Eleven here in San Diego, and that makes it *mine.*"

Taucher had a point. A good one. The al-Qaeda 9/11 cell had worked much too damned well here in San Diego. San Diego had always billed itself as America's Finest City. And there was some truth to it. It was pretty to look at, and the weather was always good, and there were beaches and mountains and deserts and farms and ranches and nice big freeways to get you around. Not too many people and not too few. We got along, more or less. Good parks. Good music and theater. Good food, locally grown.

And *power.* Naval Base San Diego, the Pacific Fleet, Camp Pendleton, Miramar Air Station. Ships and jets and men and women in uniform everywhere you looked. Plus the thousands of draftsmen and engineers and technicians and contract specialists who kept it all humming along. We liked having them, those men and women, those huge warships and roaring fighter jets. And don't forget the satellites orbiting high above it all, and the bristling antennas on the local mountaintops and all the SIGINT they harvested and stored by the second. All that, and we felt very safe. Who wouldn't?

So we lived and let live. Ours was a sunny blend of tolerance and self-absorption that allowed diverse peoples with diverse ideas to live and work here together. Have a great day. Not a problem. Waves are three-to-five at Blacks right now. Padres and Chargers looking good. Later, dog. *Mañana. Inshallah.*

And because of this, we were suckers that day. We were on our way to the beach, the job, the restaurant. The classroom, the mountains, the mall.

Distracted by our fineness.

America's.

We still are.

But now we know we are.

The ghosts of 9/11 are not just Taucher's. They belong to all of us who got fooled. She's just more tuned in to those ghosts than most. Sees them. Seeks them out. Surrounds herself with them.

"So this is mine and don't you forget it, Mr. PI," she said.

"You're welcome, Ms. FBI Agent."

"*Special* Agent. You know what I can't believe? You know what pisses me off the most about this worm-bucket and his fancy calligraphy pen? Calling himself Caliphornia. California is my state. He can't take that word. He can't call himself that. It's just goddamned *wrong.* Am I being ridiculous here, Ford? Am I?"

"I like our state, too, Joan. I was born here and they'll probably bury me here." I scanned the faces on the walls again. "Do they all live here, too?"

"Mostly. Why?"

"Persons of interest?"

She shrugged. "Some. Mostly from security cameras. Some from police and sheriff surveillance. We get hundreds of them every month. Along with thousands of tips. Just the spelling of names is enough to defeat you. Read that poster."

I followed her eyes to a poster tacked over some of the faces:

Ancestors, geography, and Islam can be used in an Arabic name in different, legitimate variations, although the personal name will almost always be included. For example, the same man may be correctly called:

AHMAD HUSAIN

AHMAD HUSAIN MUHAMMAD

AHMAD BIN HUSAIN BIN MUHAMMAD

AHMAD HUSAIN MUHAMMAD IBN SA'UD AL-TIKRITI

AHMAD HUSAIN AL-TIKRITI

ABU MUHAMMAD AHMAD HUSAIN

ABU MUHAMMAD (UNLIKELY ON OFFICIAL DOCUMENTS)

She gave me a satisfied nod. "Not to mention Hussein, Muhammad, and dozens of other names with different spellings. It takes twelve agents just to surveil someone twenty-four/seven. Did you know that? How resource-depleting and expensive it is? I'm two months behind on my Wall of Fame—just hanging the faces. Let alone figuring out how to spell their names. Or if they pose a threat. Or if I should just take a little closer look."

"I have one more for you," I said.

"Another face?"

"Better." I smiled.

"It better be better," said Taucher.

4

I REMOVED MY COPY of Rasha's thank-you note to Lindsey. Then told Taucher about him: acquaintance of Lindsey's, American Saudi, father of a student of hers, widower. And about their horse-ride and sunset-appreciation moment, complete with salami and cheese and a folding knife to cut them with, and two silver goblets engraved with Arabic calligraphy.

It took Taucher about five seconds to read the note, register the signature, then hurriedly place the card next to the life-threatening letter. She leaned in. "Similar."

"I thought so, too."

"There's no point system for questioned document analysis. You can disguise handwriting. It isn't like fingerprints or DNA." She pulled her keyboard close and went to work. Short entries—tap, tap, tap, tap, tap. Username and password, I guessed. Then another. And one more. A long pause. Then a slight change of light on Taucher's face—access granted to one small cubby within the FBI's vast electronic citadel. She unleashed a twelve-stroke flurry followed by the slightly different clunk of the enter key. Her first grab through the ether at Rasha Samara.

"So," I asked, just to be clear, "you wouldn't be able to say for sure if the same guy wrote both letters?"

She stared at the screen, eyes darting, voice flat. "Forensically, no. But there are other things we can get. From questioned documents. If we had, for instance, original documents instead of copies, like the ones you gave me." She looked up at me, flatly.

"Possibly I could help you there," I said.

"I was hoping the originals were on your person."

"Maybe. I'm asking you to keep Lindsey Rakes as protected as you can. From harm, and from unwanted scrutiny."

"I can promise nothing."

"I understand that."

"Then consider my nothing promised, Roland."

"Thanks, Joan."

"And here's what I'll need from you."

Her conditions: I would give her all of Lindsey's numbers, and tell Lindsey to expect a call from FBI special agent Joan Taucher at 11:45 a.m., two hours from then. I would inform her, Taucher, of any communication with Lindsey and pass on any pertinent information, especially Lindsey's exact location; I would suggest to Lindsey in certain terms that she would be much better meeting face-to-face with the FBI than using a smartphone or an insecure landline. I would say nothing of this interview to any person, press, media, or law enforcement agency, *especially* the Las Vegas FBI. I would supply her, Taucher, with all of my personal and business numbers, and a home address. I would be available to take Taucher's calls 24/7. I would be welcome to a validated FBI visitor parking stub, available at the lobby security counter. I nodded along, ecstatic not to be employed by, partnered with, or married to Joan Taucher.

"I want one more thing, too," I said.

"*More?* For holding out on *me*?"

"Just the basics you have on the screen in front of you. Is Rasha Samara on your watch list? Is he a person of interest? Is he violent? Should Lindsey be in a budget motel in the Vegas area, or in protective lockup?"

She rolled back again in her chair, studying me. Not far enough back to snatch and fire another dart. Though her expression was about as sharp as one. "We're looking at him."

A sinking of heart as I reached into my coat pocket and handed her the genuine thank-you card and the death letter, each in its envelope, all locked in a freezer bag.

"Thank you, Roland. You've done the right thing."

"Lindsey didn't realize she had evidence in her hands. I touched them, too."

"About what I'd expect," she muttered, with the smallest hint of humor in her eyes. We stood, traded business cards. "I can offer you a very small thank-you in return for bringing this evidence to me. But I'd need a promise of silence from you. Total and absolute."

I considered. I rarely agree to things yet unstated. But in that moment I believed whatever Joan might offer would be in my best interest to accept. A brief nod.

"Look where the dart stuck," she said. "Then go two faces down and two faces to the right. That's where I was aiming."

"Nice throw."

"Thanks. I'm a tournament player. What do you see?"

"A dark-haired, dark-skinned guy with a pleasant face, thirty, maybe. Looks like it was taken from video. He doesn't know he's on camera."

"He came to our attention through our friends at one of the mosques," said Joan. "He's not Arabic at all, but an American of Mexican descent.

Hector O. Padilla, age twenty-eight. His behavior at Al-Rribat mosque has been striking some people as strange. My agents have their hands full right this minute. They are not welcomed with open arms at the mosques anyway. And it was you who made me think of Hector Padilla just now."

"How did I do that?"

"He's a regular customer at World Pizza."

I collated this information while trying to vet Taucher's reasons for giving it to me. I doubted that it sprung from the kindness in her heart. I didn't believe for a second that her agents were too busy to follow up on a good lead. Why send me? There was something in it for her, but what? Just another free set of eyes and ears?

"May I shoot his mug?"

A pause, then she turned away to face a window as I took a phone picture of Hector Padilla, made sure the focus was good, shot him again. When I was done I stood beside Joan, looking out at San Diego, some-how tidy—for a city of a million three—against a silver Pacific. Christ-mas decorations up and a big sleigh with Santa and reindeer and boxes of gifts lifting off from the NBC building.

"You've moved up in the world," I noted.

"Same world. Different window."

I looked at the pictures on the wall again. "A few minutes ago I was thinking San Diego hasn't changed that much. That something could happen again. Something big."

She turned to face me. "Big? Big will absolutely happen again. I promise you that it's being planned as we breathe. My job is to keep it from happening *here*. In my city. San Diego will not become my San Bernardino."

She shook my hand. Cold as ever. Strode toward the door. "Roland, I know it's more than late, but I'd like to give you my condolences on your wife's death. I thought of sending flowers but decided against it. It's not that I didn't feel or care."

"I understand."

She held the door open. "Thank you."

"When will you get an opinion on that handwriting?"

"Soon. I won't be sharing much with you."

"Unless you've got a great reason to."

"Such as?"

"It's my job to find things people want."

Ocean Beach—OB in local dialect—is seven miles from the JTTF offices downtown. It's one of California's last truly funky beach towns—rebellious, charming, and a tad long in the tooth. It seems to me that the developers who came up with the name Ocean Beach could have used some of those brain-stimulating exercises they advertise on the radio. Under "Citizenship," an OB report card might say "doesn't play well with franchises." But OBecians don't sweat the small stuff. It's live and let surf. Suds and board shorts. Women on wheels. Endless summer.

I sat in my truck across the street from World Pizza, watching the sidewalk patio fill up. It was almost noon. Popular place. I'd seen their billboard advertisements up and down Highway 395, halfway up the state of California: Pizza on Earth, Pizza Be with You, Wanna Pizza Me? Lately, artisan beers had exploded in popularity here in San Diego, and through my truck window I could see the big hand-chalked beer menu standing in one corner of the patio.

On one side of the restaurant was a squat antiques store with

Christmas garlands framing the windows. On the other stood an oddly slender three-story building with a sun-blanched mirrored door and a row of faded flags drooping from a second-story planter box. The words *International Hostel* were faintly visible from where I sat.

I took a two-top inside, got a big slice of today's special and a pint of stout made right there called Gnarly Barrel. The pizza was excellent and the stout had "notes" of tangerine and cedar in it, and tasted better than it sounds.

When the check came I counted out the bills and overtipped, as usual, having tried and failed at waiting tables in my junior year of college. I sat and looked around the restaurant again, inside and out, for Hector Padilla, but I knew the chances of seeing him were slim. I wondered what Special Agent Taucher's questioned-documents expert would say about the similar writing on the death threat and the thank-you note. It occurred to me again that any man who signed his name on a thank-you note, then a few days later handwrote an anonymous death threat and mailed it to the same person, was certainly one of the stupidest ever born. Certainly Rasha Samara was brighter than that.

Which left me with these fragments:

An apparent Middle Eastern overlap between Caliphornia and Rasha Samara.

A threatened knife.

And a real knife, deftly wielded on a picnic.

Golf courses all over the world and a San Diego postmark.

And the fact that Taucher's handlers were looking at Samara.

Just as Lindsey Rakes had been looking at him, though in a very different way.

Into this strange brew I tried to factor in a distant but perhaps freshly pissed-off ex-husband.

And a Mexican American acting weirdly at San Diego's well-known mosque—weirdly enough to catch the attention of fellow worshipers and the FBI. Enter one Hector Padilla—who was also a big fan of World Pizza.

Where I now sat. It seemed more than strange that someone out there had used this very address to help deliver a death threat to a friend of mine. Maybe Lindsey's wannabe beheader lived in OB. Or used to. Maybe he had just passed through and had a good pizza. Maybe he'd stayed at the International Hostel with the faded flags. Possible, too, that he had never set foot in San Diego and that a confederate such as Hector Padilla had mailed the letter. Maybe our beheader wanted that San Diego postmark just to throw Lindsey and everyone else off his trail.

A man calling himself Caliphornia. Had to be a man, didn't it? Terror. Vengeance. A gruesome threat. A very personal lust to it. Intimate? Jump to a son of Saudi parents building golf courses, nimbly cutting salami with a folding knife while watching a beautiful desert sunset with Lindsey. Same guy? This was possible. I felt uneasy that the world—having once been so vast and free—now seemed so small and crowded.

5

HOME FROM WORLD PIZZA, I sat in front of the west-facing window in my upstairs office and looked out at my rancho. Twenty-five acres of hills and valleys. Oaks and sycamores, chaparral and coastal scrub, bold granite outcroppings. Some of the oaks are huge. No neighbors in sight, though there are other homes beyond. The nearest town is Fallbrook. My high ground is held by a large Spanish-style adobe-brick hacienda built in 1894. There is a barn, a workshop, various outbuildings, and six small casitas built along the shore of a spring-fed pond. Roughly a century ago it was given the name Rancho de los Robles—Ranch of the Oaks.

I did nothing to earn this generous land grant except marry Justine Ann Timmerman. Rancho de los Robles was our wedding gift from her parents. It had been in the Timmerman family for decades, one of their several holdings in our American West. Justine and I had loved each other fiercely for those few months we were given, and when Justine died in a light-plane crash, I tried to give the rancho back to the Timmermans. They said I was family and the place was mine.

And so it is.

The rancho aspires to its early California graciousness but is still in formidable disrepair. It feels interrupted by Justine's sudden departure. I'm not sure if it's haunted, but I do see her at times—never the whole her, just a movement, a wisp, a presence. I hear her voice occasionally, too: not words, but sounds in her key and timbre, mixed in with the groan of old pipes or wind hissing through the casement windows.

My upstairs office is hushed, and the tall windows are operatically draped. The hardwood floor is bare of the Persian carpets that litter the rest of the house. Justine's parents traveled to Iran before the fall of the shah, to hand-pick and collect them, circa 1975. The office has rustic, locally crafted furniture that is handsome and not quite comfortable. Modern upgrades include a high-speed Ethernet connection—not inexpensive in this sparsely populated part of the grid—a powerful computer assembled for me by a friend, and a wheeled task chair, much like Joan Taucher's, that I often carom around the room on.

I shoved off the western wall and coasted back to the monitor on the massive oak desk.

Rasha Samara's Internet existence was sparse but interesting. He had led a partially visible public life, but I could find only three photographs of him, no video, and a total of four attributed media quotes that totaled nine sentences.

The *Las Vegas Sun* article was informative. Rasha was born in Orange to prosperous Saudi immigrants who had settled in Irvine and naturalized. The father was eventually tenured at UC Irvine (molecular biology), the mother at UC Riverside (philosophy). Rashad—which means "integrity," according to the reporter—had spent his childhood and school years in the United States, with summers in Riyadh with his extended family. He called himself Rasha rather than the full Rashad. Rasha's father was interested in golf and horses, and so was his son.

He had graduated from UC Irvine with a degree in botany and a minor in architectural studies, gone on to study sustainable arid soil agriculture and ornamental horticulture at UC Davis. He had moved to Las Vegas at twenty-six to start his own landscape architecture company, TerraNova, with loans from his parents and distant relations in Saudi Arabia.

According to the *Sun*, TerraNova was now an international company specializing in golf course and public park design, worth an estimated twenty-five million dollars, privately owned. Much of his business was done in the Emirates, where his fluency in English and Arabic helped.

The picture above the *Sun* article showed Rasha Samara four years ago, at age thirty-six, attending an Arabian Horse Association competition at the Clark County Fair and Rodeo. With Rasha was his wife, Sally, and their six-year-old son, Edward.

Sally was accepting an award for the Samara family's generous sponsorship of the AHA Western States Youth Programs. She was wheelchair-bound and smiling widely. The *Sun* article said that Sally and her "reclusive" husband, Rasha, had been honored by the AHA for their "tireless work, enthusiasm, and generosity" on behalf of Arabian horses in the USA. In the picture with his wife and son, Rasha looked annoyed. Black-haired, clean shaven, and intense. European-cut suit, white shirt and tie. His son looked very much like him, but with lighter hair. When the *Sun* reporter asked why he sponsored AHA events, Rasha had told him, "Because I love Arabian horses," but he was late for a business meeting and had to run. The reporter noted that his phone calls were not returned.

A *Sun* article dated six months later announced the death of Sally Samara, age thirty-two of Las Vegas, from lung cancer.

All of which meant that Rasha Samara and Roland Ford had some things in common.

Born in California, schooled in California.

Close in age—Rasha forty and I'm thirty-nine now.

Both widowed in our thirties.

Self-employed.

Tight-lipped, prickly, and private.

We were both prosperous, too, what with Rasha Samara's twenty-five-million-dollar TerraNova bringing golf to the planet, and my private investigations—half of which involved a missing twenty-two-pound cat named Oxley.

The Arabian Horse Association newsletter from October 2016 had by far the longest quotes from Rasha Samara:

Arabian Horse Association: What is it that draws you to the Arabian horse?

Rasha Samara: Stamina and spirit and loyalty.

AHA: Loyalty?

RS: When Muhammad finished one of his journeys through the desert, he set his horses free so they could race to the oasis for water. The animals were crazed with thirst. As a test, he called them back. Only five horses turned and came. Mares. These loyal mares became known as *Al Khamsa,* which means "the Five." Legend has it that they became the founders of the five strains of Arabian, but you know how unreliable legends can be. The horse is the thing. The horse is always the thing.

AHA: How many Arabians do you own?

RS: That's private information.

AHA: What can the AHA do to increase the popularity of the breed and develop new interest in it?

RS: Well, stage competitions and contests and give big prizes, I guess. I don't think a breed has to be popular. It has to speak to you, personally. Arabians are proud and intelligent and don't put up with bad trainers or riders. They're not for everyone.

Like most PIs, I subscribe to some large-caliber information-peddling services. They're all online now. My choices are www.tlo.com, www.tracersinfo.com, and www.IvarDuggans.com, though I use others, too. These services are expensive and good at what they do. Their best clients are banks, collection agencies, insurance companies, and law enforcement, so my sole-proprietorship is very small potatoes to them. But as a licensed PI I get good access so long as I pay good money. And they are fast.

Basically, they work the same way. If you're a small business like me, you pay per transaction. You log on with your username and password, which gives you access to their databases. You input your subject name—even a partial name, or a phonetically approximated one, will often work just fine. Proprietary algorithms kick in as you stare out the window at a red-shouldered hawk circling in blue sky on a cool December afternoon. As you look at the cattails along one side of a pond and wonder where the blackbirds went. As you wonder what an algorithm actually is. As you think about people you have loved and some of them lost. As you wonder what a single thirty-nine-year-old male with a degree in history and an honorable discharge from the U.S. Marines and a one-fight pro boxing career and a license to conduct investigations in the state of California might be better doing with his life.

IvarDuggans.com took thirty minutes to kick back most of the basics—full name, DOB, history of home and business addresses, phone, fax and email, Social Security number, current vehicle registrations, websites, neighbors, roommates, relatives (many), known associates (many), professional licenses, fictitious business names, tax liens, registered watercraft and aircraft (none current), and corporate records for TerraNova since its inception.

Plus, this bonus highlight for Roland Ford, PI:

CRIMINAL RECORDS: Subject arrested for brandishing a weapon (curve-bladed janbiya knife) at UC Irvine Pi Phi women's fraternity party, October 1998. Partygoers later blamed misunderstanding between intoxicated fraternity members and subject. No charges filed.

That sent a cool tingle to the scar above my left eye. The scar is Y-shaped and it came from a big right in my first and last pro fight. Saw it coming but didn't have the legs left to escape. I was outclassed and knew it.

I launched myself back on the task chair, timing my rotation to put me facing the western window again. Looking down, I saw the palapa and the pond. On the patio, two of the Irregulars were engaged in table tennis. Burt Short versus the newly arrived Dale Clevenger. Lindsey watching as she leaned against one of the palapa poles, the poster of green-eyed Oxley tacked to the pole just above her shoulder.

Grandfather Dick and Grandmother Liz reclining on patio chaise longues, their backs to the competition, apparently arguing. I wasn't in the mood to watch Ping-Pong.

I pedaled back to the desk and read the CRIMINAL RECORDS entry again. What possible good could come from taking a large knife to a frat party?

IvarDuggans also included three pictures of Rasha—one at his high school commencement in 1995, another riding in an AHA endurance competition in 2002 when he was twenty-four years old, and a casual newspaper portrait taken with newly engaged bride-to-be Sally Meadows. Even as a graduating high-schooler, Rasha Samara looked calm, serious, and focused. Slender and handsome. In his newspaper engagement photo he wore a mustache and Vandyke, neatly trimmed, and his black wavy hair long.

I could hear the Ping-Pong ball faintly clicking back and forth outside. Followed by Burt Short's cackle, then Clevenger's homey drawl.

I thought of one Hector O. Padilla and the Masjid Al-Rribat Al-Islami on Saranac Street, San Diego, where Padilla had apparently been active lately. I'd been to this mosque several times as part of my rounds as a JTTF foot soldier back in 2010 and 2011, doing my best to ingratiate myself to people who were suspicious and afraid of me.

IvarDuggans.com gave me a brief profile on Hector O. Padilla, age twenty-eight, of El Cajon, which bordered the city of San Diego not far from Masjid Al-Rribat. Five feet six inches tall, one hundred seventy pounds, single. Padilla was born in the border city of San Ysidro. High school graduate, some community college courses, no degree. Failed physical requirements for U.S. Marines and Army, subsequently employed as a dishwasher, landscape maintenance worker, janitor, door-to-door cutlery salesman, and veterinary hospital night-shift worker, with workers' comp and state disability checks helping in between. Bad back. Currently employed as custodian at First Samaritan Hospital in San Diego. Included was a picture slightly better than the one Taucher had thrown her dart at. Padilla looked unremarkable. I wondered what had led him to Al-Rribat in recent days. Nothing came to mind, except for the idea that Hector O. Padilla had apparently spent much of his life more or less adrift.

The Al-Rribat Al-Islami Web page contained basic information:

TODAY'S CALENDAR

EVENING PRAYERS—MAGHRIB—AT 5:08 P.M.
FELLOWSHIP DINING 6 P.M. TO 7 P.M.
QUR'AN STUDY 7 P.M. TO 8 P.M.

VISITATION INFORMATION

VISITORS, PLEASE REMOVE YOUR SHOES WHEN ENTERING
THE PRAYER HALL. SHOES CAN BE WORN IN OFFICES,
THE LIBRARY, OR THE MULTIPURPOSE ROOM.

VISITORS, PLEASE KNOW THAT IN THE ISLAMIC
TRADITION, MEN AND WOMEN DO NOT SHAKE HANDS
WHEN INTRODUCED TO EACH OTHER.

THERE IS A SEPARATE PRAYER HALL FOR WOMEN, UPSTAIRS.
THE PRAYER HALL FOR MEN IS LOCATED DOWNSTAIRS.

VISITORS, PLEASE DRESS MODESTLY AND KNOW
THAT IT IS RESPECTFUL FOR A WOMAN TO WEAR
A HEAD SCARF, ALTHOUGH IT IS NOT REQUIRED.

PLEASE KEEP VOICES RESPECTFUL.

VISITORS, PLEASE CHECK IN WITH FRONT
OFFICE BEFORE ENTERING THE CENTER.

WE LOOK FORWARD TO HOSTING YOU AND OTHERS IN
A SPIRIT OF BROTHERHOOD, PEACE, AND UNITY.

I knew, as did most of San Diego, that Al-Rribat Al-Islami was a Sunni mosque, notorious as a place of worship for two of the 9/11 hijackers, and for its charming and outspoken one-time imam, American-born Anwar al-Awlaki. According to Taucher's FBI, al-Awlaki had covertly encouraged jihad in the months leading up to the 9/11 attacks, and had closed-door meetings with the two San Diego hijackers. Sitting in my office here and now—seventeen years after the attacks—I could surmise that al-Awlaki was at the top of Joan's regret list, right behind the two hijackers themselves, who were actually living with one of her FBI informants. Although these two soon-to-be hijackers were not on the radar of Taucher and her FBI confederates, the CIA had been watching them closely for months, as they conspired with other suspected al-Qaeda terrorists and received combat training in Yemen. Of course, the CIA had failed to share this minor intel with the FBI, and a few weeks later America woke up to what started as a pleasant September morning.

And al-Awlaki had been right here in the heart of America's Finest City, quietly encouraging his foreign brothers to bring this country down in flames. Interestingly, the jihadi firebrand had twice been arrested for soliciting prostitutes, and pled guilty the second time. I remember that he left the United States in 2002, just after I joined the Marines. He went to England, then two years later to Yemen. There, he became the first American citizen to be officially assassinated by the CIA. A drone strike in September of 2011.

I thought of Lindsey and her Headhunters. *We flagged some bad guys.* Al-Awlaki? A fat chance and a long shot, but those things occasionally help me make a living. I went to the western window again. Lindsey was no longer watching the Ping-Pong battles.

Then footsteps on the stairs and a moment later she was standing in my office doorway, her cell phone in her hand, her face pale. She stepped inside and closed the door.

6

"RASHA SAMARA JUST CALLED," said Lindsey. "He was polite and didn't sound like he wanted to cut off my head with a knife. He said he understood why we shouldn't see each other again. He has complications in his life, and so must I. Then he said complications do not interest him. I interest him. He asked me to meet him in Tucson on Friday for an Arabian horse exhibition. His son is riding. Separate hotel suites for us, of course. Separate *hotels*, if I would prefer. He would pay for my flights, room, everything. I am free to bring a friend."

"What did you say?"

She slumped onto a handsome, uncomfortable cowhide sofa. Reminded me of the way she'd landed on that barstool in the Pala Casino those two and a half years ago. I sat back down at the desk.

"I said I'd think about it," she said.

"Were you afraid?"

"Yes."

"Did he sense it?"

"I don't know. I was surprised. Unprepared."

"How did he get your cell number?"

"I gave it to him before our date in the desert. A just-in-case thing. What's that on your monitor? A mosque?"

"Al-Rribat Al-Islami. It's in San Diego."

She gave me a funny look. "Terror central."

"Al-Awlaki."

"Weasely fucker. Whore buyer."

"Did the Headhunters kill him?"

She smiled, tiredly. Shook her head. "Not us. That was 2011. We didn't exist until later. What should I tell Rasha about Tucson?"

"Tell him no. But suggest that you'd be open to him calling you again."

"Keep in touch? Enemies-closer kind of thing? I have to admit it, Roland—more than half of me is on Rasha's side. I don't want him to be a guy who wants to kill me. I want Caliphornia to be a bloodthirsty jihadi I can shoot between the eyes with a clear conscience. Someone I can hate."

"And what if he isn't?"

She shrugged. "That Taucher lady is one tough nut. I could practically feel the cuffs going on, just by the tone of her voice."

"She'll want to see you face-to-face at some point, Lindsey. I bought you a little time today, but I'm not sure how much. But you can trust her. Consider talking to her yourself. You don't need me."

"Yeah, I do. You make me feel safe and capable."

"You're both of those and more, Lindsey."

"Exactly what more?" Her black hair was down and it put her face in partial shadow. I could see her eyes twinkling in that half-light, and something of her Indian mother in the bones of her face.

"You have strength," I said. "Endurance, resolve."

"A plow horse has all that."

"A warrior does, too."

She smiled again, less tiredly, I thought. Seemed to consider something for a second.

Outside, the Ping-Pong ball tick-tocked unevenly, like a wounded clock. "What about you, Roland? How do you feel?"

"Good. Solid."

"I knew you'd say something like that," Lindsey said. "You hold it all inside. I vent."

"Different ways to put one foot in front of the other."

"How long since Justine now?"

"Three and a half years," I said. Didn't have to think about it. Another kind of clock.

"Any prospects, Roland?"

I shrugged. I was coming off an affair that had started with a spark and ended in flames. Ghosts in the closet. Hers, not mine. Wasn't inclined to get into all that with Lindsey.

"I never liked the shrink," she said.

"I know you didn't." The shrink was Dr. Paige Hulet, another long story, part of the helicopter shootout that Taucher had mentioned. The shrink had taken a bullet for one of her troubled patients. The shrink and I had had a thing, but I'm not sure exactly what it was.

"Have you moved Justine's things out of the bedroom?"

"Not really. I did the bathroom and dresser."

"Her closet will be tough," said Lindsey. "Let me know if I can help. I could go through her stuff, maybe be more practical about it. Less . . . attached."

"That's good of you."

"Maybe sometimes it's good not to think about her."

"Sure," I said.

"It's a big old house you've got."

I pulled open a desk drawer and got out a prepaid burner phone, Walmart, $49.99, brand-new and still in its box. "No GPS on this thing, Lindsey. Set it up and give the number to Rasha and anybody else you *have* to talk to in the next few days. Especially Taucher, or she'll have both our skins."

"You really think Caliphornia would ping me and track me down?"

"That's what bad people do."

We stood and she took the phone and gave me a look. "I like casita three," she said. "I like those old Laguna paintings with the droopy eucalyptus trees and the sudsy waves. What's rent, by the way?"

"Don't worry about rent now."

"I prefer worrying about it."

"A thousand, then, with the running-for-your-life discount."

"What's with this Clevenger guy?"

"Old friend of Burt's," I said. "New Orleans, originally."

"What's he do for work?"

"Documentary nature journalist, he says. TV. Award-winning."

"All TV people are award-winning."

"He's making a show about the coyotes of Fallbrook."

"Plenty of subject matter around," said Lindsey.

"He uses drones to shoot video."

"You don't do background checks on your renters, do you, Roland?"

"I believe in privacy."

"That's crazy, coming from a PI," Lindsey said.

"Life is contradiction."

"Hmmm." Lindsey looked around my office. It's filled with stuff I like. Books on history. Totems from the Northwest. Pottery from the Southwest. Photographs by Ansel Adams and Beth Moon. Pictures of my parents and siblings. Collars and tags belonging to the dogs I've had. A striking portrait of Justine by a well-known photographer, commissioned by her mother and father for her twenty-first birthday. Shots of Justine in *Hall Pass*. A maple stand for my fishing rods, reels, and related tackle in the drawers below. A model made from a picture of a large trout I caught in the Sierras, the fish jumping through a clear acrylic river, splashing clear acrylic water into the air. A genuine saber-toothed cat skull I accepted in trade for a job. A gun safe.

"Any leads on the cat?" she asked.

Tammy, the cat's owner, had been given my number by a semiharmless sociopath I once helped out of a jam here in town. He thought I would be kind enough to help her, even though she had little money. Tammy had broken into tears in my living room. Oxley meant the world to her.

Now Tammy reported any and all possible sightings to me, as well as helpful stories and speculations from people she had talked to. Tammy was a talker. She had raised quite a posse through the Fallbrook Friends Facebook page.

"A possible sighting on Stage Coach," I said to Lindsey. "Near the high school. Another on Alvarado. The best news is nobody's found him dead on the road."

"I don't like the idea of coyotes tearing apart that poor tubby thing."

"That's another thing you've got, Lindsey. A good heart."

She looked at my computer monitor. "Are you going to the mosque?"

"I need to."

"So if Oxley and I are your two open cases, the mosque visit must be for me. Watch your back, Roland."

"Always. Tell Rasha no on the horse show, but let him know you're open to communication. On your swanky new Walmart flip phone.

Call Brandon Goff, too. Tell him you're still strongly in favor of joint custody. Tell me how he takes that."

"It's not Brandon."

"Help me help you."

When Lindsey had shut the door behind her, I checked the Arabian Horse Association website events calendar. All five of their big national events had already taken place for this year, from early summer through fall. But there was a Western Region "Native Costume" exhibition coming up next week in Tucson, Arizona. Among the featured competitors in the youth division was rider Edward Samara and his mare, Al Ra'ad. A check of Arabic names revealed that Al Ra'ad means "the thunder."

As in *The thunder is coming for you.*

7

THE ARABIC WORD for mosque is *masjid*. Masjid Al-Rribat Al-Islami is on Saranac Street in San Diego, twelve miles from the San Diego Joint Terrorism Task Force building downtown.

It is a two-story stucco structure, rectangular and off-white, with pale blue tile accents. A chest-high stucco wall with small wrought-iron archways surrounds it. The main entryway to the compound is protected by metal gates with lancet arches in the same pale blue as the tile. It is neither defensive nor welcoming. Six years since I'd been there.

Today's sunset prayer ended at 6:38. I watched the men exit the downstairs prayer room, a spacious, high-ceilinged, red-carpeted area with no furniture and few windows. The ceiling was stained glass, but at this hour winter's early dark owned the colors. I smelled lamb and garlic faintly easing in from the dining room, felt my stomach approving.

The youth activities imam was the last man out. He'd put on some weight since I'd last seen him. Early thirties, bearded in the Muslim custom, dressed in a white *thobe* that reached the floor and a white turban tied at the back. We shook hands.

"A good thing to see you again, Roland."

"And you, Hadi. Thanks for seeing me on short notice."

His office was upstairs, small and warmly lit, two of the walls lined with leather-bound books. Hadi Yousef had always been open and candid with me—as far as I knew—and I had always kept his name out of larger JTTF circulation. He had been a very young imam in charge of youth activities when I first met him. He humbly dodged media and law enforcement in all of its many forms. He was my source because he had come to trust me. I'd done little to earn that trust, except state my respect and pity for the citizens of Fallujah while I was deployed there. Good enough. Yousef had been born in Iraq and thought terror was a scourge that infected not only America but also Islam. He told me once that the saddest time in his life was when the United States abandoned Iraq, leaving Islam to declare war on itself. He had told me something that rings true: that Islam is terror's biggest hostage.

After pleasantries dictated by respect and distance, I came to the reason for my abrupt visit. "I've heard about a Latino man who has been coming here recently. I've heard that his behavior is causing some concern."

"This came from Agent Taucher," he said.

I nodded.

Hadi set his elbows on the desk and touched his fingertips softly. He wore heavy, black-framed glasses that looked old and unfashionable on his young face. "Hector Padilla. He has been coming for prayer and worship for two months now. Not every day, but two or three times a week. I don't know where he lives. He is in his late twenties, and not married. He introduced himself as a lapsed Catholic. He said he had spiritual emptiness. He said he had recently broken up with a Muslim woman. He had purchased a Qur'an and some booklets on Islam. One was 'Welcome to Islam.' He also had an Arabic language learning program on

CDs. He brought them all with him in a backpack the first time he visited us. He poured them out of his pack, right onto my desk here, as if showing me proof of his devotion. During his first few weeks here, he appeared meek and inquisitive. Earnest. He was interested in meeting single Muslim women. We have informal singles activities which are supervised, and Mr. Padilla has attended some of them. I'm not here for those, generally. I guide the youth, as you know."

"Mind if I write some notes?"

"If you must."

I slipped my leather notebook and a pen from my coat.

"How did that go over?" I asked. "Mr. Padilla being openly interested in the women here?"

Hadi flared his fingers and gave me a "you never know" expression. "Some of our worshipers find his interest in Muslim women to be . . . *inappropriate.*"

"Do you?"

"I try not to judge. But I find Hector himself to be annoying."

"How so?" I asked.

"His willingness to renounce his own faith in favor of mine."

"Do you sense falsehood in it?"

"I sense weakness."

Hadi regarded me from behind the thick lenses of his glasses. Calm but alert, the same keen forbearance I'd seen in most of the various priests, ministers, rabbis, and other holy men I had dealt with in my thirty-nine years. It must come from being closer to God than I am.

My relationship to God would have fallen into the "needs to improve" category until April 7, 2004, at 2:17 p.m. in Fallujah, Iraq, when a skinny boy threw a homemade bomb at my feet and it didn't explode. Which got me thinking that God might be a lot closer than I'd thought, and maybe He even kind of liked me. I believed that until April 21 of 2015, when Justine's custom-painted pink Cessna 182—*Hall Pass*—crashed into the Pacific Ocean not far from Point Loma. Mechanical failure. Fuel pump. Low hours on it. An accident. Whose accident? I was infuriated with God and am still not completely over it. I try to forgive Him. I listen and try to hear Him. The worst of my fury is gone.

"Has anyone said anything to Hector about his behavior here?" I asked.

"Not that I know," said Hadi. "I think the imam is considering what to do. Of course, we are open to new believers. But not men of low quality."

"Are you expecting him again, on a certain day or time?"

He sat back and folded his hands over his middle. Like many Muslim holy men, his hands were expressive and emphatic. I wondered if this was formally taught.

"He lingers in the brothers' prayer room during the sisters-only Tuesday Qur'an classes," said Hadi. "To glimpse them coming and going. So, tomorrow at one thirty. He also has attended the Wednesday and Saturday beginners' Arabic classes, after evening prayer. Please do not confront him directly here at the masjid."

I nodded, then wrote "Caliphornia" across a notebook page, tore it out, and handed it to Hadi across his desk. No facial reaction whatsoever.

"I have never seen this word spelled in this way," he said. "What does it mean? Where did you see it?"

"Someone is using it as a name," I said. "He signed a death threat using it."

"A death threat against whom?"

"I'm not free to say."

Again, the patient stare. "Is Hector suspected of the threat?"

"No. He came up in the net."

"He strikes me as unusual and maybe lost," said Hadi. "But not murderous. *Caliphornia*. Such a strange name. Tea, Roland?"

"No, thank you."

"I read about the shootout at your home last year and I was glad you were not killed or wounded." A wry smile. "You are becoming an action figure. Such as my sons see on TV. You are now famous for three things in San Diego."

Yes, my fame. Most recently augmented by last year's helicopter shootout and fiery crash, as referenced by Joan Taucher earlier in the day. In this debacle, one notorious celebrity had been burned dead, and one psychiatrist wounded. On my property. My watch. Much media and speculation, and a lot of truth left untold.

Another part of my notoriety was the fatal shooting of a young black man by a San Diego sheriff's deputy back in 2009. The deputy was my partner and I was standing not ten feet away when he shot. I had drawn but held fire. I told the IA investigators why I decided not to shoot. My words cost my partner his job. And cost me my reputation within the department. Coverage and controversy. Lots of bad blood. My assignment to the JTTF was widely and correctly seen as a form of punishment for breaking rank, shattering the blue brotherhood, costing a good man his job.

The third pillar in my local notoriety is the plane crash that killed Justine. Much coverage on that, too, though of a different kind. The media was actually brief and respectful of my privacy, and quickly onto the next stories. I was envious of the ability to move on.

"It's been a year and a half since my most recent disaster," I said. "I enjoy the quiet life."

"May it continue, *inshallah*."

"And you, Hadi? How are you and Masjid Al-Rribat in these heated days?"

He leaned forward and touched his fingertips again. "I am small in the eyes of Allah and smaller in the eyes of America. I enjoy this smallness. But the masjid? So many eyes are upon us. It is very hard to be a Muslim in America. There is some tolerance, yes. But there is suspicion, too. And beyond the suspicion there is fear. And fear can turn to hate, as we all have seen. So we worship our god and we take care of our own. There is much about this life we cannot know."

"Amen to that."

"*Alhamdulillah*."

"Yes. God be praised."

We stood. I looked down at Hadi's shiny glass desktop, in which I saw a distorted reflection of his trunk and face, and decades of nicks and scratches. Followed by a sudden errant thought: "So did you say when Hector was up here he emptied his backpack on your desk? Poured the contents right out in front of you there?"

"Exactly."

"Why?"

"He is impulsive. I think he wanted to display his . . . commitment."

"By showing you what?"

Hadi recapped for me: a newly bought Qur'an, the Noor Foundation edition. And two pamphlets written by an Orange County imam named Mustafa Umar—"Welcome to Islam" and "How to Pray." Hector's pack also contained a rubber-banded stack of invitations to the "Treasures of Araby" collection at a showroom in Solana Beach.

Hadi indicated the table beside him. "As you see, he left a few of those. He also had an Arabic language CD program still in its box.

Mr. Padilla assured me that he had bought the program used online, at a good price." A small smile.

"That was all?"

"No. There was also an energy drink, two chocolate donuts with peanuts in a plastic box with a top, so they wouldn't be crushed. There was a clear Baggie of brown tablets. I have no idea what they were. And he had a sharpening stone in its box. The box cracked loudly into the glass desktop, but only made a small mark. The stone itself spilled out."

"A sharpening stone."

"Yes, Roland. A whetstone. With which someone might sharpen a knife."

A jump in the heart rate. "Describe it."

"The stone was maybe three by eight inches, with a wooden base. I can't remember who the maker was. My impression of the box and the stone was that they were new."

When Hadi had finished his description, I asked him to describe the whetstone again. Patiently, he did. The scar on my forehead tingled. I wrote down his words in my notebook as accurately as I could. I have big hands and write slowly with a pen. Finally, I rose and slipped my notebook into my pocket. "You've been generous with your time."

Hadi stood, too, handed me one of the "Treasures of Araby" flyers that Hector had given him. "I actually might go to this. It looks interesting and that gallery has a good reputation. The opening night reception is free and open to the public."

I glanced at the rugs and vessels and jewelry pictured there. *Gallerie Monfil Presents the Treasures of Araby.*

The stairs creaked as we walked back down. The smell of food was stronger and the young Muslims were already assembling for Hadi Yousef's class. They looked at me, some curious, some appraising.

"You will always be suspicious here, Roland. But always welcome."

"Thank you, Hadi."

He walked me outside. "Your soul is troubled."

"Beheadings trouble me."

We stopped at the front gate. Hadi put his hands behind his back and contemplated me. "Beheading. Caliphornia?"

I nodded.

"So, your keen interest in Hector's whetstone. There could be an innocent explanation for the stone."

"That would be wonderful."

"I will pray for your success in preventing violence, Roland."

"Help me if you can, Hadi."

"I will try, Allah willing."

"He should be."

8

I PARKED ACROSS the street and three houses down from Hector O. Padilla's home in El Cajon. The moon was a waxing crescent and a tall palm reached toward it, and for a moment I was in Fallujah in the spring of 2004.

This was an older neighborhood with streetlights few and far between and the trees grown tall. There was a good breeze and I could hear the sycamore leaves hitting the hood of my truck. No car in Padilla's driveway and the door of his garage was shut.

Light came from inside the house and garage. The front yard was small and square and marked by a low wall overgrown with ivy. I raised my night-vision binoculars. The world went green and dreamy, somehow less than real. I focused through the autumn-bare branches of a liquidambar tree. A security-screened front door. Address plainly visible on the stucco house front, no mail visible in the open black wall box below the numbers. Padilla's window blinds let out only a thin frame of light.

Watching for someone who doesn't know you're there is a strangely powerful thing. Such intimate detachment. My truck has barely legal blackout windows, which make me even less apparent. Lindsey told me she felt like God Herself when she was flying a drone mission and the Reaper cameras and sensors would relay all the live, nearly real-time activity taking place on the earth below. Seven thousand miles away. God Herself, watching her kill-list target crawl across the desert on his elbows, trying to collect the legs that the Headhunters had just blown off him with a laser-guided Hellfire missile. Which meant the man was functionally dead. Which meant Lindsey had accomplished her mission. Which filled her with satisfaction. And horror. And eventually drove her mad.

My fast-food tacos weren't bad. Still warm in the bag and plenty of hot sauce. Extra napkins. Had an energy drink, checked messages on the phone, listened to the radio news. I spend a lot of time watching people. I enjoy it. It's like a movie you haven't seen. Some are better than others, of course. You learn to let the hours just be hours.

With my mind free to wander, I wondered what kind of brown pills Hector was toting around in his backpack. I thought of the Captagon tablets we found on many of the insurgents in Fallujah. Powerful amphetamines, good for temporary strength and stamina. Fighting pills. All sorts of stories about how crazy and brave they made you. Manufactured in rustic labs. If you can make them in Iraq, you can make them here.

But what if Hector was just a well-meaning, innocent man who was searching for something to believe in? What if the whetstone was because of his interest in creating his own sashimi? What if the brown tablets were multivitamins or weight-loss potions? It's easy to be cynical. In my line of work it's a virtue.

Just after nine o'clock the garage door rose and an older black Nissan Cube backed out. It was clean and freshly waxed and shone handsomely in the weak garage lights. Through the binoculars I could see the top of the driver's head, the rest blotted out by the headrest of the seat. A man, almost certainly, dark hair, medium length and wavy. Padilla-like. By the time the Cube was almost out of the driveway I had gone into the PI slouch—sliding down the seat far enough to see my prey between the dashboard and the top of the steering wheel. Legs splayed, arms out, head back. It's uncomfortable for a big man, and somehow demeaning, too, and probably comical if it isn't you doing it. Just before the Cube passed I slumped to full invisible and watched the headlights play across the headliner of my truck.

Just enough traffic for an easy tail. Interstate 8 to 163, off at Genesee, a medical borough. Hector O. drove just under the speed limits and signaled every turn. The Cube is an amusing vehicle. They look so toylike and somehow all wrong, but they will accommodate seven adults, or so I've read. I wondered if Hector had ever carried six passengers at once. He seemed so solitary. Maybe the room for six was wishful thinking. But maybe he filled his shiny black Cube up with six people every weekend night and went square-dancing. I liked that idea. I like to dance. Makes me feel graceful. I took it up when I quit boxing. I've won a couple of trophies at amateur ballroom dancing contests. My specialty is the waltz, though I truly love a good samba.

First Samaritan Hospital was a seventies-era smoked glass rectangle with a big plastic stork perched on top, dangling a blanketed newborn in its beak. I fell back and passed the main entrance just in time to see the shiny black Cube veer toward employee parking.

I was halfway home when Taucher called. "Questioned documents wouldn't go to court on this, other than to say those two signatures probably didn't have the same author, but they might have."

"Not very FBI-like," I said.

"I told you, handwriting isn't like fingerprints or DNA," Taucher said. "Speaking of which, I messengered the letter, note, and both envelopes back to Washington. I'm hoping for results too good to share with you."

"I feel treasured."

"What have you found on Padilla?"

"Nothing at all," I lied. I wasn't in the mood to share, either.

"So you're on Interstate Fifteen, just south of Sabre Springs, it looks. Heading north for Fallbrook, I'd bet."

"Pinging my call," I said. "That's what I miss about law enforcement."

"So apply to the Bureau," she said. "We respect honest deputies who don't shoot mentally disturbed, bizarrely behaving subjects five times."

"You also work until past midnight on Monday nights."

"I don't have anything better to do," said Joan.

"I know that feeling."

"Hmmm. Later."

The long driveway from the road to my home is protected by a hefty steel gate. It's controlled remotely from the house or by a keypad set at car-window level. I could see my house atop the rise, half hidden in towering oaks that seem to guard it. At night the houselights glitter through the trees, and if there is a breeze they blink like fireflies. Waiting for the gate to open, I watched the few lights twinkle and I remembered the way I used to feel, knowing that Justine was up there in that house somewhere. It's still hard for me to bend to the fact that someone of such importance can be instantly and forever gone.

As I headed up the drive I could see the row of casitas that face the pond, and the palapa over the picnic table and the big built-in barbecue. The barbecue is stout and U-shaped, decked with cobalt-blue tile, and there are barstools all around—our natural watering hole in good weather. But most of the outdoor lights were off. With winter close upon us, the Irregulars were hitting the sack early. In Lindsey's casita a light was on and I could see Burt Short standing outside her door, hands on his hips, watching my truck.

Something wrong.

He intercepted me outside Lindsey's casita, the door of which stood open behind him. Burt Short actually *is* short. And heavily muscled, with a calm eye and an indefinite past. Shaped like a bull, big in the head and shoulders, small-footed. He looked up at me. "She's upset."

I looked past him and saw Lindsey packing a suitcase that lay open on the bed. She looked at me, face pale and eyes dark, then back to her task.

I closed the door behind me. Watched her set some folded blouses in the bag. Then a plastic toiletries case. She wrapped the cord around the nozzle of a hair dryer, her hands trembling.

"Talk to me, Lindsey."

"Kenny Bryce," she said. "Our intelligence coordinator? Not only a Headhunter, but a good, sweet guy. He called an hour ago. He got a letter in the mail the same day I did. Fancy calligraphy, an English-Arabic mix like mine. He read it to me and it sounded pretty gruesome, Roland. Signed, Caliphornia. Kenny tried to be stand-up about it. Like it was some sick joke. He wasn't sure what to do. So he called Voss, our old pilot, up in Grass Valley. Guess what? He got a cut-your-head-off announcement, too. Same day. Caliphornia himself. We're all three meeting tomorrow at eleven hundred hours. Late breakfast and a strategy meeting. In Bakersfield, where Kenny lives—halfway between here and Voss. We're thinking that whatever we do, it should be as a team."

I understood that a servicewoman's duty to her crew doesn't end after deployment. And that loyalty to friends will shape a life.

"So," she said. "Up at zero dark thirty for this gal. And a long drive ahead."

"We'll take the Cessna."

She dropped the dryer into the bag. Wiped a tear off her cheek with the cuff of her shirt. "Thank you. Really, truly, thank you. I'm scared, Roland."

"We'll beat this."

After packing, I had a night of troubled sleep in which I dreamed of Justine's face—faintly lit, but most certainly Justine's—floating in a slow orbit around me. Then the face was Lindsey's. Over and over. When I reached toward the face it would glide away, like an airborne balloon shying away in a puff of breeze, slowly, but just out of reach.

We were in the air at sunrise. *Hall Pass 2* churned powerfully through the sky, so confident and capable and alive. I felt that way also. And somehow less bound by the laws of gravity and of men.

Two hours and four minutes later Lindsey and I descended toward the flat expanse of Bakersfield. Land of heat and oil pumps and Central Valley cotton. Land of Buck Owens and Merle Haggard and the Bakersfield sound, a style of music sometimes described as more country than country, much beloved by my combative grandparents—Dick and Liz Ford—tenants of casitas one and six, respectively, on Rancho de los Robles.

"Looks like Syria," said Lindsey, looking down with a thousand-yard stare. "I've never been in Syria. But I've spent hours and hours hovering over it with my cameras. Watching insurgents and farmers and women and children. Dogs and camels and cattle. People's homes. Daesh staged from schools and hospitals. So, hours hovering, and when we had the intel and clearance we'd laser-mark the targets for the fast movers. It's called sparkling. Their infrareds would lock on and *boom!* Game over.

"But the biggest prize of all was to take out a target ourselves. Headhunters, baby, doing our deadly best. That usually meant a target in tight quarters. In a vehicle, maybe. Or a home. Something the F-16s were too fast for. We'd use Hellfire missiles or, even better, these two-footers we called the Small Smart Weapon. Those are something. We could take out a guy sleeping in bed but his wife in the kitchen would be fine. I took lives, Roland. I'm not ashamed and I'm not proud. Saved lives, too— American and others. But I've never actually set foot on Syrian soil. I'd like to, someday. To just stand in the middle of that desert with my own two boots planted in the sand. It would make me feel vested. To have the part of me that wasn't there there. I sometimes think I owe it to them. The men I killed. I've always thought it's a little rude to kill a man from halfway around the world. Isn't that like saying, *You, sir, are bad enough for me to kill, but I don't want to set foot in your miserable country?*"

"Rude," I said. "I've never heard it put that way."

"Mom drilled us kids on manners," Lindsey said, eyes still locked on the flat tan country below us. "She was very strict. Very British. Mix that with conservative Muslim ideas of behavior and you get major manners. I've never asked her, but Mom would say it's rude to kill a man from seven thousand miles away, then head home to your baby and hold him in the rocker in the morning sun and get that nice warm bottle up to his funny little face and think about the nice future he's going to have, all safe and secure because Mommy pickled some guy in Aleppo an hour earlier. The Headhunters tried to be funny about things, to make them less horrible. Like, we invented three sought-after results when we fired on an enemy. If we got close enough to our target, we demolished him. If we hit him directly, we pulverized him. But if we hit him directly in the torso, we *demulverized* him. Demulverization—highest honors. And that's what I'd think about when I'd be rocking Little John. That's where the vodka came in. Just a way of adding even more distance to those seven-thousand-plus miles. Or sometimes it was the roulette wheels downtown. When I stepped into a casino, there was no Aleppo. No Iraq. No home, even, with Johnny crying and Brandon threatening to rat me out to Child Protective Services. None of that. Just the glide of that white marble ball around and around the wheel. And me with all my might focused on making it drop where I wanted it to. You can send a missile into a man's chest from half the world away? Why not drop a little ball into black thirty-three or red forty-eight from just a few feet back? Easy. Simple. I've done it. Those are my lucky numbers."

"But you broke that cycle, Lindsey," I said. "You clawed your way to the other side."

"Yeah, sure I did," she said softly. She still hadn't taken her eyes off the land below us.

"Baghdadi was the prize," she said. "The next bin Laden. Every grunt on the ground, every Special Forces guy, every pilot and gunner in the sky wanted Baghdadi. We spent hours looking down on Aleppo and the villages around it. We knew he was moving because that's how you stayed alive down there. Thousands of people that might be him. Thousands of vehicles that might be carrying him. Thousands of buildings and bunkers and tunnels. The Reaper can stay in the air for a whole day without refueling. The longest they'd let us work was twelve hours, then you had to head home. That meant two hours in the air, two hours off to do paperwork, eat, rest. Then back in the air for two more hours. So we flew three missions a day. Staring at that screen. On a lot of my missions it was night over there, so the infrared video was always murky. Six hours of that and your eyes ache. Get off shift and walk outside and it's just starting to get dark in Las Vegas."

I cleared our landing with the Meadows Field tower, got my approach and a standby.

"But you know about that kind of thing, from Fallujah," said Lindsey. "You know about killing somebody and what it does to you. Even when it's your job and you're doing something good and the dead guy deserved it. It still takes something away from you. Or maybe you don't see it that way."

"I still think about it," I said. "How to deal with it. How you decide to deal with it. How you deal with what you *can't* decide."

"The things that are bigger than your deciding."

"Those exact things."

She was watching me then, the earth widening below us, landing strip a distant black dash.

"Would you like to hear my story about killing Zkrya Gourmat someday?" she asked.

"You've never said a word about it."

"Zkrya Gourmat was a high-value ISIL leader, back when we called it ISIL. Killing him wasn't an Air Force assignment. It was for two of the acronyms. In this case, CTC and JSOC. They draw up the so-called 'kill list.' The formal name for that list is the 'Disposition Matrix.'"

The CIA's Counterterrorism Center and the Joint Special Operations Command, I thought—the odd couple from the feuding families of intelligence and the military. Often in bed but never married. I'd brushed up against both of them in my Marine days. And just last year I'd collided with some of them on my own property, with mortal results.

I told Lindsey I'd like to hear her story.

"Let's save it for the flight back," she said. "After you've met Kenny and Voss, it will make more sense."

9

KENNY BRYCE HAD CHOSEN a no-frills café called the Mine for the Head-hunters' 1100 hours strategy breakfast. The morning was cool and bright. I hadn't been in Bakersfield in ten years. I'd always liked its rough history and reputation. A few years ago, *The Guardian* named Bakersfield PD America's Deadliest Police Force, as it had, at the time, the highest number of per capita police shootings in the country.

Voss arrived exactly on time, as ex–military officers tend to do. He was a tall, beak-nosed man with short, back-brushed hair and quick eyes. Lindsey rose and they hugged.

She introduced us and Voss offered me his hand. "Are you taking good care of my best sensor?" he asked.

"I'm trying," I said.

"She's worth all the trouble."

"You liars," she said.

They caught up. Voss's wife, Lindsey's divorce, the kids. Then the important stuff: acronym-riddled anecdotes, comic memories, gossip and speculation. I half listened and enjoyed the warm December sun on my face. The Mine's patio had Christmas lights along the roofline and a manger scene tucked into a shady corner.

After twenty minutes and no Kenny, Lindsey left him a message. We ordered and ate. I had the Golden Nugget Omelet. The waitress brought refills. When we finished eating, Voss left Kenny another message. His annoyance hung in the air with the smell of the coffee.

Which put us at the front door of Kenny Bryce's apartment at precisely 1220—one hour and twenty minutes after his botched arrival time.

Tuscanola was a newer complex, swirled white plaster and prefab stonework and wrought-iron touches on the windows. The porch was good sized and Kenny had furnished it with a bistro set. A potted succulent and an ashtray sat on the round tiled table. I noted that the long carport across from Bryce's row of apartments was roofed with solar panels and hung with floodlights and security cameras mounted high up on alternating stanchions.

Voss knocked and waited. The door sounded solid and the peephole bezel looked shiny and new. "Remember that Christmas party when Kenny got blasted and decided to sleep in the restaurant booth?" he asked.

"I do," said Lindsey. "And how damned hard it was to get him up and out of there. Didn't the manager help?"

Voss nodded irritably and knocked again. He looked at Lindsey, at me, then took hold of the iron opener and pressed. The thumb pad clunked down and the door opened, swung in six inches, then came to a stop.

My first thought on entering a quiet home, uninvited, is: *Where are they hiding and how are they armed?*

Seven weeks in Fallujah.

Seven years as a cop.

Six years as a hardworking private investigator and the sudden, wicked surprises sometimes sprung on us.

For such surprises I carry a forty-five autoloader in a strong-side inside-the-waistband holster. I wear it far back so the gun is easily concealed by a jacket or an untucked shirt. I'm right-handed.

I made a deal with myself early on as a freelancer, one that favors my personal survival: I carry the heavy, tumorous, soul-damaging gun even when I'm not expecting to need it.

Such as now, meeting with friendlies in a public place in these peaceful and secure United States of America.

"Let me do this," I said to Voss, unstrapping the gun. He eased away as I pushed the door open with my foot. Indoor air wafting out, hard and metallic. A thick slick of blood on the tile entryway.

Adrenaline blast, game on.

I drew the forty-five in my right hand, pulled Voss away with my left, then pushed the door hard. Shivered the wall when it hit. Never step past a half-open door. I threw it wide open, jumped inside, and slammed it shut. Nothing. Spun fast to sweep the room, eyes and laser sight moving as one, across, then back, eyes focused on everything and nothing, the doorways, always the doorways, and the stairs, always the stairs, for movement and the shadow of movement concealed: Fallujah.

"Lindsey, Voss!" I barked over my shoulder. *"Trouble here. Nobody in, nobody out!"*

When you're clearing you can get a rhythm and it's the rhythm of your life. Note the big revolver lying on the carpet a few feet away from the entryway tile. Note the sand-colored carpet showing blood. You follow the blood. See the living room is spacious but sparsely furnished. Sweep across, sweep back. Breakfast nook empty. Your legs stable, eyes clear. See the small kitchen and a utility room behind it and a door to the attached garage. Garage for defense. Garage to hide. Follow the blood back to the living room. Silence outside the front door. Up the stairs slowly, one at a time, eyes and gun on the landing. Blood shows the way.

I made the landing, felt the warmer upstairs air pressing close. Scanned the hallway. A wall sconce knocked loose and dangling on its wires. One room right and another left, doors wide open. On the pale carpet a crimson drag pattern like a paint roller might make, all the way to the end of the hall, then through the open door.

Carpet is quiet. I stayed to the left of the blood. Stepped slowly, gun raised. Cleared the right-side bedroom, then the left-side bath. Stood outside the door at the end of the hall where the drag marks went through, knowing that death had gotten there ahead of me.

A quiet breath, then in.

Stillness only. Sunlight through vertical blinds, slats of light and dark on the bed. Nightstand lamp still on. Big bed, still made up, two pillows side by side, a man's head lying on one of them. Looking up. Eyes half open. Lips parted as if ready to speak. Neck severed, now a crusted red-black stump. A fly on his forehead in a bar of sunlight.

On the floor, in the narrow shadow cast by the bed, lay the headless body. Arms and legs splayed, facedown if there had been a face. Jeans and socks. Neck flared.

I cleared the bathroom and the walk-in closet and came back, stopping close to the bed. Lowered the gun. Breathed even and deep. Heart in my throat. Tire hiss outside. A fly in the room.

And cop training:

UNSUB, black male, 30–40 years old.

Decapitated.

Height and weight TBD.

Defensive wounds on arms and hands.

One long slit over the heart, probably an entry wound, the blade apparently wrenched upward to cut the aorta and vena cava, then swept up and out.

Which had happened so fast Kenny Bryce didn't have time to fire his weapon. And would have left him only a few seconds of waning fight. Which would have caused the first lurch of his blood to land on the entryway tile, where I had seen it, where he was stabbed. And allowed it to surge and spread and sink in as he was dragged across the living room, up the stairs, down the hall, and into the room in which he slept.

What strength to accomplish all that, I thought. In another man's home. What ferocious resolve. What stone calm. And speed. Kenny Bryce's heart was Caliphornia's first strike. Deep and final. The beheading was a ritual. Something to inspire terror in the living.

Which it did.

I headed down the stairs, weapon face-high and pointed up. Felt the jab of panic, whirled. Heart racing and ears screaming. Empty stairs. Empty landing.

I cleared the garage, came back inside to the front door, and looked through the peephole. In the distorted distance, Lindsey and Voss had taken opposite ends of the porch. They stood in oddly similar postures, arms crossed and feet wide. Lindsey in the sun and Voss in the shade.

I cracked the door. "Kenny's been murdered," I said quietly. "Don't come in. You'll contaminate more evidence. Stay put. I need a few minutes."

"I came here to see Kenny," said Lindsey. "I'm coming in."

"Think," I said. "The police are going to question all of us, long and hard. I'll take the heat for going in. You stay ignorant. A tampering charge won't help your custody fight."

"We didn't know it was a damned crime scene," said Voss.

"That's my best defense," I said. "So let me go collect some things we'll need. We'll never get them if I don't get them now. A few minutes. Then we'll call the cops."

Lindsey looked to Voss, defaulting to the old order.

"He's right," said Voss.

She glared at Voss, then at me. "Did they cut off his head?"

I nodded, shut the door, and turned the deadbolt.

Got my phone into camera mode and shot the bloody tile and the bloody inside of the front door, and the revolver on the floor, and the carpet and steps and landing and hall and bedroom. The terrible bedroom. Shot his head and body. Macro to close-up. Video.

Then to the bed stand, where the reading lamp spread its cool light. Where waited Bryce's phone, charging, and placed to hold down the top of a handwritten letter that looked very similar to Lindsey's. An AF Falcons money clip, thick with bills, anchored the bottom.

Dear Lt. Bryce,

To cause another's death is to cause your own.

I am going to decapitate you with my knife. Like the swords of the great Saracen warriors, it has a name. It is Al Ra'ad. The thunder.

Watch for us. Listen for us. Believe every fearful thought.
Your end is our beginning.

Sincerely,

Caliphornia

I rattled off ten shots on auto-drive. Ten more. Wanted that letter cold.

The spare bedroom was Bryce's office. The desktop computer was sleeping. I tried some passwords based on Kenny Bryce's name, and Headhunters, USAF, and Air Force Falcons, which were featured on a wall poster, a coffee mug on the desk, even a mouse pad, in addition to the money clip. No luck. Looked over the last three months of a hardcover appointment calendar and found nothing of particular interest. Dinner with Ron and Kaya last Saturday. An appointment with Dr. Leising one day previous. Haircut next week. I shot the September through December calendar pages anyway.

In the bathroom I tore off some toilet paper, then went back to the meaty hell of Kenny's bedroom. The horror of a body and its severed head is not describable in the language that I know. There, I hovered over Kenny Bryce's cell phone. Hoped he'd left it on while charging. Figured the chances were fifty-fifty. Covered my fingertip with the toilet paper, hit the screen control. Clean blue light. Icons. A fly buzzing. Such a lucky day for Kenny and me and the world. I opened Contacts and scrolled down for Ron and Kaya, then Dr. Leising, wrote their numbers in my notebook. Noticed that my handwriting was forceful and shaky. Searched his contacts for anyone of obvious utility. Got Mom and Dad. I chose a few first-name-only contacts at random, on the theory that they were close to him. Brandon Goff's name jumped out at me like a clown from a dark closet.

Back downstairs I went through the mail on the kitchen counter. Found the envelope that the letter had come in—postmarked the same day as the threat to Lindsey, with a San Diego postmark and a return address belonging to World Pizza of Ocean Beach. Shot that and looked through what else was there.

I rolled off a paper towel and dampened it under the sink faucet. Cleaned my prints off the garage doorknob and the front-door deadbolt. Squeezed the towels dry over the sink, set the soggy wad in my coat pocket. I'd faithfully confess to America's Deadliest Police Force the basic truth of what I'd done, but I saw no use in advertising my curiosity. *No, sir. I had no idea what I was walking into.*

I stepped outside and closed the door behind me.

Lindsey was leaning against the porch railing. She offered me a hard stare and smeared a tear off her cheek with her palm.

Voss stood beside her. "We've just broken a bunch of laws," he said. "I think we should at least get our stories straight."

"Don't get creative," I said. "Tell the cops exactly what happened. I'll take point. When I'm done sending these pictures to myself, I'll call Bakersfield PD."

And Taucher.

"Lindsey, you need to answer a very important question. What was Brandon Goff's relationship to Kenny Bryce?"

"Friends. Air Force. We had us some times."

"Did they have a fight or a falling out?"

"Never."

"Was Bryce trying to get close to you since the divorce?"

"Absolutely not."

I glanced up toward the early-afternoon sun, a dazzling orange ball high in the blue. Wondering, if I could take away the roof of Kenny Bryce's upstairs bedroom, would that powerful sun burn away the blood and the bones and the horror? Burn them right down to nothing? I knew the answer, though: not in my lifetime. But if I could replace the roof with a magnifying glass of the same size—stupendously heavy and thick and perfectly proportioned and polished—maybe then? In the end I figured if I really wanted it all cleaned up right, I'd have to pour a gallon or two of gas over it and light the match.

I lit a cigarette instead, sat in one of the little bistro chairs and started tap-tap-tapping on my goddamned phone, bouncing images of headless Kenny Bryce from one point on planet Earth to another.

10

TWENTY-SEVEN HOURS LATER I was back home, outside on a chaise longue, bundled in my barn jacket and watching the black-orange December sunset. My grandfather Dick had just delivered to me a bruising bourbon. Just a splash of water. Dick doubts my well-being when I don't have a cocktail in my hand, and this time he wasn't totally wrong. I couldn't get the Bakersfield images from my brain. I wondered if I ever would. I wanted that drink.

"Judging by your face, I'd say your trip was not a huge success," said Dick. He sized me up over his highball glass, took a sip, and sat down on the chaise next to me.

"No, not huge."

I'd been detained and questioned for ten hours over two days, since calling 911 from Kenny Bryce's front porch. At the end of the first day I'd talked our way out of an overnight discretionary hold and into the Marriott downtown. A little sleep, then round two. I felt bent and folded and torn, but I had not yet been charged with any crime.

"Lindsey looked ready for the grave," Dick noted. "Might I have an executive summary of events?"

"No," I said. "Events involved a freshly slaughtered human being. That's all I'll say. And keep it to yourself."

I watched orange and black compete low in the western sky, black winning out. Listened to the clink of ice in Grandpa's glass. His wife, my grandma Liz, walked past him without a look and sat on the other side of me. She carried a balloon glass half full of red wine. They've been married fifty-something years, raised three children, helped to spoil eight grandchildren, and now reside in respective casitas at opposite ends of the pond.

"Welcome home, Rollie," she said, studying me. "Looks to me like you and Lindsey must have closed the nightclub twice."

"I wish I looked better for you two."

"Honey, can't he just enjoy a sunset?" asked Dick.

"Overall, though, Lindsey is quite fetching these days," said Liz. "And apparently her custody battle is going in her favor, too."

I nodded, sipped the bourbon. "It's nice to have her back," I said, regretting it immediately.

"I would think so," said Liz, swirling her glass.

"In what way is it nice, Roland?" asked Dick.

"In the way that a strong young man likes having a lovely woman around," said Liz. Another lift of her balloon glass.

"I've forgotten," said her husband.

"Fifty-one years of marriage and Dick lost interest halfway through," said Liz. "Garaged the car with plenty of miles still left on her."

"Do we have any noise-canceling headphones around here?" I said.

"I've got a pair in the house," said Dick. "Believe me, they're well used!"

Liz sighed and leaned back on the chaise. "Rollie, just FYI? The electrical in my place is acting up again. My brand-new microwave sparked and fizzled out last night. Had to drink my hot toddy cold."

"Why not use the stove?" asked her husband. "You remember how to boil water, don't you?"

"This Chilean wine I found must be really good. Halfway through and even you seem funny, hon."

"What's the latest on the cat?" asked Dick.

Owner Tammy Bellamy had left me four emails when I was closing nightclubs in Bakersfield. There had been two false sightings yesterday, Tuesday, and two more today. People were reporting average-weight gray striped cats—not twenty-two-pound Oxley. One was not even gray, and only one of them had Oxley's green eyes. Tammy said that the brief rain shower on Monday night had ruined most of the posters. Would I take a few minutes to replace the soaked posters with fresh ones from my stack?

"Tammy needs some help putting up new posters," I said. "You guys up for that tomorrow?"

"There are hundreds of them," said Dick.

"The rain ruined them," I said.

"She should never have let that cat get over ten pounds," said Liz.

"Tammy needs our help."

"You're making the big money off of this cat, not us," said Dick.

"I've got some of Tammy's apricot-brandy jam and you're welcome to it."

Dick shrugged. "Okay. Liz and I will put up more posters. But it's been what, ten days? Every time I hear those coyotes yapping I think Oxley just got lunched. What a racket those things make. And almost every night. Maybe Dale can shed some scientific light on why those animals are running around unchecked. Maybe find a way to cut their numbers down. Dale's won awards, you know."

"Coyotes have to make a living, too," Liz pointed out.

Dale being Dale Clevenger, award-winning video-journalist now residing in casita number two. Who, judging by the lights already on in the barn, was hard at work on his next program.

After the last strip of orange had blipped out over the black hills, I got a handful of LOST CAT flyers from my office and brought them down for Dick and Liz. They were disputing the truth of the "flash of green" in Key West sunsets: Liz pro and Dick con, on and on as always—poster models for how not to grow old. Or maybe they had it right: the secret to longevity was dispute.

Liz took the flyers and squared them on her lap. "We'll find this kitty."

Clevenger and Burt were in the barn. Radio news playing low, every light on. Clevenger had taken over one end of the space, arranging two long utility tables in a wide V shape for a workstation. One table for his three custom-made computers, three monitors, a bank of wireless speakers, and an audio mixing board. The other table for his drones and their corresponding tools. He had four, five, or six drones—the number kept changing. Tonight it was five, three of them whole and two taken apart for maintenance or repair.

Clevenger stood inside the V like an impresario, looking up from one of the monitors when I walked in. He's husky, curly-haired, and thick-armed. Hangdog eyes, big and expressive. Glasses always out of kilter, an air of benign intensity. He reached down to the audio mixer and the barn filled with the sound of yipping coyotes. It's a high-pitched sound, wild and inscrutable. Starts and stops abruptly. Eerie. Sounded like there were ten of them right there in the barn with us.

"How many of them are there, Roland?" he asked in his soft Georgia accent.

I'd been told that one coyote can make much more noise than you think. This sounded like a platoon. "Four."

"You're close. What's the most you've ever seen together, here in Fallbrook?"

"Four," I said. "Parents and two young ones, by the look of them."

"Check these guys out. Got them out near Winterwarm Street last night, that big field where the longhorns are pastured."

I came to the monitor to see six coyotes moving across a moonlit meadow, shot from above by drone. The light was weak and the animals looked ghostly. They had the familiar, light-footed coyote trot, and their heads were up. As if on cue they stopped, listened, then started yipping and howling again. Paced nervously. Something out there. Snouts raised, they howled at the drone. The camera panned to a half-dozen Texas longhorns—staunch and imposing creatures kept for nostalgia by a Texas-raised Fallbrook resident—watching the coyotes with little apparent interest.

Then back to the coyotes, silent and spreading into a loose half-circle to work their way across the pasture. Noses down. Noses up. One by one, disappearing into the thick scrub of an arroyo. Consumed, they struck up their inquisitive yipping again, their voices braiding together. I could barely see the forward shiver of brush as their bodies pushed through.

Suddenly the yips turned urgent, a crazed blast of determination rising in pitch. Then came to a perfect stop. Hushed snarls as the bushes quivered in the darkness. A rabbit shrieked and a puff of dust rose in the moonlight. Then the snarls of the five hungry coyotes snapping at one another while the lucky one tore into his prey. Beneath the soundtrack, the radio news ran on, Redskins in L.A. against the Chargers on Sunday. Clevenger stopped the show.

"How was Bakersfield?" asked Burt.

"Slow."

Clevenger gave me a look: curiosity and concern behind his crooked glasses. "Why don't you come out with us tonight, Roland? I could use another hand. We're going back to the longhorn pasture, but this time I've got floodlights set up. Enough to light up a soccer practice. Sometimes when you light these critters, they give you dirty looks and high-tail it. Sometimes they just keep on doing whatever they're doing. I've got the cameras and mikes, infrared binoculars, and two drones ready. We'll call the animals in with the varmint recording."

Clevenger touched a keyboard and the sounds of the coyotes killing the rabbit filled the barn again. I was sick to my soul with death. The brush parted and the coyotes looked straight up at the drone overhead.

"No Oxley?" I asked.

Clevenger shook his head. "Didn't see him. But I'm ready if I do. Got my Kevlar animal gloves and the crate out there in the van."

"I'll pass tonight," I said.

"It's cold and boring, mostly," said Clevenger. "But you're welcome to come along anytime."

Burt walked me across the barnyard, toward the house. He's small and takes short, fast steps and I'm tall and take long, slow ones. If you added us together and divided by two you'd get an average man. A year and a half ago, we were little more than landlord and tenant, agreeable strangers. Then he'd offered to help me out of a very tight situation. Two capable men had wanted to do me harm. There's a story behind it, like there's a story behind everything, but the punchline is that Burt and I prevailed at great cost to my tormentors. The cost to ourselves, we have not discussed. But in that muzzle-flashed moment, we become something new to each other. I trust him with my life, and I owe it to him.

"Someone's threatened Lindsey," I said. "That's why she's here."

He looked up at me, matter-of-fact. "She's jumpy."

"Someone wants her head, Burt. Literally. He decapitated a guy in Bakersfield two nights ago. One of Lindsey's old Air Force buddies."

"One of the Headhunters?"

I nodded.

"Hunter becomes hunted. You think this beheader is working alone?"

"I think he's got help. Just my gut on that."

"Where did it happen?"

I knew he'd talked to Lindsey, but I gave him the basics anyway. He nodded along. Burt gets things quickly, including some things other people don't. "Samara," he said. "The Prince Charming she dated one time in Las Vegas. The one with the handwriting that looks like the threat. I wonder if he was in the Bakersfield area two nights ago."

I told him the FBI was looking into that.

"I'll make sure Lindsey's door and window locks are sound," he said. "And install a wireless security system in her casita, something she can monitor by phone. I'm up most nights anyway, so I can keep an eye out. You might think about moving her every few days. Motels, cash, new IDs. I've got a friend who breeds Cane Corsos—that's 'dog of the guard' in Italian. Very capable and well-trained animals. He leases them out for protection. He could have one here in a day or two. Does Lindsey still have that pistol?"

I nodded.

"Tell her to be careful with it."

We continued along the pond, then doubled back toward the casitas and the main house. I could see lights on in Lindsey's casita number three. Apparently, Liz and Dick had gone to their respective corners. Casita four was vacant.

I sensed that something was bothering Burt. He's never been one for an evening stroll, or walking me home. "Saturday, the day before Lindsey got here, I went to Joe's Hardware for a space heater," he said. "Noticed a nice black C-Class Mercedes SUV behind me. Big guy at the wheel, long black hair, sunglasses. Wearing a blue leather moto jacket. Very fashionable for this hick town. Fine. Got the heater, put it in my trunk in the parking lot. I went east on Main for home, and by the time I'm to Mission there's the black Mercedes SUV behind me again. Fashion boy at the wheel. He followed me two vehicles back all the way here. Waiting at the gate, I watched him in the rearview. He went right on by, not a pause.

"Two days later, on my way to golf, same black SUV fell in behind me on Old 395. Same guy. I pulled into the club, he went by. Shot nine rounds—one under—went to the restaurant for lunch, and when I left he was sitting in his car in the lot. Same blue moto jacket. I got into my car and drove home. When I came to the gate I punched the code and came through and pulled in behind the bougainvillea. Sure enough, here comes Moto Man. Slowed down when he went past your drive. Took a long look in. Gate still open. I'd already figured he wasn't looking for me. He had me, twice. And if he just wanted to draft in past the gate behind me, why didn't he? First, I thought Clevenger. He had some trouble back in New Orleans, moons ago. Then I thought Lindsey— something to do with her ex, maybe. The custody dispute."

I hadn't seen a black Mercedes SUV around Rancho de los Robles, or in any other place that might stand out. I thought back to the previous morning, when I'd driven Lindsey and myself to the Fallbrook Airpark. Still before sunrise. Darkness and empty winding roads. No hundred-thousand-dollar German SUVs that I noticed.

"Think about that Cane Corso," said Burt. "Best guard dog there is."

"So you say."

"My friend Bruno? He trains them right and contracts them out for people who need protection. Expensive, and kind of limiting, a large beast like that in your face twenty-four/seven. But Lindsey in casita three with a Cane Corso napping on a pad inside the door? *That's* security, Roland. The beheader would never know what hit him."

I sat in the dark in my office for a while, ailing from what I had seen in Bakersfield. Ugliness causes ugliness, happiness makes happiness. Opposite momentums. Joy is easy to ride, the way I had ridden it with Justine. Higher and higher. Until. Icarus? But so hard to ride death. Which led me to Justine. Which led me to Kenny Bryce. Which led me to the rabbit screaming briefly on Clevenger's video. Leading me, of course, to my own death, whenever and however it might come. Death. One and whole and undefeatable. Spirals inside spirals.

My mother, who is only occasionally softhearted and almost never sentimental, told me something once that had the ring of truth to it: when you feel bad, do something good for someone else.

I told Burt not to let Lindsey out of his sight or off the property until I got back. Then got a handful of LOST CAT flyers from my office desk, then a staple gun and a hiker's headlight from the barn.

It was a cool night and dark. A quarter moon. Fallbrook's country roads are curving and unlighted, and the shoulders are thin, and the vegetation grows right up to the asphalt on both sides. The canopies of large old oak trees join hands from opposite sides of the narrow roads. Minor moonlight blinks by overhead and there is really just the faint white line to guide you through the curves. Headlights appeared behind me, coming fast. I pulled over to let a Porsche convertible howl past. A blonde in the passenger seat, hair streaming.

I stopped along Old 395, left the engine running and the headlights on while I pulled a rain-faded Oxley poster from a power pole and stapled up a new one. In the beam of my hiker's headlight, Oxley's hypnotic green eyes regarded me. I made another stop on 395 as I worked my way toward Fallbrook. I tried to make a rational assessment of the obese cat's chances of survival after nearly a week and a half of coyotes, dark roads, and fast cars. Not good chances, by my reckoning.

I sensed a tail a mile from town, made a stop anyway. Got a gun from the locked toolbox in the bed of my truck, pocketed it in my barn coat. Stapled an Oxley poster to a white post-and-rail fence. A black Mercedes SUV passed by. I continued onto Mission, passed it, and pulled into a deep, oak-roofed turnout. Saw headlights in my rearview mirror two curves back. Not terrific tradecraft.

When I hit town I hung fresh LOST CAT posters outside Vega's Tailor, El Toro Market, and the Mission Theater. Put the old flyers and the hiker's headlight on the seat beside me. Looked down at Oxley, blanched by rain, fading into history. I fought back the pessimism. Heard Mom's voice. Something good for someone else. Hoped her travels with Dad were going well. This month: Florida.

I'd just stapled a poster on the wall of the Main Street Café when the black Mercedes SUV pulled to the curb and parked in front of my truck. Burt Short's fashion man stepped out, eyed me across the hood of his vehicle, then started my way. No blue moto jacket, just jeans and a black car coat against the December chill. His hair was black and unruly, much longer than he had worn it as a San Diego sheriff's deputy during our two months as partners.

"Hello, Jason," I said. "What brings you out tonight?"

"Lindsey Rakes. Your new tenant."

"You mean my former tenant?"

"Maybe we should talk."

I considered the pros and cons of having to lie to my old partner, now a licensed private investigator himself. And I was more than a little interested in what had brought him here. "Right this way."

11

JUST A FEW STEPS down Main Street was my new downtown office. New to me, at least, as of late last year when I decided I needed a place away from home to meet with clients—attempted murder, gunfire, and justifiable homicide being things best left outside the rancho.

The office is next door to the Dublin Pub, open but quiet at this hour. I could smell the fish and chips, hear the jukebox. I put the old-fashioned key into the old-fashioned door lock and let Jason in. Fallbrook is an old-fashioned town.

The lobby was small and neat—a directory, mail slots for each of the six offices in the building, a small table with a display of silk flowers. Old crate labels hung on the walls, brightly colored images of oranges, sunny groves, smiling young women holding out ripe fruit. And, interspersed with them, a few of my Oxley posters. I straightened the "California Girl" frame.

"Impressive office building," said Jason.

"It gets better."

I hit the lights and we climbed the creaking stairs to my second-floor office. The sound of shoes on carpet, then hardwood, a wide landing and three closed doors: Anders Wealth Management, Rick Topp Construction, Ford Investigations.

"I figured you for something more contemporary," said Jason.

"None of that around here," I said.

My office is spacious, with a coffered high ceiling and views up and down Main Street. It really is a Main Street, too—in the small-town sense—mom-and-pop shops, a candy store, a barber shop with a spiraled pole outside, a hardware store, a café with a fountain. Even a playhouse and some art galleries. But some modern touches, too—an Internet cafe, a craft brewery, hot yoga. I looked up and down the now dark and quiet street below. Switched on a lamp, set the Oxley posters on the credenza. Pulled over a chair for Jason, then sat behind my desk.

He hadn't changed much in the last nine years. Same cut-from-stone face, ready eyes, and deep voice. He had always looked like an untalented actor playing a cop. Like he couldn't quite emote. In the two months we'd spent as partners-in-uniform, I didn't get to know him well. Five years younger than me, a wife and daughter. Drove an overpay-grade BMW even back then.

With a shared past like Jason Bayless's and mine, there is almost no room for small talk. Nine years ago we had lived through a terrible moment together, seen it different ways, and behaved accordingly. Recounted and relived it accordingly. And because of its terribleness it became not a moment at all, but a lifetime.

"Do you still think about it, Roland?"

"Not often," I said.

"I would do it my way again," he said.

"I'd do it mine."

And with that, of course, I was forced to think about it.

In my memory, that three p.m. in Imperial Beach is always clear and precise. December 22 and cold, Deputies Bayless and Ford on their foot beat—specifically, we're in a dirty alley behind a low-rent strip mall. There, in a patch of sunlight angling down through a gray-black sky, one Titus Miller backpedals away from us in his too-big overcoat and mismatched athletic shoes. One blue and the other red. Titus, homeless and occasionally violent, often high or drunk, sometimes clearly deranged, a man with nothing but his foul-smelling clothes and a bundle of possessions he had lashed to a wheeled cart with plastic newspaper bags tied end to end. Titus, age nineteen, black. Titus, who would smile and cry real tears for the ten dollars you gave him. Titus, cussing us badly and letting go of his cart and backpedaling, throwing open his too-big overcoat with both hands to get at something in his waistband, something hand-sized, dully black but metal-shiny, too, and maybe it was snagged or stuck, very hard to tell in that bright sun.

We both drew down, Jason cursing Titus while I ordered him to freeze, and Titus not freezing, still trying to get that shiny thing out of his dirty layers of clothes.

And again I see, with the same unvarying clarity as always, Titus freeing that dull/shiny black thing with both hands and extending it toward me as he stops his retreat and drops into a shooter's stance. I see his expression as he looks at me over the sights of my weapon. Nothing in his eyes but fear and nothing in his hands but a wallet. Five shots from Jason—concussive, gun-range close, bullets twang-sparking off a waste bin behind Titus. Titus in wholesale collapse, the wallet falling from his hands, still lashed to his belt by its shiny chain.

"I'd like it to go away," said Jason.

I nodded.

But taking a life becomes a life of its own. Becomes a different life, for all involved.

December 22.

Peace on earth, goodwill toward men.

Protests in Imperial Beach, San Diego, L.A., San Francisco, and Oakland. Most peaceful, some not. Rubber bullets and bricks on cop cars.

The biker-style chained wallet was found to be empty, and was a recent acquisition of Titus's, according to a liquor store clerk who had sold it to him at a steep discount as a Christmas present.

The crime lab found a badly rusted .22-caliber six-gun buried deep in Titus's cart. Loaded.

Six months later, the Internal Affairs deputy-involved shooting investigation was complete, and found that Deputy Roland Ford had acted properly within the law and the scope of his authority. And that Deputy Jason Bayless had used excessive and unnecessary force in the death of Titus Miller, nineteen, emotionally disturbed and unarmed.

"You never understood that I was afraid for *your* life, too," said Bayless. "Not just mine."

"I did understand that, Jason."

"I was trying to save my partner from a man with a history of violence and a loaded firearm in his possession."

"We don't need to go through it again," I said.

"But I want to, now that time has given me a chance to hate you less."

"Okay," I said. "What happened that day is, I saw a wallet and you saw a gun and tried to save me from it."

Jason leaned forward, his stone-cut face beveled in the lamplight. "When IA asked your opinion of my judgment, you did not stand by me."

"You're right," I said. "I did not. I saw a terrified man brandishing a wallet. You saw a criminal with a history of violence about to shoot your partner. I can't change what I saw and neither can you. The only difference is my eyes were better than yours that day."

He sat back and considered me. "You took my life as I knew it. I tried to protect you. And in so doing became a murderer. A pariah. A despised man. What's left besides hate?"

Then a long silence in which I sensed in Bayless the stirrings of revenge and dreamed-of violence, long knotted inside.

"I wish it was different, Jason."

"Those words mean nothing."

I looked straight across at him. "So how do you like the PI's life?"

Which is where Jason Bayless and I had both landed. At very close to the same time.

"It pays the bills," he said.

"Yes," I said. "Mostly."

"I have no heiress's fortune to spend."

I nodded and said nothing.

"Although, Roland, I'm sorry for what happened to her. I felt bad for you, even."

A moment of respect for Justine and the memory of her. "So what's this about my old tenant?" I asked.

"I've been hired to locate her," he said. "Her name rang a bell, so I started with the same kind of search a fourth-grader would do for a report. Took me to your helicopter shootout with Briggs Spencer last year. I confirmed a few things with friends that I still have in the department. As you know, among the players on your property that day was tenant Lindsey Rakes, a then-unemployed twenty-nine-year-old female, former U.S. Air Force and divorced mother of one. I can't help but wonder if she came back your way."

"She moved back to Las Vegas a month after the shootout with Spencer."

"Tracersinfo.com told me that much," he said. "She moved to Vegas, where, according to Clark County Court records, her custody tug-of-war for son John Goff, age nine, continues. Trouble is, she left town last Thursday and I think she might have landed here. Where she knows a few people. Like you. So if you could just tell Lindsey to call me and confirm her whereabouts, then I can get paid and cancel this case and buy my family some neat stuff for Christmas."

"Who hired you?"

"Jesus, Ford—I can't tell you that."

I had a notion. "Goff. Her ex. Paper to serve?"

Jason leaned back in his chair again, his car coat falling open like a gunslinger in a western. Instead of drawing a six-gun, he opened both hands in a show of peaceful refusal to answer my question.

"I thought about going to a county service for Miller, but there wasn't one," he said. "Just an indigent remains disposition. They actually call it that. Cremation."

"I looked into it, too."

"I'd like to wake up and feel blameless for a day," said Jason.

A moment of silence, in memory of the seconds that change our lives forever.

"Who hired you to find Lindsey?" I asked again.

Jason shrugged.

"If I knew, I might be able to help you out," I said.

"But you haven't seen her in a year and a half. Remember?"

I leaned across the desk toward him. "Jason, there's some real bad stuff in the air for Lindsey right now. Terrible stuff. And you might be playing right into it."

"My job is to find her," he said. "If you don't help me, maybe *you're* playing into it."

An interesting idea. One I did not like.

He stood and I walked him to the door. Picked a few Oxley posters from the credenza and gave them to Jason.

"What's with the damned cat anyway?" he asked.

"Something my mom taught me."

"My mom taught me loyalty until the bitter end," said Bayless. "She's Irish."

"So is mine."

12

JOAN TAUCHER STARTED OUT half a step ahead of me on the Embarcadero, her boots tapping a cadence on the boardwalk. We were southbound in the brisk morning, too early for tourists, under a gray blanket of clouds that looked heavy enough to lie on. A cold Pacific storm from the north was due by noon. I'd had my morning run into the hills, my half-hour alternating the heavy and speed bags in the barn, some sit-ups. Felt clear and ready.

"Thanks for the early call and the pictures," she said. "I don't think those images will leave my head anytime soon. Of all the stuff I've seen—plane wrecks to crime scenes to autopsies to cartel snuffs—those were the pure worst."

"They're stuck in my head, too."

"Oh, Christ," said Taucher, stopping and looking at me. "I'm sorry. I shouldn't have said plane wrecks. I wasn't thinking."

Planes and wrecks. My heart beats faster when I hear an older Cessna 182 churning through the sky above. Taucher had no way of knowing that I'd first laid eyes on Justine Timmerman during a cold winter storm like the one about to hit us. At a holiday party in the Grand Hyatt hotel, which was just a few blocks from where we now walked. I looked up at that hotel, a mirrored wedge atop the skyline. Remembered red-haired Justine in her red party dress and the rain lashing the windows of the banquet room.

Taucher reclaimed her half-step lead. "My bedside manner has always sucked," she said. A gull wheeled and cried and Joan's boot heels thumped along. "Anyway, I sent your picture of the Bakersfield threat letter to our questioned-documents section. Match. Same writer as Lindsey's and Voss's threats. No doubt of that. And speaking of Lindsey's threat, the original you so heroically salvaged for me—the lab found DMSO on the letter and the envelope."

"Horse liniment."

"I thought of Rasha Samara's Arabians, like you are right now," she said. "But no DMSO on his thank-you note or envelope. DMSO is also a remedy for aching humans, and you can get it at any feed and tack store. The trace particles left on the paper were clear. And don't forget, our documents section could *not* establish that Samara wrote the threat to Lindsey. Based on comparison with a perfect handwriting sample—his thank-you note. To which he signed his own name."

The cruise-ship terminal was coming up on our right. I could see the impressive *Emerald Empress* at dock, the gangplanks being moved into place. The cloud blanket had not visibly moved in the heavy pre-storm stillness.

Taucher turned to look at me, then slowed her pace. "Now, the calligraphy pen used to write the letters was likely the same instrument. Note I said *pen,* not marker. Our writer is a fascinating combination of artist and amateur. His instruments could be considered professional grade, but his execution is fair at best. Self-taught, probably. With a how-to calligraphy book and a good sample of Arabic writing to work from, most people could do what Caliphornia did."

"Maybe he *is* Arabic."

"Back to Rasha? Maybe. But Rasha Samara is native-born and Caliphornia's phrasing sounds slightly foreign. *I want to decapitate you with my knife . . . to cause you death.* The Bakersfield threat was less stilted but stuffed with Islamic references. The writer used a one-millimeter stainless steel nib, with minute flaws that both our stereo-microscope and spectral comparator picked up. The tip is iridium. The lab thinks the nib used on both threats was a Brause Hatat, which the Brause catalog recommends for Hebrew and Arabic writing. More comparison testing to come, but the same flaws showed up on both documents. They're like tool marks on bullets or cartridge casings. Same writer, same pen. Same ink, also—an acrylic shellac suspending the pigments and dyes. The ink is animal-free, which means likely a high-end maker."

We continued down the boardwalk. Joggers and walkers and a few moms with strollers. "Why are you telling me this, Joan?"

Which brought us to a stop. And got me a flat stare.

"I'm helping you, dumbass."

"Why?"

"I respect what you're trying to do for Lindsey Rakes," she said. "I respect your loyalty to her. She told me you're not charging her for protection, investigation, anything related to this."

I thought of Jason Bayless's charges against my loyalty, and was momentarily glad to have a differing opinion from Taucher. Deep loyalty has two very sharp edges. In truth, when I resigned from the Sheriff's

Department, I questioned my loyalty, too. It was always Us against Them. And I'd willingly ditched the Us. So what did that say about me?

"More important, Ford—I'll help anyone who can help *me* cancel Caliphornia's ticket here in my Golden State. You are my citizen and I need your help. That terrorist son of a bitch is cutting off American heads on my watch, and I can't even build a decent suspect profile. He's out there, and he's ten steps ahead of us. And, as my father liked to say, *that frosts my balls.*"

I looked down at Taucher as she regarded the ships on the water. In the cloudy coastal light, her heavily made-up eyes were raptorlike. Light brown in the iris, and unblinking. Startlingly clear. I wondered if she dreamed only of work and of terror and how to banish it from her city. Though I knew that wasn't likely, I couldn't guess or even convincingly imagine *what* she might dream about, other than that. I didn't care exactly, but for some reason I wanted to know.

She was right about not having enough knowledge of Caliphornia to effectively cast even the widest of nets.

"You know I'm in," I said.

She nodded.

"Did Bakersfield PD show you the security video?"

"Indeed they did," said Taucher. "It's grainy. Isn't security video always grainy? From liquor stores to international airports. They haven't improved the common security video camera in what, thirty years?"

"Why are you torturing me, Joan?"

She actually looked surprised. "Well, male—we saw that much. His race is iffy. Maybe Caucasian, but just as easily a light-skinned Semite, Latin or Arab. Rule out black and Asian. When I said grainy I wasn't kidding. And the angle is terrible. There are six and a half seconds of recording. Two seconds show him in profile, from the side as he comes into the camera, moving toward the apartments. The last four and a half seconds are of his back. He looks somewhere in his twenties or thirties, six-feet-one or -two, one hundred seventy to two hundred pounds. Dressed like a surfer or a boarder—flannel and loose pants, those big clunky board shoes. And a half-zipped U.S. Air Force hoodie, which is maybe why Kenny Bryce opened his door. The hood was up in the video, hiding his hair and most of his face. A cool-dude walk. Light gait. Well balanced. The video was taken from high up and mostly behind. He'd obviously cased the place and knew where the cameras were. On his way back into the carport, he trotted, hood up and head down. That light gait again, like an athlete. The detectives told me it was the only camera that caught him. No one saw such a man come or go that night. Caliphornia arrived at eleven ten and departed at eleven twenty-six, according to the video time and date stamp."

I remembered the cameras on the carport. "All the front doors would be off-screen," I said.

"Yes," said Taucher. "Unfortunate for us, but a valid privacy issue. Because from the blood, it looks like Caliphornia stabbed Bryce in the heart before he even got past the door. Before Bryce could even fire his gun. Imagine the stones it would take to do that with a porch light shining down on you. And the door open. You're in plain sight."

"I'm surprised Kenny Bryce opened his door," I said. "The peephole worked well enough."

Taucher nodded. "Here's where the path forks. If you take the right fork to answer why he opened his door, you get the Air Force hoodie logo. Bryce would immediately register a friendly. I saw all that Air Force stuff in his office. Or maybe Caliphornia flashed a convincing law enforcement ID. Such as the Air Force Office of Special Investigations."

"What if the ID was genuine?" I asked.

Taucher cut me a sharp look. The idea of American agents becoming murderers or terrorists does not sit well with American agents, even those in agencies who refuse to cooperate or even get out of each other's way. I'd touched her federal nerve.

"For that matter, maybe Bryce knew Caliphornia," she said. "Saw him through the peep and swung the door right open."

I had thought the same, and realized that Lindsey might know him, too.

"He *seems* to know them," said Taucher. "He used the word *personal* with Lindsey. He accused Bryce of causing death—most likely a reference to his war experience. The same with the threat to Voss."

Consequences and calculations came at me in silence then, as we strode south down the Embarcadero. A cold breeze broke the stillness, blurring the smooth water of the bay. I heard the halyards and lanyards ringing from the yachts.

"And if you take the left fork to answer that question?" I asked. "Why Bryce opened his door to Caliphornia?"

Another unhappy glance. "Someone walked past that security camera thirty seconds ahead of Caliphornia. Headed the same way. A woman. Again—terrible video. Young, judging by her movement and posture. Dressed in layers. Like maybe a sweater and shawl for the cold. Or a full-length overcoat. Carrying something up against her left side. A package? A twelve-pack? A bundle of mail? You can't tell. She was right at the edge of the picture. Four seconds and gone. The manager didn't recognize her. Neighbors didn't, either. Was she with Caliphornia? We don't know. Did she knock on Bryce's door? We don't know. We can't even say where she went once she passed out of the camera's field of view."

I said the obvious: "Kenny might be more likely to open his door to a woman."

"Exactly."

The breeze rose, rippling the bay.

"Lindsey's with you, right?" asked Taucher. "Physically on your property? None of this motel-room-in-Las-Vegas bullshit?"

"She's with me."

"You think you can protect her?"

"Yes, I do."

"You see what you're up against?"

"I see it."

"I hate amateurs, Roland."

"I do, too, Joan."

"My medical examiners say Caliphornia is a good beheader."

"What is a good beheader?"

"It was relatively fast and clean," she said. "Done with a long-handled, fixed-blade knife that was very sharp. They can tell by the length and depth of the cuts, and how cleanly the vertebrae were severed. 'A sashimi-sharp knife wielded by a two-hundred-pound weightlifter' is how one of them put it. Our MEs have such atrocious senses of humor."

Very sharp, I thought. As a knife sharpened on a whetstone might be.

"The MEs won't rule out two attackers, even though the crime scene people say one," said Joan. "Two different sets of angles on the slashes."

"Or one man with two knives," I said.

"A ninja-style beheader?" asked Taucher. "Doubtful."

"Maybe he's high," I said. I was thinking of fenethylline, a powerful amphetamine manufactured in Syria and Iraq, and sold to fighters on both sides. Fighting pills. The popular name is Captagon and it was once manufactured for profit in the United States. Coming from makeshift labs in the Middle East, Captagon is a crude brown tablet. In Fallujah we found bags full of them on insurgents. Captagon is alleged to stimulate unnatural strength, stamina, and cruelty in whoever takes it.

Taucher looked at me unhappily, as if I were adding to her problems. "Captagon?"

"Or something like it."

"You think this guy is Middle Eastern?" she asked. "Careful what you say. They'll start calling you phobic and obsessive. A burned-out witch on a mission."

"Read the threats again," I said. "The language of them. If you need reminding."

"I don't need reminding, and I can't shake the image of Kenny's decapitation. The lab said Caliphornia was able to use his victim's weight—and gravity—to accomplish his mutilation. Really put his back and legs into it. The average human head weighs sixteen pounds."

A surprising levity in her voice. Gallows humor? One way to deal with horror. Then shoes on the boardwalk, coming fast behind us. Taucher wheeled on the runner huffing past, eyes wide and not a little wild.

"Okay," she said, her voice possibly one small degree more hopeful. "I'd like to thank you again for the Bryce pictures and the early heads-up. You helped me. You didn't have to."

I told her she was welcome and immediately asked her where Rasha Samara had been the night Kenny Bryce died.

She glanced at me, then away. "We're working on it. We're good at that kind of thing. But not even the FBI can watch everybody every hour. Think of all those faces on my office walls."

I did, nodding.

"I'm sure you've gathered the basics on Samara," she said. "What more do you want?"

"I want to know why you're looking at him. He builds golf courses and rides horses."

"Because he's a rich American of Saudi descent who travels frequently to the Middle East, is widely known and connected, and has relationships with Saudi-Arabian political and business players. These people have money, rivers of it, all flowing down to them from oil. Rasha associates with some people whom the Bureau is *this* close to classifying as sponsors of terrorism." She turned to me mid-stride and raised one hand to brandish a quarter-inch gap between thumb and forefinger. "*This* close. And this ends the Rasha Samara discussion we didn't have."

"Understood. I thank you for your help."

"I don't dislike you and I want you to protect Lindsey."

"I'm glad you don't dislike me."

"I do permit myself certain emotions."

"Name one, Joan."

I saw the flicker of humor on her face. Our pace slowed just a little. Taucher tried to get back on task but some of the fight had gone out of her voice. In its place was something new. Resignation? Disappointment?

Then ten steps each in silence, more or less synchronous, taking us farther down the boardwalk. Don't know why I counted them. The fretful bed of gray clouds had still not seemed to move, even as the breeze came faster.

"I will now share a confidence with you," said Taucher. "I don't like being seen outside."

"Why not?"

"Because of my makeup. You've noticed that I wear heavy makeup."

"Yes. Why?" I asked. I felt like a compass needle unable to settle.

"Well, the makeup on my face is to hide what's under it," she said. "But around my eyes, the makeup is to show them off. My eyes are my only good feature."

"I've never suspected you of vanity."

"Doesn't it scream out?"

"Your eyes look good, Joan. But what are you hiding?"

"I'll tell you. I used to get kicked and punched in my face a lot in MMA. Goes with the territory, like with your boxing. One day, in a match, I got kicked really hard. Didn't see it coming. Knocked me down but I got right back up. Won that fight, too. The downside was this acute hematoma that developed on my cheek. Kind of like a blood blister but deeper. Left cheek, over the bone but spreading down almost to my mouth, and up into my left nostril. And the hematoma never went away. It faded some. And it got a little smaller. But it turned from liver red to this cadaver-gray, raised, pore-dotted splotch that would look like hell on any person's face. But this is *my* face, so I use the makeup. Of course, you can't make up only a part of your face without calling attention to your secret. You have to go all in. That's me. I've gone to dermatologists and cosmetologists and clinics and classes and consultants, all to learn how to put on makeup like a pro. I traveled to Tokyo to study makeup with an actual Geisha. I've *worked* at it. Still, when I'm outside, especially on a cloudy damp day like today? Well, if I'm not perfectly and heavily defended with my makeup, I look like an aging woman who got kicked in the face too many times and too hard. Which is what I am. I wish I didn't have to make myself up like a whore. I dislike my vanity. But not as much as my hematoma. Does any of that make any sense at all?"

She laughed, brief and dry. Then turned to face the bay. The rain hit hard and suddenly. Slapped heavy on the water, raising mist like steam. We stopped under a metal restaurant awning built to protect waiting customers from the sun, raindrops roaring down.

"How are you going to handle Bakersfield with the media?" I asked.

"Publicly, we're not involved," she said. "I'm leaving it all to BPD. Their show."

"Are they going public with the mutilation?"

"No," said Joan. "Not with the threat, either. Just that he was found stabbed to death in his home. We weighed the value of telling the whole truth against the terror it might cause. It felt really good to deny this bag of dirt his moment in the sun."

"He doesn't seem to want publicity at all," I said.

"You watch," she said. "He'll change, now that he's followed through with Kenny Bryce. Classic pattern of radicalization. Anger, disillusionment, curiosity, commitment, action, escalation. He's got confidence now. He'll seek credit. He'll be vulnerable to recruiters. We'll hear some kind of communication from him. I expect it. I dread it."

She dug her phone from her coat. She held her device up close and it chimed and a cool glow played off her face. I looked for the hematoma but couldn't make it out. Wondered if it prognosticated dire events, like my own scar did. Her pale raptor's eyes seemed to draw the light from the screen as her thumbs flew and the glow from the phone changed colors. She stared at the screen for a long moment, then slid the phone back into her pocket.

"Sorry," she said. "My handlers like a short leash these days. Your turn now. What did you learn about Hector Padilla?"

I told her about my conversation with youth imam Hadi Yousef, and the odd behavior of Padilla at Masjid Al-Rribat Al-Islami. His interest in Islam, and in finding a Muslim woman. His loitering outside the women's prayer room. When I told her about the large sharpening stone that had fallen from Hector's upturned backpack and landed on Hadi's desk, Taucher's breath caught. "Who carries around a fucking sharpening stone?"

"Hadi said it looked new."

Taucher's eyes narrowed, and, heavily made up or not, sparked with anger. "Is he still working at that hospital on Genesee?"

"He works a midnight shift," I said. "And yes, he worked the night Kenny Bryce was killed."

She betrayed some small hint of appreciation of my professional reach. "You have a source at First Samaritan?"

I shrugged. One of my old deputy friends was their head of security. For him, a call to the janitorial subcontractor was all it took.

"I need one more thing," I said.

"You're the neediest informant I've ever run."

"I have to see the surveillance video from Kenny Bryce's place."

An SDPD police cruiser came by, tires swooshing through the quickly rising rainwater. The patrolman gave us a look.

"That's physical evidence," she said. "They'd have my head. God, I have to stop saying things like that. Anyway, the surveillance video is a tall order, Ford."

"I understand."

"Maybe you don't," she said. "The video is FBI property and I can't let it leave the building. Not physically, not electronically. Either one gets me written up, demoted, or canned."

"Send me a self-destruct file," I said. "Then I can't betray you."

Exasperation. "They'll see it the second I send it."

"Have someone else send it."

Spy versus spy, I thought. Until now, I'd never thought of Taucher as at risk from her own organization. I'd thought of her as a rock. Now I wondered about her short leash. But as I considered it, I saw that she would have her internal enemies, just like any other ambitious employee. Maybe more. Her fierce attitude. Her blunt humorlessness. Her legendary obsession with 9/11. The fact that she could never quite be a part of the old-boys network.

"And," she continued, "if I bring you back to JTTF again to show you that video behind closed doors, heads will turn. 'What's with Taucher and that PI? What's the paranoid old hag up to now?'"

I told her I knew what it was like to work in a large organization. What happens if it turns on you. "You might enjoy private work, Joan. Like mine."

"Is that supposed to be funny?" But before I could answer, she said, "But you should see it—the Bryce video. I'll think of something."

"Six and a half seconds," I reminded her.

"I've got an idea," she said. "But get off my back, Ford. I don't negotiate."

I nodded and watched the rain pelting the bay, half amazed that Joan Taucher would put herself at risk to help her neediest informant. I'd been a genuine help to her so far—I'd *brought* Caliphornia and his threats to her instead of to her superiors—but how much more favor would that earn me?

And I was puzzled, but somehow pleased, that heavily made-up Taucher had chosen to be seen outside by me. I wasn't sure why I was pleased. Maybe something as simple as not disliking her. Maybe something as simple as being on the same side. "It's all about risk and trust," I said.

"What is?"

"Heading into a storm you know is there," I said.

A glimmer of mirth in her eyes. "It doesn't rain in San Diego," she said.

13

PSYCHIATRIST JARED LEISING had seen Kenny Bryce approximately twenty-four hours before his death. Bryce had been in treatment with the doctor for four years. Kenny had left the Air Force two years previous, to do landscape maintenance for Kern County, but apparently he had thought highly enough of the doctor to drive the four-plus hours from Bakersfield to Las Vegas once a month to see him.

Leising was wiry, in his early fifties, with a pair of rimless Freudian glasses and a sharp Vandyke to complete the psychoanalytic look. He had told me over the phone that Kenny Bryce was one of his favorite people, and he was shocked by what had happened. He had been expecting a call from the Bakersfield PD, not from a PI from San Diego.

Hall Pass 2 had landed me here in Las Vegas just in time for a $7.99 all-you-can-eat breakfast buffet at a minor downtown casino and a short Uber to Dr. Leising's office. The storm had passed and the late Las Vegas morning was cold and sunny.

Leising's consulting room was crisply lit and furnished in a fifties desert style—orange carpet, an aqua-colored couch and chairs, and lime-green wall assemblies in various geometric shapes. I took one of the aqua chairs and Leising the other.

He crossed his legs and set his notepad and pen on the white cylindrical stand beside him. "I don't know where to start or what to say," he said. "Can you ask me the questions? Rather than what usually happens here in this room?"

"Tell me how you met Kenny."

It was four years ago, Leising said, while Kenny Bryce was flying Headhunter missions out of Creech AFB. Kenny had come to him on the advice of his pilot, Marlon Voss, and his sensor, Lindsey Rakes, both of whom were seeing Leising occasionally to work through "combat-related stresses."

It surprised me that Lindsey had never mentioned her psychiatrist. But I'm a believer in the right to keep and bear secrets. Which is probably why the Headhunters had taken their burdens to someone outside their own Air Force mental health system. Combat stress is hard enough; the stigma of PTSD is a military career killer.

Dr. Leising's voice was clear and his words seemed to be amplified by the hard, brightly colored surfaces of the interior. He said that he thought he could help Kenny, because Bryce's symptoms were not unlike those of Voss and Lindsey, and a number of other RPA—remotely piloted aircraft—operators that Leising had treated.

He said that his general approach with combat stress was to go light on drugs and heavy on talk, exercise, and clean living. Mostly talk, he emphasized. He was old-fashioned in that way.

"What were Bryce's symptoms?" I asked.

"Fatigue. Anger. Anxiety. Sleeplessness. Confusion. Like many other people, Kenny tried to self-regulate with alcohol and marijuana. Which exacerbated the symptoms and dulled his performance as a flier. And later, in his job with the county, in Bakersfield."

I thought of what Lindsey had told me of the Reaper team's long and tedious hours in flight, the fruitless patrols and surveillances, the many weeks spent watching one man on the ground, miles away, a known terrorist, surrounding himself with innocents because he knew that to be alone meant death from above. Then the moment when he needed to move into the open, and the sudden violence the Headhunters unleashed. If the mission took place at night, the crew would see their target explode in the eerie infrared light. If the mission was during the day, they would see their target blown apart in a post-pixelation high-def gorefest intimate in its closeness and focus. And if there was any doubt that their target had been destroyed, they'd send down another missile to make sure. She told me that often, four or five Reapers at once were deployed on a targeted kill. Their firepower was lethal and accurate and meticulously recorded. That was Lindsey's job as sensor operator. She may have been flying from a trailer at Creech, but her unblinking vision was *right there when the missiles hit, Roland*—collecting the images and sending them back to her ground-control station. Lindsey had told me that those mental pictures were part of their take-home pay. You took them home and tried to find a place to hide them.

"Lindsey told me that drone fliers see things that other fliers don't see," I said.

"They see what grunts see," said Leising. "The RPA crews have more in common with the boots on the ground than the fighter pilots who drop the bombs. On top of that, the more glamorous conventional pilots consider themselves the only 'real' pilots. They're full of swagger and pride. They are celebrated in movies and TV. While RPA fliers are often very disturbed by their killing. So there's no joy in a flight trailer, Mr. Ford. No rush of velocity. No beers after with your crew. The RPA fliers go home after twelve hours and try to live their lives."

The word *cost* came to mind. The cost that Kenny had paid. And Lindsey was still paying. How you measured and weighed it against the good it was intended to do.

Leising picked up his notebook and pen, patiently wrote, then closed the booklet and set it back on the white stand. "Pardon me. I'm writing a book about all this. Robotic warfare and what it does to the human being. It's a story that should be told."

"I'll read it."

"My wife has promised to also," said the doctor. "Which gives me two preorders with which to entice an agent." He looked at me in frank assessment. "You served?"

"Marines."

"Then you understand the burden drone fliers share with all other men and women in war—that sometimes innocent people die."

"I understand that burden," I said.

Leising waited, letting the silence be. "It is the deepest gulf between the expectations of the RPA fliers and what they experience in combat. Because, in spite of what many politicians and generals and the public like to believe about the 'surgical' precision of drone warfare, the truth is not so simple. So, on top of the discrete challenges of hunting human beings from thousands of miles away, drone teams have the up-close experience of watching their munitions blow up the wrong people. There's a twelve-second lapse between the time the pilot says 'Rifle!' and the moment the missile destroys its target. Kenny liked to say that those twelve seconds are the longest twelve seconds in sports. Joking, of course. He always was. But the truth is that those twelve seconds could be when the target leaves the room and his wife comes into it. When the child walks from the courtyard into the impact zone. When a boy rides up on a bicycle. When the target answers a knock on his door from an innocent neighbor."

Another cost, I thought. I had seen innocents killed in Fallujah. Their blood was on my soul but not on my hands.

"Innocent blood was a heavy burden for Kenny Bryce," said Leising.

Lindsey had never spoken to me about collateral damage. And I had respected her privacy enough not to ask. Soldier to soldier, she knew that I would at least understand the context of the thing. But a soldier's secrets are hers to keep.

"As combat fliers, I suppose the Headhunters spilled their share," I said.

He looked at me over the top of his small round spectacles. "I only tell you this because of what has happened to Kenny. And with the hope that it will save Lindsey and Marlon from such a horror. It took Kenny two years to come to the point where he could tell me what I'm about to tell you."

I waited.

14

"**DO YOU REMEMBER** reading about the Doctors Without Borders improvised hospital in Aleppo? In April of 2015?"

"Collateral damage?" I asked.

"One of four improvised hospitals in the eastern half of the city," said Leising. "A known Islamic State terrorist named Zkrya Gourmat was using it as cover because it was allegedly off-limits to both Assad's Air Force and coalition drones. Zkrya was a young man, intelligent and charismatic. French born and tech-savvy—a good recruiter. Called his group the Raqqa Twelve. Gourmat was believed to be third in line in domestic IS operations in Syria, behind Baghdadi. The Joint Special Operations Command and the CIA put him on their kill list, no surprise."

Leising recrossed his legs, sighing. "Gourmat would sneak away from this hospital to make his rounds, and was rarely seen outside. This hospital was a collection of inflatable operating rooms erected within a cave, and other improvised hospitals were little better. One was concealed in a chicken farm just outside of the city. Doctors Without

Borders supplied and funded them, but they—the doctors and aid workers themselves—were not officially permitted inside Syria. The hospitals were known as IH-One through IH-Four, and IH-One was Gourmat's hospital. But he would never stay for more than three days. Then he would appear somewhere else."

I'd seen pictures from some of those hospitals. Calm doctors trying to put the wounded back together in medieval quarters. "But the Doctors Without Borders volunteers staffed those operating rooms anyway," I said.

"You bet they did. Such brave people. And while they tried to save lives, Kenny and his Headhunters watched from above. Kenny called it Whac-A-Mole. Gourmat always stayed very close to the doctors and nurses and the White Helmets, who are humanitarian workers, of course. They were his shields. The people of east Aleppo hung on desperately. They even tried to pacify IS by obeying sharia law. Strange as it may sound, Gourmat was actually well liked, Kenny said. The Headhunters would watch him outside the inflatable surgical tent, AK slung over his shoulder, talking and laughing with them. He was banking that the U.S. drones wouldn't fire on him when he was among innocents, and Assad had granted provisional protection to some hospitals. This was before the Russians came in, and nothing in east Aleppo was spared. It took Kenny and his Headhunters several months, but they realized that Gourmat had to be using footpaths obscured beneath the rubble, and tunnels.

"One day he came up in broad daylight, driving a motorcycle down a dirt path toward a mosque they were using to store arms and ammunition. Kenny contacted the Reaper Operating Center and reported that they'd finally flushed their extremely high-value target. This initiated the ROC 'kill checklist,' which establishes all of the conditions, prerequisites, and circumstances needed to take a shot. Gourmat went inside the mosque, and he spent over ten minutes there. But ROC would not approve a launch at or near any mosque or holy site—the same protection afforded to the hospitals. So the Headhunters were ordered to catch Gourmat on the road, alone on his motorcycle, for a collateral-free kill. Gourmat sped back toward IH-One on his motorcycle. Still no approval from the ROC. A common frustration. The American command is careful about such strikes. The CIA, less so. So while Kenny and his flight mates waited for clearance, Gourmat made it all the way back to IH-One. Finally the clearance came through and Voss fired two missiles. But suddenly, and for no apparent reason, Gourmat lost control of the motorcycle and it went into a skid that ended in a pile of rubble not fifty yards from the operating tent. No problem for a laser-guided Hellfire missile. Medical people came pouring out of the hospital to see what had happened. They gathered around Gourmat to see what they could do. Within seconds the missiles hit, and they were all either killed or badly injured.

"Later, Kenny and the Headhunters learned that two of the dead were Doctors Without Borders surgeons, three were nurses, and four were Syrian volunteers. Without them, two hospital patients expired on their cots, awaiting treatment. IS fighters stormed the inflatable shelter to steal painkillers and anything else of value. Back here at Creech, Kenny and his crew watched the spectacle in high-definition color. As I said, it took him two years to tell me about it."

Hollow silence. A car door slamming in the distance, the soft whine of the heater coming on. Dr. Leising made another short entry in his notebook, then set it back.

War and its secrets. I have mine. And maybe because of them, I'd seen evidence of Lindsey's torment that first night we met, when she was on her fortune-wrecking roulette-and-booze bender at the Pala Casino. And during the year or so she lived in casita two at Rancho de los Robles, Lindsey had confessed much to me regarding her vices, her failing motherhood, her anger and fear and self-disgust. But not this. A terrorist on a motorcycle and Aleppo field hospital IH-One—at core, the heart of her darkness.

"How was Kenny doing?" I asked.

"He was doing well," said the doctor. "He'd come a long way in four years. He had stopped the drinking and recreational drug use. He began to like his job—being outdoors rather than cooped up in a flight cockpit trailer. He had begun to date again. So, when Lindsey called to tell me what had happened to Kenny, I felt especially bad. He was thirty-four years old, Mr. Ford. Young, strong, and bright."

Another silence, this one dedicated to Kenny Bryce.

Leising sighed. "When I saw in my mind's eye what was done to Kenny in his home, I became sick. His body. His head. The brutality. It took hours for that first wave of nausea to pass." He smiled wanly. "I apologize. I should find someone to talk to."

"Talk to me."

"Lindsey told me about the threats," he said. "The handwritten letters to all three of them. Can you protect her?"

"She's safe," I said.

"Her heart is good," said Leising. "But she is willful and has been self-destructive. Kenny and Voss internalized. Lindsey acted out."

I nodded.

"There is such a familiarity in the death letter to Lindsey," he said. "I hope you don't mind that she showed me hers. As a picture attached to a text message, I mean. As did Marlon."

"Theirs to share," I said. "Be very careful what you do and say. This man is the coldest killer I've ever run across."

The ex-cop in me felt my control of this case fraying. So I let it go. When you turn private, the legal pillars break down, from Miranda to the chain of custody. Sometimes this is good. Lindsey and Voss shouldn't have shared evidence with their former psychiatrist, but there was no getting the toothpaste back into the tube.

"You're right about the familiarity in the threats," I said. "I think that Caliphornia knew all three of them. Or pretends to. He refers to past transgressions in all three Headhunters. Did any of them mention enemies?"

"No," said Leising. "Kenny had a bar fight not long after he mustered out of the Air Force. Charges were dropped. Lindsey ran up gambling debts but managed to pay them off. Voss, no. He's very self-controlled. A family man. No enemies that he spoke of."

"Did they know other people in common?" I asked. "Friends, co-workers, shared contacts or acquaintances. Other than you."

Leising eyed me, smiling. "Well. They all shared the same chain of command at Creech. I remember a colonel that they all spoke of. A captain as well. I can get names for you. But, really, the Headhunters had all of the United States Air Force in common. Many of them remain in touch with each other. Organizations, clubs, reunions, the Air Force Academy."

I wondered who else might know them well enough to be aware of their mistakes and misdeeds. I drew blanks. My IvarDuggans, TLO, and Tracersinfo services might help me make connections. I even tried out the idea that the man before me was a clever sociopath staging deadly games with his patients. Which meant Caliphornia was one of them. Sounded like a movie I'd seen.

"Enemies," I said, as much to myself as the doctor.

"Here's an outside possibility," said Leising. "A few years ago, Kenny told me he had been quoted in *The Washington Post*. A Sunday feature article about the new esprit de corps that the USAF was fostering within the unhappy RPA community. The drone teams were being encouraged in friendly competition against each other. They were allowed to give themselves combat team nicknames, and to create morale insignias for their uniforms. In the article, Kenny told of creating the Headhunter name and patch. There was even a picture of it—a grinning skull with wings of fire. Toward the end of the piece, he deflected questions about widespread dissatisfaction among RPA personnel. And refused to comment on a drone strike alleged to have gone wrong at a field hospital in Aleppo. The *Post* tallied the dead, citing research by the British group Syrian Observatory for Human Rights.

"Kenny was furious when the story ran. But there was his name, in black and white, and a picture of the Headhunters patch, associated with the dead doctors and nurses. He ill-advisedly threatened a lawsuit."

"But the camel's nose was already inside the tent."

"It most certainly was."

This was bad news, and the more I considered it, the worse it got. A casual newspaper reader might or might not link Kenny Bryce to a drone attack in Aleppo. But, fueled by the possibility of that connection, a determined actor could discover that Kenny and his Headhunters had fired the missiles. And from Kenny, it was two short lines to Marlon and Lindsey.

"Ladies and gentlemen," I said. "Please welcome the Headhunters, as inadvertently presented in *The Washington Post*."

Leising leaned toward me. "Cali*phornia* read the *Post* article?"

"Any fourth-grader can find the *Post* article."

"Okay, but *why*?"

"Nine innocents and one terrorist killed in a drone strike," I said.

"So Caliphornia might be a friend or a relative, taking revenge for IH-One?"

"Yes."

"Or is he a terrorist taking on the U.S. Air Force?"

"Both."

He frowned, peering at me through the small round lenses.

H*all Pass 2* churned through the cold post-storm air as I flew southwest for home, the engine droning and gently buzzing my bones. I thought about Zkrya Gourmat losing control of his motorcycle and the catastrophe this had led to.

I had only faint memories of the attack at IH-One, as reported by the media. The story had broken at nearly the same time that Justine's sudden death was sweeping me down its dark, deepening tunnel. The fate of the innocents on IH-One had barely registered on me.

Now, as the green hills of Fallbrook eased by beneath me, I considered that a major player was missing from the story of Zkrya Gourmat and IH-One. Someone who had taken the life of one Headhunter and threatened two more.

Caliphornia.

Astride the world with a knife in each hand, I imagined, with one foot in Aleppo and the other in Bakersfield.

Look for him where he started, I thought. *Look for him in the rubble.*

ather than go straight home from the airport, I drove the hour south to Point Loma, paid my admission to the Cabrillo Lighthouse Monument, parked, and climbed my way to the whale observation area. The late afternoon was blustery and cold, and the dauntless tourists were few in number and thickly wrapped. I stood at the wall and looked west out over the Pacific, heaving, gray, and endless. I looked for whales as I always do up here, saw none, which is how many I always see. As I strolled past the lighthouse, a peregrine falcon dropped into a hundred-mile-an-hour stoop and out of sight behind the wall in front of me. I figured that some elegant sea bird was about to become the falcon's meal. Around me, the sage and brittlebush shivered in the wind and the gulls cried and wheeled.

I looked out to the approximate place where Justine had gone down. I lit a cigarette and watched the sun set, an orange ball melting on the curve of the far horizon.

A moment of peace, or something like it.

Until an arriving Telegram message chimed on the phone from the depths of my pocket. It was from Bakersfield detective Marcy Brown, who wrote only "Courtesy of JT."

I touched the link, saw the brief "Property of Bakersfield Police Department" statement, and then the video played.

Taucher had been right about grainy. The Tuscanola apartments parking area. Poorly lit, filled with vehicles, locked in shadows.

Caliphornia was just as she had described him. Indeterminate race. Twenties or thirties by his posture and movement. Six-feet-plus or-minus, average build, one hundred seventy to two hundred pounds. Dressed like a surfer or boarder, the baggy pants and cloddish board shoes. A flannel shirt under the Air Force sweatshirt. Hood up. Light on his feet in spite of the shoes. Athletic. The two seconds of Caliphornia in profile suggested sharp features and heightened alert.

I watched it again.

Went back for thirds but the screen pixelated brightly, then self-destructed to black. *Like one of the Headhunters' targets*, I thought.

I tried to find it again, but it was gone.

15

LATE THAT NIGHT, in the privacy of my home office, I poured an assertive bourbon and put on some waltz music. I sat in front of my computer monitor, entered my search words, then closed my eyes and let the music move through me. Stood and took a few three-beat turns before opening my eyes to the "Syria improvised hospitals" search results waiting for me on the screen.

As the waltz went undanced to, I read the thirty-five-page list of articles, news broadcasts, radio stories, books, videos, and blogs related to my search. Each page contained approximately a dozen entries, and each entry's first sentence. I opened and read the most promising. Many contained multiple references and links to source material. Most were related to the bloody 2016 siege of Aleppo. But I was after something on the IH-One drone attack of a year earlier.

An hour passed slowly. Another. I sipped and scanned, clicked and read, translated and printed, followed links on hunches, detoured, closed and opened anew. At one point I launched myself in my wheeled chair à la Joan Taucher, rolling across the old hardwood floor to land at the western window of my office. Where, looking down from the second floor, I saw the glassy black pond and the staunch palapa and the horseshoe-shaped barbecue and the chaise longues and the Ping-Pong table covered by a tarp against in-blowing rain. Grandma Liz had convinced Grandpa Dick to string Christmas lights along the edge of the palapa roof. The little twinkling bulbs seemed lonely against the vast dark beyond.

Surprisingly, Lindsey reclined on one of the chaises, facing the pond in profile, wrapped in a heavy coat, a watch cap over her ears. She took a drink from a coffee mug that did not steam, though the breath from her nostrils did. Even from this distance I could see she had the thousand-yard stare again. I felt equal parts pity and alarm.

I knew that she had left the property this afternoon, in her car, for approximately one and a half hours.

This intel courtesy of Burt. He'd tailed her from here to a nature preserve in Fallbrook called Los Jilgueros. It's a pleasant place, big sycamores and lots of native plants, some trails and ponds. I fly right over it, in and out of Fallbrook Airpark.

According to Burt, Lindsey had parked her Mustang, gotten a backpack from the trunk, and headed into the preserve. Burt followed covertly, letting a "loud family of five with two dogs" run interference. Lindsey had strolled to a bench overlooking one of the ponds, unslung her pack, and taken out her phone. Burt hunkered cross-legged in a thicket of matilija poppies and watched Lindsey while a weasel watched him. She worked the phone, fussed with the backpack.

Ten minutes later, a boy of about nine and a man in his thirties came down the same trail. When Lindsey spotted the boy she stood up and ran toward him. The boy ran to her and they embraced. "She swung him around and around," Burt had told me. "I'd never seen Lindsey Rakes actually happy until that moment."

Burt said that Lindsey and the man seemed cordial but chilly. All three went back to the bench, where Lindsey pulled wrapped gifts from the backpack and the boy opened them. One of the gifts was a small drone, which the boy had no problem piloting through the trees, along the edge of a pond, across a grassy meadow, and back to the bench, landing it deftly.

"Obviously in his genes," Burt had said, grinning, his lower teeth straight and small.

After a forty-five-minute visit, they returned to the parking lot for a long good-bye. Burt told me that Lindsey appeared to be pleading with her ex-husband.

She got into her car and threw up some mud in the dirt parking lot. Burt had followed her to Daniel's Market in nearby Bonsall, from which she came a few minutes later, carrying a green reusable shopping bag that she swung somewhat heavily into the trunk of her Mustang.

That was when Burt had seen Jason Bayless in his black Mercedes SUV, watching the market, too. Which told us that Bayless had located Lindsey, and that Brandon Goff wasn't the one who had hired him.

Now I looked at her through the window again and told myself that no matter her demons, she needed my protection. Maybe *because* of her demons. And she had been located. Anyone determined to find her— Caliphornia, for instance—would draw a short, straight line between Daniel's Market and here. If necessary, I could get her off the property and stowed elsewhere in a matter of minutes.

After talking to Burt I'd taken another crack at Bayless, by phone, to see if I could find out who had hired him. He'd hung up.

I looked down at Lindsey yet again.

Then pushed myself across the floor and back into bloody Syria.

The listings were wide-ranging and only somewhat chronological.

So I had to read every one of them. As in a boxing match, inattention could mean defeat.

Thus:

"SYRIAN FIELD HOSPITALS: A CREATIVE SOLUTION IN URBAN MILITARY CONFLICT COMBAT IN SYRIA" —*Avicenna Journal of Medicine*, sponsored by the Syrian American Medical Society

"IN SYRIA'S CIVIL WAR, DOCTORS FIND THEMSELVES IN CROSSHAIRS" —*The New York Times*

"SYRIANS' ALTERNATIVE TO A HEALTH CARE SYSTEM: FIELD HOSPITALS" —*Avicenna Journal* again

"SYRIA: HOSPITALS OVERWHELMED AMID ALEPPO BOMBINGS" —*Médecins Sans Frontières* / Doctors Without Borders.

Another hour, another bourbon, but I was getting closer:

"U.S. LAUNCHES SECRET DRONE CAMPAIGN TO HUNT ISLAMIC STATE LEADERS IN SYRIA" —*The Washington Post*

"U.S. DRONES ARE FLYING OVER ISIS AREAS IN SYRIA— WITHOUT ASSAD'S APPROVAL" —*Business Insider*

Midnight came and went. The coyotes started up in the distance, though at first I thought they were police sirens. I wondered how Clevenger was doing on his coyote epic. He hadn't gone out yet tonight.

I watched the Christmas lights glowing along the edge of the palapa roof. *'Tis the season,* I thought. Comfort and joy. But where exactly do you find them? I glanced at the short stack of Oxley posters still undistributed, though I'd plastered Fallbrook with them as best I could. I wondered if the cat would make it through the holidays, if Tammy

Bellamy would ever see him again. I wondered why Lindsey had been careless enough to leave the premises in broad daylight so soon after Caliphornia had done to Kenny Bryce exactly what Caliphornia had promised to do to Lindsey. Which led me back to who had hired Jason Bayless to locate her. So much for comfort and joy.

Then, deep down on page twenty-six, I found what I was looking for.

The Doctors Without Borders website had reported in May of 2015 that one of their MSF—Médecins Sans Frontières—"field" hospitals, located in the Farafra neighborhood of Aleppo, had been hit by drone-fired missiles on April 22. Nine dead: two doctors, three nurses, four volunteers. Details were few, because IH-One was a very small improvised hospital consisting of three inflatable sterile operating rooms and ten beds tucked back into the bowels of a cave. Because the government of Assad considered Doctors Without Borders to be enemies of the state, said the news release, no MSF personnel were allowed in the Syrian Arab Republic. An enterprising photographer had managed to smuggle out a brief video of the aftermath of the missile blasts: fire, smoke, the twisted carnage of bodies and body parts, what looked like a motorcycle tire poking out of the rubble. I watched it four times, concentrating on every detail I could take in.

The report continued:

> The target of the attack appears to have been Zkrya Gourmat, a French-born suspected Islamic State leader. IS has exponentially increased its numbers during Syria's three-year civil war. The group has imposed strict sharia law in the eastern, rebel-held half of Aleppo. As the civil war escalates, Syrian, Russian, and Coalition air strikes are increasingly replacing the so-called

"targeted" coalition drone missions. Coalition drone strikes have resulted in civilian deaths, but the numbers of collateral casualties are disputed.

MSF-supported field hospitals such as IH-One have become necessary in Syria because the Assad regime has tortured and executed 120 Syrian doctors, 50 nurses, and 65 medical aid workers since late 2011. Over four hundred Syrian doctors have been imprisoned.

Both of the physicians and all three of the nurses killed just outside IH-One were Syrian. The four dead humanitarian workers were from France, Germany, Italy, and Syria. Names have been withheld pending notifications, according to MSF policy.

I found another article about IH-One on the Physicians for Human Rights website, based on the MSF release. No new information.

And another piece from NPR, in which two IH-One volunteers were interviewed. Little more.

But what struck me was *how* little. There was a short, back-page *Washington Post* report based on the MSF release but not published until June 15. A similar piece was published in *The New York Times* the next day. I found a *Los Angeles Times* feature on the White Helmet volunteers in Syria, one of whom cited the drone attack on an Aleppo field hospital in 2015 as one of his inspirations for doing humanitarian work at the risk of his own life.

I changed the search words to "Syria field hospitals," with little variation in the results.

Then to "Syria makeshift hospitals," but the same thirty-plus pages of entries kept coming up.

I spent some time on the Doctors Without Borders website, but even their coverage of IH-One in Aleppo ended with the May 2015 posting. It was easy to see that small, makeshift, improvised IH-One—supported but never staffed by Doctors Without Borders personnel—had been figuratively buried by the brutal government siege of Aleppo that began less than a year later. The suffering and deaths of so many people at the hands of their own government had commanded the attention of the world for nearly three months, finally upstaged in the United States by the election of Donald Trump. I thought back to those dark months, the only light I could come up with being the Cubs breaking their eighty-one-year World Series drought in seven dramatic games.

I shrugged and sipped the booze.

By the end of 2016, IH-One had been literally buried and forgotten.

16

I STOOD AND STRETCHED and went to the window again. Lindsey was gone and the lights in her casita were on. I wondered if maybe she'd gotten snack food on her market run, or orange juice, or maybe energy drinks. Maybe a nice bag of brown potatoes. What was wrong with wishful thinking?

The barn lights were on, too, indicating Dale Clevenger and maybe Burt. By my casual estimate, Burt slept four hours a day.

Back at the computer I stared at the monitor until the screensaver came on. Rubbed my eyes and yawned. Considered another drink but told the bartender I was fine.

Bring this story to life, I thought. The living have their versions—but what about the dead?

What would they say?

You don't even know their names.

I wanted names.

I wanted faces.

The Doctors Without Borders page had declined to publish names, nor had other mentions of the attack identified the victims. I went back to the links at the ends of the articles I'd printed, but nothing looked promising.

Change it up, I thought. *Come at it another way.*

I found mountains of government statistics of both military and civilian deaths in the Syrian Arab Republic. I narrowed to "air strike deaths" and found numbers but not names. I narrowed again to "drone strike deaths" and found the same. I bored an even smaller hole: "medical workers dead in Aleppo," which took me back to the Doctors Without Borders releases.

The Free Syria group had its own version of the drone strike outside IH-One, but it listed none of the dead by name. Again, victims' nationalities—Syrian, French, German, and Italian—were noted. Then something caught my eye, a link hidden in a thicket of them at the end of a Free Syria release:

Martyr Statistics—Published by the Syrian Revolution Martyr Database http://syrianshuhada.com.

I hit the translate button and watched English replace the Arabic writing.

On the home page was a map of Syria and a "martyr count" by province. The site listed a staggering 151,888 martyrs killed in Syria through April of 2016—*before* the bloody siege of Aleppo. I thought about that number for a moment, knowing that the number of Syrians forced to leave their homes was many times more.

On the left side of the home page was a long table of contents. My heart sped up:

MARTYR COUNTS BY GENDER

MARTYR COUNTS BY CIVILIAN/MILITARY

MARTYR COUNTS BY PROVINCE OF DEATH

MARTYR COUNTS BY CITY OF BIRTH

MARTYR COUNTS BY NATIONALITY

STATISTICS OF CHILDREN MARTYRS

STATISTICS OF FEMALE MARTYRS

STATISTICS OF MARTYRS FROM CHEMICAL AIR BOMBING

And on and on. I clicked on "Martyr Counts by Week," found that forty-four civilians had died in the city of Aleppo the week of 4/24/2015. Of these, eighteen had died in "Bombardment by air."

Next I went to "Martyr Counts in Aleppo City by Neighborhood" and found that Farafra—home of humble IH-One—had been the neighborhood of death for nine martyrs the week that the Headhunters had drawn down on Zkrya Gourmat.

My heart sped up, solid and eager.

On a separate sheet of paper I wrote down their Martyr ID numbers, then began in alphabetical order.

Monique Alaly was a twenty-two-year-old French woman with a black hijab and a winning smile. She was listed as a volunteer medical worker. A short video showed her in a classroom, teaching science to a roomful of girls.

Mhood Amin was a Syrian doctor. Male, no age given and no picture or video.

Ibrahim Azmeh was a forty-nine-year-old Syrian doctor with a sharp, ascetic face and straight black hair. In his video, the doctor sat in an outdoor café in what looked like Damascus, smoking a cigarette and looking calmly at the camera.

Noor Mofq was a forty-year-old Syrian nurse, female, no photo or video.

Dieter Njar was a thirty-year-old German volunteer medical worker. In his dark-framed eyeglasses he looked scholarly. The short video showed him kicking a ball down a soccer field.

Nurse Ahmad Radhah was Syrian and twenty years old, his face plump and cheerful. He sat astride a scooter on a dusty city street, his helmet too small and riding high up on his head.

Nurse Ramy Salim was bearded, twenty-eight, Syrian.

Omar Soad was an Italian volunteer worker, mustachioed and handsome. The video showed him smiling, his arm around a young woman. No age given.

Syrian volunteer Nady Warim was eighteen and wore a light-colored hijab.

I printed each martyr's page, read them carefully, then again. I logged off syrianshuhada.com and on to my IvarDuggans site, on which I spent the next hour searching the nine last names. I set the search parameters for people eighteen to sixty years of age, hoping to snag siblings and/or parents who might have come to the United States. Only four of the last names came up nationally: one hundred fifteen Alalys, two hundred forty-five Azmehs, eighty Radhahs, and three hundred eighty-seven Salims. I ran Gourmat also: seven hundred thirty-two across the nation.

Making a risky assumption, I narrowed the search to California residents. This cut the list by roughly two-thirds. When I cast an even smaller net—restricting the search to five years or less of residence in the state—my third was halved in a keystroke. Which left me two hundred thirty-four men and women living in California who may or may not have been related to one of the ten people who died in the Headhunter drone strike on IH-One on April 22, 2015.

More risky assumptions landed me one hundred seventy-one people in Southern California: thirty in greater Bakersfield and sixty-six in San Diego County.

Next I cross-referenced all ninety-six individuals through the "known associates" search. As I expected, many with the same last names were family. Google Maps allowed me to see their homes and neighborhoods. I found clusters in Northeast Bakersfield and in El Cajon, east of San Diego. I wondered how many were on the walls of Taucher's JTTF office.

Choosing four of the San Diego names at random, I printed out home address histories, aliases, email addresses and phone numbers, vehicle ownership, fictitious business names, and evictions. And again, I found familial interconnections where I expected to. The information came forth quickly. IvarDuggans was worth its salt on the easy things.

But it took me another full hour to search the criminal records of the four lucky people I'd chosen. The IvarDuggans criminal and court records databases are notoriously slow. I longed for my former Sheriff's Department access to the state and federal agencies, the best data often being the bones the FBI threw your way.

By then it was after two o'clock. I stood and stretched, knowing that IvarDuggans didn't have the tools to do the hard labor of separating terrorists from innocents. But I knew who did.

"Up kind of late, aren't you, Joan?" I asked.

"Ford? Has something happened?" By the time she'd finished asking the question, her voice had gone from dull to sharp.

"We need to run some names."

"It's two fifteen in the morning, you ape," she said. "Learn some manners."

"Listen."

I told her about the Headhunters' accidental catastrophe at IH-One in Aleppo. How that piece of bad luck had cost nine innocent lives. How Kenny Bryce's conscience had clamped on and shook him like a bulldog for years. Lindsey's, too. And probably Voss's.

Taucher listened but said nothing.

So I took a leap of faith over miles and years, landing on the eerie sense of familiarity and blame that Caliphornia's threats contained. What if Caliphornia had originally been forged in that misbegotten air strike? So much of what we knew about him pointed to Middle Eastern roots and culture. What if he was a relative or friend of someone the Headhunters had killed? A brother, even. A father?

In the presentation of my thesis I began to see its wobbly structure. What if what we thought we knew about Caliphornia was invented as distraction? Were we being played? As if to strengthen my premise, I told Taucher the search criteria I'd used. I sounded exhausted even to myself. Doubted that I was making sense. Doubled down with false bravado.

"I've got thirty names in Bakersfield that need to be checked," I said. "Sixty-six here in San Diego. Run them for me, Joan. I need this. I cut the list from seven hundred."

Silence from her, the slot machine whirring. "You were right this morning about risk and trust."

Heading into a storm you know is there.

I still wasn't sure what had brought those words out of me as the rain poured down on us. Part of it was seeing the Grand Hyatt, where I'd first laid eyes on Justine Timmerman in a similar, spectacular storm.

But the bigger part was a storm of a wholly different kind— Caliphornia and his bloody Thunder. I had felt him down on the waterfront in the rain. A force of will. Gathering himself right here in my state and my city. For an attack against my own.

"Okay, Roland. Email the names to me. I can search phonetically, but it helps when the names are spelled correctly and consistently. I spend too much time trying to account for the quirks of Arabic and Farsi."

"I owe you."

"I'll never get back to sleep now," she said.

"You can brew up some coffee and watch the sunrise."

"I'll be in my office hours before the sun comes up," she said. "I usually am. Doing more important things than watching the sun do what it always does."

I heard her quick wispy laugh, then the line went dead.

Taucher returned my wakeup call at five fifty, just as the sun was pushing the darkness from my bedroom. I'd fallen asleep on the bed with my clothes on.

"One of the victims of the drone attack on IH-One has relatives living in California," she said, speaking fast. "Dr. Ibrahim Azmeh was survived by nine children. Three live in France, three in Syria, and three live in Los Angeles, where they were born. Two brothers and a sister. We'll interview them tomorrow afternoon. The older brother filed a State Department complaint after his father's death and got twelve thousand five hundred U.S. dollars in condolence pay. He's not on our radar and don't ask me why. Pick me up by the elevator on the third level of the Horton Plaza parking garage, tomorrow, noon sharp. You can drive. I hate the L.A. traffic."

"Good morning, Joan."

"There's no such thing as good, Roland," she said. "Rasha Samara was in Bakersfield the day Kenny Bryce died. He bought an Arabian horse for two hundred and forty thousand dollars."

I hadn't even formulated a reply by the time that Taucher, master of the short good-bye, was gone again.

I stood in the kitchen waiting for the coffee to percolate, two hands on the counter, looking out at the grainy light that was trying to buoy the day. I'd been up most of the night and maybe that's all it was, but Taucher's dire pronouncement had moved me. Moved me from doubt and melancholy to some rough hybrid of anger and frustration.

There's no such thing as good.

Thirty-nine years on this planet. Why hadn't someone told me?

My phone rang and Jason Bayless's name and number came up.

"Okay, Ford," he said. "I found her. As you no doubt heard from your little friend. I gave my client your home address and collected a nice bonus I'd worked into the deal. The reason I'm calling is to say that my client is not my client anymore. When I told him that Lindsey Rakes appeared to be residing on your property, he wanted to know the layout of the place, which room was hers, when she was most likely to be home. He tried to hire me to get inside and take photos or video, or maybe fly over a drone. I told him I don't fly fucking drones. He made a joke about her not needing a place to live for that much longer. Actually laughed. Ford, I didn't like this guy from the start and I like him less now. I don't know what your Lindsey has gotten herself into, but this little fart is bad news. Just my guts talking."

"What's his name?"

"Hector O. Padilla. El Cajon."

No such thing as good?

"Talk to me, Jason."

"When he hired me he said he was Lindsey's cousin," said Bayless.

"Later he said Lindsey and he had been married once and he was paying child support and had to talk to her. He gave me those two different stories and I wasn't even pressing him. Then he said Lindsey was important to his boss. Boss? Who exactly am I working for here? I had a bad feeling about him. I realized no, I can't do any more work for this shitbird."

"Where did you leave it with him?" I asked.

"Professional and cordial."

"Did you talk in person?"

"Once. Then Telegram, mostly. Why?"

"I don't know," I said. "More bad feelings. I get 'em, too."

17

AN HOUR LATER Burt's dog-breeder friend, Bruno Zacardi, came up the drive in a mud-splattered white crew cab and parked in the sun of the barnyard. The company logo on the truck was a bronze-colored Roman battle shield with an armored dog in the middle. *Zacardi* was arched over the top of the shield in ancient Latin letters and *Cane Corsos* at the bottom. There was a phone number and a Riverside, California, address.

As Lindsey, Burt, and I walked down to greet them, I could see the head of a large dark dog looming over the people in the front seat.

Bruno dropped from the vehicle and landed lightly, a small man with black hair sprouting out from under a newsboy's cap, and a thick black mustache. A woman worked her way down from the passenger side. She was large and blond, wearing overalls over a blue plaid shirt, and black rubber mud boots almost to her knees. She slung a red backpack over one shoulder, then set her fists firmly on her hips as she looked around.

"That's his wife, Rose," said Burt. "And little Zeno there in the back."

As we crossed the barnyard toward the truck, Bruno motioned for us to stop. He and Rose continued forward to meet us well away from their truck, in the backseat of which Zeno's massive head and sharply cropped ears presided in keen stillness. He looked to be a pale gray. Burt introduced us and we shook hands all around.

Then a moment of silence as Lindsey stared at the dog in the truck. She stuck her hands into the pockets of her red Navajo blanket coat.

"The dog," said Bruno. "At first he can be distracted by so many people. We leave him for a moment of thought. Lindsey, you are very lucky to have Zeno. You will be safe. You will come to love him very much. And of course he will be devoted to you, too."

"Is he really as big as he looks from here?" she asked.

"Seventy-five kilos. Large for his breed," said Rose. Her accent was not as pronounced as Bruno's. "But the Italian mastiff is not a big mastiff. They are trim and athletic and extremely focused on their loved ones. They descend from the Molossers, Roman war dogs that are now extinct. Then the Italian mastiffs themselves almost became extinct. Our lines all derive from stock in southern Italy—from Basilicata, Campania, and Apulia. It has been our life work to preserve them. As you probably know."

"Yes, I've read about them," said Lindsey. "And about you."

"The old Molossers were the best war dogs out there," said Burt. "The Romans liked to starve them before battle, then set them loose on the enemy. Some riveting accounts about Roman legions employing the war dogs in Sardinia. Dragging the locals out of caves and such. Recommended reading."

Bruno smiled largely. He had a wide nose that seemed to divide his mustache. With his accented English, newsboy cap, and too-small wool sweater, Bruno could have just arrived at Ellis Island. "Burt, you forget Cane Corsos' great loyalty and love. Be careful to not change Lindsey's mind!"

"No chance of that," said Lindsey. "Can I meet him now?"

Bruno looked to Rose, who set her fists on her spacious hips again as she turned to survey the pond and the countryside beyond. Her fine blond hair lifted in the breeze. "This is your land, Mr. Ford?"

"Yes."

"So there's no sudden arrival of humans or dogs?"

"Very little. It's fenced and posted."

"We'll use it for the imprint," she said. "It will work well, Bruno."

Bruno smiled. "Yes, Rose. You come with us, Lindsey. But—with respect, Mr. Ford—you and Burt wait here until I come back. It will not be long. The imprint must begin naturally and happen at Lindsey's and Zeno's pace."

Bruno took Lindsey's arm in one hand and Rose's with the other and guided them back toward the truck. The women towered over him.

They stopped about ten feet short of the driver's-side door. Bruno was talking to Lindsey, gesticulating with his small stubby hands, but I couldn't make out his words. Lindsey nodded, then nodded again. Rose—taller even than Lindsey and half again as wide—looked at Lindsey with what looked like a critical eye. I could see the dog's huge block of a head and his eyes glimmering far back in the truck.

Bruno's hands and arms flew as he explained. Lindsey nodded along, bent respectfully to Bruno's shortness. Then Rose strode three long steps to the back door of the crew cab and swung it open with a sharp command. She stepped back and tapped her thighs with both hands and Zeno launched to the ground.

What struck me first were his large sculpted muscles and imposing head. Sleek bulk. He looked metallic. Even from here I could see that his eyes were the same light gray as his brindling. He had a small white triangular blaze on his chest. With his stubby tail wagging, he circled Rose happily, nose to the air, then nose to the ground. He looked very heavy, though not tall at the withers. But light on his huge feet. When he bumped Rose's legs I could see his formidable weight and strength shudder through her.

"A gray-masked *formentino* brindle," said Burt. "Light gray brindles on fawn, leaning toward cream. Very striking. The dog is classic Cane Corso—ears cropped equilaterally to stand erect at all times. Tail docked at the fourth vertebrae. The lower lip hanging below the jawline. As Rose pointed out, this breed was nearly extinct in the late 1970s. A few families, such as the Zacardis, rescued them. I stayed with Bruno's uncle Anatoly and his family in Basilicata one summer long ago. Fantastic people."

Zeno then stopped and locked on to us, tail erect, motionless. When he looked at me straight on, I could see the soulful wrinkles of his forehead, both vertical and horizontal, heavily converging on his prodigious eyebrows. Beneath which the pale gray eyes registered me with a somber intelligence.

"That dog will bond with Lindsey in less than five minutes," said Burt.

Zeno lumbered along on Rose's left side as she walked back to Bruno and Lindsey. No leash. He nudged Bruno's hand while looking at Lindsey, tail not wagging. Lindsey opened her hands and the dog looked up at her, then returned to Rose's feet to rule the space between his master and this stranger.

Then Rose slung the red backpack over both shoulders and, with Zeno close on her left, strode off across the barnyard with Bruno and

Lindsey in tow. They followed the dirt road to the south shore of the pond, moving briskly, stepping around the mud puddles left by yesterday's storm. They rounded the pond and continued south into the hilly grasslands that make up most of Rancho de los Robles.

Bruno stopped at the crest of a rise and watched the others continue down. Rose was in the lead, with Zeno walking close to her left and Lindsey a few yards behind. After a moment Bruno started back toward us, while Rose, Lindsey, and Zeno vanished into the swale and dropped out of sight.

"I had a quick look around Lindsey's casita last night when she was out on the patio," said Burt. "Two quarts of Stolichnaya—a plain and a pepper—sitting right out on the kitchen counter. Some good-looking smoked almonds, and a pile of Ghirardelli seventy-two-percent-cacao chocolate bars. Two of those crescent-roll tubes and a tub of whipped butter. She must be quite the midnight snacker."

I nodded but said nothing. I wasn't expecting she'd bought the orange juice or energy drinks I'd hoped for.

"Any thoughts on who hired Bayless?" Burt asked.

"I'll get back to you on that, Burt."

"Excellent, Boss."

I watched Bruno traipsing back around the pond toward us. He veered not one step to avoid the puddles, splashing right through them instead, like a boy. A plume of smoke trailed behind him from the cigarette in his mouth.

Beyond him, Rose and Zeno climbed upward into my view again, Lindsey now on Rose's right and Zeno still on her left. A moment later they went around an outcropping of granite boulders and back out of sight. A couple of hawks circled in the clear blue sky.

Bruno approached, flicking his cigarette butt to the wet road and hopping to squash it. "It is going very well. Zeno is very interested in Lindsey. It helps that Lindsey is of good size, like Rose, because Zeno has always loved big women. He does not care for men. Rose was his first and his constant mistress. Lindsey will be his fifth."

"The others rented him and sent him back?" I asked.

Bruno nodded. "One kept him for almost a year. The others only a few months. Immediately after a mistress returns him, Zeno becomes depressed and confused. Rose heals him. I was that way when I was young and had a broken heart, too."

"How will Rose transfer that affection and loyalty to Lindsey?" I asked.

Bruno crossed his arms and looked across the rolling hills to where the trio had disappeared behind the rocky hillock. The hawks had shifted in the sky to circle above the dog and women, alert for flushed birds and game.

"The affection and loyalty are natural," said Bruno. "The Cane Corso heart is the biggest of all the dogs. As is his courage and intelligence. So Lindsey will have to give the dog attention, respect, affection, and food. Attention is most important, and food is second. She must always have for him occasional treats and meals twice a day, eight a.m. and eight p.m. I have brought her one month's supply. Zeno also loves being talked to. This may sound foolish, but I believe he understands fifty percent of what he is told. Fifty percent he is absolutely the master of. The other fifty? Well, he has no idea—because he's a dog!"

Bruno exploded into laughter at his own joke. "Come to my truck. I have the food and dog treats that Zeno loves."

"Why haven't they come out from behind the rocks yet?" I asked.

Bruno squinted out at where we'd last seen them. "There is a small blanket and dog treats in Rose's pack. She and Lindsey will find a dry place, spread the blanket, and sit too close together for Zeno to get between them. They will talk to each other in quiet, intimate voices. They will touch each other and perhaps embrace. As sisters would embrace. Zeno will try to force his way between them but Rose will not move away from her new dear family member. She is as determined and nearly as strong as Zeno is, believe me! Before long, and with the help of the food for bribing, Zeno will give up and move to Rose's free side. After all, her closeness is what he wants most. And that is when Lindsey will join him on *his* side of Rose and sit down close beside him. So now Zeno is in the middle. He has won—but he still has to comprehend it! At this point, he will either stay or growl tremendously and go to Rose's free side again. If he stays, Lindsey will scratch his throat and give him food, and the first stage of the imprint is nearly complete. If he goes back to Rose's original free side, then the whole thing starts over again. This beginning method of imprint goes back many generations in the Zacardi family. In the very old days, if the Cane Corso would not imprint with family members, or important friends, after three tries on three days, a dog would be castrated and sold. A bitch would be locked from the grounds to fare for herself in the town or the woods."

I watched Lindsey, Rose, and Zeno emerge from behind the boulder-strewn hillock. The women walked side by side, relaxed and conversing, the dog between them, with a muscular glide to his stride.

"Zeno has accepted Lindsey into his family!" said Bruno, clapping his hands. "He is very intelligent. He has always loved the women."

I watched Zeno charge off after a rabbit, which easily out-legged him into a patch of prickly pear cactus. The dog stood at the edge of the cactus patch, tail wagging, nose lowered.

"Rose will give Lindsey the list of commands," said Bruno. "They are Italiano, of course, and they explain themselves. Zeno has been trained to follow them instantly and fully. Even in the face of death he will follow his commands. Here, I brought a list for you, too."

From his rear trouser pocket Bruno handed me a smudged and wrinkled sheet of paper. I unfolded it and looked down the menu of Italian commands and their English translations.

The two women and their proud protector came toward us on the bumpy dirt road. Zeno's prodigious head, sharply cropped ears, and heavy brow gave him a wise and monstrous bearing. His legs were trunklike, I saw, much thicker than the legs of the Labrador retrievers I had had as a boy. His feet were enormous and he splashed as casually through the puddles as Bruno had done. His light *formantino* coat with the dark gray brindles caught the crisp December sunlight as his muscles bunched and stretched beneath. The bright white blaze on his chest seemed jaunty. I heard the women's voices as they approached. Rose said something ending in a rise of pitch, and Lindsey laughed.

"Lindsey is expecting genuine trouble?" he asked.

"Pretty damned genuine."

"Zeno increases her advantage dramatically."

I nodded.

"A man experienced in killing with a knife is Zeno's most dangerous enemy," said Bruno. "Such men are old-fashioned. Rare in this technological country. I brought his body armor. It protects against a knife and bullets. He enjoys wearing it. He knows that he is going into battle."

Later, as Bruno and Rose walked toward their truck, Zeno took up his usual position on Rose's left, timing his stride to hers with all his power and grace.

At the door, Rose lifted a finger and Zeno sat and looked up at her.

Of course, he was ready for her to open the back door and let him jump in. But instead, Rose knelt and threw her arms around the dog, laid her head against his. She looked past him at me, tears streaking her face. Then she stood, turned her right palm to face the ground, and Zeno lay down. Bruno opened the door and his wife swung into the cab, drawing her heavy rubber boots in last. Zeno issued a gigantic sigh with a sorrowful yelp tucked inside it. Bruno pet him once on the head and walked to the driver's side of the truck. He climbed in and Rose's window went down.

"Call him to come and tell him to sit," she said to Lindsey. "Firmly."

Lindsey held her sheet of commands out and ready in one hand, shading her eyes with the other. "*Vieni*," she ordered. Zeno swung his massive head to regard Lindsey, then turned back to his true master. Didn't budge.

"*Vieni!*" called Lindsey, with more force.

Zeno came.

"*Siediti.*"

Zeno sat before her but still looked at Rose.

I saw the dog in profile, his slightly upturned muzzle, which Bruno had told me lay at a breed-perfect one-hundred-and-five-degree angle from the upright plane of his forehead. Moreover, I saw his eye, the beautiful pale gray eye that matched the brindles of his coat. And in that eye? It's easy to humanize a dog, but they have strong emotions and no interest in hiding them. In this case: heartache and resolve.

"*Bravo regazzo*," said Lindsey, gently. "Good boy."

He sat very still and never took his eyes off Rose as she rolled up the window and Bruno backed up the truck and drove away.

18

LATE THAT BLUSTERY AFTERNOON, I sat in my truck across the street and a few doors down from Hector Padilla's home. I had a hunch and time to bet on it.

It was Friday and this El Cajon hood had a bustling, home-from-work feel. Christmas lights were up and some already turned on. A minivan pulled into the driveway next door to Hector's. The garage door went up. A woman unleashed two young children, who spilled past her through the sliding door. All three gathered at the rear of the vehicle. The lift gate opened and they wrestled out a tightly wrapped noble fir, which they lugged into the garage. The girl had on pink rubber boots and a pink fur-lined coat, and the boy wore floppy black board shoes and a silver quilted parka. I pay attention to children because Justine did. We wanted one. For starters. We had happily set ourselves to the task of creating one, just hours before she took off in *Hall Pass* that final day.

My slick, fold-out invitation to opening night of the "Treasures of

Araby" exhibition and sale—a gift from Padilla to Imam Hadi Yousef, then from Yousef to me—lay on the passenger seat.

GALLERIE MONFIL PRESENTS

The Treasures of Araby

Collectible Art, Artifacts, and Antiques

From Exotic West Asia

The opening-night party, to which the bearer of this invitation was welcome, was set to begin in two hours, at six p.m. in Solana Beach.

I took my time reading the invite copy and looking at the pictures again. I braced it on the steering wheel so I could read and still see activity at Hector's house. The booklet opened into four panels on each side, for a total of eight pages. Two panels were dedicated to each of four exhibits:

OF CARPETS & MAGIC

CENTURIES IN TILE AND TEXTILE

ART, SENSE, AND SPIRIT

THE SWORDS OF ARABY

The pictured carpets for "Of Carpets & Magic" made me think of the collection of Persian rugs that had come with the house I live in. The carpets had been collected over the years by the various Timmerman family occupants of Rancho de los Robles, many of whom took their carpets seriously. Some of the invitation pictures looked very much like the rugs I unmagically traipsed over daily.

The pictured tiles were intricate and beautiful, most of them Arabesque variations of flowers, plants, and animals. The elegant calligraphic script reminded me of Caliphornia's handwritten correspondence.

The image for "Art, Sense, and Spirit" was a reprinted sixteenth-century Iraqi painting titled *Prince Conversing with a Mythical Bird*. It was done pre-perspective, making it oddly flat and swirling.

"The Swords of Araby" pictured an Arabic *saif* sword, curved in deadly grace, handle and hilt intricately engraved with calligraphic script and songbirds. I thought of Kenny Bryce and the threat letters to the Headhunters. How could I not? Something alien and cold stirred inside me.

I looked up from the sword to Hector Padilla's quaint El Cajon home. I imagined his Qur'an, his energy drinks, these invitations, and the large sharpening stone spilling from his upturned backpack to Hadi's desk. I thought of Taucher's cogent question: Who carries around a sharpening stone? A seemingly hapless hospital janitor who wants to become a Muslim and learn Arabic in order to find a Muslim woman?

At five sharp, Hector's garage door rose and the shiny black Cube backed out into the mid-December dark. I fell in behind it. Hector drove as he had driven before, exactly the speed limit, signaling turns well ahead of time, waiting at least three full seconds at each stop sign. He picked up Interstate 8 west to the 5 north, headed for Solana Beach. I was pretty sure where he was going. *Nice work, Ford.* I stayed two cars behind in the heavy traffic. Predictably, Hector drove only in the slower, second-from-the-outside lane. The Cube, freshly washed and waxed, gleamed in the lights of the exit signs.

Hector exited Via de la Valle, loafed his way to South Cedros Avenue, and turned right. Cedros Avenue was an upscale retail zone: galleries, furniture, lifestyle purveyors, the Belly Up nightclub, where I had spent a number of nights with Justine—and, later, without her. Hector circled the crowded area patiently, finally finding a place. I parallel-parked half a block down, keeping an eye on him.

Not difficult. By the time he had gotten out of his car and made it to the parking meter, which seemed to be puzzling him, I had paid and caught up. I'd never really seen him before, except pictured on Taucher's wall or sitting in his car. He appeared less than average in height. Bushy dark hair and a small pot belly. Jeans too small and Raiders hoodie too big.

I window-shopped a contemporary art gallery, fingering the GPS tracker in my coat pocket. Nifty gadget: reports the host vehicle's location to your phone every second while in motion, so you can become invisible. It never needs a line of sight. Gives you time/date/address for every stop, sleeps when your target isn't moving, waterproof, with a built-in magnetic fastener strong enough to keep it secure on a car chassis. Fifty hours of charge, one hundred ninety-nine bucks.

I'd had a good long look at the paintings in the window by the time Hector solved the meter, locked up his Cube, and headed down Cedros, tapping what looked like a rolled-up magazine against one leg. I gave him a good lead, then followed, kneeling to activate the GPS tracker and attach it to the rear chassis of the Cube. It jumped to the metal frame with a heavy clunk.

The Gallerie Monfil was a big corner building, a three-level gallery/warehouse I'd visited several times. They specialize in folk and primitive art and crafts from around the world, handmade furniture, ceramics, weaving, textiles, carvings, vessels, and jewelry.

Hector walked toward the entrance. Well-dressed people bustled in around him, winter finery finally on display in sunny San Diego County, and I was surprised by how many visitors there were. Hector stood in the line, the invitation protruding from his magazine, which he leafed through as he waited. He paused and checked his phone, then looked at the people around him, a half-smile on his face. I held back, watched a woman in a green dress stride by, diamonds in her ears, a faux-mink stole on her neck, a man with a phone in tow. She looked at me unhurriedly. A calligraphic sign announced *The Treasures of Araby—Level Three. Docent-guided tours at 7 and 9 p.m.*

I drifted into the building a minute or two after Hector. Claimed a free glass of champagne off a table in the lobby. Heard the holiday music coming from the PA. Then climbed the wide maple-and-stainless-steel stairs to level three.

I entered a spacious rotunda buzzing with visitors. Dramatically elevated in the center was a life-size bronze Arabian charger with a warrior astride it, scimitar lifted high. The sculptor had captured speed and balance. Around this centerpiece stood lesser statues, metal sculptures and wooden carvings and large, free-standing ceramic vessels. From amid these rose tapestries and fine fabric pavilions and lilting silk banners, and the walls were hung with carpets. Each object had an orange price tag on it. Beyond all this I saw that four salons branched off in four directions, spokes from a hub, each bannered overhead with the names of the collection's four exhibits.

Hector stood at the clogged entrance of the "Of Carpets & Magic" salon, looking back toward me and the central rotunda. The Raiders sweatshirt would have been provocative here two years ago, when the Chargers were still in town. He checked his phone quickly again. Then scanned the crowd before he turned and walked in. I gave him a minute, then followed.

Big room, rugs piled high on the floor, and three walls fitted with hangered carpets that glided left and right at a customer's touch. Docent-salespeople busy answering questions. Lots of interest in these beauties.

In the middle of the room teams of young men and women unrolled rugs for viewing, and carried the rejects back to the stacks and racks and the winners to the cashiers down on level two. Faux-Mink Stole looked down at a rug, diamonds swaying, a forefinger to her lips as she considered a purchase. Caught me looking. Hector seemed fascinated by a blue-toned Persian carpet with a background of pistachio green. Sensing my interest in him, he turned and I looked away.

As if he was suddenly bored, Hector walked out of the salon, tapping the rolled-up magazine on his leg again. I watched him go into the rotunda, look up and around at the other salon entrances, then, stepping around the bronze warrior on his Arabian horse, cut diagonally into "The Swords of Araby." I studied the crowd for a minute or two, then tailed him in.

The "Swords of Araby" salon was more crowded, full of a strange energy the carpet salon had lacked. The centerpiece was a majestic tapestry suspended from the center of the ceiling, depicting a hunter fighting a lion. Both man and lion were much larger than life, especially the lion, which towered on its hind legs over the hunter and everyone else in the room. But the turbaned, high-booted human looked poised and confident, having planted his knife in the animal's chest. Blood was jumping as the lion snarled, teeth bared. In snippets I read the placard below it, while keeping track of Hector. "Mihr Killing a Lion" had been faithfully re-created from an 1830 silk tapestry woven in Persia. It illustrated one of the adventures of Mihr (the Sun) and his best friend, Mushtari (Jupiter), from a poem about their friendship. You could own this re-created tapestry for twelve thousand dollars, professional delivery and hanging included. I glanced up again at Hector, then away, an eye blink before his gaze hit my face. The holiday music stopped.

A man's amplified voice filled the room. "Ladies and gentlemen, please give me your attention as I point out the highlights of 'The Swords of Araby.'"

I saw the speaker, small and sleek, move into the center of the room to stand under the great tapestry. He wore a trim dark gray suit, an open-collared shirt with red and white stripes, a lavender handkerchief, and a small mike attached to his lapel. His hair was short and glistening, his complexion ruddy. He stood on a carved wooden chest that looked plenty strong enough to hold him.

"Thank you, thank you," he said, his voice forceful and clear and lightly accented. "Hello, my good friends. For those of you who don't know me, I am Bernard Monfil, owner of this gallery. I welcome all of you and wish you a wonderful experience here tonight. Araby, as you know, is not a place that you can locate exactly on a map, or a word that you will find in a modern English dictionary. Rather, *Araby* is a word coined by James Joyce—an *idea*—deriving from the collective and unrivaled histories, cultures, and arts of the mysterious Middle East. Araby is treasure and learning. Araby is romance and—"

Hector listened, nodding. He dropped his magazine and snatched it up again, rolling it tight.

Which gave me just enough time to recognize it—*Rumiyah* magazine—the "official" publications of Islamic State. The title is Arabic for Rome. Rome—as in the fall of. Rome—as in jihadis must not rest until they are resting in the shade of the olive trees there. Rome—as in the United States. The magazine instructs American "lone wolf" terrorists on such things as how to build concealable micro-bombs, set effective forest fires, and hide weapons in street clothes.

I knew all this because I'd read the current issue online, to see what Caliphornia might be reading. Or even writing. Hector's issue was the same one I'd read, and I recognized the cover—a bloody knife blade fresh from a kill. The related cover story was titled "Just Terror Tactics," and it covered "choosing the right weapon and targets." One line of this bloody how-to article had stuck in my mind. Something like: "People are often squeamish about the idea of plunging a sharp object into another person's flesh."

As Monfil continued on about the Swords of Araby, Hector strolled into the knife gallery.

19

HECTOR ENGAGED THE SALESWOMAN, who had set a number of the decorative *janbiyas* on a glass countertop. I pressed in closer. The *janbiya* is the classic Arab knife, with a short, curved blade and a raised medial ridge running its length. The hilt is relatively short, made for one hand. I could see that each knife was safely housed in its own scabbard. An informative stand-up cardboard graphic said that the *janbiya* is a dagger used in the Middle East and India but is most closely associated with Saudi Arabia and Yemen. Many boys in those countries begin wearing such a knife at age fourteen as "an accessory." The design and materials used to make the blade, the handle, and the scabbard are a measure of the owner's status.

Hector's back was to me, but I could see that he was talking to the saleswoman with some animation. He'd rolled his *Rumiyah* magazine tight and stuffed it into his wallet pocket. The clerk had a skeptical expression and a guarded smile. Looked at me quickly, then back to her customer. One dark-suited security man watched from behind the counter.

Hector perused the knives before him. Asked a question, got a brief reply. He picked up one scabbarded dagger in his right hand, then another with his left. Raised them up as if he was about to stab something. Then set them back down and crossed his arms.

I sensed female company hard on my left and half a step behind. "Do you think he's dangerous?" asked Faux-Mink Stole. "Or just insane?"

"Definitely."

"You look familiar. But then, I collect faces." Cinnamon hair, loosely up, eyes blue. The faux mink had a fair, elegant neck to ride on.

"My face is common as a clock's," I said.

"No, you're wrong," she said. "I love that scar. But I really am concerned about this little man. Playing with knives. What if he's packing?"

"He could be."

"I *have* seen you," she said. "On the news last year. Fallbrook. A helicopter."

I raised one finger to my lips. Her smile of recognition quickly turned to surprise, then confusion, then embarrassment.

"I am so sorry," she said, leaning closer, her voice a leafy rustle. "I have terrible manners sometimes. I truly beg your pardon. And please know that the man you watched me walk in with is a client."

From a black clutch she drew a business card and a short jeweled pen, wrote something on the back of the card, and handed it to me. Then she smiled and backed into the crowd, latching the clutch as she looked at me, blending easily, as if she had another set of blue eyes on the back of her head. I looked down at the card:

WYNN RENNER AGENCY
Talent, Media, and Performance Arts

Underneath that, a Santa Monica address, phone number, and website. On the back, no handwritten phone number after all, just: "Sorry. Do call." When I looked up again she was gone. Should have asked her if she danced.

After more talk and knife-handling, Hector decided on two *janbiyas*. The clerk rang him up. One knife came in a silk scabbard, decorated with leaping lions. The other scabbard looked like heavy sand-colored cotton with subtle stripes and triangles woven in. The saleswoman accepted his sheaf of bills with unsubtle disgust, counted them quickly down to the glass countertop, gave Hector his change. Then wrapped the knives in red tissue, set them in a twine-handled Gallerie Monfil shopping bag, dangling it out to Hector on the farthest possible tip of one forefinger.

Hector O. Padilla, owner of two *janbiyas* and a stone to sharpen them on. *Janbiyas*—possibly the type of weapon used to decapitate Kenny Bryce.

Hector O. Padilla, reader of *Rumiyah*, recently broken up with, interested in Muslim women.

Hector O. Padilla, owner of Lindsey's current address, professionally provided by my old partner, Jason Bayless.

I followed Hector from the knives, to the swords, to the spears and lances. He didn't seem to have serious interest in any of them. Standing under the ceiling-mounted "Mihr Killing a Lion" tapestry, Hector set down his treasures of Araby to consult his phone again. This time it took longer than it had before. He read, thumbed in a reply, then slipped the phone back into his rear pocket and took a deep breath. He headed for the salon exit. Hustled back a few seconds later to get the shopping bag he'd left behind.

Following him was easy. Plenty of people out on Cedros that night. Not that he seemed to practice universal awareness all that often. He walked past my truck with a relaxed air, tapping his terrorist magazine against his leg. I climbed in a few moments later, watching from two hundred feet away as he got into his gleaming black Cube. I set up my smartphone with the tracker codes, keeping an eye on Hector.

He U-turned and came toward me. I did a full PI Slouch, watching his headlights pass across the headliner until they were gone. Started her up, gave Hector a few seconds while I confirmed his location on my phone, then cranked a U-turn of my own. The tracker GPS updated its location every second on my screen—street, address, city, state. Best hundred and ninety-nine bucks I'd ever spent. Bought two.

He made a series of right turns, which brought us back to where we started. I couldn't figure why, other than some kind of evasive maneuver he'd been told would work. I thought of him forgetting his bag of treasures of Araby. Separated by ten seconds, I tracked him north to Lomas Santa Fe, east to Stevens, south to La Colonia Park, where he circled a parking lot and came back out. This could have outed me if I hadn't been trailing far back. I parked, shut down, and slouched again while his headlights slid over me.

Then another U-turn and a low-speed tour through residential Solana Beach. I fell far back, lost sight of him, let the tracker do its job.

At last Hector broke out and took a mile-long straightaway on Villa de la Valle. Past the racetrack and the fairgrounds, both dark. His taillights, way up ahead. A left turn on San Andres and a right on Flower Hill. Then he stopped. I pulled over. Five seconds. Ten. Twenty. I drove slowly toward his current location, spotted his Cube parked far out in the Flower Hill Promenade lot. Just a few other cars there, this far from the retail stores on a cool, dark night.

I parked in the lot, on higher ground, a full hundred yards away. Killed the engine, got my night binoculars from under the seat. Rolled my window down. Hector got out and started toward a Toyota 4Runner parked one space over from the Cube. It was a dark, older vehicle and I wrote the plate numbers in my notebook.

The Toyota driver's window was halfway down. A stand of eucalyptus trees bordering the lot blocked the moonlight. As Hector approached I could just make out the shape of someone behind the wheel. A pale face in a dark interior.

They talked, Hector saying little, nodding. The window rose and Hector went to the rear, opened the 4Runner's lift gate, and let it rise. Then back to his Cube, where he swung open the rear cargo door.

20

HE LOOKED AROUND BRIEFLY, reached in and hefted out by its handle a green metal canister. I knew what it was instantly. I knew it to be rectangular, just under twelve inches long, six inches across, and seven high. With a fold-down metal handle, heavy lid, hard-to-open latch plates that lock tight to defeat sand, moisture, time itself. I'd seen more than a few of those during my days as a Marine. I glassed the yellow print:

420 CARTRIDGES

5.56MM

M16

LOT WRA 22416

Hector lugged it with both hands to the 4Runner, set it in the cargo area, pushed it forward. The driver, still locked in darkness, didn't appear to move. Hector clap-dusted his hands on his way back to the Cube.

Repeated the activity.

Four trips.

Which meant sixteen hundred and eighty rounds.

Or, accounted another way, two and a half minutes of fully automatic fire through an M16. Although M16 barrels melt at around two hundred straight rounds.

Rumiyah says to rest your gun. Which is fine, because you need to reload anyway. You have to stop firing to step over bodies. Which is good, because it lets the barrel cool. Why not post some video? Show the world what a badass you are, and what you're doing to make it a better place? By then, you're good to go again.

If you kill only one person with every ten rounds, you've taken one hundred and sixty-eight lives in your two and a half minutes of fully automatic glory.

Add an accomplice and the numbers can double.

A case of four hundred and twenty M16 rounds will cost you about what I paid for my GPU vehicle tracker—around two hundred dollars. Best deals are online. Shipping is sometimes free.

I glassed the SUV driver again, sitting very still in the dark interior. Him or her? Young or old? Something in the vague shape of the face said young and male. My night-vision binoculars couldn't illuminate, but they enhanced my eerie phantom and his surroundings in counternatural green.

Hector wasn't finished. From the front passenger side of the Cube he pulled out his fashionable Gallerie Monfil shopping bag, rummaged through the red tissue paper, and removed one of the knives. Walked it over to the 4Runner and held it up to the half-open window. Nodded, said something, shrugged, returned to the Cube. Standing by the open door, he drew out the blade and slashed the air around him, his free hand out for balance, which he nearly lost.

Then back to work.

Four more trips, four more ammunition canisters. I saw that these contained nine-millimeter cartridges, usually used in handguns. Smaller shells. One thousand rounds per canister. Hector was breathing deeply by the time he shoved in the fourth case and slammed the 4Runner's lift gate shut.

Dusting off his hands again, he approached the driver's window. The driver turned. And in the moment before Hector blocked my view, I saw that he was indeed a lean-faced young man, wearing a dark watch cap and a dark plaid shirt buttoned to his chin. It looked heavy, maybe flannel, against the cold. A tremor of recognition rattled through me as I pictured the Kenny Bryce surveillance video. Surfer. Boarder. In the brief moment I saw him, he gave Hector a blank stare. Splinters of light for eyes.

A moment later Hector backed away from the 4Runner. The driver's window was already up and white exhaust coughed from the muffler. No interior lights, but the headlights came on and the 4Runner pulled out. Hector tried to follow, realized his rear doors were still open, got out and slammed them shut, then hustled back behind the wheel.

I watched them go. In the shopping center lights I could see that the 4Runner was dark gray. Fell in behind them as Hector's location registered on my phone. Backtracked to Via de la Valle, to Interstate 5. The Toyota hit the southbound on-ramp fast, blowing past the one-car-per-green light, heading for traffic. Hector chugged along behind him and of course stopped at the red light. My heart sinking and racing at the same time. An eternal red light. The Cube rolled away, my turn next. I ran the light, swept around Hector's left and barreled past him, taking the middle lane and hitting the gas. I knew my chances were poor: too fast and he'd know something was wrong, too slow and I'd never catch up with him.

But I had good lines of sight from the middle lane. Stayed right there and gunned it. Eighty miles per hour, a hair faster than most of the flow. Eyes steady, breath even, high on hope. It was a wide freeway, two lanes on either side of me, traffic fast but light enough to give me a good view of the 4Runner.

But no 4Runner by the time I came to Del Mar Heights Road. Highway Patrol stopped on the right shoulder behind a Corvette, so I slowed down. Model citizen.

And no 4Runner by the next exit sign, either. That sinking feeling. But I regained my eighty miles an hour, blinders on for everything but what I wanted to see. And maybe because of that, I passed the Carmel Valley Road off-ramp just as I saw the dark gray Toyota climbing that ramp toward a very lucky green light that would take it over the freeway, then back onto it, heading in the opposite direction—north.

Disappointed and not a little pissed off, I sped the long half-mile south to Sorrento Valley Road. I knew that by the time I'd reached it, my mark would mostly likely be on his happy way northbound, doing the speed limit with nearly six thousand rounds of ammunition in the back, chalking up the miles between us. And almost impossible to find.

I exited at Sorrento Valley, pulled over when I could, called an old San Diego Sheriff's Department friend who might be willing to run the 4Runner's plates for me. I got a firm maybe.

Then Taucher. Who, when I told her about the ammunition, hissed a string of profanities. "We can rattle Hector's cage first thing in the morning," she said. "Friendly little knock and talk."

"You might rethink that," I said.

I told her I'd put the tracker on Hector's car, that we knew his address and work schedule, and if left unmolested, odd Hector just might lead us somewhere even better than a knife buy and an ammunition transfer. But if we let him see our shadow, he'd go down his hole. And whoever was the receiver of said ammunition—maybe even Caliphornia himself—would go down his hole, too.

Taucher liked that. Then she was gone.

I stepped outside and had a smoke. Heavy breeze from the Pacific. Moon caught in the marine layer. Watched the cars speed by below me. Interstate 5 goes all the way from Mexico to Canada, where Canada names her 5 also and lets her run into the Rocky Mountains. I drove through British Columbia once. Beautiful. You might not know that California is longer than Texas is wide. Almost got into a bar fight about that, in Fort Worth, from where Lindsey hails.

I got back on the freeway, northbound for home. Still disappointed and a little pissed off. Reminded myself that everything happens for a reason. Reminded myself that I've never believed one word of that sentence.

But this I knew: I would stop Caliphornia and his loyal dunce Hector from whatever they were planning for Lindsey and Voss and whomever their almost six thousand rounds were for.

Halfway to Fallbrook I got a call from a number not in my contacts. It came in at exactly eleven o'clock, from a Las Vegas area code. I hit the earpiece button and waited.

"Mr. Ford, my name is Rasha Samara. I live in Las Vegas. I'm looking for Lindsey Rakes. She's missing."

Ring of ear and thump of heart. "What is your relationship with her?"

"We're acquainted socially," he said. "I am a businessman. Lindsey Rakes taught my son in school."

His voice was full and smooth. A slight accent. My imagination readied for liftoff, but I kept it on the ground. So many salient details about Rasha Samara: IvarDuggans had told me that he'd been questioned by UC Irvine campus police for brandishing a *janbiya* at a party. Taucher had told me that the FBI was looking at him. My own eyes had told me that Samara had handwriting very similar to Caliphornia's.

"I've been trying to contact her for four days now and she hasn't responded," he said. "Maybe she simply doesn't want to communicate with me. If that's the case, I'm fine with that. Still, I'm worried."

He sounded reasonable and believable, I thought. "If something is wrong, do you have any idea where she would go?" I asked.

"I think she might have gone back to her previous address—your home in Fallbrook," said Samara.

"Why do you want to find her?"

A beat. The Oceanside Boulevard exit sign rushed by above me.

"Why do you care? You find people for money."

"Let's say I care, Mr. Samara. We're friends, and I value friends."

"I value her, too. She's important to me. Have you seen her?"

"Not in a year and a half."

"Then I would like to hire you to find her."

No way I could shield Lindsey and do an honest job for Rasha Samara. But I wanted him close, so I gave him my routine: twenty-four hundred dollars to start, cash only, good for three full days of work. If I got lucky before three days, he'd get a refund. If not, I charged one hundred dollars an hour for additional work. Major credit cards and PayPal accepted.

"Why cash to start?" he asked.

"So I can see the face I'm dealing with," I said. "And change my mind if that face doesn't look right. *Right* is kind of a broad term."

We set the appointment for eight in the morning. Rather than use my Main Street office, I wanted Rasha to see my property, to see for himself that I had no Lindsey to hide.

I hung up, voice-dialed Burt, told him about tomorrow's visitor. Asked him to get Lindsey and Zeno a motel for a couple of nights—something pet-friendly, not too far away but not too close.

21

SAMARA'S WHITE RANGE ROVER came up my driveway at seven fifty-nine the next morning. I'd had my run and punched the bags hard and well. Burt, walking down the drive with a cup of coffee, waved Samara through an open post-and-rail gate and into the barnyard. From where I sat under the big palapa I saw that Rasha had brought a second.

Samara got out of the passenger side and shut the door, then stood still, sizing up the ranch. Snapped his jacket arms down over his shirt cuffs as he considered. He was on the tall side, slender and wide-shouldered in a shimmering gray suit. Athletic and poised. Something like the shape of the man in the Bakersfield video. Sharp-faced, too, like the 4Runner's driver the night before.

His confederate was an economy-sized block of muscle in a black polo shirt and chinos, with a gun in a paddle-style, inside-the-waistband holster at the small of his back.

I watched Burt introduce himself, shake hands, and motion toward me, Roland Ford, California Bureau of Security and Investigative Services license number PI 537668, firearm permit number 081211, six feet three inches tall, two hundred ten pounds, brown and brown, DOB 1/13/79. College grad, former jarhead, former professional boxer, former sheriff's deputy, former husband. Likes: dancing, fishing, skiing, hiking, finding missing people, digging up the truth, a good bourbon, a good book. Dislikes: rudeness, ignorance, entitlement, cruelty, irresponsibility, cheating, sloth, parking tickets.

I felt good about myself right then. Early on a cool bright December morning. Watching the men come up the path toward me. I had a full set of teeth, a good cup of coffee, and a bright future so far as I could see. But there was something more, and it was this: last night, when I'd seen all that ammunition and understood that it was very likely to be used for wickedness, I'd felt needed. Needed to protect. To prevent. To vanquish. Nothing better than being necessary. I hadn't felt that since the day Justine died. But last night, seeing Hector and his partner—whoever he might be—had jumped my adrenaline and my will. Now I felt light and nimble on my war footing. I'd been called again, and was soon to be deployed. My crusade. Roland Ford, paladin.

Rasha's handshake was rough and strong, contrary to his sleek appearance. We sat opposite each other, midway down the long picnic bench under the palapa. I gave him the pond view. My view was of the old adobe brick house. The casitas stretched along the shore, Lindsey's number three now without Lindsey, who had departed with Zeno and Burt at daybreak for a Best Western in Oceanside. I'd ordered Dick, Liz, and Clevenger not to interrupt in any way my meeting with Mr. Samara. To my right, Burt and Rasha's bodyguard—Timothy—stood at ease by the barbecue, talking quietly. The top of Burt's head came only to the midpoint of Timothy's torso.

"This is all good," said Rasha Samara, looking out to the pond and beyond. "It's good you left it native and drought-tolerant."

"I pretty much leave it alone," I said. "You build landscapes for a living."

"Golf courses. Nothing like this. How old is the house?"

"Well over a century."

He smiled, more with amusement than warmth. "Americans have a shortened view of history."

I shrugged. "A century is long to me," I said. "This whole property was a wedding gift from my wife's parents."

"I've read about her and the accident," he said. "Very sad. My wife died of cancer just a few years earlier. Both of them were robbed. So were we. We have a lot in common."

I nodded. Rasha offered me a cigarette from a silver case. I declined. He lit the smoke with the case and slid it back into his suit-coat pocket. Through the slow-moving cloud I saw Burt and Timothy looking back at me. Timothy had taken on a new alertness, back straight, his big fingers intertwined softly in front of him.

I opened my briefcase and set between us a pen and two copies of my standard contract. It's a simple document, stating the purpose of the investigation, responsibilities and limitations of both parties, and compensation. It sets forth the basics of my insurance policy—California requires one million dollars of insurance for any PI who carries a firearm while working. It covers injury and destruction of life and property. It felt odd to be taking twenty-four hundred dollars in advance for locating a woman who was living in one of my own rentals.

Rasha glanced through one copy without patience. When we had both signed and dated them, I gave him one, then checked the signature page of my copy. It had the same patient, artful, Arabic flair with which he'd signed his card to Lindsey. I put the contract and the pen back into my briefcase, set it on the pavers at my feet.

"Should I continue to call and text and email Lindsey?" he asked.

"Yes," I said. "Obviously, I'll need to know if she responds. But if she's choosing not to communicate with you, do you have an idea why?"

He ground out his cigarette in my hand-collected clamshell ashtray. "We dated one time. Then she said, No more. She could think I'm stalking her now."

I thought about that, let the silence sink in. "Tell me about it."

"Lindsey was one of my son's teachers," he said. "At the back-to-school night I saw that she was strong and intelligent and beautiful. She also seemed to be in turmoil. I saw her for parent conferences. I saw her at fundraisers for the school, and some of our son's athletic events. It was two years later that I asked her to go riding. That was just a few weeks ago."

"How did it go?"

"I love Arabian horses," he said. "The more time I spend with them the less time I want to spend with people. I'm not quite half joking. We rode from the stable where I live. It's beautiful desert. Very Arabian. I was born in the U.S. and I learned English as my first language and modern Arabic as my second. But Arabia is in my blood. Like the horses are. My family spent many weeks there when I was a child. Whole summers. Parts of the American West remind me of the Saudi Peninsula. The weather, the flora, the geology. So we rode. Lindsey and I. She's very good. We rested the horses. Talked. We shared cheese and salami, drank wine, and watched the sunset. When we rode back, we hardly said a thing. I think we were lost in our own pasts, but something told me this was a beginning. That someday soon, I would be able to introduce Lindsey to Sally. In my heart. You probably know what I'm talking about."

Burt led Timothy to the Ping-Pong table, and together they lifted off the fitted plastic cover. Burt got the paddles from a hutch and set the box on the table. I could see his bottom-toothed grin as he tightened up the net and big Timothy pawed through the box for the right paddle. Burt is a ferocious player, torqueing his short, muscular body into almost every shot, starting low and ending high. Mid-rally, he's a lateral blur. Plays far back from the table and lets her rip. I try to crowd the table and hit early. Take away my opponent's time. I can beat Burt, but not often. Timothy held up a dimpled/smooth two-sided paddle and a ball. Nodded. Lumbered smoothly to one end of the table, bouncing the ball on his paddle.

"Yes," I answered. "You want to forget and remember. Sometimes, the same things."

"The daily torture," said Samara. "I dated a lot after Sally. Many expensive restaurants and destinations. And then I'd had enough. Something broke or healed. I don't know which. It doesn't matter. Then I spent three hours with Lindsey Rakes and welcomed myself back into the world again."

Then came the *ticka tocka, ticka tocka* of Ping-Pong.

"How long did she live here?" asked Samara.

"One year."

He studied me, sharp eyes in a sharp face. I thought of the phantom image behind the wheel of the Toyota the night before.

"How many casitas do you rent?"

"Five," I said. "There are six, but I keep number three available for friends. Emergencies."

"Which was Lindsey's?"

"Two."

Rasha regarded the casitas. Similar shapes. Different-colored doors and window trim. "Are these the rules, or are they a joke?"

He was looking up at my posted rules, framed and protected by clear plastic and screwed to one of the palapa's thick palm-trunk uprights. When I'd first started renting casitas—two years ago now—I'd been serious about posting rules. It seemed to make good sense, to let everyone know what was expected and what wasn't. Rules would put me in charge, but I could still be a nice guy. I watched Samara read them, something between a smile and a smirk on his face.

GOOD MANNERS AND PERSONAL HYGIENE

NO VIOLENCE, REAL OR IMPLIED

NO DRUGS

NO STEALING

QUIET MIDNIGHT TO NOON

RENT DUE FIRST OF MONTH

NO EXCEPTIONS

"They started out serious," I said. "But now I'm not so sure. I haven't had any rotten renters yet."

"What about possession of guns and knives?" he asked.

"Implied by rule two," I said, thinking: *Interesting, the knives.*

"Alcohol?"

"Rule one."

"Obscenity and lewd conduct?"

"Rules one and five."

I smiled, but Rasha didn't. "Why is it that when I go online and to the *Fallbrook Village News*, I find no information about rentals here?"

"It's all word of mouth," I said. Which was true.

"Casita three is open?"

"Three and four," I said. "People tend to sit tight for the holidays."

"May I see one?"

"No. They're not ready for tenants yet."

He gave me a dark look. Maybe darker than the moment required. Maybe that was part of Lindsey refusing a second date. As much as fearing her own attraction.

"Do you love her?" asked Rasha.

I'd wondered if that question was coming. "As a friend."

"But as more, when she was here?"

"Friends then and now."

"You were so close to her beauty and power," he said, eyes brightening. "You must have wanted them."

I remembered the near-total wreck that was Lindsey Rakes when I first saw her at the roulette wheel that night. And the long weeks here as she tried and failed and tried again to put herself back together. She was beautiful in her damage, yes. Powerful? No. She was staggering. I had wanted to help her, and respectful distance was required.

"I tried to help her put herself back together," I said.

"For yourself?"

"For her."

"You behaved well."

I looked out to the barnyard, and the long driveway leading away from Rancho de los Robles, then up to two red-shouldered hawks keening as they circled the pond.

"Now," I said. "Why don't you tell me about the UCI frat party in '98? When you were arrested for brandishing a *janbiya*."

22

SAMARA'S DARK LOOK grew darker.

Ticka tocka, ticka tocka.

"How do you know about that?" he asked.

"Anyone with a phone and a little money can find that out."

Rasha shook his head slightly, then reached out and tapped his fingers on the table. "The party was called 'Come as Your Own Cliché.' This was before Nine-Eleven. I wore the knife in its scabbard in plain sight, on a belt, outside of my caftan. The *janbiya* was a dull family heirloom. I also wore a turban with a big fake diamond and a blue ostrich feather. I grew a crafty little goatee and trimmed my beard down to a thin outline of my jaw. A friend of mine, Anton Webster, came as an Eighteenth Street Crip, dissed me. Called me wooly-headed camel jockey. I drew my knife. He pulled a black plastic squirt gun on me, and I slashed at him. With much playful drama. Our acting was good enough for a call to the campus police from one of the Pi Phi sisters."

Burt and Timothy had both moved back from their respective ends of the table. Burt moved in bursts, fast and animated. Large Timothy bounced on the balls of his feet, squatting deeply into his shots, easy of swing, head steady. The rhythm of their paddles on the ball slowed, as the ball arched higher across the widening distance, then dropped deep steeply to the table.

"Do you still have the *janbiya*?" I asked.

"Somewhere."

"Do you know Kenny Bryce?"

A pause. "No."

"Marlon Voss?"

"You're accusing me of something."

"I asked if you know Marlon Voss."

"*Why?*"

"Do you know a man who calls himself Caliphornia? Spelled with a *p* and an *h* instead of an *f*? As in *caliph*?"

"Is he a singer or a comedian or something?"

"He's a murderer who uses a knife."

The dark look again. "Now I understand you. You are another fearful American who thinks every Arab is out to slaughter someone. I am Caliphornia because I own a decorative *janbiya* that I was dumb enough to take to a fraternity party over twenty years ago."

Ticka. Burt, a corkscrew and a white tracer.

Tocka. Timothy's topspin shot dropping like a stone.

I stared at Rasha the same way I used to stare down my opponents in the ring. I wasn't looking for fear or weakness in him. You won't find them in a fighter. Uncertainty is the best I ever got, and that, only rarely. Anger was next best because it made people behave stupidly. Rasha Samara stared back, as focused and determined as any opponent I'd ever faced. No hint of fear, but a nice dose of anger.

I threw a combination.

"The worry is he's sponsored," I said.

Another baleful stare, then his face relaxed. He smiled and sat back. "Why didn't you just tell me, Mr. Ford? That I, through my family and its ties to other powerful families in Saudi Arabia, am a sponsor of Caliphornia, a knife-wielding terrorist?"

"I said nothing about terror."

"I came here hoping to find a woman I think may be in trouble."

"I've agreed to help," I said.

"Yes, you have," said Rasha. He squared his copy of the contract before him, gave it a long look, then tore it into quarters. Swept them into a loose pile, facedown. From his jacket pocket he took a small plump envelope, pulled out a hundred-dollar bill, and slipped it under the pile. "This will cover the hour of mine you just wasted."

I left the bill where it was, but I turned over the top quarter-page of the contract, where we had signed and dated. "Where did you learn your penmanship?" I asked.

"My mother," he said. "She bought me a calligraphy kit when I was ten. Of course, you know that all Arab knife assassins train in calligraphy."

Rasha rose, buttoned his suit coat, and nodded to Timothy. The big man let the ball go past him. Burt tossed his paddle to the table and kept his eyes on Timothy, not me.

"I think you're covering for her," said Rasha. "I think she's been here."

"I heard you were in Bakersfield on Monday," I said. "And bought yourself a beautiful horse."

Samara shook his head, his bitter humor spent. "I bought the mare at a Bakersfield auction by proxy. Her name is Clementa. Personally, I was in Bahrain that day."

Timothy gave his paddle to Burt and they shook hands with some earnestness. I watched the big man and Samara march into the barnyard, Samara a step ahead. I watched him closely, gauging his light-footed gait against the balanced walk of Kenny Bryce's killer. Captured on a very poor grainy black-and-white video. Similar? Somewhat. And his face, how similar to one I saw last night in the darkness of the vehicle? Enough to count as more circumstantial evidence that Caliphornia was now crossing my property toward his SUV? Maybe.

Burt came to my side, watching the two men board the white Range Rover. "That your cutthroat?"

"I don't know yet."

"Timothy said his employer has a temper," said Burt.

"He didn't quite hold it."

"We split the first two games and I was up eighteen–fourteen in the third."

"Good work, Burt."

"Timothy says Samara was overseas all week. Not in Bakersfield at all."

"So I heard."

"I wouldn't expect a beheader to drive a Range Rover," Burt said. "Too showy and easy to remember. And they break down every other week."

We watched the too-showy SUV trundle down the rain-pocked dirt drive toward the gate. A flock of starlings lifted off from a flat tan puddle.

Burt and I collected the breeze-blown contract pieces and covered the Ping-Pong table. I put the hundred-dollar bill into my wallet, wondered if I should mail it to him. I looked again at Samara's contract signature, picturing the ugly threat that Caliphornia had so beautifully written to Lindsey. I thought of what Samara had said about Lindsey's beauty and power, and how I must have wanted them for myself.

A few minutes later Burt came from his casita and loaded his golf clubs into the trunk of his car. Perhaps because of his shortness, Burt drives an enormous old Cadillac, a red Coupe deVille convertible with majestic fins, a white interior, and white sidewall tires. He could stretch out and nap in that trunk, no problem.

I watched him drive away, thought of another red convertible that had gone down and up that driveway so many hundreds of times. Until that day in April when it left here and didn't return. A Porsche Boxster, music blaring, a redhead at the wheel, her hair in a black scarf. That car was still out in the barn, washed and polished and under its cover. But impossible for me to drive or sell.

I got another cup of coffee and sat upstairs in my office, checked my messages. Fielded a worried call from Tammy Bellamy, who had received a text about a gray cat seen walking along Stage Coach Road, not far from the high school. Less than half an hour ago. Tammy asked if I could please go find the cat, and, if it was Oxley, "save" him. I explained that I could not. But I felt the need to apologize and did. Hung up feeling like a heartless son of a bitch.

I did have my reasons. I was just a few hours from my noon rendezvous with Joan Taucher in the Horton Plaza parking lot and our planned journey to Los Angeles. Where we would interview two adult children of slain Doctors Without Borders physician Ibrahim Azmeh. Dr. Ibrahim Azmeh, accidentally blown into eternity by Lindsey's Headhunters.

No sooner had I forgotten my heartlessness than my friend at the San Diego Sheriff's Department called with news of the 4Runner's license plate check. The plate had last belonged to a vehicle totaled in a collision, and had likely ended up in a scrap yard. Salvage operators were required by law to return currently registered plates, but . . . I thanked him and told him I owed him one.

I sat awhile, contemplating through my western window the pond, the long drive leading down to the gate, the rain-greened hills. Possibly the same flock of starlings that had flown up when Rasha Samara drove past now came back to land around the same puddle.

I saw the black Ford Expedition turn off the road and stop outside my gate. Saw its exhaust lifting slowly in the still cool morning, and a hand reach for the keypad.

I answered the intercom but said nothing.

"Mr. Ford? This is Directing Special Agent Darrel Blevins of the Federal Bureau of Investigation. We need just a few minutes of your time. Now."

My good mood was being shot to hell. First by Rasha Samara, then by Tammy Bellamy, and now by the FBI.

"Badge, please," I said. "Hold it up to the camera by the speaker button."

He did, sighing. My security video streams into my house with a one-second delay but is state-of-the-art compared to Kenny Bryce's.

The gate rolled open and the Expedition surged onto my property in a way that could only be federal. Feds surge. They always surge. Directing Special Agent Darrel Blevins didn't need no stinking badge.

23

IN THE SUN-DAPPLED BARNYARD: four suits, three hastily flashed FBI badges, one handshake from Directing Special Agent Darrel Blevins. Tight faces for concealing thoughts, loose coats for concealing guns, polished dress shoes flecked with moisture from the dewy grass, young agent Mike Lark trying to shake the droplets off. Patrick O'Hora was white and built, Darnell Smith black and trim.

"We need to talk to you about your relationship with FBI Special Agent Joan Taucher," said Blevins.

"I'm innocent," I said. "And I have an appointment soon."

"Thank you for making time for us on short notice, Mr. Ford." Blevins smiled. All implants, perfect and white. He had downy white hair and a fissured face. "We'll be as brief as possible."

We sat beneath the palapa, where Rasha Samara had fired me a little more than one hour ago. Blevins removed a small digital recorder from his briefcase, set the briefcase on the ground and the recorder on the table between us. He clicked it on, ran a quick test, then stated the time, date, and players. Asked each of us to confirm when he spoke our names.

Dale Clevenger rolled up the drive, parked his van in front of casita two, finally home from his night of filming. He waved at me, pulled one of his drones from the van, and went inside his home. In a charged silence, all four agents stared at him and his camera-armed aircraft.

"Who's that and what's with the drone?" asked Blevins.

I explained.

"You rent those cottages?"

Explained again. Liz and Dick sat on Liz's porch, apparently arguing, both dressed for tennis, gear bags at their feet, cups of coffee steaming. Dick looked our way with exaggerated nonchalance.

I was hoping I could hustle this thing along. "What can I say about Joan Taucher that you don't know already?" I asked.

"Well, let's see," said Blevins. "Did you have a personal relationship with her in 2010 and 2011, when you were part of the San Diego JTTF?"

"Not personal, no," I said.

"Tell me what you did for JTTF," said Blevins.

I filled him in on my duties, sure he already knew.

"Was Joan a good superior?" asked Blevins.

"All business."

"What do you mean by 'all business'?" asked Mike Lark. He was young, square-jawed, boyish.

"No, Mike," said Blevins. "No."

"Sorry, sir."

"Where were we?" Blevins asked, turning back with another flash of his flawless substitute teeth. I wondered what had destroyed the originals.

"All business," I said.

"Did she ever bend the rules or overstep her boundaries?" asked Blevins.

"Taucher was scrupulous. We had lunch a few times. I remember her counting out the pennies and nickels for her exact portion of the bill."

Blevins nodded. "How would you describe Agent Taucher's attitude toward her job? Her attitude toward terror?"

"Loved her job. Hated terror."

"Did you ever hear her referred to as Joan Wayne?" Blevins asked.

"Everyone called her Joan Wayne."

"Ever see her in an MMA cage bout?"

"No. I saw pictures of her in her fighting gear."

"The online stuff that got her so pissed off?"

I nodded. "She wasn't happy about that."

"Did Joan ever share information with you?" asked Blevins.

From his poor attempt at sounding off-hand, I knew Blevins was finally getting to his real point.

I had to think about that for a moment. To the FBI, information is the Holy Grail, and despite post-9/11 "changes," sharing intel outside the Bureau can be a mortal sin.

"Share information?" I asked. "Isn't that what everybody does at the JTTF?" I'm sure they heard the sarcasm.

Blevins stared down at his recorder as if expecting it to say something. When it didn't, he picked it up, seemed to examine it, then set it back down.

"Let's bring this narrative up to date," he said. "Five days ago you brought us the Lindsey Rakes threat. You bypassed the San Diego agent-in-charge and went right to the FBI Special Agent Joan Taucher. I understand that. You had worked with her before. You had a relationship. A business relationship. On Monday, according to Joan, she agreed not to interview Lindsey Rakes personally. This because of some legal entanglements regarding the custody of Lindsey's son. Correct?"

It was up to me to separate what Joan had told Blevins from what Blevins was *claiming* she'd told him. I drummed my fingertips on the old wooden table, gave Blevins my weigh-in stare. "Yes."

"Again from Joan," said Blevins. "She admitted that we, the Bureau, were looking at one Rasha Samara as a person of interest in the financing of terror."

"She didn't use the words *financing* or *terror*," I said. "She said you were looking at him and that was all."

"Oh," he said curtly. "Not quite the story we got."

"You might run it by her again," I said.

"Don't try to negotiate with me," Blevins snapped. "We do not negotiate. Now—again according to Joan—that same day she told you about Samara, she also suggested you do some background on one Hector O. Padilla. This because he had been behaving oddly at a San Diego mosque *and* was a regular customer at World Pizza in Ocean Beach— the alleged return address on Caliphornia's threat letter to Lindsey."

I nodded, wondering exactly what these esteemed colleagues of Joan Taucher's were looking for.

"And she allowed you to photograph Padilla's picture with your phone, inside her JTTF office," said Blevins. "Correct?"

"I shot pictures of the photograph."

"With Joan's permission?"

"She allowed me to," I said. "So I could see what I was doing, so to speak."

"And maybe as a thank-you for bringing her the Lindsey Rakes situation?" Blevins asked.

"I doubt that."

"Because of the personal relationship you and Agent Taucher do not have," said Blevins.

"Precisely." I wondered if these fine gentlemen had bugged her office, or if Joan had already told them all this. The best thing I could think to do was to let Blevins throw his net. See where it landed.

"Now, later—this from Joan again—she told us she shared FBI lab results with you. Specifically, that the signatures on the Caliphornia threat and the Rasha Samara note were probably from two different writers. That would have been Monday night."

While I was driving home from my stakeout of Hector Padilla, I thought. Which meant either Joan had told them about our conversation or these guys were monitoring her cell phone—probably SOP for agents' work-issued smartphones. I looked at each of Blevins's underlings in turn. Three faces, bland and unreadable.

I wondered, if they knew all this, why did they need my recorded corroboration? The answer hit me hard: so I could help them throw Taucher under whatever bus they had in mind. In their eyes, I was a high-value asset—a private contractor who had come forward because Joan Taucher was leaking information. Information on terror. Which made her a danger to our national security.

"She gave me the documents examiner's opinion of the signatures," I said. Wondering again exactly what Blevins had in mind for Joan Wayne. The Bureau. Suspicion wrapped in suspicion. Cunning wrapped in cunning. While Caliphornia moved through their defenses like a ghost.

"We're almost done here," said Blevins. "Just a few more questions. Now, moving along to two nights ago, Thursday, you were contacted by an officer of the Bakersfield Police Department regarding surveillance video taken at Kenny Bryce's apartment complex. You were sent a self-destructing Telegram video. Six and a half seconds, Joan said. Did you in fact receive and view such a video?"

Again I wondered how they knew this. Her office landline? Her cell? Did it matter? Like anyone—from model citizen to terrorist—I was pleased to know that the self-destructing video had left no trace in my phone.

But I clearly remembered Joan's words about agents handing out FBI property, and I knew what Blevins was thinking. Joan allowing me to view the Kenny Bryce video was comparable to her smuggling papers out of JTTF headquarters in her briefcase. Or a video stick in her purse. As she had said: *That's physical FBI evidence. They'd have my head.*

It looked to me like they were trying to do just that. I saw no choice in what to say. "No. I've gotten no *Mission: Impossible* Telegrams."

Three of the men sat back, as if on cue, exchanging glances, sighs. Only Lark, the young upstart, remained fixed on me.

"Think about that again," said Blevins. "I'd like to give you the opportunity to remember correctly."

"No. Final answer."

"We have what we need," he said, looking past the pond to the green hills beyond. "Is that where you guys shot down the helicopter with Briggs Spencer in it?"

"The very place."

He nodded. The violent death of psychologist Briggs Spencer here at Rancho de los Robles had made headlines across the nation.

"Spencer was a complicated man," said Blevins. "And part of a complicated chapter in our history."

"I've heard those platitudes before."

We stood. Blevins clicked off his recorder but he didn't put it back into his briefcase. I walked them past the Ping-Pong table and the barbecue, toward the railroad-tie steps that lead down to the barnyard.

Silence. Sweet smell of grass in sunshine. Agents two by two, PI Ford leading the way, listening for the click of the recorder's "on" button. Heard it just before we started down the steps. Blevins the crafty.

"You sure you didn't see that Bakersfield surveillance video, Ford?" he asked from behind me.

"I'm very sure."

"Lying to a federal agent is a crime."

Zeno had left a sizable pile in our way. I stepped around it, turning as Blevins walked straight toward it. I slowed and held his look and let him continue on his course.

"Oh, shit," he said, stopping.

Everyone else stopped, too.

"I'm sorry, Mr. Ford," said Lark. "But may I use a restroom before we leave?"

"Christ, Mike, can't you just *hold* it?" asked Blevins. His face was florid and he had both hands out for balance, sweeping one shiny cap-toe dress shoe across the slick, unhelpful barnyard grass. Raising an invisible mountain of stink.

"I can't, sir," said Lark. "And it looks like you might be a minute."

I led Lark across the damp grass and into the barn, pointing out the bathroom back in the corner behind the tractor and the Bobcat. Clevenger's worktables had their usual collection of drones and drone parts, cameras and monitors. The agent stopped and stared at them before turning to me.

"Blevins doesn't work with us in San Diego," he said. "He's from Washington. Where he and his people want to transfer Joan. Where they'll hold a pillow over her face and call it a promotion. Joan and I work together. I've tried warning her. I've tried talking to her."

"And?"

"She doesn't listen to me."

"Sounds like her."

"She's a great agent," Lark said. "I want to help her but I don't know how. I'm not even sure there's anything I *can* do."

"I hope you think of something," I said.

He looked at me for a beat, as if waiting for a suggestion. "Me, too. I'm twenty-four. The same age as Joan was when she first started here in San Diego. Just before Nine-Eleven. I was seven when I saw those planes coming down."

The moment of silence we all know.

"God, that was funny," said Lark.

"Nine-Eleven?"

"No. Darrel stepping in the dog shit."

24

IN THE EXPECTED PRIVACY of my pickup truck, I told Joan Taucher everything that had happened two hours earlier. The Saturday traffic was light and we were almost to Camp Pendleton by the time I'd finished.

Taucher sat hard-faced, looking out the windshield through aviator sunglasses, her makeup heavy and her white bangs trimmed bluntly at her brow. No hematoma in sight. Black suit with a flag lapel pin, black blouse, gun and holster temporarily on her lap for comfort. A charmless black purse on the floorboard in front of her.

"I know all about their crude tricks," she said. "Frosts my balls. Lark's a good kid. He tries to help me, but I see through him like a window. I don't know about my office being miked, but I know the work phones are monitored. Randomly, they say. Policy. It just piles up in the Cloud. Metadata. Useless mountains of crap in the Cloud, generated by us. Nobody can listen to it all. Hell, we can't even keep up with the domestic terror tips. You saw my walls. I watch what I say, wherever I am. The stuff I shared with you was small potatoes. They haven't written me up for anything. Yet."

"I'm surprised you take it so well."

"And my choice is what?"

I thought about that and saw her point. I couldn't picture Taucher doing anything other than what she was doing here and now in this city. Guarding the citadel. Tracking the ghosts. She was where she belonged. By fate, luck, or design. Blessing and curse.

As if at a loss for meaningful law enforcement activity, Taucher removed her gun, looked at it for a moment, then pushed it into the holster and snapped it shut.

Marah Ibrahim Azmeh was twenty-four years old and single and lived in Torrance, southwest of L.A. She worked for the County of Los Angeles Public Social Services Department, in payroll. She wore a yellow dress, yellow flip-flops with white daisies on them, and a pretty smile as she welcomed us to her small tract home. Taucher had told me that Marah meant "happiness," and that Marah had been born to Madiyah and Dr. Ibrahim Azmeh while he was a resident at Centinela Hospital Medical Center in Inglewood. Dr. Azmeh himself had helped deliver her. She was a graduate of Cal State Northridge.

Waiting for us in the small living room was her older brother, Alan Ames. My quick IvarDuggans.com search revealed that he had been born in Inglewood as Alim Ibrahim Azmeh, and changed his name when he was eighteen. He was twenty-six years old, married, and a father of two. Employed as a surgical nurse at the UCLA Medical Center, where—I noted—his father had studied. Arrested for aggravated assault three years prior, charges dropped.

He sat at one end of a white couch, looking calmly over his teacup at us when we came into the room. He stood briefly, nodded without speaking as Taucher and I introduced ourselves, then sat back down. He was husky, dressed in jeans, a rugby shirt, and white athletic shoes.

"Tea?" asked Marah. "Juice?"

Taucher and I declined and Marah settled onto the couch opposite her brother. Their blood relationship was easy to see—slender faces, expressive brown eyes, coffee-with-cream skin. Their hair was black and straight, Marah's streaked with henna. They both resembled their father in the one picture of him I'd seen. Not striking similarities, but even so. Different degrees of his aquiline nose.

The house was small, mid-fifties, probably three small bedrooms and two baths. Built in the era of Eisenhower, Elvis, and Khrushchev. Black-and-white TVs, green front lawns. Sears and Roebuck, Briggs & Stratton. Skinny ties and showing-top flattops. My grandpa Dick as a boy, playing catch in the street, Liz jumping rope.

Now a sun-filled living room. Polished windows. Facing the couch sat two wooden armchairs with red-and-gold Arabesque upholstery—one for Taucher and one for me. Persian rugs on a dark laminate floor. An entertainment center along one wall, a few CDs and DVDs and a modestly sized flat-screen TV. Bookshelves on another wall: college textbooks, sociology, psychology, American history, economics, art. More art. For the serious reader, I thought. For the searching young mind of Marah Azmeh. The other wall was densely hung with framed photographs—family and friends, at a glance.

Taucher thanked them for agreeing to meet us on short notice, although—she pointed out—it was their duty as American citizens to be vigilant against terror. Marah nodded. Alan didn't.

"Tell us what happened to your father," she said.

"You know exactly what happened to him, Agent Taucher," said

Alan. "You probably know more than we do. He was blown to pieces by an American drone on April twenty-second, 2015."

"I'm sorry for your loss and I understand your anger," Joan said briskly.

"You certainly do not," said Alan. "I have less than one hour before work."

"I'll be direct," said Taucher. "An assassin has murdered one of the three drone operators whose targeted strike killed your innocent father and eight others. That drone operator's name was Kenny Bryce. We know that this assassin intends to murder both of the other operators as well. He has called his actions 'justice' and 'vengeance.' So we are here to find out—do you know who this assassin might be? Do you know any relatives or friends of the collaterals who died that day and who are angry enough to kill in revenge? Have you heard of any such person, perhaps even secondhand? A rumor, even. A suspicion."

I wondered how Taucher's calling their father a "collateral" would sit with them.

Marah collected Alan's empty teacup and excused herself to the kitchen. I could see her back and hear the clink of porcelain and the faint sound of liquid being poured.

Alan Ames folded his hands on his lap. "I do not murder. My sister does not murder. We do not associate with murderers. Are we finished?"

"But you have other brothers and sisters overseas," said Taucher. "Uncles and aunts and cousins. Have any of them ever communicated anything about avenging your father's death?"

"Ask *them* if they are murderers," said Alan.

Marah returned with Alan's teacup and saucer and set them beside him. She sat again, her face passive, looking at me.

"They're half a world away," said Joan.

"Mr. Ames, do any relatives or friends of your father live in the United States?" I asked. It was certainly possible. My IvarDuggans.com search had failed to reveal both Marah and Alan as related to Dr. Ibrahim Azmeh, yet here they sat.

Alan's face closed on his sister. "Marah? Speak to these people."

She leaned forward. "Friends, certainly. Dad was a great man. He was fun and outgoing and popular. Tons of friends. Friends from his childhood in Damascus have immigrated here. Friends from his college days in Paris. People who laughed and argued and smoked and hugged you and talked about ideas and politics. And he had even more friends from medical school here in L.A. Like, I couldn't count them if I had to."

She cleared her throat. I sensed truth and gentleness in her, in the way her words and emotions and expressions came out as one. Authentic and undiluted. "He left my mother and the United States to return to Syria when I was ten years old. Which meant more friends and more children for him. He married twice again, but not through divorce. This is legal in most of Syria. I can't even guess about my father's friends in America, but none of his children are here that I know of, except for Alan and me and Ben."

I glanced at Taucher, who eyed me back.

"Correct," said Alan. "Our father was the stereotype of a Muslim woman-owner. He wasn't devout. But he liked the three-wives idea. He was still married to all of them the day you slaughtered him."

Marah took a deep breath and a shamed glance down, then politely changed the subject. "Ben is the youngest," she said. "Benyamin. He lives in Santa Ana. I didn't hear back from him about this meeting."

"We'd like his address," said Taucher.

"Yes, sure," said Marah.

"Is there anything else to talk about, then?" asked Alan.

I hit him with a quick jab: "Did you ever think of getting vengeance for your dad?"

He considered, eyes hooded. "I was furious when I heard. I would have probably killed the messenger if it hadn't been Marah. But serious, actual revenge? No. Impractical. I couldn't see myself going up against the U.S. Air Force, or the CIA, or whoever was responsible for firing that missile into a group of doctors and nurses."

"Never fantasized that you could get away with it?" asked Taucher.

A consideration, then a smirk. "We all have our fantasies, Agent Taucher. Maybe even you."

"You're a rude dude," she said.

"I'll be happy to report that remark to your superior."

"I'll give you his name and direct number before we leave."

"Which will be soon, I hope—"

"*Alan . . .*"

Alan stood. "I can't be late for work. I don't want your boss's name or number. I loved my father and you killed him for no reason. We received twelve thousand dollars for him. I will never forgive and never forget."

Alan embraced his sister and whispered something in her ear and did not look back on us. The front door slammed. Marah sat back down on the couch, sat forward and lowered her head, then snapped back her mane of copper-black hair and looked at us.

25

"SORRY," SHE SAID. "Alan's, like, really pissed at America for not doing enough in Syria. Yet managing to kill Dad. Dad loved America. That's why he came here to study and start a family. We'd visit Syria to see our relatives and roots, but he thought America was our future. Alan hated the drones long before Dad was killed. For Alan, it became a point of honor to collect the condolence payment. It was very difficult to get. Interview after interview. Delays. He felt like a suspect in a crime. One of the conditions was that we couldn't speak in public or to the media about the payment. They didn't tell us the amount being offered until after we had signed everything. When the check for twelve thousand five hundred dollars came in, Alan just about choked, he was so mad."

"I might have, too," I said.

Taucher gave me her battle glance. "It's war. Things happen in them."

Marah faced Taucher with a nod and silence.

"Does Alan talk about vengeance for your dad?" I asked.

"Some angry threats at first," said Marah. "Then nothing. He doesn't have room for that. He's a busy father and his wife is pregnant again and his job pays well. They live just one block away."

"Is he always that hostile to the authorities?" asked Taucher.

"He gets along well with the local police," said Marah. "He helped operate on an officer in the ER a few years ago and they became friends."

"So he's just reacting to my fizzy personality?" asked Taucher.

A small smile from Marah.

"Is your mother still in the U.S.?" Taucher asked.

"She lives in France."

"Tell us about Ben," I said.

"The baby," she said. "He's twenty-two now. Two years younger than me, and four behind Alan. Ben is our free spirit. Very American. He travels and studies what interests him. Likes art and adventure. Stays in campgrounds. Surfs and climbs rocks. Some college, too. Serial girlfriends until lately. Works but always needs money. Odd jobs, usually in the health-care field. Dad's doctoring had a big influence on the three of us."

"Is he political?" I asked.

A pause. "More spiritual than political."

"Explain 'spiritual,'" said Taucher.

"He's a searcher," said Marah. "We were born into Islam, but when Ben was a teenager he accepted Christ. Then he rejected Christ and became a Jew. Then he came back to Islam."

"When did he return to Islam?" asked Taucher.

Marah looked out a window, apparently in calculation. "Just over three and a half years ago."

"When your dad was killed," said Taucher.

Marah nodded. "Ben changed. He went from outgoing to quiet. From happy and carefree to solemn. Ben had been a lot like our father—energetic and loveable and fun to be around. When Dad died in Syria, the Dad part of Ben went away."

"That's very unfortunate," said Taucher.

A beat from Marah while she ordered her thoughts. "Well, misfortune lies beneath everything that's happened in Syria. Millions of misfortunes, many of them final. We know the doctors were not the targets. Our State Department said that the doctors ran to help Gourmat, the Islamic State leader, in the time it took the missile to travel from the sky to the ground. So there's luck involved, too. Bad luck."

"So, back to Ben," said Taucher. "Around the time your father was killed, Ben returned to Islam and became withdrawn?"

She nodded. "But a few months after leaving, he began to send emails, and call and text. He even sent me a snail-mail letter just a few weeks ago. He seemed to be moving on."

Taucher and I traded looks: Ben's letter.

"After leaving where?" asked Taucher.

"Oh, I'm sorry," said Marah. "Leaving here. Ben lived here with me for about a year. That would have been from the middle of 2014 until a couple of months after Dad died. I miss him. We really had some good times. And recently, he's started to sound more like himself. I think he's getting okay again."

"In the calls and texting?" asked Taucher.

"And letter and emails, too. I think he's healing. Grief can't last forever, can it?"

"When did you see him last?" I asked.

"The day he left here," Marah said wistfully. "So, June of 2015. Time zooms right by, doesn't it?"

I sensed the timing was right to ask a big fat favor of Marah. She was leaning. And I wanted to beat Taucher to the punch before her fizzy personality took over again. "Can we see his room?" I asked.

"Sure," said Marah, standing.

A short hallway, bath on the right, scent of soap and shampoo on my way past. On the left a closed door that Marah opened for us. I followed Taucher in. Small and square, a mattress on the floor, a blue sleeping bag for a bedspread, one pillow. The light fixture in the middle of the ceiling was covered in a Japanese-style paper dome, orange. The floor rug was thick underfoot and brightly colored, a budget Persian-themed knockoff. Posters on the walls, neatly tacked: Yosemite's Half Dome at sunrise, two Hapkido fighters, the Great Mosque of Damascus, Beyoncé onstage, waves lined up at Rincon, hillsides covered in what looked like California golden poppies. A wooden desk sat before the room's one window, through which a grape-stake fence half covered in ivy was visible. No electronics on the desk—rather, two stacks of paper, one white and one colored. A small brass incense holder with a fresh stick. Faint smell of sage. A Rastafarian-colored beanbag humped in the corner by the closet.

"So he left in April of 2015, after your father's death?" asked Taucher.

"Not until June," said Marah.

"Is there a picture of him?"

"Just a second," she said, heading down the hall. She came back with her phone, tapped up the photos, and held the screen so Taucher and I could see. Ben's face looked like his siblings' and father's. Same sharp face and expressive eyes. His long black hair was spiraled and coppered— a surfer's sun-bleached dreads. Ben smiling next to a pretty dark-haired woman. Then a blonde. Ben in a martial-arts *gi*, getting into a small gold-colored pickup truck. Ben with a surfboard under his arm. Ben at the desk in this room, turned to face the camera, pen in hand.

As Marah swiped from image to image, I pictured that face, recessed in the dark interior of the 4Runner that night at the mall in Del Mar. And in the grainy Bakersfield video that Joan Taucher had shared with me at her professional peril. Very possibly the same man. Nothing stood out as fundamentally different. But nothing stood out as identical, either. If it doesn't fit, you must acquit. Or must you?

Taucher's look said *maybe*, too.

"Here," said Marah. "This is Ben's latest Telegram text, from three days ago. 'Chillin' here, sister. Need money for wedding and down payment on a house. Want to marry Kalima and have us a baby! You'll love her. Let me know if you have fifty thousand dollars for me! We have a small humble home in Riverside County in our sights. Will pay you back! A rich private lender would be better, if you know such a person. My credit is bad and Kalima's is worse.' That is so Ben. They met on Facebook."

"Sounds like a cool guy," said Taucher. "Can I see that?"

Marah held the screen up and Taucher read through the message again. I knew what Taucher was doing, but Marah apparently didn't.

"How much money have you given him?" asked Taucher.

"Maybe six hundred dollars over the last few years."

"Where are you going to get that fifty grand?" Taucher asked with a dry smile.

Marah rolled her eyes.

"What kind of car does he drive?" I asked.

"A small gold pickup truck," said Marah. "I don't know the maker. It's old. You know, it's fine that you're so interested in Ben, but whoever this terrible assassin is, it can't be Ben."

"Why can't it?" asked Taucher, her combat face back on.

Marah's eyebrows rose in a mask of pleading disappointment. "He's the *baby*. He's golden Ben and he's never hurt a living thing in his life. He hasn't eaten an animal since he was fifteen. I understand it's your job to be suspicious, but you want to be correct, too. Right?"

"We have to be correct," said Taucher. "And we appreciate your efforts to help us be correct. So, with your permission, we would like to look through this room. Desk, closet. All of it."

The disappointment on Marah's face now deepened. I watched her will it away. A strong young woman wrestling with a weighty opponent—herself. Stoic acceptance then, and a flash of anger in her dark eyes. "I'd have to be present," she said.

"Of course," said Taucher. "You've done the right thing, Marah."

"Alan would kill me."

"Alan has issues that help no one," said Taucher.

Alan's issues struck me as more dangerous than that.

26

TAUCHER MADE FOR THE CLOSET and I sat at the desk. The two stacks of paper were neat and the glass desktop had been dusted recently. I turned on the lamp and opened the top middle drawer. Pens and pencils, paper clips, a stapler and staples, index cards in a rubber band, a yellow highlighter.

Farther back in the drawer was a faux-leather folder bulging with loose papers. I slid it out and opened it. A complimentary bank calendar with a red stagecoach speeding through a green valley. A paper-clipped batch of printouts and magazine pages related to rock climbing, surfing, and nature photography. A flyer for a public gun range in El Monte—rates and hours. That caught my attention. It looked like the stuff that Ben might have swept off his desktop just before leaving.

From the corner of my eye I saw Taucher's blurred form at the closet. I could hear the clothes hangers rasping on the wooden rod, Taucher impatient and forceful. I went back to the folder in front of me, listening over my shoulder.

Taucher: "Marah, would you mind reading me a few of Ben's texts and emails? Just so I can get to know him a little while I'm having a look here?"

A pause that grew longer and longer. The women silent. The hangers no longer scraping on the dowel.

Marah: "I'm sorry. I think I've made the wrong call. I don't feel right about letting you do this."

I slid the folder back where it had been and quietly closed the middle drawer. Felt our friendly citizen slipping away fast.

I opened the top left drawer, found hanging folders labeled "Bills," "Surfing," "Climbing," "Campgrounds," "Shooting," Music," "Truck," "Computer."

All empty.

Marah: "I think I've been an idiot. To allow you to go through Ben's stuff."

Taucher: "You've been smart and fair with us. We're not here to bust anyone. We're here to scratch people off our list. To establish Ben's innocence."

Marah: "Is innocence in your vocabulary, Agent Taucher?"

Taucher, her voice softer: "Marah, you certainly don't have to share Ben's communications with me. I understand your feelings, and I apologize."

The bottom drawer had no folders at all, just two neat stacks of *Surfer* and *Alpinist* magazines reaching nearly to the top of the drawer. I slid it shut and looked at Marah just as Taucher spoke.

"Marah? Has Ben been just a little bit not himself lately?"

Marah's eyes narrowed slightly. "Not at all. He sounds happier than he's been since Dad. You heard his text. He wants to get married and buy a home. He's *never* talked about settling down before."

"Have you met the prospective bride?"

"No," Marah said softly. "Not yet."

"He's had serial girlfriends, right? So this Kalima may or may not be serious."

Back to the desk. In the top right drawer I found a plastic bag containing bars of surfboard wax and a surfboard leash, tightly wound and held fast by its own ankle strap. I wondered if Ben had stopped surfing. And if so, why.

The bottom right drawer was empty. I stood.

"We're almost done here, Marah," said Taucher. "And I can't thank you enough for putting up with my obnoxious attitude and occasional bad manners. It's obvious to me that your brother Ben has nothing to do with our investigation. As I said, half our job is clearing people. The *pleasant* half, I might add."

"Okay. I'm sorry to be suspicious of you."

"If we could just see that letter from Ben," said Taucher, "we can finalize this deal."

"Finalize what deal?"

"We have a sample of the assassin's writing," said Taucher. "Handwriting is like fingerprints in that everybody has their own unique signature. Mr. Ford is very familiar with handwriting analysis. Right, Roland?"

Marah looked to me for confirmation.

I nodded, disrespecting myself for manipulating a half-willing ally.

Suspicion clouded her face again. But something else overrode it, and I wondered what. "Handwriting. Okay."

"The price of liberty is eternal vigilance," said Taucher.

"Patriotism is the last refuge of a scoundrel," said Marah.

"We are not scoundrels," said Joan. "And believe me, the aforementioned vigilance doesn't pay much. The hours are long and we make mistakes sometimes."

"I get a decent salary from Los Angeles County."

"Great," said Taucher. "So if you could just show us Ben's letter, we can let you get on with your day. You mentioned that he sent it just a few weeks ago. So his current Santa Ana address is on it, right?"

"You people are relentless," said Marah. "You're enough to make good Americans not want to help you. Which is what we are. Al, Ben, and me. Good Americans."

"Marah?" asked Taucher. "I couldn't be more satisfied that none of you have anything to do with the man we're after. Federal policy requires me to get the handwriting sample and address. Do you have anything to add, Roland?"

"Only thank you."

Once more, those layers of conflict crossing Marah's lovely face, like clouds at different elevations. "You're not FBI, right?"

"I'm a private investigator, as Agent Taucher told you and Alan."

"Why are you here?"

"I love working Saturdays."

A smile.

But what better answer than the truth? "The killer we're looking for is brutal and efficient," I said. "He's threatened a good friend of mine, a wonderful woman. She has a beautiful son. I don't want her to be decapitated."

"She and her crew killed Dad?"

"And nine others, including one Islamic State terrorist."

"I'm sickened by what your friend did to Dad and the others," said Marah. Her face had flushed. "And I'm sickened by what could happen to your friend, too."

She took my card and she offered me her hand. Her shake was warm and firm.

"I'm curious," I said. "Did you three siblings get twelve thousand five hundred dollars each for the death of your father? Or did you split it?"

"We split it evenly between his nine children," said Marah. "About fourteen hundred bucks apiece. I donated mine back to Doctors Without Borders."

Coincidences intrigue me. "Nine dead and nine siblings," I said.

"I saw that, too," Marah said. "I used to wonder if the repeating nines were a way to understand Dad's fate or luck. Fate and luck are opposites, as you know. I went to my Qur'an for help. I used to read it to Ben, but I hadn't picked it up in years. I remembered one of our favorite surahs, about free will and fate, chapter thirteen, Al Ra'ad. I opened to Al Ra'ad, closed my eyes like we used to—so, like, your blindness is fate and your finger is free will—that's what Ben and I made up, anyway. And I blindly put my finger on the page. The verse was 'The Messenger has companies of angels successively ranged before him and behind him. They guard him by the command of Allah. Verily, Allah does not change the condition of a people until they first change their ways and their minds.'"

As my pulse hammered, Caliphornia's elegant calligraphy to Lindsey came crashing back to me: *The thunder will come for you.*

As did the name of Caliphornia's knife: Al Ra'ad—the thunder, as *handwritten* to Kenny Bryce.

And the name of a horse owned by Rasha Samara and ridden by his son? The Thunder.

I looked to Taucher, her face flushed, her eyes sharp and pitiless as an eagle's.

"What did that passage say to you, Marah?" I managed.

"That Allah is all-powerful, and people are free to change their ways and their minds. Both are true. It made me want to join Doctors Without Borders and go to Syria and continue Dad's work."

"Why didn't you?" I asked.

"I was afraid to die."

"You made the right decision," said Taucher. "Now, if you can just let us see that letter, we'll get out of your hair."

Marah left the room with a loud sigh. I heard her yellow flowered flip-flops slapping on the hallway floor.

"I can get a phone warrant for Ben's bill stubs and personal papers in an hour," said Taucher. "The FISA courts still love us. Unless you think you can sweet-talk them out of her."

"I think we've outstayed our welcome," I said. "Leave them for another day."

Flip-flops in the hall on their way back. With an almost palpable reluctance, Marah handed her brother's letter to me. I set it on the desk. The envelope was a good-quality, cream-colored paper, and Marah's name was written in a hurried-looking printing in black ink. The return address was legible. I pulled the letter out, set the envelope aside, and held the letter open in the good sunlight coming through the window.

Elegant Arabic-styled calligraphy.

Slanting neither backward nor forward, but upright.

Feet and tails raised like candle flames.

Taucher's hawk eyes unblinking.

Dear Marah,

I hope this note finds you well. Look at my calligraphy. I've been practicing for months. So much has changed since those happy times I spent with you. I've found a new passion. Bigger than me. Bigger than Allah. Maybe I will introduce you someday. I am well and strong. I am still in need of money, but I know that you're not exactly rich working for the county. We are only as strong as the walls we climb.

Love,

Adams

Marah broke the silence. "Ben found something," she said softly. "He was always searching."

"Who the hell is Adams?" asked Taucher.

"Ben makes up names for himself," said Marah. "Sometimes I do it back to him. Since being kids. Adams is one of his favorites. And Anderson, and Abraham. Always with an *A*."

I thought: *Whoever he's calling himself, he needs money.*

"You would have to know him," said Marah.

"I think I'm beginning to," said Taucher. "May I photograph this? Better yet, can I take it?"

I watched another dispute play out on Marah's face. Family versus duty? Love versus fear?

"Take it," she said. "Go."

"And that picture you showed us," said Taucher. "The one of Ben and his dark-haired lady friend? Will you text it to me?"

"When I get a chance."

"How about now? I've got my phone right here. The woman is Kalima, correct? The one he wants to marry? How is it spelled?"

Marah spelled out the name.

"Last name?" Taucher demanded.

"I don't know," said Marah. "We've never met. But I do know that I'm sorry to have met you."

We spent the hour's drive south to Santa Ana in discussion of the brothers Azmeh. I was very interested in Alan's aggravated assault three years ago—around the time of his father's death—and his clear and present anger. Family man or not, his anger was real. Was it real enough to take him on a journey to Bakersfield? Taucher thought Alan was a "pissy hothead" and was more intrigued by baby Ben's several mysteries. Most of all, his sudden silence after his father's death, his handwriting, and his need of money.

Then miles of silence as we barreled south into Orange County. For a long while I didn't read the road signs. Didn't listen to the news. I was chewing on the big question: Whoever he was, one of the Azmeh brothers or not, how to get Caliphornia to come out into the open?

I worked long and hard on it, like a dog on a chew stick.

Kept chewing. That's what PIs do.

27

BEN AZMEH'S ADDRESS WAS a Santa Ana apartment not far from the Civic Center. The street curbs were dense with the cars of working people home for the weekend. A lunch truck was doing slow business in the shadow of the jail. Taucher and I ate standing up, burning through the napkins, watching the occasional jail visitor come and go. I think she caught me looking for the fabled hematoma under her makeup.

"Fifty bucks this address is a shell," said Taucher. "Like World Pizza."

"I'll bet it's a good address."

"You're such a Boy Scout."

"Indian Guides. Comanche."

"My mother wouldn't let me join the Girl Scouts because they were too soft."

"Maybe not a good fit for you, Joan."

"I wanted soft. I was a girl."

Del Sol Apartments was two short blocks south. Ben Azmeh's unit was ground-floor, at the end of a two-story building. Taucher and I stopped well short, standing beneath skinny palms with shaggy heads. Some of the apartments were strung with Christmas lights. I looked along the sunlit stucco wall of the building, at the first-story patios and second-floor decks crowded with barbecues, bikes, toys, potted plants. Poinsettias in gold- and red-foiled pots, strings of lights on the balconies. The grass along the sidewalk was foot-trampled, and I thought of Blevins stepping in Zeno's business. Felt happy.

"Follow my lead here, Roland," she said. "If he's cooperative, it's just a friendly FBI talk with old Ben. We're wondering how he's doing. Wondering if he might have any concerns to share with us. Like, about fellow Muslims. I'll get him onto Doctors Without Borders, Aleppo 2015. My guess is he'll blather heatedly about that, if he's anything like his brother. If we get inside, it's strictly a plain-sight. Don't touch, whatever you do. Don't, *don't*, put on any heat. Nothing about Lindsey, Kenny, or Voss. Nothing about knives, calligraphy, ammunition, or Hector Padilla. I lead. Let him answer my questions. Got it?"

"Got it."

Taucher gave me a brittle grin. "A short leash for you, Roland. Just like they give me. Now, if Ben won't cooperate, we'll be back to fight another day. If he resists, threatens, or makes any kind of aggressive move—I'll accept your physical help. If this is the guy who killed Kenny Bryce, then I'll *need* it. We cuff his butt and call the nearest resident agency, which is less than half a mile from here. We can hold him seventy-two hours as a domestic terror suspect, no Miranda needed. You've got a gun back in the truck?"

I nodded.

"Get it."

My leash was long enough to reach the toolbox bolted into the bed of my truck, from which I took my .45 autoloader, snug in its clip holster. Which I slid between waistband and flank, right side, grip resting in the hollow below my rib cage, snug and easily hidden by my coat. I have a two-shot ankle cannon, too—a four-ten shot-shell over a very hot .357 magnum—prodigiously lethal and made for only the most desperate of straits. I decided against it.

Taucher stood under the thin palms in her black suit, her back to me as she watched the apartment. Square of shoulder, platinum of hair. A businessperson, perhaps. A professional. An undertaker. She struck me as alone in her world, a solitary hunter, though she could have a rich family life, close friends, and strong interests that she had never once mentioned. And why should she? I probably had her all wrong.

We were halfway to unit 24-A when I saw the red "For Rent" sign hanging in the front-porch window. We stopped and for a long silent moment let the defeat sink in.

Caliphornia, I thought: dancing away, a step ahead of us.

As in Bakersfield.

As in last night after the Treasures of Araby?

In this moment it felt like Caliphornia could stay ahead of us for quite a while. I chose not to imagine the carnage that he could deliver with six-thousand-plus rounds of ammunition and a few guns to fire it with.

Who are you?

How can we bring you to us?

What will you fall for?

What do you need?

"So is this bad luck or fate?" asked Joan. "Maybe I should consult Al Ra'ad like Marah and Ben. I bought a Qur'an right after Nine-Eleven. Trying to get a feel for what I was up against. Maybe that was politically incorrect, but I reasoned that religious extremists start with religion. There's a lot of violence in that book. It's real us-against-them kind of stuff. I read parts of it. Not the whole thing."

I thought of the good Muslims I'd run across in my life. From Fallujah to San Diego. "Islam is the hostage," I said, quoting Hadi Yousef.

"Maybe."

"Blame the terrorist, not the excuse," I said.

"I'm *trying* to. Now this son of a bitch moves out of his apartment on me."

We stood on the porch. Taucher knocked and rang the doorbell anyway, but the silence inside wouldn't budge. I looked through a crack in the beat-up plastic blind, saw a sparsely furnished room. Beige carpet. A defeated leather sofa. Fast-food litter.

I tried the door but no luck.

"There's that optimistic Boy Scout again."

"I told you I was a Comanche."

"They were sport rapists and torturers," said Taucher. "They didn't even *need* a religion to blame it on."

"They did it for homeland security," I said.

"Like me," said Taucher. "At work they call me Joan Wayne but they think I don't know."

When I turned away from the window I saw that Taucher was dialing a number on her phone. "Yes, hello, this is Joan Taucher and I'm here on the front porch of unit twenty-four-A in the Del Sol Apartments. I want to see it right . . . Yes, well, that's not good enough. I need a place to rent *now* . . . Thursday is fine for move-in, but I have to make a deposit today. I need to see it right now. I love the neighborhood, the palm trees, the lunch truck . . . everything."

She looked at me and rolled her eyes. "So how long can it possibly take you to get here and show me this place?"

She looked at me again, then at her watch. "You're kidding . . . Really?

Wonderful! I'm here with my business partner right now. We'll see you in just a moment."

Joan swiped off with a flourish, dropped her phone back into her bag. "Joan Wayne speaks, people listen."

The manager was a middle-aged man named Ernest Robles. That his name meant "oaks" I took as a good sign. He was thick-bodied and gray-eyed and his silver-black hair was brushed back from a ruddy, pleasant face. White shirt with the sleeves rolled up, tucked into pressed jeans, square-toed cowboy boots. We introduced ourselves and shook hands. He gave me a long look—stoic and calm—letting me know that he was not afraid of me. Big men get this often from smaller men. It took me some years to realize it's a warning wrapped in respect.

He let us into a cool room that smelled faintly of tobacco and lamb.

"The tenant left early this morning," he said.

Taucher gave me an unhappy look, then moved into the middle of the small living room, hands on her hips in a proprietary stance. "What about the smoke smell?"

"I'm painting on Monday," said Ernest. "The new carpet comes on Tuesday. And full cleaning Wednesday. It won't smell."

"What a relief," said Joan. "The former tenant was a man, I take it. By the bad housekeeping."

Ernest nodded, looked for my reaction. "Not the cleanest tenant. Not the worst, either. Not by far."

Taucher turned to him. "What's rent?"

"Seventeen hundred a month. Thirty-four hundred moves you in."

"No wonder the poor stay poor," said Joan. "How long was the smoker here?"

"Six months."

"Hard on the carpet, too," she noted, looking down. "Where did he go?"

"I don't know," said Ernest. "He told me late last night he was moving out. He was paid up until the end of the month."

"How old was he?" Joan asked.

"Young. Early twenties."

Taucher held her phone up for Ernest to see. "This him?"

Ernest looked hard at the screen, at me, then Joan. "If you're cops, just say so."

"Yes or no?" she pressed.

"I want no trouble."

"You'll get trouble if you don't answer me," said Taucher. She held the phone closer to him.

I wondered how Joan had gotten so good at handling people so badly. Part of Fed 101? She would happily make sows' ears out of silk purses all day long, and nobody could stop her. She had what Grandpa Dick called "countercharm." I wondered, not for the first time, if she even knew it.

"Yes," said Ernest, cool and offended. "That's him. But that's all I can say."

"It certainly isn't," Joan said.

"Are you serious about renting this unit?" he asked. "I have an obligation later today."

"Business partner," said Taucher, turning to me. "Maybe you can explain this best."

I nodded. "Mr. Robles, can I have a word outside with you?"

That look again, telling me he wasn't afraid. "I don't want trouble."

Outside in the cool afternoon sun I told Mr. Robles who we were. And that we were looking for a very dangerous man who may or may not be his former tenant. That got his attention and his interest. He wanted to know if this dangerous man might come back here. "If we could have a look around, and ask you a few questions, it would be a big help. I don't have to tell you this, but you should know that a woman's life is at stake."

He scanned my face with his gray eyes, then looked past me, back into the unit. "I thought you were a couple at first."

"No," I said.

"You must be very relieved," said Robles, with a small smile. "The tenant, his name was Ben Anderson."

Because he always made up last names, I thought. Always started with *A*.

"May we look through your apartment?" I asked. "Maybe photograph a few things?"

"Yes. He was an interesting young man. I'll tell you what I know."

28

BACK INSIDE, Taucher and I went through the kitchen as Ernest Robles did as promised.

"He was pleasant but said little about himself. He had a soft personality, like a priest. He never smiled. His clothes were always the same—sweat shorts or sweat pants and athletic shoes. Flannel shirt, plaid. Sweatshirts with hoods. A wool cap if it was cold. His hair was long and black but bleached by the sun. Like a surfer, but I never saw a surfboard. He worked during the day, but I don't know where."

"What did he drive?" I asked.

"A gray SUV. Toyota or maybe Nissan."

Taucher shot me another glance. Then looked at Ernest. "Which?"

"Hard to tell apart. But that's good evidence? The old gray SUV?"

"Yes, good," I said. "Did Ben have friends or visitors?"

"A woman. Never smiling."

Joan held out her phone again, close up to Ernest's face, as if he were visually impaired.

"Yes," he said.

"Name?"

"I never met her," said Ernest. "She would come over when he got home from work. And on the weekend. Sometimes I would hear music inside. Mostly it was quiet. When it was warm out and the windows were open I could smell cooking. Lamb. Vegetables being fried. Affectionate voices."

"What kind of music?" I asked.

Ernest pursed his lips and frowned. "At first, American rock music. But lately, different. Egyptian? Persian? Strings, but not like a guitar. Not American or Mexican."

"What about men friends?" I asked.

Taucher was snapping pictures with her phone again.

"Sometimes another man," said Robles. "They seemed like friends or maybe brothers. He was shorter than Ben, who is tall. I don't remember what he looked like, except his hair was dark."

My first thought was brother Alan. "Age?"

"Sorry," said Ernest. "I only saw him coming and going. Maybe twice or three times."

"Did you see his car?" I asked.

"No. Parking is behind."

Taucher and I opened the kitchen drawers, the refrigerator and dishwasher, the cupboards, the tall, narrow broom closet. All empty except for a bottle of sparkling water, a half-carton containing two eggs and four shells, and a crisper full of vegetables no longer crisp.

"So," I said, "no garages with the units?"

"Only a carport. Assigned spaces."

"Did you ever see Ben bringing cases in or out? Heavy cases?"

"Like beer or wine?"

"Like beer or wine."

Ernest pursed his lips again and shook his head. "No. Once he brought longer boxes from his SUV into the apartment. Maybe . . . three or four feet long. The next day he drove away with the same boxes. He said they were new blinds for the bathroom and bedroom. But he returned them because he didn't like them."

"How many long boxes?" I asked.

"Maybe four."

Taucher turned from the broom closet. "He's probably got a storage unit somewhere," she said.

"I don't know about any storage unit," said Ernest.

Taucher gave me a cold glance, then walked past us into the living room. Where we moved the beaten couch away from the wall, pulled the pads off, pushed and pulled them for contraband. Down in the main couch crack we scored a quarter and a penny and a few loose peanuts. We sprung the sleeper, lifted the thin mattress, put it back, and folded the couch shut.

"He danced at night alone," said Ernest. Waited for our attention, which he got. "I did not spy. I believe in privacy for my tenants. But sometimes when I was walking around in my complex I would see him through the blinds. Just the shape of his body. He appeared to be dancing or writhing. He had rhythm and a sense of purpose, but no pattern that I could see. His arms would be out and he would leap up and squat down. He had his hands raised, with his fingers up and together, like for chopping. Like blades. He was graceful and slow and flexible. He would bend backward as if trying to touch the floor. Then straighten and jump up and land lightly. Legs out, then together, like a ballet dancer. Not a sound from where I stood. I saw him do this several times. It was hard not to watch. It was hypnotic."

Taucher looked pleasantly stunned.

"Several times," she said quietly. "Like he was practicing for something?"

"Practice, I don't know," said Ernest. "It looked like exercise. Or meditation. Maybe yoga."

The bedroom was small and square, with only one window. There was a row of colored pushpins along the top, which had apparently held up a cover or curtain of some kind. I could see fabric dangling from one of them, likely from someone ripping it off. Joan produced a pair of surgical gloves from her purse, worked them on, and carefully removed three of the pins. Placed them in a small plastic bag, locked it.

There was a twin mattress and box springs along one wall, no sheets, covers, or pillows. Empty closet, and a flimsy plastic shelving unit inside it, empty, too.

"Didn't leave much," said Taucher.

The bathroom was small and messy, white counter smeared with toothpaste, sink half coated with dried soap, whiskers, and shaving cream.

"DNA central," said Joan. She produced a larger plastic bag from her apparently bottomless purse. Used cotton squares to swab the sink and the tub drain. Pulled a wad of dark hair from the drain screen and wiggled it into a third plastic bag. "To be cool is to be equipped," she said.

Ernest issued a puzzled smile.

Taucher shot phone pictures of the bath, while I went back to the kitchen and went through the mail on the counter. Buried down in the junk mail was a flyer from Free World Hapkido here in Santa Ana, addressed to Ben Anderson. Set it aside. On the bottom of the pile was something I'd seen before and that Taucher had apparently missed—the glossy invitation to the opening of "The Treasures of Araby" in Solana

Beach. No postage, no addressee. Hand-delivered by Hector Padilla? Or had Ben Azmeh picked it up himself?

Joan, suddenly beside me. "A shadow-dancing beheader who calls himself Caliphornia, uses a knife, and has six thousand rounds of ammo stashed somewhere? I can't wait to punch this guy's ticket. Look what I found."

She dangled a clear plastic evidence bag before me. I followed the left-and-right pendulum of a toothpaste-sized cylinder with the letters DMSO on it.

"Horse liniment for his Hapkido aches and pains," said Taucher. "Easily transferred to paper he was writing on."

As the circumstantial evidence against Ben Azmeh continued to mount, I looked out the dirty kitchen window, past the shaggy-topped palms, still working on my favorite chew stick. We needed a way to get Caliphornia into the open. If Ben was our man, what about his plea for a money-lender in his letter to Marah? Money. Something he needed.

Beyond Joan's shoulder Ernest's pleasant face rose like a moon. "I take my wife to Mass on Saturdays," he said. "It's time for me to go get ready."

"Mass? Say a prayer for us," said Taucher.

"You think Ben Anderson is this dangerous man?"

The silence of confession.

"Then I will pray for you," he said.

Master Don Kim was a fifth-degree black belt who ran the Free World Hapkido dojo in Santa Ana. He had a warm smile and cool eyes and was about to start his Saturday adult class when Taucher and I walked in. The grown-ups warmed up, gis snapping. Kim was short, burly, and neatly groomed. About my age. He kept his smile and nodded when I asked if he knew Ben Anderson.

"Yes, he's a very good student. Why?"

Taucher badged him. "Five minutes in back?" she asked.

Smile gone, Kim gave orders to his ranking student, a lean, bearded, middle-aged man with a black belt that had one gold bar on it. Then led us past his students, through a split white curtain with a red-and-blue Hapkido emblem on either wing of it, and to the men's locker room.

Two rows of lockers and benches, three shower stalls, one wall draped with training gear hung from pegs: padded gloves and vests, fighting sticks and swords, extra helmets, dummy handguns, nunchuks, bats and clubs, throwing stars, throwing knives.

"Tell us about Ben Anderson," said Taucher.

Master Kim was soft-spoken and chose his words carefully. He smiled often, but his eyes were humorless. He said Ben was an excellent student, a second-degree black belt. Ben had trained at other studios over several years, said Kim. He had been coming to Free World Hapkido for only approximately one year. Ben was good with the younger students. He occasionally taught them, working off his own costs. Ben did not engage socially with his peers at the dojo. Very polite. Master Kim said that Ben talked sometimes about surfing and rock climbing and photography and art. Kim didn't know what Ben did for work, but twice Ben had asked if he could be late with his monthly payment but still attend. Kim had agreed both times because Ben was dependable. Ben did very well in competitions. He was tall and strong, which made him powerful yet vulnerable. He generally attended the weekday five o'clock open sessions for red belts and up.

"He was not here this last week," said Kim.

"Is it unusual for him to miss?" asked Taucher.

"Very unusual. He almost always tell me when he would miss. But not this week."

"Did he talk much about religion, politics, world events?" asked Joan.

Kim shook his head thoughtfully. "No. He like sports. Boxing and baseball and tennis."

I nodded toward the equipment wall. "Is Ben proficient against weapons?" I asked.

"More than proficient," said Master Kim. "He is excellent with the knife. Defending against the knife is what I mean."

"Do you teach knife combat?" I asked.

Kim held me with his steady gaze. "Only for students who request it."

"Has Ben requested it?" asked Taucher.

"Ben teaches it," said Kim. "He is better than me. I do not like knives."

Taucher gave me a quick look that Kim did not miss.

"I have students to teach," he said. "What has Ben done?"

"This is just a routine background check," said Taucher. "He's applied for a federal job. Don't say anything to him—we don't want him to get his hopes up."

"You should hire him," said Master Kim. "He is a good student and a strong young man, and he will be able to pay me on time."

Master Kim smiled. We thanked him and he held open the curtain, then walked us to the dojo door.

29

THE TRAFFIC WAS HEAVY back to San Diego. Holiday shoppers and travelers, a pileup in Tustin. Interstate 5 took us down through Camp Pendleton, my days as a Marine tackling me with their usual blunt force. Out the window I saw the "Afghan village" set up on the bluff overlooking the Pacific, tan "mud" huts with my young combat-clad brothers going door-to-door. Helicopters hovering. A simulated fight for life. I knew that every man and woman out there was eager for the real thing. Their chance to fight. I'd been. Couldn't wait to get out there and do what I'd been taught. Lots of training. Weeks and months. Still wasn't expecting that clenched gut or those cold rattling knees that carried me into my first action.

When I came back from Fallujah in 2004 I knew that someday soon Saddam Hussein would hang, and the new Iraq would flourish, and the Middle East would retreat from war. I knew that no more of my friends would die or be mutilated in that blistering desert. Then the ancient hatreds took over. The sudden chaos. And from its flames rose men far more primitive, resourceful, and bloodthirsty than any I'd dreamed of in nightmares. To found their state. State of fear. State of terror. State of death.

"Do you remember every minute of it, Roland? Fallujah?"

"I used to. I let it go."

"But look at all those young Americans who can't," she said, looking at the magnificent new Camp Pendleton Marine Corps Hospital, towering mirror-bright in the east. "Look at that, Roland. What we bring them home to. Our children. I wouldn't trade one American finger for the whole country of Iraq. Or Afghanistan. Or any other place."

"I didn't know you were a peacenik, Joan."

"I'd nuke 'em before I sent one more American over there. I really would. You probably don't have the stomach for that, do you, Roland?"

"Not at the moment."

Just the hum of the air conditioner as we passed the hospital and the traffic broke up and we headed south for the city.

"I respect that," she said. "Your non-bloodiness. You seem to have a good heart."

From the periphery I saw her look my way, dark aviator lenses on a white face.

"Although," she said. "There *is* the psychologist you blew out of the sky last year, who burned like a match in your front yard. And it's safe to say you spilled blood in Fallujah."

"Guilty twice, Your Honor."

"Don't," she said. "Only you can judge yourself. None of Joan Wayne's goddamned business, that's for sure."

The sun got lower and the shadows longer. We sped past North County streets with pretty names: Vista Way, Las Flores, Tamarack, Poinsettia. Taucher's silence was like Justine's used to be—hyperactive and eager to break itself.

"I think Ben Azmeh is Caliphornia," she said. "Beyond the circumstantial evidence, he feels right and he's acting right. Conflicted upbringing—born Arab in America. Bright kid, but always reminded he's different. Chip on shoulder gets heavier and heavier. Worships father, father the strong, father the good. Father slaughtered by infidels. Loner on a faith quest. He's physical enough to do what Caliphornia has done, too. Strong and balanced and fast. He likes the risky stuff—rock climbing and martial arts. Likes *knives*, for the holy sake of Christ. He's got motive, means, and opportunity. *But . . ."*

She checked her phone, dropped it back into her jacket pocket and looked out the passenger window. "But I still do not have proof. If I take this hunch to my superiors, what will happen, Roland, is this. First, we apply to FISA for a warrant to track Ben Azmeh's cell phone. Probably granted, possibly not. But if Ben resorts to burners, we won't get far with a phone tap. Whatever FISA decides, we'll have a long, drawn-out huddle about how we proceed. Lots to consider. Many moving parts. For instance, what the lab comes up with on all that evidence from the apartment. Take him down or watch him? A week of twenty-four/seven surveillance takes twelve agents and thousands of dollars, and if you think we're not on a budget, you're wrong.

"I love football. It broke my heart when the Chargers jilted me and the rest of my city. So let me put this in football terms. Once San Diego FBI has finally agreed on an action, we run the ball off tackle, up to Los Angeles Division for approval. More layers. There's not only the special agent in charge but *an assistant director in charge.* Possible fumbles everywhere you look. But say we're lucky. They like the plan. That means we throw a long bomb all the way to Washington. Where the ball bounces fingertip to fingertip and ends up in the hands of our beloved director, who must eventually *lateral* to the DOJ so the whole fed bureaucracy can legally CYA before flipping the ball to the White House. Hoping somebody's home. In the end? Everyone is professional, meticulous, thorough, and slow as a tortoise tied to a tree. So the clock will run out on us. Caliphornia will kill Lindsey and Voss and use his guns and ammo on innocent people. I feel it. I know it. Son of a goddamned bitch, I *know* it, Roland."

"Or?" I asked.

"We keep Ben to ourselves and nail his ass fast."

"If it *is* Ben, Joan."

"Christ, Roland, of course if it is Ben."

"I still like Alan's anger," I said. "It's up front and real."

"He's a family man."

"So was bin Laden."

"Okay, then I like Alan as brother Ben's right-hand man. I like him as Caliphornia's Zawahiri."

"Brothers in arms," I said.

"It makes perfect sense."

I drove into the carpool lane and set the cruise control. My thoughts were on the move again, in and out of light and shadow like Clevenger's coyotes in the floodlit night.

"The money," I said.

"I think so, too."

"Ben asked Marah for money," I said. "Twice."

"I heard it," said Taucher. "*Loudly.* So if the brothers are in this together, we only need one. I vote Ben. We approach him online, just like Islamic State would. Get him on the encrypted apps, offer the money through an IS or al-Qaeda sympathizer. Remember, Caliphornia is already on high alert. He'll be very careful. But if we bait the hook just right and he takes it—game on."

"You memorized Ben's cell number when you asked Marah to see his text."

"Crafty old Joan," she said.

I thought it over. Taucher going rogue, with my help. After suspects we could not identify with certainty and had little physical evidence against.

"If it goes wrong, the Bureau will bust you down," I said. "And cook me for obstructing a federal investigation."

Taucher stared out the windshield, then folded her hands back over her purse. "Yeah. They'd find me a desk somewhere quiet and miserable. Make room for the new. They've been wanting that for a while. San Diego's a plum with a history and I'm part of it. Just yesterday the SAC told me I might find a change of territory refreshing. I couldn't believe what I was hearing. And told him so."

She made no acknowledgment of my own risk here. Not that I needed it. I wasn't close enough to Taucher's world to discern the fine borders between leadership and manipulation, insight and paranoia, fear real and fear imagined.

My first responsibility was to Lindsey Rakes. My second was to Voss and the thousands of other people who could receive one or more of the bullets delivered by Hector Padilla to Caliphornia. *Probably* Caliphornia. My third was to keep myself out of federal prison long enough to complete missions one and two.

"We're a good team, Roland."

"I'm glad I don't work for your people."

"Mostly they're good people and in the right," she said. "We stand for the rule of law and we protect the innocent."

I weighed Joan Taucher's smallness within that great Bureau against the bigness of her spirit and her fight.

"Now, help me compose a solicitation to Ben Azmeh," she said. "From Raqqa Nine—an extremist organization offering him money."

"Zkrya Gourmat's recruitment network?" I asked, remembering Leising's story.

"As re-created and updated," said Taucher, with one of her small dry smiles.

"By you," I concluded.

"Of course."

Our fearsome Bureau, I thought, *trolling for terrorists.*

I pondered my mission for a moment. Then ad-libbed: "'Dear Mr. Azmeh,'" I said. "'We are Raqqa Nine. We operate in the spirit of Allah and Zkrya Gourmat. As you know, we finance terror in America against the infidels. How can we help you succeed?'"

"That's good," said Taucher. "But if Ben is driving around an SUV full of ammo, taking routine evasive action on Interstate Five, he is very wary. And now that Marah and Alan have probably both told him about their terrible experiences with the FBI today—he's even warier. Suddenly, Ben gets a solicitation for free money, just for being called a promising young jihadi? No. It has to be something that will speak *directly* to Ben Azmeh-Adams-Anderson."

I thought about that a moment. "Okay. 'We are Raqqa Nine. We seek to finance homegrown terror in America, against the infidels. Your name has come to our attention through a mutual friend whose brother died at IH-One in Aleppo in April of 2015. I cannot reveal his name at this time. However, the link below is to an encrypted app where we can communicate securely. We can arrange to meet at a time and place where ideas can be exchanged, cash can be transferred, and security is without question. Sincerely . . . Warrior of Allah.'"

Taucher turned and raised her sunglasses to stare at me unfiltered.

"It's beautiful. I love the 'Warrior of Allah' touch. I can have it to Ben Azmeh as soon as I get home."

Home, I thought: *where she can keep her confederates in the digital dark*. I was surprised at her crude guile.

Taucher's email to me arrived one hour and forty-five minutes later. I was upstairs in my home office. She had logged the property from Ben Azmeh's apartment into evidence, then "sped" home and sent him a Telegram "Secret Chat" message from the Warrior of Allah, offering support, enthusiasm, and money for his jihad.

On her email to me, she had signed off:

Thanks for being a genuine help.

Best,
JAT (the A is for Annabelle)

30

OUT IN THE BARN, I banged the heavy and speed bags for a long while. Then showered and joined the Irregulars for cocktail hour under the palapa. They had a big fire going in the pit under the high part of the thatch, where the flames couldn't catch it on fire. Dick poured me a forthright bourbon and added a few drops of water. We sat on chaise longues facing the hills. The night was cool and the stars were post-storm bright.

Dick swirled his glass and the ice clinked. "If those weren't four feds sitting at that table this morning, my name's not Dick Ford."

"Friendly neighborhood FBI."

"And what did they want with my favorite grandson?"

"Dirt on one of their own."

"That's low," said Dick.

"I thought so, too."

"Who was that earlier?" he asked. "The dapper Arab with the bodyguard."

"Not important."

"Something about Lindsey, I surmise," he said. "And that's why you sent her away for a while."

"Need-to-know, Dick. Sorry."

"I'm cool with that," he said. "But I'm not sold on that dog of Lindsey's. I don't like him, and he senses it. Looks at me like he wants to eat my balls. Well, off to see how Liz is doing. That knee of hers doesn't love the tennis court as much as it used to."

I waved Lindsey over and she took Dick's vacated chaise. Zeno lay between us, head up and facing me, a gray-eyed sphinx.

I told her about my visit from Rasha. That he physically resembled what I had briefly seen of Kenny Bryce's killer. That his temper had boiled. That he had admitted to brandishing a *janbiya* at a college party. I told her that his claim of being out of the country on the night of the murder was yet to be vetted. She reminded me of his handwriting, so similar to that of Caliphornia's.

I told Lindsey that I could find no motive for Samara to take Kenny's life, and no reason for him to threaten her. I admitted that I found his interest in her genuine, if possessive and impulsive.

"My gut tells me he isn't our man," I said.

"How sure are you?"

"I can't make any claims there," I said. "Rasha could be enough of a sociopath and a liar to fool us all."

"Comforting, Roland."

I said nothing of Ben Azmeh.

The fact that we had only circumstantial evidence linking him to Caliphornia dripped in my mind, the sound of water hitting water. A constant reminder that something isn't right.

I looked out at the placid black water of the pond and saw Ben's strange dance behind the cheap plastic blinds of Del Sol unit 24-A.

But Rasha's voice is what I heard, when I'd asked him if he still had his old *janbiya: Somewhere.*

Such are the vagaries of an uncertain soul.

L indsey and I took on Burt and Clevenger in Ping-Pong, best of three, fought them to a one–one draw. Lindsey served to open the third. Burt's high, long-distance spin-bombs made up for Clevenger's slowness and poor motor skills. Lindsey had remarkable reflexes but was tactically unsound, trying to make winners of almost every shot. I stayed in close to the table, bringing my six feet and three inches to bear, hitting the ball early and flat at tough angles.

Zeno lay under the table on Lindsey's and my end, positioned, of course, as close to Lindsey as he could get without being stepped on. I looked at him occasionally, a large, brindled, gray-eyed beast patiently sizing me up. A ball went off the table and *click-click-clicked* on the uneven pavers, finally rolling to a stop between Zeno's huge front paws. I kneeled and thought whether or not to reach in. He studied me. Eyes inscrutable within the heavy folds of his face.

I didn't know what to make of Zeno yet. I told him so.

He must not have known what to make of me, either, because he didn't move when I reached in and took the ball. Just looked at me as if I was not really there.

Burt and Clevenger beat us in the deciding third game, twenty-four to twenty-two, a heartbreaker decided by cloddish Clevenger's shot that came off his paddle *and finger* at an unintended angle, nicked the white baseline in front of me with an audible *tick*, and dropped uninterrupted to the floor at my feet.

I wanted to knock out Clevenger with an uppercut, but I'm a good sport, so I couldn't, even if the bourbon suggested that I *could*. Instead I dropped the paddle to the table, went to the fire, did an Ali shuffle, and threw some punches into the flames. Felt good, hands and feet working together, heavy as they were from the workout. This drew hoots and claps from the Irregulars, who broke into Zevon's "Roland the Headless Thompson Gunner," a song I'd always liked but that now struck a hideously raw nerve. It's an Irregulars favorite, along with "Money for Nothing," in which they diss their landlord for charging rent but doing nothing. I might add that none of them except Burt pay on time. I have never once collected all rents by the first day of any month, as mandated by the rules posted on the palapa caisson not ten feet from here. But they have a point. I really *do* do almost nothing, though I always warn them of that before we sign a lease. Those Irregulars. You never know quite how they'll come at you.

Grandpa Dick presented me with a fresh drink. "That Clevenger's a lucky prick."

Clevenger waved guiltily and headed off for the barn and his coming night of coyote hunting. Limping Liz and Dick took their towering drinks and reclined next to each other on the padded chaise longues, quickly falling into an argument about whether to ice or heat a sore knee: Dick for heat but Liz all ice.

When my phone vibrated in my pocket I hoped it was Joan saying that Ben Azmeh had responded positively to our offer of cash. Instead it was Tammy Bellamy, just to let me know that the gray striped cat spotted walking along Stage Coach Road turned out to be plain gray, and not Oxley at all. So he was still out there, somewhere, and Tammy was really hoping I hadn't given up. A full moon was coming, and I knew what that meant. She asked me to keep an extra-sharp eye out, and offered to pay for my gasoline if I ever wanted to fill her up and patrol Fallbrook. I told her not to worry, said I'd keep an extra-sharp eye out, not to sweat the gas.

Lindsey, Burt, and I put on our coats and walked the pond under good clean moonlight. Zeno traveled at Lindsey's left side, matching her pace exactly, anticipating her turns on the meandering path, a darkness within the dark. Breeze in the cattails. An owl sweeping low past us from behind, hefty but silent.

"About those bottles of Stoli on my kitchen counter," said Lindsey. "They are there for a reason. They're unopened, so that I can see them and they can tempt me. I can beat them. I'm a boozer, but I know I can. And Burt was in my casita, Roland. We've discussed it. One of Clevenger's drones recorded him in high-def. I was in the barn looking for a Phillips-head and wasn't supposed to see him."

Burt cleared his throat. "I won't apologize twice. I was trying to help you."

"I know," she said. "But it's between me and the bottles now."

We rounded the west bank and came to the outcropping of boulders that mark the halfway point from the house. "Thanks for sticking with me, guys," said Lindsey. "We're going to beat Caliphornia. I'm going to get joint custody of John. I'm going to be a good mom. But I'm not going to hit the bottle again. I feel a little bit stronger every hour, every time I look at those things. Sometimes I'm so damned thirsty for it my body wants to turn inside out. But I refuse. It's not one day at a time, it's one second at a time. Then the second passes and I think about tomorrow being better. Because it's going to be. And you guys are bearing me up on your shoulders. I love you both."

She stopped and knelt and scratched Zeno's ears with both her hands. "I love you, too, Zeno. Yes, I love you, too."

She jumped up and loped off toward her casita, the great gray protector bounding along beside her.

"Just FYI," said Burt. "She drove back to Los Jilgueros earlier today, so she could see Johnny again. She asked me to ride shotgun and said she was going with or without me. I actually did bring a shotgun—the little sawed-off model you're familiar with. Zeno in the back. Lindsey well protected. Her ex brought her flowers."

Upstairs, I hit the computer hard, retracing my way through the many folders on "Martyr Statistics," published by the Syrian Revolution Martyr Database to http://syrianshuhada.com, searching for Caliphornia's companion, Kalima. I remembered Taucher's office poster of the dizzying variations that a single Arabic name can have—in pronunciation and spelling. I followed the same twisting path through Aleppo, April 22 of 2015, to the page of the names of those martyred in the air strike on IH-One. I knew that a matrilineal first name would be an unlikely miracle, and in fact there was no Kalima killed that day. So I followed the names of the dead back to the Martyr Statistics for any mention of family. It took almost an hour, but when I tracked down the martyr profile for Dr. Mhood Amin, killed by the Headhunters that day in Aleppo, I found that he had been survived by four children, one of them a daughter—Kalima Amin.

I found six Kalima Amins on Facebook.

One of them was the dark-haired beauty who matched the picture we'd gotten from Marah.

Where on earth could I find her?

I struck out with TLO and Tracersinfo.

But did much better with IvarDuggans.com, which listed Syrian national Kalima Amin as a legal visitor, on a fiancée visa issued in February of the previous year. Age twenty-eight. Her U.S. address was the apartment that Ben Azmeh had abandoned less than twenty-four hours ago. Surprisingly enough, Kalima Amin's fiancée-sponsor-retriever was not Ben Azmeh at all. It was Caliphornia's cryptic associate, Hector Padilla. Her visa photo was included.

My heart thumped away with the thrill of the hunt—a solid connection between Padilla and Ben Azmeh. And thus between them and Caliphornia. I rolled back a few feet in my chair, then found the picture of Ben and Kalima on my phone again. Confirming the match.

Ben looked solemn and proud. So did Kalima.

I consulted my computer for the meaning of her name in Arabic.

Truthful witness.

I wondered if Hector had acted on orders from Ben, to secure the fiancée visa for Kalima, travel abroad, and bring her to America. As an employed, native-born U.S. citizen with no criminal record, as well as being a non-Muslim, Hector would qualify to obtain the special visa. Leaving Ben in the shadows.

Of course, I couldn't let go of Alan Azmeh. Not with that white-hot rage surrounding him like an aura.

I ran him through my services again, keen to the "Known Associates" listings and any financial irregularities. I found the arrest report for the assault complaint that was eventually dropped. The officer had written that Azmeh had apparently been provoked by racial epithets and a "yank of" his headscarf. I saw that the alleged provocateur had been arrested as well.

Interesting. I wrote down the cop's name and made a note to call him the next day.

I was back on the patio early the next morning, sun warming me through my sweats, coffee in hand, and bullish on the day. My plan was to run two miles through the hills, beat up on the speed bag and the heavy bag in the barn for a few rounds.

Then my phone vibrated, Taucher's name and number greeting me. My first hope was that she was reporting that Ben was ready to do business with Raqqa 9. Or maybe she had found a home address for Kalima Amin.

I knew this day would be good.

"Voss went out for his usual sunrise run this morning," Taucher said. "Another runner found him dead on the trail half an hour ago. He was lying on his front side, with his head removed and propped up on his back, between his shoulder blades. IS style. No witnesses. I'm checking the commercial manifests from Sacramento, Reno, and the Bay Area. Amtrak and Greyhound, too. No Ben Azmeh, and no Ben Adams or Anderson. Not yet. I've got his name on the hot watch. Son of a *bitch*, Roland! How long to fly us to Grass Valley?"

"Three hours," I guessed. "I'll be waiting for you at Fallbrook Airpark. Dress for the cold."

A door banged shut behind me. Burt, starting down from casita number five, short and bow-legged, one arm swinging, the other bringing a cup of coffee to his face. Burt senses distress as surely as a shark. I told him what had happened and not to let Lindsey out of his sight.

"Don't worry about Lindsey," he said, clapping a strong little hand on my shoulder. "You just do what you have to do. You're in a war, my friend."

31

WE STOOD near the snow-dusted footpath where Marlon Voss had died, watching as the Nevada County sheriffs cleared the scene. A surprisingly large group had gathered behind the yellow tape, heavily bundled against the Sierra Nevada cold. Two old volunteer deputies in Day-Glo green vests talked solemnly with the onlookers. A creek rushed past, loud. Smell of cedar and pine. I'd paid the taxi driver to wait and I could see him parked along the road, checking his phone.

Voss's body was gone and the decomposed granite trail was thoroughly stained with his blood. One detective, two uniformed deputies, and a crime scene tech were the only law enforcement left. They didn't seem to mind us being there. The tech squatted to take pictures of a small red flag that had been poked into the trail eight or so feet from where Voss had died.

"What caliber?" asked Taucher, her words a frosted exhale past the raised collar of her peacoat.

"A nine-millimeter."

"How many?"

The tech looked us over. Big-faced, freckled, and young. "Just this one. I'm surprised he left it here."

"Maybe it was too dark," said Joan, looking up at parallel ridgelines of the canyon.

"Sunrise was seven nineteen," he said. "But that eastern ridge blocks first light. So it's more like seven thirty right here. Enough light to see a shell casing? Hard to say."

"Did he see anyone?" I asked. "The man who found the body?"

"You should talk to a deputy," he said, swiping the flag off the ground and standing. "I'm not even sworn. But I can tell you one thing—this is the most sickening killing I've ever seen."

Dave Bridgeman, the detective, had spoken to Taucher earlier by phone. He confirmed that Voss had been shot at least once and beheaded, neither of which had been confirmed yet to the media, or to Voss's widow or children.

"But we couldn't get him covered before two more runners saw the whole gruesome mess," said Bridgeman. "Everyone's buzzing about it and the media's all over us. The guy who found the body went into shock and we took him to Memorial."

"I need to see him," said Taucher.

"Sierra Nevada Memorial Hospital on Glasson. You can't miss it."

She drew her phone, voice-dialed, and waited for the call to go through. I looked at the bloody swatch of gravel and listened to the creek roar past. This was once serious gold country. I tried to picture big lazy gold nuggets rolling downstream along the creek bottom. Tried to picture anything but Voss. Snowflakes slowly fell.

"What's a PI doing here with the FBI?" asked the detective.

"Trying to help a friend," I said.

Taucher turned her back to us, apparently in disagreement with someone.

Bridgeman put his hands into the pockets of his winter jacket. "I'm told there was something down in Bakersfield I might want to know about."

"Ask Joan."

"Don't think I'd learn much," he said with a small smile.

Joan's voice was rising. I thought a moment, decided to take a chance on doing a good deed for what seemed like a good cop. What did I know? "Bakersfield PD detective Marcy Brown is a reasonable sort. You can use my name, but it might backfire."

"I understand."

The lobby of Sierra Nevada Memorial Hospital bristled with reporters and camera crews trying to beat the cold. Taucher walked through them with her head down. I got to the elevator first and held the reporters off while Joan stepped in.

In a second-floor room sat the man who had discovered Voss at first light. He looked to be in his late seventies, probably trim and fit beneath the layers for warmth. He wore a hospital robe with a parka over it, and a fresh pair of light blue pajama bottoms. Patient-issue white terry-cloth slippers. There was a nurse in the room with him and a sheriff's deputy outside the closed door.

He rose and shook my hand. "Bill Immel," he said. "And you are?"

I introduced myself and Agent Taucher, whom Immel scrutinized with sharp eyes. He had a handsome but pugnacious face and a head of brown-gray hair.

"Sorry, I pissed my pants," he said, pulling on the legs of his baggy blue pajamas. "Haven't done that since the day Oswald shot Kennedy. But not because of Dallas. I was in a recon Huey over Quang Tri and the gooks hit us with fifty-caliber. That gets your attention."

The nurse was a petite Filipina who gave Immel a flat look as she wrapped an old-fashioned blood-pressure cuff around his upper arm.

"I like you, Alma," he said, sitting on the bed. Alma squeezed the rubber inflator. "Sorry about the 'gook' remark. I'm not racist. But I'll tell you two, when I saw that man on the running trail with his head lopped off I fell to my knees and peed. It just happened. I was in the middle of a good run, too. Who came in behind you just now?"

Taucher and I both looked back at the closed door, then to Bill Immel.

"There's no one," said Taucher.

"Behind you, I said."

"No one, Mr. Immel," said Joan.

Alma released the pressure and took the reading.

Immel squinted at each of us knowingly. "Have you made an arrest yet?"

"No, Mr. Immel," said Taucher. "Did you see anyone else on the path this morning? Before or after you found Mr. Voss?"

"I did not," said Immel. "I'm always one of the first ones out there. Along with the decedent."

"So you had seen Mr. Voss before?" Taucher asked.

"All the time. Always running opposite directions. Nodded but never spoke."

Alma hung the pressure cuff over one shoulder and entered something on her tablet. "Still high, Mr. Immel. You lay back on the bed and relax."

"I will not," said Immel. "I'm trying to help these people. So listen up. It was seven twenty-eight a.m. when I found him. I don't know why I looked at my watch, but I did. Kneeling there, my heart was beating very hard and my whole body went cold. There was nothing I could do. His head . . . Kay always used to tell me . . . well, a lot of things."

"Did you hear a gunshot?" asked Taucher.

"No. The path runs along the creek. Loud with all the run-off. The first part of the month was warm for these parts."

Taucher nodded. "Did you hear or see a vehicle when you were kneeling beside the body?"

"I saw a vehicle parked off the road. Sometimes the runners park there in summer, when it's crowded. It seemed out of place there, because this morning it wasn't crowded at all."

"What kind?" asked Joan.

"Toyota 4Runner," said Bill. "Two thousand two, gray. I've got one, too. Love it. Oh, and I almost forgot—there was someone behind the wheel. Possibly a woman."

Taucher and I traded looks while Immel peered at us. "You're like watching two lemons that just lined up on a slot machine," he said. "But the third lemon never comes. Meaning you don't pay off. Meaning you don't tell me anything."

"Describe her," said Taucher.

"You try describing a smudge behind a windshield two hundred feet away with snow coming down," said Immel.

"Did you touch the body?" asked Taucher. "Mr. Voss, I mean?"

"No," said Immel. "I saw no profit in that. I think that's the whole point of these beheaders, to make you feel helpless."

"That's an excellent synopsis of the terrorist mind-set," said Joan.

"Jihadis in Grass Valley?"

"I did not say that," said Joan, giving me a "me and my big mouth" look.

"Did you call nine-one-one?" I asked.

"Wouldn't you?"

"Did you have your phone with you?"

"Always. Jacket pocket. One that snaps."

"So you were there when the first deputies arrived?"

"I feel like I still *am* there," said Bill Immel. "Blood has such a strong smell, especially that much of it. His eyes were half open. Dreamlike. Go away! Alma? I think I will lay back for a few minutes, if you don't mind."

He sighed and stood and hovered by the bed while Alma turned down the sheets and propped up some pillows. "Were you serious about jihadis, Agent?"

"We haven't ruled anything out yet," said Taucher. "But I very much want to thank you for your help."

Immel worked his bulky layered body into the bed and Alma covered him with a sheet and blanket. "Warm enough, Bill?"

"Just a chill."

"You would be more comfortable out of those clothes."

"I'm keeping my clothes on."

"Hot soup?"

"That would be real good," said Immel. "I wish I could stop seeing what I saw. But you can't unsee things. If enough people in America saw what I saw this morning, it would be bad for the country. Very bad. Productivity would go down."

I set a business card on his bed tray and told him he could call me anytime for any reason.

"I'm only seventy-eight," he said. "I'm strong as a goat and my mind is not wholly gone. But something changed back there on that running trail. I am changed."

"You are still in shock, Bill," said Alma. "You eat soup and you feel better."

"Bring it on, beautiful."

I found us a way out through the ER so we wouldn't have to deal with the reporters again. Out back on the entrance ramp, a Nevada County Fire and Rescue truck idled in a pool of pale exhaust. Our taxi waited out front.

Taucher stopped under a snow-laced pine tree to take a call. I watched the snow and hoped it would stay light enough for takeoff. The airport was a few hundred feet downslope and I thought my chances were good.

Taucher shoved her phone into her coat pocket and gave me a look as cold as the day. "Nothing from Ben Azmeh."

We stood there for a long minute in the dainty snow. Letting the silence be.

"This guy's heading south for Lindsey," I said.

"We'd be foolish to think anything different."

I tried to subtract what else we knew from all we didn't know, to reduce things to the essential: a ten-hour drive from where we stood to Fallbrook, where Lindsey was hunkered down with Zeno and the Irregulars. So, if Caliphornia had left here promptly after killing Voss, he'd make Fallbrook by five thirty in Sunday traffic.

"And when he gets to San Diego," I said, "he'll want to see a helpful, friendly face."

By the time the taxi driver got us within sight of the Nevada County Airpark, Taucher was calling in the 4Runner's stolen plates to the California Highway Patrol, requesting an all-units-be-on-the-lookout notification *and* a message on every Amber Alert emergency-message sign in every county of the state.

It was too late to tell her they wouldn't do the Amber Alert, though she probably knew this already. Amber Alert is for missing or endangered children—period. There's Silver Alert for missing oldsters and a Blue Alert for cops in danger. But no alert for someone who has just beheaded a citizen on his morning run.

Taucher started to argue, voice rising. In the rearview mirror I saw the cabbie look back at her.

But to my surprise, she silenced herself, listened for a long while— breathing like a bull in a rodeo pen—then thanked them and hung up.

"We got the damned BOLO at least," she said.

As we pulled into the tower I called Burt and Lindsey and put them on my own personal Ford Alert. Lindsey sounded worried, but Burt said they were "ready for anything."

Next I talked to Clevenger, who quickly agreed to hover one of his drones over the casitas and monitor the video feed for intruders. Then he apologized for the lucky shot in Ping-Pong. I checked in at the tower and we trotted out to *Hall Pass 2* through pinpricks of snow.

32

HECTOR PADILLA'S HOUSE, at twilight: dark inside but the porch light on. If we were right about Caliphornia's destination—and if he'd driven fast—he could be here in under an hour. We were parked half a block down from the house, shrouded by my blackout windows and a sycamore still trying to hold on to its big yellow leaves.

As darkness fell, most of the other houses on the block came alive with Christmas lights. Santa's sleigh took off from a roof. A trio of lighted angels, winged and posed in song, stood on a lawn not far from us.

"Where would he be by now?" asked Taucher.

"North San Diego County. Maybe closer."

Taucher had set her tablet on the floorboard, screen dimmed but angled optimistically up to her in case of a response from Ben Azmeh.

My phone stood upright in a cup holder, still logged on to Facebook, where we had followed Marlon Voss's murder in Grass Valley. The online buzz was minor until the mainstream media caught Bill Immel leaving Sierra Nevada Memorial.

We watched the two-minute CNN video: Bill in a wheelchair in the hospital lobby, Alma behind him at the handles, and a uniformed guard trying to give Bill some space from the reporters. Hair awry, still bundled in his sweatshirt and parka. His mind wandered. He told about running almost every day, then this morning finding the headless body. He described the snow falling and the steam still rising from the bloody pool on the running path and the half-open eyes of the dead man. The reporter asked him how it felt to see such a thing.

Helpless and sick, Bill Immel answered. Then he said he'd forgotten the question.

"My dad got like that when he was about Bill's age," said Taucher. "Scattered. Scared. Lost his courage. Then dementia started to creep in. It really seemed to start when he fell from a ladder. Putting up Christmas lights. And the fall didn't hurt him physically, according to the doctors. No concussion, no breaks, just a twisted ankle and a bruised shoulder. But it *scared* him. It made him think how fast things can change and what a hostile thing a commonplace ladder can be. And that's what I saw in Bill Immel having to see Voss. Like falling off the ladder. You see something terrible, so fear rushes in, and you can't easily get rid of it. And terrorists know that—one act makes a million fears. Tens of millions. Look at Nine-Eleven. Or the IS execution videos."

A vehicle came down the street slowly, passed. I watched it in the rearview. Fog rolled in from the west.

On Facebook, Marlon Voss's widow, Danella—apparently standing on the front porch of a home in lightly falling snow—said that her husband had been, ". . . a great husband and father. A great Air Force pilot. He was brave and patient and funny. He was the love of my life." A twentysomething man who looked a lot like Marlon Voss appeared in the doorway behind her and gently pulled her back in.

Something in that moment got to me. The woman turning back into the house with her son. People and a house forever and terribly changed. The math was so wrong. Start with a brave and selfless doctor in Syria. Then a well-liked young man working as a landscaper in Bakersfield, a man with a lot of life still ahead of him. Now a pilot and his family. All of their relatives and friends. Next, a young mother? The math of vengeance, never balanced or even. Never finished. The scar on my forehead itched. I rubbed it.

A live local feed featured Nevada County sheriff's detective Dave Bridgeman confirming that local Grass Valley resident Marlon Voss had been found beheaded on a running trail outside of town. No arrests had been made. He asked citizens to be alert to strangers and unusual activity but not to alter their daily routines. No, they did not recover a murder weapon, and he wouldn't speculate on what specific type of weapon had been used.

Sacramento FBI spokesperson Minerva Dakis followed up, saying that they had found no evidence of this murder being a terrorist act, but the Bureau was not ruling anything out. She asked that anyone who had been in the area that morning report anything unusual, explaining that the first twenty-four hours are critical in crimes such as this. The FBI tip number ran as a footer across the screen.

"Minerva being there makes this look like a terror investigation," said Taucher. "It's the right call, though. It gives Caliphornia a stage to act upon. Puts his name on the playbill. But it puts pressure on him, too. We need the pressure."

"He still hasn't taken credit for Kenny or Voss," I said.

"He will."

There were several more Facebook posts and Tweets by Grass Valley residents. Some had stood behind the crime scene tape, posting videos and selfies as the sheriffs worked the murder site. Others had formed an ad hoc "Vigilance Committee" in the saloon of an old gold rush–era hotel—Victorian lamps and high-backed smoking chairs and bottles stacked behind the bar. The committee chairman said they were concerned that Voss's murder could have been "terrorist in nature," although the small Muslim community in Nevada County was known as peaceful and hardworking. He pointed out that there was also a "biker population," though this didn't seem like "their kind of crime." Several of the Vigilance Committee members knew Marlon and Danella Voss, and spoke highly of them.

Taucher shook her head and sighed.

"Life is waiting, Joan."

"How can you be so young and act so old?"

"Years of practice."

She gave me her sharp-eyed predator's once-over. "So what's with that scar on your head? You touch it when things bug you. Then you furrow your brow like you're expecting an explanation."

"There's a story behind it."

"So cough it up."

While we waited for Caliphornia to show, I told Taucher about my one pro bout. It took place in the then Trump 29 Casino down in Coachella, of all places, in 2005. This was when I was Roland "Rolling Thunder" Ford. Twenty-six years old, fighting heavyweight. I'd been out of the service for only a few weeks. Still thinking I was the world's toughest Marine. I'd never been knocked down in a Marine Corps bout. I hadn't lost life or limb in the hell of Fallujah. I'd never really been defeated at anything, in my own eyes, at least.

My opponent that night was Darien "Demolition" Dixon, and I knew after ten seconds of the first round that he was twice the fighter I was. He toyed with me for a time. I went down in the ninth to the jab, a cross, and a big left hook. I lay there flat on my back, still conscious and aware of the noise, the bright lights, and the ref counting over me. Time went slowly. I knew I could beat the count, get up and fight. Or stay where I was and call it quits. What bothered me most was realizing that my invincibility was gone. Even half knocked out, I was fully astonished by this. I was mortal. Utterly so.

Defaulting to Ford stubbornness and Marine Corps training, I got up, bounced on my feet, and glared at the ref, nodding. Bring it on. He held my gloves and stared back, then let me go. Demolition hit me with a big right hand I didn't have the legs to slip. I saw it coming, all right. Saw my mouthpiece, too, flying through the lights. What I remember next is a bunch of faces looking down at me. A background of brightness. Then I was watching me sitting on my stool, somewhat pleasantly stunned and childlike, both outside myself and inside myself at the same time. A state of detachment and wonder.

The hospital, an MRI, twelve stitches to close the cut from the knockout punch, which left a nickel-sized, Y-shaped scar up on my forehead, left of center.

Sometimes I look at the scar just for a reality check. A mortality check. To remind me that sometimes it's okay not to get up before the bell. Okay to not let blind reflex drive you into the punch that puts you down.

When I'm worried or afraid, that scar acts up. Itches, burns, tingles, grows cold—depends. On what, I haven't figured out yet. But it's both a reminder and a warning, and I value its input. Sometimes, a lot. And sometimes I feel again that odd state of post-KO wonder come over me, and I'll be sitting on my stool once again, and at the same time observing myself from a safe distance.

"In some light, you don't really see the scar," I said. "Then, in other light, you can't miss it."

She listened with her stony expression and said not a word until I had stopped talking. A vehicle passed us from behind. Right taillight out. "I know all about that," said Taucher. "How something can be almost invisible, then a second later you can't take your eyes of it. Mine is about quarter-sized, shape of an oval."

I thought it would be rude to look for the hematoma now, but somehow also rude not to. As if I wasn't interested. Instead I stared out at Hector Padilla's dark, still home.

"Don't feel obligated to look, Roland," said Taucher. "You can't see it in a dark car. And thanks for telling me about the knockout. Your scar tells you to be deliberate and mindful of consequences. I admire that. After I got kicked down in my MMA match, my fear broke. It just vanished. So I really went after her. In the end that fight was mine and she was the one who never fought again. So what my scar says is never quit. Never negotiate, even with yourself. Isn't it funny how similar experiences mean different things to different people? Maybe that's why we work so well together."

We watched the street.

Waiting for Caliphornia to show.

Waiting for Ben Azmeh to take the bait.

Waiting for Hector.

But no text messages to the Warrior of Allah, and no 4Runner just in from Grass Valley. I hit the wipers to clear the fog off the glass. Hector's house sat squat and dark down the street. The angels continued their silent caroling on the lawn and Santa's sleigh rose from the rooftop.

"Ben *has* to answer us," said Taucher. "He's Caliphornia. I know it."

"Patience."

Taucher studied me sullenly. My optimistic word seemed to hang in the quiet. A van went by. A young couple came from the house across from Hector's place, nicely dressed, got into a small white car. On Taucher's lap the tablet went to screensaver. I had the unpleasant realization that all our earnest striving and good tools and clever plans might not be enough. Taucher looked at her watch. The likely hour of Caliphornia's arrival had come and gone and we both knew it.

"Patience was pure Dad," said Taucher. "He was all patience. Me, you know—the opposite."

We ate jerky and apples and energy bars we'd picked up at a convenience store. Stared at Hector Padilla's house in silence, like it was the Church of the Holy Sepulchre and we were expecting a miracle.

Mind adrift, I thought about Justine and hoped that God was taking good care of her. Recalled my strong emotions just a few hours ago as I had landed *Hall Pass 2* at Fallbrook Airpark. Just as I had done so many times with Justine in those brief and beautiful days. I like to drift, remembering the good and forgetting the bad.

Taucher brought me back to earth, stating that American Latinos were the fastest-growing group of Americans converting to Islam. Had their own mosque in Houston. Two hundred thousand Latino Muslims in the States right now. Mostly women, but guys like Hector, too. I wondered out loud why Islam was appealing to Latinos. She had no facts but said that Muslims and Latinos both felt like second-class people in America. Plus Latinas could then wear a hijab and hide their true ethnic identity, or some blemishes or scars, such as her own "pestilential" hematoma.

A light went on in the back of Hector's house, then another in the living room. A faint human shape moved behind the curtains and was gone.

"Well, well," said Joan. "Does he work Sundays?"

"He's not scheduled, but he fills in a lot," I said. This from my contact with the company that did security for First Samaritan Hospital.

Five minutes, then ten.

A Miata came past us, top down in the cold, older guy in a knit cap, surfboard riding beside him, heater probably pegged. Retirement in the Golden State, I thought, endless summer.

Fifteen minutes later Hector's garage door rose and his gleaming black Cube backed into the foggy night.

33

HECTOR WORKED HIS WAY through the neighborhood, signaling long before his turns, always at or below the speed limit, going extra-slow in the fog. I stayed well back, the signal on my GPS tracker strong.

He merged onto Interstate 8 with the determination of a bed of kelp. Taucher cursed him under her breath as she monitored her phone and the tablet at her feet, throwing its cool light up at us. "No man should drive like that," she muttered. "It's a sin."

No sooner had he hit sixty miles an hour when Hector signaled to exit. Off at Los Choces toward Lakeside. Hector took the right lane, of course, his Cube glimmering even in the fog.

"Maybe he's going to the Walmart supercenter," Taucher said. "I get all my household stuff there. Save a bundle."

And sure enough, Hector pulled into the Walmart supercenter at Camino Canada. He parked far out in the lot. I pulled forward into a space with a good view of him. He sat in the driver's seat, his head bowed to his phone, his distant face uplit by the screen.

"All yours, Joan," I said. "He'll recognize me from the Treasures of Araby."

"Need anything?"

"I'm fine for now."

She got out, set the tablet on her seat, and shut the door. I watched her and Hector converge on the entrance. Taucher had her black purse slung over a shoulder, her peacoat and sweater and duty boots. A black watch cap snugged down. Strong legs, long strides, poise and balance. I didn't know what to make of her. Never had. Some big part of her remained unknown to me—to the whole world, for all I knew. Attracting but not welcoming. Walled but not hidden. Taucher's words expressed my feelings, too: *I don't dislike you.* But who, really, are you?

Then Hector, angling from her left in his too-big Raiders hoodie and too-small jeans. A puffy wad of plastic Walmart bags in each hand. He stopped to look at the window decals on an SUV. Hiked his jeans and wiggled his hips as he read, grocery bags flapping in the breeze. A multifaceted man, Hector. A football fan. A Cube owner. A seeker of Allah, a student of Arabic, an admirer of Muslim women. A reader of the jihadi magazine *Rumiyah*, owner of two new *janbiyas* and one large sharpening stone, deliverer of five thousand six hundred eighty rounds of new ammunition in weatherproof cases. Now trying to stuff the plastic bags into one bag as he ambled into Walmart to stock up on Allah knew what.

I watched the American shoppers come and go. Baskets and bags of loot. Each time Taucher's tablet went to screensaver mode, I touched the space bar and brought the screen back to life.

Not going to answer the Warrior of Allah, Ben?

Wouldn't you like some easy money? Oh? How much?

Nearly forty minutes later I saw Hector pushing a well-burdened cart through the sliding exit door and heading toward his car. He stopped and answered his phone. Someone backed toward him and honked to get him to move. Hector waved, walked behind another car, stopped, and continued talking.

Taucher came briskly from the store, a plastic bag dangling from one hand, peacoat unbuttoned and watch cap off. Hector was off his phone and back en route for the Cube when Taucher threw open my truck door and climbed in. She slung her bag into the back.

"He bought holiday party stuff," she said. "Red paper tablecloths and napkins, green drink napkins, green and red plastic tumblers, 'Happy New Year' placemats with champagne glasses and top-hat designs on them. Quantities of all. Enough plastic flatware for two hundred and fifty people. Tins of those wretched holiday sugar cookies. Other than that, no food or drink, just the supplies and decorations. I timed my purchases perfectly to be in the next line when he paid up. He dropped two hundred and eighty-six dollars and thirteen cents. See, you really can save a bundle here."

While Hector tied each bag snug and loaded it into the back of his Cube, we speculated. Was the Muslim wannabe throwing a Western-style holiday party? Was it a First Samaritan Hospital employee event? Did Hector have two hundred and fifty friends?

He got back into his Cube and took the interstate west toward his home. Passed his exit. Held a solid fifty-five miles per hour in the slow lane. I-8 west to the 163 south, to I-5 north, exiting Fifth Avenue, then west toward the fog-shrouded Pacific Ocean and a left turn on North Harbor Drive.

He parked along the Broadway Pier, short of the Cruise Ship Terminal. I went past him and found a place. This is one of San Diego's postcard views—the bay and the yachts with their masts jutting up against the flanks of the downtown high-rises. Off in the distance an immense aircraft carrier sat at anchor off Coronado. Closer in, the Cruise Ship

Terminal, and a big Viking Line ship being readied for a morning departure. Closer still, the smaller commercial ships—Hornblower vessels for lease, bay cruisers, party barges, and private yachts. The lamps on the boardwalk made halos in the mist.

Hector locked his Cube with the fob and headed down the boardwalk. Taucher and I followed far back. When we came to the Cube, Taucher faked a call with her phone, pacing the boardwalk while I knelt behind the car and replaced the GPS tracker with another—battery fully charged and ready to go.

A hundred yards ahead of us, Hector stepped off the boardwalk and onto a private dock. The yacht beside it looked large. He stood outside a white picket gate and entered a code on a keypad. The gate swung open and Hector traipsed down the dock toward *Glorietta*.

She was an older motor yacht—a vintage dining ship that might have been working the San Diego area for decades. Three decks. She appeared strong and capable and well cared for.

Hector took out his phone and began shooting pictures of the ship. I could see the flash blipping through the lesser lights of the dock. He went bow to stern, composing his shots patiently.

Then he walked up the gangplank and boarded. A few minutes later his flash was going off again inside the dining ship, white blips behind the smoked-glass windows.

"Hector has bought decorations for a holiday celebration," said Taucher. "Let's just say it's going to take place aboard a party ship. *Glorietta*, for example. Which he is now photographing."

"It makes me think of the ammunition he delivered to Caliphornia," I said.

A pause, then we spoke the same words at the same time.

"*San Bernardino.*"

A moment later, Hector came back down the gangplank and started up the dock toward the boardwalk.

"You know," said Taucher. "If Ben Azmeh is Caliphornia, he's the first Syrian American terrorist to take lives on American soil."

I thought about Ben, the American-born kid who read the Qur'an with his sister and made up last names that sounded American, who couldn't settle on a faith, who liked art and practiced calligraphy, surfed and snowboarded and climbed rocks and learned Hapkido. And I thought of a U.S. drone strike—flown in part by a friend of mine, from Creech Air Force Base in Las Vegas—that left nine innocents dead in Aleppo, Syria, seven-thousand-plus miles away, one of the dead being Ben Azmeh's much-loved father. No acknowledgment by the United States until later. Along with a small condolence payment delivered in enforced silence.

Which led me to remember Rumsfeld's cogent inquiry on war in the Middle East: *Are we creating more terrorists than we're killing?*

And a line I found on the Internet one night: *Don't think of a bomb as going down and destroying stuff. Think of it like a seed that goes into the ground and grows insurgents out of it.*

I shut my eyes and imagined a map of the world, with red lines across time and space, connecting what had happened that day at IH-One to what had happened before and after. I saw the red line from Dr. Ibrahim Azmeh's Damascus all the way to UCLA, and another to Lindsey Rakes's Fort Worth, another across the American desert to Las Vegas, one stretching across the world to Syria again, then coming back to connect Torrance to Santa Ana to Bakersfield to Grass Valley to San Diego, where this complex collision of fates and nations and families was still happening before our very eyes, right here on the waterfront.

"And if Ben Azmeh is our first Syrian American terrorist to kill his own citizens," said Taucher, "then I'm responsible for stopping him. This is what I do and this is where I do it."

I opened my eyes. The Cube started up and Hector backed out. We followed him to the 163 north, past Balboa Park, and under the stately Cabrillo Bridge. Hector exited Clairemont-Mesa Boulevard and drove the speed limit to the Spotted Jaguar adult club, where he parked far out in the lot, as was his habit. A moment later he was shuffling toward the entrance, hiking up his jeans again, looking up at the sky.

"The red lines back and forth across the world just extended to a strip club in San Diego," I said.

"I don't see any red lines," said Taucher.

"They're imaginary but real," I said. "They connect everything that's happened with everything that's still to happen. An improvised hospital in Aleppo to the Spotted Jaguar. Dr. Ibrahim Azmeh to Hector O. See? Connections. Three out of the last five end with O."

"So do 'mumbo' and 'jumbo.' You're just tired."

"I'm tired of severed heads," I said.

"Your duty right now is to stay alert, Roland," she said. "I shall be taking a power nap. That's any nap under thirty minutes."

Taucher released her seat belt, reclined her seat, buttoned up her peacoat, set her watch cap over her eyes. "Dad told me stories before sleep. Made them up on the spot. Most were funny. I'd always demand one more story, so Dad saw how short he could make them. My favorite was 'This is the story of a snail who tried to cross a busy freeway.' That was it. The whole story."

"I like that one," I said. "You like your dad a lot."

"Worship," Taucher said, her voice losing volume. "Mom, too. But I hung Dad's moon and that means everything to a girl. I was his star and everybody knew it. If he'd been blown to pieces by a drone, I'd track the guilty parties down, too. So I *get* Caliphornia on that level."

"I don't know what I'd do," I said.

"Where do you think he is right now?"

"Sleeping," I said. "I wonder if he has people he can trust, beyond Hector. He has to cache his weapons and ammunition and whatever else he's got. A storage unit. A cheap apartment. Friends."

"We need to reach out to him again," said Joan. "Make sure he knows we're interested."

"He knows," I said. "He's probably checking out Raqqa Nine and the Warrior of Allah every way he knows. Let your Bureau website fool him, Joan."

"But what if we scared him off?" she asked. "Should I just apply for the FISA warrant, give my evidence to Blevins, let the old boys take over my operation and run it into the ground? Remember, if *I'm* the one who stops this son of a bitch, then *they* can't transfer me out of *my* city."

I thought about that. "You'll have to bring in the Bureau at some point, Joan."

"Yeah, yeah, yeah," she whispered. "I know. Here I thought you were on my side."

"I'm on whatever side gets us all out of this alive," I said.

"Not my side?"

"You can call it your side, Joan."

"Good. Because I'm the one paying you the big bucks." A catch of breath from Taucher, then a long sigh. "Wake me up when party boy comes out."

An hour and a half later, just past one a.m., Hector traipsed from the exit of the Spotted Jaguar to his car.

Taucher cussed me for letting her sleep that long. I followed Hector back onto the freeway and all the way home.

Then drove the hour back to Fallbrook Airpark for Taucher's car, parked in foresight outside the locking gate. Before climbing out of my truck she turned and offered me a tired smile. "Night, Roland."

"Night, Joan."

"Roland and Joan are French heroes," she said. "You a legend and me a saint."

"It's all making sense now."

She took a deep breath, trying to pump herself up for the foggy hour's drive home.

The new-message tone dinged from the device at her feet. It sounded faint and far away and harmless. She looked down at it with unusual Taucher deliberation. My scar itched.

She brought the device to her lap, squared it, and checked the inbox. A catch of breath.

"Dear sweet Jesus God in heaven," she said quietly. "We have a reply to our solicitation of Ben Azmeh."

She turned the screen toward me in the darkness.

34

Your solicitation is an insult. Are you trolling for idiots? I'm genuine. I'm centuries ahead of you. I am Caliphornia. Know me by my dead. I need $50,000 to finish my journey and begin my jihad. Don't waste my time, you alleged Warrior of Allah.

"Caliphornia" appeared at the top of the Telegram secret-chat screen, below it a clear circular graphic of a black *janbiya* and a crescent moon on a red background.

"Telegram secret-chat mode," she said. "End-to-end encryption means only we will see his message. It will self-destruct when he wants it to. My heart is pounding, Roland. This guy is real. I didn't make him up. What do we say back?"

"Our Warrior of Allah should be a tough sell," I said.

"I agree. And you might be better at this than me. I'd just lose my temper and scare him off."

I settled the tablet on the console between us and wrote:

> **WARRIOR 2:37 A.M.**
> We deal with thousands of liars and
> cowards. From that crowd we have to
> sponsor who is authentic. We hope
> that you are genuine. You are young so
> you brag about your actions. Tell us
> more about yourself, Caliphornia.
> We like your clever name. But we
> don't know your dead.
> Impress us.

Taucher read it twice, hit send with a firm poke of her finger. My rebuke hit the screen immediately. Telegram is not only heavily encrypted, it's able to synch messages to all your devices at once, and it's fast.

I watched the fog coil and roll past the windows.

> **CALIPHORNIA 2:39 A.M.**
> I now introduce myself. Link to story
> and follow-up.

I linked to an article on page three of the *Bakersfield Californian* for December 12. It was a brief piece and a picture of smiling Kenny Bryce:

COUNTIAN STABBED
TO DEATH IN HOME

*Kenneth Bryce, thirty-four, a Kern County employee, was found
dead of apparent stab wounds in his Bakersfield apartment
yesterday . . .*

The follow-up link took us to a page-seven article in the same newspaper, two days later:

NO TRUTH TO MURDER
RUMOR, POLICE SAY

Bakersfield Police say there is nothing to substantiate a rumor that a recent murder victim had been decapitated.

Kenny Bryce, thirty-four, was found dead in his apartment Tuesday afternoon, victim of multiple stab wounds. Bakersfield PD says there are no suspects and no arrests have been made.

However, two Kern County Medical Examiner and Coroner's Office contractors have said that Bryce's body was decapitated when it arrived for autopsy. Neither contractor would speak on the record or give a name to this publication . . .

My turn again:

WARRIOR 2:47 A.M.
Do you claim responsibility?

CALIPHORNIA 2:48 A.M.
I claim glory.

WARRIOR 2:49 A.M.
But where is your proof? Maybe you only read these stories as we just did.

Caliphornia answered the Warrior of Allah with two brief and hideous video clips.

One of Kenny Bryce's head dangling over his pillow, an anonymous hand clutching his hair.

The other of Marlon Voss's head being set on his back, the head rolling off, then two gloved hands putting it back and getting it balanced.

A long silence.

Failure of words. Pause of will.

My anger building. *Lure this cutthroat bastard in.*

> **WARRIOR 2:52 A.M.**
> **Why doesn't America know you? Terror must be seen to be valuable. Where are your posts and Tweets? We do not sponsor crime, we sponsor fear. America must hear from you. If God allows. Inshallah.**

Ten minutes passed. With a sinking feeling that I had asked him to do something he wasn't ready for. And lost him.

> **CALIPHORNIA 3:02 A.M.**
> **No publicity yet. Stealth and secrecy. One more U.S. drone killer to behead. Then I'll bring the terror America has earned since 9/11. Inshallah, Warrior of Allah, whoever you are. I will launch my jihad with or without your bags of money!**

> **WARRIOR 3:05 A.M.**
> **Drone killers? American soldiers?**

CALIPHORNIA 3:06 A.M.

Why aren't you talking about my money?
Why are you so slow? Are you believers or
the FBI?

WARRIOR 3:10 A.M.

We ask the same of you. Life is risk. We
have the money and are eager to invest in
the right people. Acts in America are
more valuable to us than acts at home.
We need heroes and martyrs. We need
great warriors, not shy killers. We need him
who will take the head of the unbeliever
and hold it high, dripping blood on
the world!

CALIPHORNIA 3:12 A.M.

If you want real American terror, be
ready to move very quickly. Fifty
thousand. It must be delivered by
an Arab man who speaks Arabic. A
man of the book. I'll message you with
instructions when and if I decide
to trust you. If you contact me
before then, you will never hear
from me again.

Half an hour of silence from Caliphornia, Taucher staring out the window, lost in something.

"He's real," she whispered. "He actually does these things."

"We found him, Joan."

Another deep breath from her. Decision time.

"You found," she said. "But now I have to take him back to my tribe."

"I know."

"I don't want to. There, in the tribe, I'm Taucher the paranoid. Taucher the haunted and hysterical, Taucher the beat up and made up. Soon to be promoted out of her job and her city. But before that happens, I need the Bureau for fifty thousand cash and a takedown team. What I want most on earth is to crush Caliphornia. I'll do what I can to keep your hand in, Roland. You brought him to us and I need you to push his buttons."

35

FOUR HOURS AND NO WORD from Taucher. Maybe Caliphornia had ducked for cover. Maybe I'd simply been cut from the team. Maybe both.

Too tired to sleep, brain on spin cycle, I sat under the palapa in the cool morning.

Noted the evidence of last night's party: take-out boxes from Vince's Pizza in town, beer and soft drink empties, Ping-Pong table left uncovered. Zeno's water bucket by the barbecue.

Clevenger's drone hovered above the casitas, streaming me and everything else that moved within its field of view back to one of Clevenger's computers. I was glad to have it protecting Lindsey. I flipped it off anyway.

Moving slowly, I dropped some pizza boxes and foam salad containers into the trash. Listened to the red-shouldered hawks screaming in a chill, unsettled sky. The storm that almost chased us out of the Sierra Nevada, I thought, making its way down to us. I looked out at the pond for a while, where a snowy egret stalked. If you want to see patience, watch a snowy egret stalk.

Then the slapping of a screen door, and a muscular gray beast emerging from casita three. Followed by a tall black-haired woman in a Navajo-style coat, jeans, and boots. She raised her coffee mug at me, then they started down the railroad-tie steps.

Zeno arrived a few yards in advance, stopped and beheld me. Head up, legs wide, chest full. Brindled flank like a tiger's stripes in sunlight. Soulful brows, gray eyes focused only on me. On me, but somehow detached from me. Without judgment.

Lindsey approached from behind him. She stepped around him and came toward me, but Zeno bumped past her and sat down between us, facing me.

"Guess I'll say good morning from here, Roland."

"Morning, Lindsey. Looks like you and Zeno are getting along."

"Like peanut butter and jelly," she said.

"I see you had a pizza party without me."

"We waited for you as long as we could," she said. "Grass Valley?"

I nodded.

"We've contacted him," I said. "Caliphornia. He's close."

A cloud crossed her handsome face. She lifted the handgun from the pocket of her robe by its grip, then let it drop heavily back in.

"Take a walk?" I asked.

We started up the gravel path around the pond, Zeno between us and keeping our pace. The sun was still low but warm through my coat.

I told her what I'd learned about that day in April of 2015, in Aleppo, where the Headhunters had been cleared to take out Zkrya Gourmat. I told her about the local doctor who ran the improvised hospital—a man beloved by many friends and family—one of the volunteers who died.

"Yes," she said. "Dr. Ibrahim Azmeh."

"Caliphornia is his son."

Lindsey stopped. Zeno did, too.

"Benyamin," I said.

I was just now beginning to fully understand Lindsey's take-home from the war. Post-traumatic stress, to be sure. We combat vets all had it, just in differing degrees. We handle it in different ways. In Lindsey's case, the stress wasn't something the enemy had done to her or to those around her. It was something *she* had done to the enemy. An act that could feel eternal and could not be forgotten or changed. A psychiatrist friend of mine had written about this kind of stress. She called it "moral injury."

"Ben didn't just snap," I said. "He's been preparing himself for this. He might be planning other things, too, but we're not sure what or when."

I told her about Caliphornia's martial-arts and knife training, his time spent at gun ranges, his communications with the FBI's "recruitment" site, loyal Hector, the ammunition.

"How old is Ben?" she asked.

"Twenty-two."

She hugged herself against the morning chill, then we continued around the pond, dog between us. She was locked in thought, eyes to the ground, her footsteps measured and slow. We were halfway around the water before she spoke again.

"A Muslim trying to kill a half-Muslim," she said. "But this isn't about religion, is it?"

"No. It's personal. Like he said in that threat to you."

"Personal," she said. Then, a few steps later, "Can I tell you something personal? Flying Predator drones for recon is tedious business. Hours of cruising and hovering. You follow a man. You follow a technical—that's a truck with a machine gun mounted on the bed. You hover and watch. You're like a cop on a beat. You get to know the people and their habits. You know their faces. Some by name. It drove me bats, not knowing all their names. You watch them go about their lives, do their jobs, trying to survive. Some are moms or dads, and you see a guy hugging his kids before he heads to work, or to the market to get food, knowing that he might not make it back. Of course, he knows it, too.

"But things can change. Fast. You finally get the guy out in the open—a terrorist you've been looking for, month after month. You find him in the right time and place, and as soon as you're cleared hot, you're going to light that fucker up. It's why you're here. It's what you do. So that day in Aleppo, when Zkrya Gourmat took off on his motorcycle, we Headhunters went from zero to ninety in a heartbeat. For weeks we'd been the watchers, but suddenly we've got our pistols drawn and we're running straight into a gunfight. I stayed cool, Roland, because that's what all your training says. Cool, methodical, open-eyed. The sensor operator's job is to guide the missile to its target. You use a targeting laser, which is one very temperamental piece of technology. It has a grip like a pistol but bigger. Trigger for acquisition, buttons for adjustment, set and reset, and a keypad for altitude, azimuth, distance, and closing speed. If you breathe wrong, you throw the laser off-target. If you flinch or twitch, you can put that Hellfire on the house next door, or into the group of old guys smoking cigarettes in a courtyard, or on a kid on a bike, or into a mosque at prayer. When Zkrya lost control of his motorcycle, I had that laser right on him. Followed him down and into the crash. When the doctors and nurses came running out of the field hospital, I saw I had to get that laser off Gourmat or we were going to kill them all. I could see it was going to happen, sure as sunrise. The timing was perfect. The distance they were covering. The seconds until the Hellfire hit. *But it wouldn't come off!* My laser wouldn't respond. I tried everything to get it off Zkrya, lying there on the ground in the rubble by his smashed-up motorcycle, but it wouldn't come off target. Like it had its mind made up and I had no say in the matter. I watched my screen. Saw the people trying to help Zkrya. And then my screen pixelated. A second of white fire. When it came back to life a few seconds later, I saw the bodies and parts of bodies burning and smoking, and the few people still alive crawling through the blood and dust. Hell. Fire."

She stopped and looked at me. A tear ran down her cheek and she ground it away with a balled fist. "Kenny and Marlon knew how hard I tried to get that missile away from the people. They knew what a good sensor I was. I need someone alive on earth to understand that fact. That I was a good sensor. Kenny and Marlon are dead. So now maybe you can carry that truth for me, Roland."

"I'll help you carry it, Lindsey. You know that."

"*Resti*," commanded Lindsey. Zeno lay down on the path and watched her come to me. When she got close, he sat up, cropped ears alert.

Lindsey kissed my cheek and took my hand. "You're a friend, Roland. Someday you will be whole. Until then, know that you're my brother in arms. And if you need me, I'm yours. I might even pay my rent on time. Someday."

Zeno growled.

"*Silencio!*"

Went silent and stared at me.

"Rasha called," said Lindsey. "He apologized for scaring me with his calligraphy and his college stupidity. Said to call him if I wanted a man to talk to."

On a hunch I called Liam Flaherty, my contact at Pacific Security, which provides security for First Samaritan Hospital, proud employer of Hector Padilla. It paid off: First Samaritan's annual New Year

Harbor Cruise would begin boarding at six p.m. on New Year's Eve—on the dining ship *Glorietta.*

"It's the big fundraiser for their Children's Unit," said Liam. "A pricey ticket. Live music, dancing, a high-dollar auction. First Samaritan employees do the decorating and cater it themselves so all the money can go to the cause. What are you fishing for, Roland?"

"We need to talk."

"You sound serious, my friend. Name the time and place."

I got into my truck, checked the gauges, set my phone in the cup holder, and plugged in the charger. Still nothing from Taucher.

Had we lost him?

36

MARAH AZMEH WAS UNHAPPY to see me standing in the lobby of her County of Los Angeles Public Social Services Department building in Los Angeles. She put on a smile anyway, understanding that I wasn't here on a friendly visit. Signed me in, got me a pass, and led the way outside into the sunny L.A. day.

We sat opposite each other at a round concrete table in the big employees' patio, in the shade of a green canvas umbrella. She wore a loose gray cowl-neck sweater, black leggings, and brown mid-calf boots. A house finch with a red breast stood on the edge of the table, looking back and forth at us. It was late morning, the tables still mostly empty.

Speaking carefully and softly, I told her that her brother Ben was in terrible trouble. He had fallen in with some very bad people. We had learned a lot about him since talking with her and Alan. The FBI now had proof of Ben's involvement in two murders and they needed to find him, fast.

Her face colored in that way of hers, revealing the fear and worry inside.

"Do you mean the Air Force man in Bakersfield?"

"Him, and another, just yesterday. Part of the drone team that killed your father. Both beheaded. Ben sent us video, Marah. It's brutal."

I watched her composure crack and her eyes swell with tears. She brought her hands to her face and bowed her head. Shook it slowly, her henna-streaked black hair falling over her fingers like dark water. The finch took off.

"As I told you, he's threatened someone else, too," I said.

"The woman with the son," I heard her say.

"She's alive. And Ben is alive. And you can help them stay that way."

She raised her tear-channeled face to me, then looked off toward a black metal fence sparsely clung by mandevilla. A busy L.A. boulevard hummed beyond. "I knew," she said softly.

"What did you know?"

Her eyes back on me. "I didn't know *what*. But I *knew*."

"Marah," I said. "If you want to help him, I'm going to need more than that. You're going to have to reach back and find it. What you knew. What you saw. Time is important here."

She produced a tissue and wiped her eyes. Blinked three times. "The drone operator? In my house, when you said he'd been murdered, I thought of Ben."

"You went to the kitchen and refilled Alan's teacup."

"I was surprised."

"By?"

"Thinking of him in that way," she said. "I had never let him question my belief in him. He was always, in his heart, so young. And sweet and happy. When Dad died, Ben began to change. Sweetness and joy gone, replaced by anger. And a belief that something had to be done. I told you this."

She had, and I remembered it clearly. But I had mistaken the seeds of vengeance for a son's grief for his father. As had Marah—at first.

I told her I'd gone to Ben's apartment on Saturday afternoon, right after talking to her and Alan. Told her that Ben had moved out just hours earlier. "When you gave me that address, did you know he wouldn't be there?"

"*No.*"

"Where would he go, Marah?"

"I don't know. He hasn't answered."

In silence, I let the seconds drag past. Conscience teasers. Memory prods.

"Help me help Ben, Marah," I said. "Give me something. Something unusual. Unexpected. A pattern, or something *out* of pattern. Something he did that surprised you or made you see him differently. Or worried you. Or just made you mad at him."

She pressed the wet wad of tissue against each eye. Looked out toward the street, shaking her head. "Mad at him? The maddest he ever made me was over, like, sixty-eight dollars. So, I wasn't that mad, really."

People remember little things for a reason. "Go on, though."

"Months after he moved out of my house, I was still getting his mail. The junk mail I threw away and the rest I put in a box for him. One envelope was an overdue bill. It said 'Urgent' in red letters. I set it aside and tried to get in touch with him. He didn't answer my calls, or texts or emails. Whatever. That was Ben. He was only nineteen. I forgot about the bill, found it days later under a stack of my own bills and opened it. Apparently, he'd used his old address—my address—to rent a storage unit. A storage unit for *what*, I wondered. When he lived with me, he barely had enough possessions to fill his truck. He was always proud that he needed so few *material things*. Which didn't prevent his storage rent from getting overdue. Again, I tried to get in touch with him to see what he wanted me to do. No answer. So I got angry. Ben was always nickel-and-diming me and Alan. Letting us cover for his carelessness and immaturity. I called the number and they said the late payment was due the next day before five o'clock, without penalties, and could only be made with cash or check. The woman was rude."

"But you went."

"Alan and I went," said Marah. "I paid what was overdue, and two months in advance, to help Ben. The office was a hot, stinky, run-down trailer with two cat-litter boxes that needed to be emptied. The wall calendar advertised beer and showed a woman wearing almost nothing. I remember standing at the counter and writing the checks and being very angry at Ben for making me do that. Alan was disgusted by everything he saw, and angry at Ben, too."

I could tell from Marah's face how ashamed she was for getting angry at her little brother. I remembered how she had first described him: *He's the* baby. *He's golden Ben and he's never hurt a living thing in his life.*

Some of the early lunch folks had begun trailing into the patio with their trays and bags. The finch landed back on the table, gave us each in turn his keen attention. Hopped left and hopped right.

"Where was the storage facility?"

"Some confusing part of San Diego. Near the border."

"What was it called?"

She eyed me skeptically, searching my face for a clue to my pointed interest. Not being a suspicious woman, Marah saw nothing unusual in storing things. Not having seen Hector O. Padilla loading thousands of rounds of ammunition into the back of golden Ben's truck, Marah couldn't share my passion for Ben's storage unit.

"I'm sorry, but I don't remember."

"What name did he use to rent it?"

"Ben Adams."

A foursome took the table nearest ours. One of the men smiled at Marah and she put on a brave face, smiling faintly back.

Then the smile faded and her dark eyes searched my face, as if looking for shelter. "I wish you could have known Ben before Dad died. He was innocent and curious and happy. If what you say about him is true, then he's gone. That Ben is gone. I should go, too."

"You've done the right thing by helping me," I said.

"Right for whom?"

"The mother I told you about, for one."

"The woman who helped kill my father."

"You may be helping others, too," I said. "People neither of us know."

Marah shook her head. Disbelief? Disgust?

"Will you call Alan and explain the situation and let me talk to him?" I asked.

"When?"

"Right now, Marah. We're running out of time."

Another searching look. She found her phone and dialed. Speaking softly and urgently, Marah explained what I had told her and what I needed. She asked him to help me, and to help Ben, and any others who might be in danger. She hunched her shoulders and her red-black hair fell forward to hide her face. She went silent for a long while and all I heard was Alan's faint furious voice and the sharp intakes of Marah's breath.

She handed me the phone.

"You Got It Storage," he said. "San Ysidro."

I thanked him and hung up.

"Let me walk you back," I said to Marah.

"I would appreciate that."

We stood and the finch hunkered down on the white plastic tabletop so we wouldn't notice him. Red-breasted and dark-eyed and feet like pencil marks.

In the lobby I watched Marah disappear around a corner. I returned my guest badge to the guard and trotted across the parking lot for my truck.

37

THE YOU GOT IT office trailer was just how Marah had described it, stinky and run-down. The manager could have been the same rude woman she remembered. The litter boxes still needed cleaning and the beer calendar was now a tequila calendar.

"What can I do for you?" she asked.

"Shall I tell the truth or make something up?"

"Make up something fun. The hours drag in here."

I introduced myself truthfully, holding open my sport coat so she could see private investigator's license clipped to an inside pocket and the gun attached to my side. She squinted at me. Early sixties and holding fast to her looks—lipstick and makeup, big red hair, a low-cut tank, tight jeans. Said her name was Laney Walska. I'm a sucker for a redhead.

"That license might be made up, but the gun isn't," she said. "And I can have the cops here in under three minutes. Last time, it was under two."

"No need, Laney. The license and the gun are both true. So is what I'm about to say, so please listen carefully."

I broke it off for her as fast and neat as I could: two beheaded American airmen, another under a death threat, a cache of ammunition, and a Syrian American suspect who was renting one of her units.

"A Middle Eastern terrorist," she said.

I told her he was American born, a citizen—Benyamin Azmeh—but he rented by the name of Ben Adams. Told her I wanted to see his unit, maybe take some pictures. Then I'd go away and she'd never have to see me again.

"It's against the contract for me to let you do that," she said.

"It's against the law for me to even ask."

"Are you serious about all this, honey?"

"Every word I said is true."

She gave me a look that said she'd seen some things. The phone on the counter rang and she ignored it. She blinked twice, quickly. Twisted a strand of her super-sized hair through some fingers.

"You can't talk that lock off," she said.

"I'll find a way."

"He'll know."

"Yes, he will."

She raised her eyebrows and turned to the steel desk behind her. Sat down in front of a dirty white monitor, one of those bulbous things you can't even buy anymore. The incoming phone call went to message and one Laney told the caller she was out of the office, please leave a message, while the other Laney began tapping on a smudged white keyboard.

"The bad guys all lie," she said. "But I can print you a copy of his application if you want."

"I want."

———————

Ben Adams's unit was D-32, an "extra-value" unit. Laney led the way in a golf cart, red hair lofting, and stopped in front of the corrugated steel door. I parked behind her, shut off my engine, and stepped out.

"You don't have to stay," I said. "I've got what I need to get in."

"If you're going in, I'm going in," she said, climbing from the cart. "Don't make me change my mind. I want to see what this son of a bitch is hiding, same as you do."

She opened a large black toolbox on the rear platform of the cart, pulled on a pair of leather gloves. Then hefted out an enormous power cable cutter. A bulky, futuristic white-and-red polymer body, wide black jaws. It looked like something from a *Star Wars* movie.

"The Milwaukee Force Logic Cable Cutter with ACSR jaws," she said. It was heavy enough that she needed both hands to carry it to the door. "Seventeen hundred bucks online from ToolBarn. Delivered. I keep it charged. Stand back, please."

It was a good keyed padlock, available at most hardware and home-improvement stores. I'd seen it advertised as lock-cutter-proof. Laney cut through the shackle with a loud ringing snap, set down the cutter, and twisted off the lock in one gloved hand.

"That's satisfying," she said.

While she put her things back into the toolbox, I squatted and lifted the rolling door. Felt the shudder and clank of the jointed panels, the rasp of steel wheels in steel runners. A white curtain lilted out and brushed my face. Made my heart jump. It was too heavy to see through, split down the middle.

I considered, parted it, and stepped inside.

Laney gasped.

It all came at me in a rush, the gun racks bristling with carbines and assault rifles; the handguns dangling on pegs; Hector's *janbiyas* from the Treasures of Araby displayed like museum pieces; ammunition canisters stacked in one corner; produce crates overflowing with extra magazines, straps, and holsters; a weirdly humanoid coatrack hung with black sweaters and camouflage shirts and pants, watch caps, and balaclavas.

A large poster of the California state flag hung on one wall, the state misspelled "Caliphornia" and the iconic grizzly bear padding headlessly through his own blood.

Two card tables stood edge-to-edge in the middle of the room, littered with what looked like notebooks and loose sheets of printer paper. Fast-food bags in a trash can. Three folding chairs.

I read the careful handwriting on the cover of one notebook. "SDSU Student Union."

The penmanship wasn't Caliphornia's elegant English/Arabic calligraphy but a beginner's clumsy approximation of it—Hector, I thought— imitating his friend and mentor.

Laney had hardly moved. She stared at the flag with a sickened expression. I moved past her, turned on the lights, and pulled down the metal door, leaving it up a couple of feet for fresh air. The fluorescent tubes flickered and the curtain settled.

"I signed him up," she said. "Nice-looking young man, early twenties. A surf-dude type. Never saw him after that. I only work weekdays. I can't believe this stuff is his."

"Is his rent check always on time?"

"Late once years ago, but after that never a problem. I've had guys try to cook meth in my units. Gassed themselves pretty good. Had two young people breeding pythons. Some others shooting porn. I've had more stolen property in and out of here than I even know. But never anything this . . . scary. Can I do anything to help you?"

"Go back to the office if you need to."

"I'm sticking with the good guy and his gun right now."

"Don't touch things," I said.

"I know the drill."

I climbed into the back of my truck and opened the steel storage container bolted to the bed, behind the cab. Pulled out the blanket, then moved the CD box and the air compressor and the gallon of water and the long-handled lock cutter that seemed sticklike and primitive compared to Laney's futuristic contraption. Also moved the pistol box and the shotgun case and the road flares to get to one of my work cameras in its sturdy canvas pack. Slung it over my shoulder, locked the storage box, and hopped down.

Back inside, I put in fresh batteries, stills and video, macro to micro, and plenty of it. The guns were mostly inexpensive AR and M16 knock-offs. Plastic stocks, open sights, and high-capacity magazines. I opened one to see if it had been modified to fire on full automatic. It had. The ammo boxes were either full or nearly full of factory-new rounds. Shot pictures of the California state flag poster, and the coatrack heavy with commando gear, and the tables with the notebooks and papers strewn about.

Letting the camera hang around my neck, I picked up the "SDSU Student Union" notebook.

Page one was a sketched floor plan of the SDSU Student Union, entrances and exits noted, along with the closest parking.

Page two was an action plan, written out in what looked like a fourth-grader's simple, clear block letters. H was to enter the San Diego State University Student Union, "casually work his way to its center," and start shooting the students. When the panicking students ran out, C—"dressed in custodial clothing supplyed by H"—would be ready outside the main entrance/exit and cut them down with automatic weapons fire. When they were finished, K would be waiting in the "escape vehicle" in the parking lot nearest the Student Union entrance.

The "peek killing hours" for students in the Student Union were from eleven a.m. to two p.m., Monday through Thursday, as noted in the page margin.

The most effective weapons for H would be handguns, easily concealed in a backpack, and *janbiyas* for "close killing." For C, one fully automatic rifle hidden inside a wheeled trash can that "will fit in the car and look natural with C's custodial uniform purchased at thrift store" would be best. The trash can would, of course, be left behind in the chaos.

Inshallah, written at the bottom.

If God allows.

I set the notebook down with the others. Felt the strangest of brews running through me: adrenaline, rage, revulsion.

Laney joined me at the table. "What's all this? Looks like homework."

"Yeah, homework." I handed her the SDSU Student Union notebook.

Then browsed some of the other material on the tables. Our students of slaughter were also planning a "Clairemont-Mesa Traffic Signal" attack, where they would go car to car at rush hour on the Clairemont-Mesa on-ramp, shooting the motorists trapped in their cars. Three other on-ramps "would work, but offer less casualtys." All had "functional getaways." Someone had calculated "kill-to-survival rankings" for each potential target—no suicide missions for these holy warriors. Also a sketch of the Clairemont-Mesa on-ramp to the 163 Freeway, notes on "best traffic hours" written off to one side.

Inshallah again.

Other notebooks with other plans. I scanned through them, reading quickly:

"Oceanside Walmart."

"Kensington Preschool."

"Bowling Alley, Escondido."

All of them, *Inshallah*.

Some were detailed, others were little more than the name.

Then, what I expected but didn't want to find: a simple but clear sketch of what looked like a long, rectangular-shaped dining room. Doors and windows, round tables of clumsily drawn diners.

The next page made my pulse pound even harder:

"First Samaritan New Year Harbor Cruise."

I read quickly. The party on *Glorietta* always started at six and the ship would leave the dock at seven. The dining boat was slow and would "take a while to get into the deep water." Earlier that afternoon, Hector would be there with the other volunteers, prepping the food and decorating. He'd stash the gift-wrapped guns and extra magazines in the ship's hold. "The boat is old and slow and takes until eight o'clock to get into the deeper water of the harbor," he had written.

The plan was to "be patient" and let *Glorietta* get far out into the harbor. Caliphornia and Hector would kill the captain and crew first. Then shoot as many innocent people as they could. The people who jumped "will be easy targets in the water." Some would drown. Kalima would pick up her men in a rented skiff and whisk them back to shore and away.

I folded the pages lengthwise and put them in an inside pocket of my jacket. Then took a handful of the notebooks and threw them across the room. Flipped over both card tables, scattering the deadly plans across the concrete floor. Toppled one of the gun racks and let the rifles clatter down. Swept some of the handguns off their pegs, and the *janbiyas*, then heaved the produce boxes across the room.

I turned to see Laney push the coatrack over. "Thieves cut in," she said.

"Trashed the place and took a few guns," I said, slipping a .40-caliber autoloader into one of my coat pockets, and a nine-millimeter into another.

I locked my loot in the steel container in my truck. Then pulled down the rolling door of the storage unit and watched as Laney worked the lock back on and arranged the neatly severed shackle to appear normal. At a glance, you couldn't see the cut. All it had to do was fool casual thieves, and to make Caliphornia believe he'd been broken into when the cutter-proof lock came off in his hand.

I called Taucher to order a JTTF stakeout.

L iam Flaherty and I stood in the spacious dining room of *Glorietta*, where some two hundred and fifty holiday harbor cruisers would begin boarding at six o'clock on New Year's Eve. For a moment I pictured them, some of San Diego's finest, dressed in their best, ready to ring in a new year, overbid on auction treasures for a good cause, prepared to eat and drink and be merry.

Two hundred and fifty guests.

Crew and staff.

All of them aboard *Glorietta*, half a mile out in the harbor on dark winter water while two heavily armed men calmly take life after life, reload, kill again and again, blood running down the decks and scuppers while terrified people take their chances overboard.

I told Flaherty just enough of what I knew to bring a flush to his broad Irish face.

"How do we handle this?" he asked.

"Quietly," I said.

A hard, blue-eyed stare from Liam. "This ship we're on never leaves the dock, right?"

"New Year's Eve it doesn't."

We climbed to the upper deck and looked out at the city, downtown rising above the bay into a winter-pale sky. I was looking forward to calling Taucher with what I'd found, but she beat me to the punch. I stepped into the breeze to take her call, away from Liam.

"*Caliphornia* wants his money," she said. "*Tomorrow!* We've got an Arab American agent on his way to deliver it. We insisted on a bodyguard to protect our man and cash. You've got the job if you want it."

"Why me?"

"You've got JTTF experience, you're capable, and you're cheap. And you don't come off as a fed."

"Yeah, I'm way better-looking."

"Are you finished being a twit?"

"Yeah. So let me tell you about New Year's Eve aboard *Glorietta*."

38

FOUR P.M. THE NEXT DAY, a Tuesday. A pewter sky bellied low over Balboa Park, breeze rising and daylight falling. I had been cast in the role of armed bodyguard in this FBI Repertory Theater performance of *Busting Caliphornia*. The curtain was scheduled to rise in half an hour.

I was given no lines but was allowed to drive my own truck and pick out my own clothes and accessories. I had chosen a navy suit, white shirt, and yellow tie, my .45 handgun in my leather inside-the-waistband holster.

One hour ago I had driven into the heart of the park like any other visitor and parked near the Mingei International Museum. As scripted, a black federal Town Car was waiting. I opened a rear door and stepped in. FBI Special Agent Ali Hassan, flown in from New York, sat in the spacious backseat. He was young and trim, with black hair, a goatee, and an expensive suit. We shook hands.

Our black-suited chauffeur was none other than Directing Special Agent Darrel Blevins, who introduced the cast as soon as I sat down: Mike Lark the homeless was under the tree right there, Joan Taucher and Patrick O'Hora in the white Challenger over by the exit, Darnell

Smith circling on a damned motorcycle in case high-speed pursuit ensued.

"He'll come buzzing by here again any minute," said Blevins.

We had a good view of the benches outside the Mingei, where Caliphornia claimed he would meet Hassan and his bodyguard at exactly four thirty. It made sense that he'd choose a busy, outdoor public place with fading daylight for the cash pickup—easier for him to remain unrecognized, and more difficult for law enforcement to operate—if Raqqa 9 and the Warrior of Allah were not who they had claimed to be.

But as I looked out the darkened Town Car window, I saw that the blustery weather and short daylight had kept some of Balboa Park's usual holiday visitors away. A young couple hustled from the Mingei and across the parking lot toward their car. An old man with a cane rose from one of the benches and headed bent-backed toward the museum. A flock of pigeons lifted off the grass nearby, and the old man turned to watch. Lark, smudged and ragged, slouched against the trunk of a huge coral tree, his heavily laden shopping cart beside him. I pictured him in my barn, young and bright-eyed, stating his affection and respect for the beleaguered Taucher, telling me that he was the same age she'd been when she started out in the Bureau. And making the crack about his boss stepping in the dog's mess.

Balanced across Hassan's knees was a well-used leather briefcase containing fifty thousand dollars in twenties. He opened it so I could see. There were fifty bundles of fifty bills each, printed on five-plus pounds of paper. The Bureau had decided not to deploy exploding dye packs—too much risk that the suspicious Caliphornia would ask *Assayed* Hassan or his trusted bodyguard to handle or transfer the money first. Each bill number had been recorded, on the slim chance that Caliphornia might get away and start spending it.

"Yep," said Blevins. "There goes Smith on his Kawasaki."

I watched the leather-clad, black-helmeted agent coming down the drive and past the Mingei, the Kawasaki's stinger burping in the afternoon quiet of the park.

Blevins turned and beamed us, implants perfect and polished. "Don't screw this up, PI," he said. "Just do whatever Caliphornia says, and we'll take care of the rest. Remember, if either of you runs his left hand through his hair—we are coming in fast and hard. That's your call-in-the-cavalry signal: left hand through hair. So keep your left hands far away from your damned heads in the meantime."

Ali shot me an annoyed look as he clicked the briefcase shut. "We'll manage."

"I love stuff like this," said Blevins, turning away from us to face the windshield and the Mingei. "Gets my mojo up. What's that in your waistband?"

"The gun that any armed bodyguard would carry."

"Know how to use it?"

"Yes," I said. "Makes me feel better, too, what with all the heads rolling around lately."

A silent beat while I scanned the parking lot for a metallic gray 4Runner.

"You were in Fallujah, weren't you?" Blevins asked.

"The first one," I said.

A half-turn, and half of the dazzling Blevins implants. "When it all went to shit."

"A lot of bad things happened all at once," I said.

"That was when I finally realized how much they hated us," said Blevins. "Killing those American civilians like that."

I cocked my head, figured why the hell not. "If they showed up here with a hundred and fifty thousand troops, you might hate them, too."

Blevins growled. "So us being there excuses everything?"

"It set the table for people like Caliphornia."

"We were *helping* them," said Blevins. "You want to weigh in on this, Ali?"

"I was born in the U.S.," he said. "I married an American woman. I'd fight to the death to defend my country from occupiers. Like anybody anywhere."

"What gives Islamic State the right to cut off American heads?" asked Blevins.

"They're fanatics with no country to defend," said Hassan. "We should run them into the ground where we find them."

"You got that right," said Blevins.

Again I studied the lot for Caliphornia's gray 4Runner. And again for a black Cube. At four twenty Blevins asked if we were ready. Helpfully, he reminded us not to screw this up.

Looking through the windshield, I saw the empty benches outside the museum. A security guard came from the building, looked around for a moment, then went back in.

"Good luck," said Blevins.

Ali and I walked side by side on the nearly empty footpath, took a detour away from the Mingei, passed the visitors' center and the Prado Restaurant. He carried the briefcase in his left hand. Wore wraparound sunglasses and a blue shirt open at the collar.

We looped back to the Mingei and my heart fell a little when I saw the empty benches. No Caliphornia visible on this late blustery afternoon in a beautiful park. Hardly anyone at all.

Hassan went to a bench, lowered the briefcase, and sat. I walked across the thin grass and stood under the big coral tree, thirty feet away from him. Buttoned my coat, snugged my lapels, mentally registered the gun against my backside, then checked my phone. All of us on the take-down team had linked our Telegram apps to group-receive from Caliphornia, but only Ali would answer.

Four thirty came and went. The darkness closed and headlights came on and I could see Blevins's vague outline behind the wheel of the black Town Car. The darkened windows of the Challenger revealed no one inside at all. A moment later Agent Smith came whining down the drive on his motorcycle, revs high but speed low, apparently taking in the fetching scenery around him.

Then a buzz from my phone.

CAL 4:44 P.M. DECEMBER 18
Change of plan. Walk to Air and Space Museum. Stand outside of entrance. Your suit looks expensive. Your bodyguard's not so much.

Ali and I walked south toward the Spreckels Organ Pavilion. The amphitheater sat empty in the near-darkness. Hall of Nations to our left. United Nations Gift Shop. Christmas lights. Palms and eucalyptus towering high and lit from below. On President's Way, a blue Mustang went by, then an older 4Runner. White.

We walked along Pan American Plaza and another parking lot with more spaces than cars, our heels sharp on the walkway. Businesslike. Executive. Confident. An oncoming covey of teenage girls broke rank to let us through, lost in laughter and their phones.

"He's seeing if we're alone," said Hassan. "When he's satisfied that we are, he'll leave. My guess is he'll ditch this park altogether."

"I agree," I said. "He'll want a better crowd to feel safe."

"Are there usually more people here?" he asked.

"A lot more," I said. "The fabled San Diego weather let him down."

We stopped a few yards short of the entrance to the Air and Space Museum. The building is bulky and cylindrical, an old version of futuristic. Plenty of room for air and space. Out front, scale models of iconic fighter jets rise on pedestals—an old X-15 and a modern F-16. A huge, spotlighted banner above the entrance announced the current exhibit:

AIR WARS

Fighters in the Desert Sky

Around the building, streetlamps glowed and eucalyptus trees swayed in the cool breeze.

Under the X-15, Ali set down the briefcase, hiked a shirt cuff, and checked his watch. I walked off a hundred feet or so, stood just outside the pale pool of a streetlamp with my back to the building. Feet spread, hands folded dutifully in front of me. Roland Ford, bodyguard.

Felt like a smoke, but you can't do that here.

Had some thoughts, none of them interesting.

Ten minutes later I saw Ali walking toward me, looking down into the glow of his phone. I read the message:

CAL 5:05 P.M.
Take a seat under the Unconditional
Surrender statue by the Midway.

"That's the nurse and the sailor kissing," I said.

"Crowded?"

"Always."

Then Darrel Blevins, group-texting the team:

BLEVINS 5:06 P.M.
(619) 555-5555
TUESDAY, 12/18/18
Ali—confirm with Caliph. You and Ford
WAIT ten minutes before you leave for
Unconditional. TEN! Smith, pick up
Lark NE corner Hall of Nations and
take side streets to statue to come in
from south. JT and O'Hora wait FIVE
and come to statue from north. I'll
be waiting and watching. Be alert.

Ali and I strolled back to my truck, stood outside, and snuck a couple of his cigarettes. Kept an eye out for park security. Laughed quietly at ourselves. Schoolboys. Waited. Our ten minutes felt like an hour.

Then we launched.

39

MY NERVES WERE STEADY and my eyes sharp and my body felt light and strong. How I used to feel before a fight. Took Park Boulevard to the 163 to I-5 north. Headlights and taillights, traffic heavy but moving. Off at the Lindbergh Field exit, then all the way to North Harbor Drive, which runs along the bay and comes into downtown from the north.

The evening was clear and the stars began to emerge above the city lights. The yachts bobbed easily on the water and the traffic was steady. We passed *Glorietta*. A weak light inside.

I drove past the smaller charter boats and the pleasure craft to where the *Azure Seas*, berthed at one of the cruise-line docks, disgorged a river of tourists onto the Embarcadero. Many headed for *Unconditional Surrender*, no doubt.

"Do you think he's convinced?" asked Ali. "Or will he run us around some more?"

"If we passed his sniff test at the park, I think he'll show," I said. "He wants that money. But if something looked wrong to him, he's gone by now and he won't talk to the Warrior of Allah again."

"The damned motorcycle," said Ali. "It was conspicuous and noisy and out of place. Easy to remember if he sees it again."

Traffic thickened near the *Midway*, and we picked our way toward the parking lot. The enormous aircraft carrier presided over the city waterfront like a city of its own, multi-storied and brightly lit, a chapter of history afloat on glimmering black water. Paid my money and parked.

We made the Embarcadero and rounded the stern of the *Midway*. Then mixed in with the steady flow of holiday visitors, cruise-ship patrons, and local families out for a look at the harbor lights and the city skyline and maybe dinner. I scanned the parked vehicles for Caliphornia's 4Runner, Blevins's Lincoln, and the Taucher-O'Hora Challenger. Up ahead I could see *Unconditional Surrender*—the sailor and the nurse, locked in their eternal public kiss—brightly towering in the night.

The statue is based on the iconic photograph *V-J Day in Times Square*, which captured the sailor kissing the nurse. It was originally installed in Sarasota, Florida, but some San Diegans had to have one, too. Others did not. As they argued, private donors and city boosters ponied up a million dollars, bought another *Unconditional Surrender* statue, and installed it here on the waterfront.

Where it now loomed before us, immense and boldly lit. Twenty-five feet high. Bronze, but painted to resemble skin and clothing. An average human adult is roughly the length of one of the nurse's shoes, and comes to about the middle of the nurse's calf. The closer you get to it, the more vertigo-inducing and weirdly monstrous it is.

All of which was arguable to the scores of people milling beneath the sculpture—posing for pictures alone and together, trying to re-create the postures of the kissing couple—laughing and snacking and drinking as they ambled or stood or sat on concrete benches, craning their necks.

We worked our way to the edge of the mall in which the statue stood. The *Midway* presided to the north, the downtown hotels and offices sprouted densely to the east, and to the west I could see the twinkling necklace of Coronado on the black water of the harbor.

Ali carried his briefcase to an open bench and sat, facing *Unconditional Surrender* and the *Midway*. With his trim suit and briefcase, he looked out of place here among the tourists. Uptight and somehow false. All the easier for Caliphornia to spot. And to doubt?

Across the mall, Taucher stood with her back to the statue, taking or faking phone pictures of the aircraft carrier. Her apparent companion, O'Hora, waited not far from her with a convincing air of boredom.

From the Embarcadero, homeless Lark wandered toward *Unconditional Surrender* as if he'd walked all the way from Balboa Park.

But no Caliphornia.

I stood just off the Tuna Lane sidewalk, a hundred feet away from Hassan on his bench. Tuna Lane curved one-way past the statue and the waterfront restaurants, then back out to North Harbor. One side was bordered by diagonal paid-parking spots, much coveted during the holidays. Cars pulling in and cars pulling out, cars waiting, patience required. I scanned them, hoping that simple good luck would bring Caliphornia's gray SUV into focus. I wondered if he'd switched vehicles for this meeting. Did Kalima have a car?

Turning away, I saw Lark, already ambling down the sidewalk along Tuna Way toward us.

Then:

CAL 5:58 P.M.
**Leave the briefcase. Go back to
your car.**

HASSAN 5:59 P.M.
**I was hoping to discuss our future. We
need good warriors and we pay them well.**

CAL 5:59 P.M.
Another time.

Text to the team:

BLEVINS 6:00 P.M.
(619) 555-5555
**Ali and Ford leave case and clear toward
Midway NOW. Keep going. Others,
close only when subject has possession of
case and BEGINS exit. O'Hora and Lark
CONTACT. Taucher and Smith COVER.
Clean and fast. Collateral everywhere. Get
him down and tied and make me proud.**

Hassan stood and turned my way. I stepped around the tourists, looking for Caliphornia or anyone else who might be closing on the money. Saw a couple with a stroller and twins. And an old couple, he with a walker and she with a steadying hand on his arm. A group of Japanese tourists. A laughing boy in overalls running loose, with Mom in hot pursuit. Sailors on leave, taking selfies for families or lovers—one of them maybe the next serviceman to be immortalized by a photograph.

Ali waited, then we started off toward the *Midway* under the dress of the kissing nurse. Drifted through Taucher and O'Hora with nothing more than glances.

Then, like a guest appearance in a strange dream, Hector Padilla came shuffling across the grass toward us, his face uncharacteristically grim and his eyes raised toward *Unconditional Surrender.*

40

WITHOUT BREAKING STRIDE, I worked my phone: Hector incoming from north. Then, once out of earshot, I told Ali we had just passed Caliphornia's partner in terror.

"That little guy?"

"Hector Padilla in the flesh," I said.

"Change of plan, then," said Ali, walking faster. "When we hit the sidewalk, you go to the truck like Blevins ordered. I'm going to join the tourists and loop back to the statue."

"So am I."

"I'm ordering you to the truck, Ford."

"I'm not going. I'm in this thing, Ali."

He looked at me, nodded, then veered into the southbound foot traffic.

Up ahead of us, Hector stopped just short of the grassy mall to hike his pants, still apparently gazing at the statue bathed in light.

Ali and I drafted in behind a bunch of grunts in desert camo, followed them all the way to North Harbor. Then I branched away, angling between a big Latino family dressed in their holiday finest and a Chinese tour group, many-footed and serious. All of whom bore me back onto the Tuna Lane sidewalk and into even heavier foot traffic.

I lumbered along, Inconspicuous Ford, a natural heavyweight in a suit and tie on a collision course with one beheading terrorist, his esteemed colleague, six armed FBI agents, fifty thousand cash, and two oblivious giants making out. Kept bumping into people, apologizing softly, my eyes trained on the briefcase, visible through the legs of the passersby. Turned my attention to Hector, plodding across the mall toward the money, his phone to his ear again.

I slowed and let the pedestrians eddy around me. Over their heads I had a good view of Hector as he moved across the mall, looking up at the statue again with a worried half-smile. He stopped, raised his phone, and took a picture of the big kiss, then turned around and lifted the phone for a selfie.

A middle-aged Vietnamese couple sat down on Ali's vacated bench. Hector looked at them and shot another picture of himself. The couple talked and gestured and showed each other pictures on their phones, unaware of the cash at their feet, seemingly delighted to be alive in this time and place.

Then the man threw his head back laughing and knocked the briefcase over with his foot. Stopped laughing, leaned forward to give the case a good long consideration, then reached down and set it back upright. Said something to the woman, who said something back, and they both laughed. Another exchange. After which each of them looked out across the mall in different directions, apparently looking for someone to match the forgotten briefcase. They looked like people trying to ID a distant relative at a train depot or an arrivals gate, before the world became too dangerous for that. After a few moments of this, they stood and walked away.

Hector watched them leave, hustled to the bench, and plopped himself down. He took more pictures of the statue, lowered his phone, and looked around.

I could see Smith and Lark just beyond the statue, watching Hector from behind the nurse's gigantic white shoe. Taucher and O'Hora had moved closer in, fussing over angles as they shot their own pictures of the kissers.

Blevins to the team, by text:

What's he doing?

TAUCHER
Sitting by money.

BLEVINS
When in possession take him down.

LARK
All over him, Sarge.

Hector set his hands on his thighs and looked around anxiously. Raised his arms over his head, arched his back, and rolled his shoulders like a boxer. A small girl in pink sweats and boots charged Hector, touched his bench, then fled squealing back to her surprised parents. Dad raising an open hand to Hector. Mom petting the little girl's hair. Hector on his phone again, nodding, then sliding it into his hoodie pocket.

He reached down without looking and pulled the briefcase onto his lap. I hoped the others knew exactly what Blevins meant by "take possession." I didn't. O'Hora and Lark easing in now. Taucher and Smith, too, looking toward Hector but not directly at him.

Hector lowered one elbow to the case, raised his fist, and set his chin on his knuckles. *The Thinker.* Seemed to come to a decision. Took the handle of the briefcase in his left hand, stood, and started across the mall toward North Harbor Drive.

O'Hora and Lark closed, badges proffered, free hands on their guns, still holstered.

I moved closer. Saw Hassan at the edge of my vision.

O'Hora, not unfriendly: "Police, Mr. Padilla. We need to have a word with you."

"Who are you?" asked Hector, not stopping.

"Drop the briefcase and raise your hands, Mr. Padilla."

"But I just found it."

O'Hora, louder: "Drop the case and raise your hands, *sir.*"

Hector stopped. "I'd like to see some ID."

Lark: "That would be these badges, Mr. Padilla. Now, please *drop* the briefcase and raise both hands."

A ripple of silence widened around me, spreading from person to person like a secret. Bodies in retreat and advance. Bodies uneasy.

Shaking his head, brow furrowed, Hector walked toward O'Hora and Lark with unusual purpose, then did a funny little soccer step that angled him away from them.

O'Hora and Lark drew their weapons.

Shrieks and curses and a disordered scramble. Air taut with fear. Some held their ground and some crept closer, crouching, cell phones brandished.

O'Hora, gun steady on Hector: *"Police! Drop the case! On your knees with your hands up!"*

A young woman: "He doesn't have a gun!"

Hector, turning toward the agents but not stopping. "I found this briefcase. I can use it at work!"

A middle-aged man: "It's just a briefcase!"

O'Hora, loud: *"I am Agent O'Hora of the FBI! Padilla—to your knees!"*

Hector stopped and faced Agents O'Hora and Lark with a flummoxed expression on his face. Guns ready, Lark stepped closer to Hector while O'Hora circled behind him.

Hector dropped the briefcase. Looked around, went to his knees, and raised his hands. In a fluid rush, O'Hora holstered his firearm, charged from behind, and slammed Hector to the ground, face-first.

The agent pushed his knee into the small of Hector's back, straight-armed his face to the dirt, and raised a plastic tie from somewhere inside his coat.

The blast was sharp and loud, blowing O'Hora and Hector raggedly up and out. Concussion. Power. Cries and wails, bodies swaying like trees in a sudden gust. A hot jab to my face. Lark blown flat. Bodies scrambling and circling and frozen in place. Little girl in the pink sweats and boots screaming clumsily toward her parents. Vietnamese couple running hand in hand. Smoke and sparks and the sweet reek of burnt flesh, parts of things dropping from above, some flaming, some smoking, and a downward lilt of fluttering leaves that were twenty-dollar bills.

Time paused.

Turn of earth, dome of sky.

Time creeping back, cautious, half-speed.

I stood back up and ran into the storm.

Taucher, Smith, and Hassan were already near the blast site, weapons drawn. We faced one another over the bloody heaps of Hector and O'Hora, and I saw Taucher's helplessness and her anger, but most of all

I saw her disbelief. And with the return of my equilibrium, I realized exactly what had happened.

Instinct took my eyes to the Tuna Lane parking lot, where the door of the black Town Car swung open and Blevins jumped out just as a white sedan slowed behind him. The pop of gunfire, flashes in the darkness, the sedan jumping into the line of cars streaming onto North Harbor Drive.

I barreled through tourists, a clot of them rushing against me, toward a tour bus parked on North Harbor. Then past the Town Car, where Blevins lay sprawled faceup on the asphalt. An older woman had kneeled beside him, praying in a language I didn't recognize. I drew my weapon and angled toward the exit as the white sedan turned onto North Harbor, headed for downtown, a thousand streets, two handy freeways, and freedom.

Traffic moving. The sedan disappearing into the city.

I trudged back to Blevins.

41

I WATCHED from the comfort of my home office as Caliphornia was loosed upon the world.

An evil, a star.

At first he had no name except to us.

The social media were first: scores, then hundreds, then thousands of shared Facebook postings and YouTubes of the carnage, all multiplying dizzily—an explosion on this side of the world instantly fanning out to the other and back again.

At first it was all amateur video of carefree San Diego, America's Finest City, the moody bay and the invincible *Midway*, Hector's confrontation with O'Hora and Lark. Then the sudden, vicious, oddly small-looking explosion that ripped apart O'Hora and Hector so finally. Followed by jerky video of onlookers running in various directions, their cries and wails and many languages, the pounding of shoes and the squelch of wind on microphones, hanging smoke. Eyes wide in faces slack with fear. Money fluttering in the air. Brief, shaky video of a woman praying over a man in a parking lot. Neither one of them clear enough to identify.

Next, the professionals—networks, cable, PBS—regular program-
ming canceled or delayed. Even most of the advertising. Fast as you
could turn channels, graphic scenes of Caliphornia's violence flashed
past; the man himself was neither pictured nor named.

> *Terror has apparently struck again in America tonight, this time*
> *in San Diego, where two FBI agents, a suspect, and two bystand-*
> *ers have been killed in a wave of coordinated public attacks just*
> *moments apart . . .*

Reporters and stunned witnesses muttered under the light-blanched
Unconditional Surrender, San Diego's chief of police and mayor, a U.S.
representative, and, later, a senator all weighing in. Followed by a hur-
ried press conference with FBI, Homeland Security, and JTTF.

> *The two dead FBI agents are Directing Special Agent Darrel*
> *Blevins, sixty-three, and Special Agent Patrick O'Hora of San*
> *Diego FBI, who was forty-four . . . The dead suspect has not been*
> *identified.*

I turned on the radio, too, and every time I landed on a strong signal,
it was about the terror in San Diego.

> *Also reported dead at the scene are two visitors, possibly in port*
> *aboard the* Azure Seas.

Just before nine o'clock, the IS-affiliated news agency Amaq claimed
through Al Jazeera that "an IS detachment has claimed four lives in San
Diego, California, and one IS martyr has entered heaven."

At nine p.m. Caliphornia introduced himself to the world. He posted on the big popular platforms—encryption and secrecy be damned. He was after fame and he was ready to crow:

I am Caliphornia. I pledge bayat to
Islamic State. San Diego is mine and
Bakersfield is mine and Grass Valley is
mine. I am Caliphornia. I am a part of you
and I am inside you. You will know me by the
knife, the bullet, the bomb, and the fire.
You will know me well but not at all.
I am everything you see and fear. I am
Caliphornia. Mashallah.

His posts had pictures of a long-haired young man with his face partially covered by a scarf-sized version of the California flag—spelled Caliphornia—with the beheaded bear traipsing through its own blood. Or the same young man partially hidden by bars of shadow and light, or wearing sunglasses with palm trees reflected on the lenses. In some he was bearded, in others clean shaven.

The terrifying video clips of Caliphornia dangling Kenny Bryce's and Marlon Voss's heads stayed up for nearly half an hour on social media feeds before their cyber-security could scrub them off.

The president of the United States Tweeted his disgust at the "barbaric attacks," and promised "very massive retaliation, very quickly."

My Internet slowed to a crawl.

We are aware of this problem . . .

My mobile apps froze and unfroze and froze again.

We are working to resolve these issues . . .

We've made a star out of him, I thought. The biggest since bin Laden. Exactly what they wanted.

L et me see that snout of yours," said Burt Short.

He turned the office desk lamp to my face. Peeled back the bandage and took a long look at the stitch he'd put in my cheek. It had taken him longer to remove the small ragged shard than it had to take the stitch. My cheek burned and my right eye watered. The scar would be on the side of my head opposite the boxing scar. I wondered how many more scars I'd collect on my face in this life.

Lindsey sat on my office couch, Zeno lying bulkily between her and the world, his head on his front paws, eyes open. She had watched with me in stunned silence as Hector and O'Hora were detonated again and again.

"Where'd you learn to take stitches, Burt?" asked Lindsey.

"The Philippines."

"Were you a paramedic or something?"

"Yes," he said quietly, holding my cheek to the light. "Good. Clean. Keep it dry for a couple of days."

I turned back to the computer monitor—back up to half-speed now—where Hector was running past Smith and Lark with his funny little stutter-step. I picked up my phone, left open to Facebook, where a frozen image of Voss lay in the scattered snow on the running path.

Then looked at the wall TV, where Taucher's boss of bosses at the Western Region JTTF, Frank Salvano, said: "We consider this a terrorist attack on U.S. soil. The FBI and Joint Terrorism Task Force will bring their full weight to bear on this investigation. If this man calling himself Caliphornia is responsible for these heinous crimes, we will bring him to justice, and we will do so with relentless pursuit and conviction. We have no higher priority at this time."

Salvano was tall and almost gaunt, with short silver hair and rimless glasses. The anger in his voice was substantial. He offered a hotline number, which trailed along the bottom of my TV.

Then Taucher called, finally. I shooed off Burt and Lindsey, closed the office door.

She was at the hospital with Lark and Smith. She and Lark had been far enough away from Hector to avoid shrapnel, for which she thanked God. Smith had been hit, but his motorcycle leathers had protected him. Hector's micro-bomb was made with carpet tacks—cheap, sharp, and heat-retentive. Joan's voice sounded thin and spent.

"Our special agent in charge just left here," she said. "Turns out our Washington friends have some, um, deep reservations about my idea to lure a known murderer into a public place. And the resultant loss of life. Although—of course—all of us involved last night, from the SAC on down, couldn't wait to nail Caliphornia's butt to the floor. SAC said I should consider a voluntary reassignment to Washington. Said he didn't want to write me an official reprimand—just yet. I demanded they let me finish this out with Caliphornia. Then I insisted. Then begged. I'm still in. Skin of my teeth."

I couldn't think of anything reassuring to say.

"They've been waiting for something like this," she said. "I put body and soul into protecting my city. Now that I've failed, all I feel is tired."

"People won't die aboard *Glorietta*, thanks to you."

"They died tonight instead," said Taucher. "And Caliphornia got away."

I felt the moments moving by. Heard something in the background, radio or TV or the chatter of hospital staff.

"So, how can Raqqa Nine get our young terrorist to trust us again?" she asked, almost dreamily. "Do we blame him? Claim that the FBI was watching *him*, not us? We could say that moneybags Hassan is furious and on his way home. That our fifty thousand dollars are gone. That we are out of faith in *him*."

"He won't trust Raqqa Nine again," I said. "Not after this."

I glanced at my phone and the computer monitor, both still devoted to the death and destruction. Bodies on the ground, covered. Twenty-dollar bills falling through the air. I'd seen the real thing, but I still couldn't take my eyes off it. *Hypnotic*, I thought. For the whole country. For the world.

On my TV BBC news feed, Amaq, again quoted by Al Jazeera, stated that "donations to Islamic State have been flooding in . . ."

"On the hush, Roland," said Joan, "we think Hector's bomb was detonated by remote. This is preliminary. Very."

"Why kill Hector?" I asked. "It cost Caliphornia a soldier and fifty grand."

"Look at this spectacle! Caliphornia's introduction to the world, through the martyred Hector. Think like a terrorist, Roland."

I listened to her breathing, soft and slow.

"Okay," she said. "I'm still in this game, whether the SAC wants me here or not. Look, we know that Caliphornia is murderous, suspicious, and completely out of trust. Is he going to blunder into our You Got It stakeout? Doubtful. *But*, if there's any way we can get to him, the Bureau is a thousand percent ready. No expense spared, nothing they won't consider. Is there something personal to Benyamin Azmeh, maybe? Something important enough to get him out of his hole? He's hot right now. He's lucky, therefore risk-tolerant. Maybe you can exploit that. Think of a way, Roland. You're good at this kind of thing. The Bureau has trouble thinking outside the box sometimes. Hell. We *are* the box."

"Lindsey," I said.

A beat. "Bait?"

"Let me think."

Later that night, the SDPD identified the suicide bomber as Hector O. Padilla of El Cajon, and the two dead innocents as Mr. and Mrs. Glen Nguyen of Miami. Pictures of all three. The couple was the one I'd seen, much in love and delighting in their travels and amused by the mystery briefcase at their feet. Hector looked his usual self, pleasant and befuddled.

The San Diego chief of police also said that "the murder of Agent Blevins and the suicide attack by Hector Padilla were coordinated acts of terror." She added that "radical extremism is behind these acts," and that so far as her department could determine, "Caliphornia, and the gruesome videos accompanying Caliphornia's taunting claims, are authentic. We will stop this person or persons," she said flatly. "It's only a matter of time."

Then, after a two-hour hiatus, Caliphornia himself stormed onto the digital stage again, boasting through a new Facebook post that his jihad had just begun and that *the Kuffar will have their throats cut as they sleep at night. Allah-hu Akbar! Hector is in Paradise! You will know me again before forty-eight hours have passed.*

Quickly followed by a fresh Tweet from newly minted @Caliphornia Dreamer, his avatar now changed to a *janbiya* raised in a black-gloved hand. *All people of the Book rise up against America, this whore of Satan. The martyr Hector is smiling on us from Paradise! Forty-eight hours!*

Then a YouTube video from Caliph2ReVenge of Kenny Bryce's head on his bed, and narration in Caliphornia's strangely inflected, surfer-Arabic English: *Two down and one left to go. Pleasant dreams to you tonight, Lindsey, and all the unclean infidels you mate with!*

YouTube took it down after five minutes, but it was already in the ether, the damage ongoing.

Which of course unleashed speculation on the identity of "Lindsey." A specific woman or even man? A generic nickname for . . . a Western woman? A nonbeliever? An old lover? A prostitute? Why her, specifically?

Minutes before midnight, Frank Salvano, the tall and now haggard Western Region JTTF director, took to the lectern again while the cameras flashed and whirred. This time he had a large monitor beside him and a remote in his hand.

"We have identified two suspects in the murder of FBI agent Darrel Blevins in San Diego this evening," he said.

The monitor blipped to life with a blowup of smiling Ben Azmeh and Kalima Amin, the image downloaded to Taucher's phone by well-meaning Marah Azmeh. Their names were superimposed beneath them. Salvano spoke their names anyway, and said their last-known address was an apartment in Santa Ana. Next came an outdated DMV mug of one Ben Adams sporting dreadlocks and a humorless glare—clearly Ben Azmeh. Then a State Department head-and-shoulders photograph of solemn Kalima Amin, staring out from behind her hijab with just a hint of contempt.

"This picture of Kalima Amin was taken from her application for a fiancée visa, issued by our State Department in 2016," said Salvano, the TV lights flashing on his glasses. He described the suspects physically and said they were last seen at approximately 6:30 p.m. leaving the parking area on Tuna Lane in an older white Ford Taurus, near the *Unconditional Surrender* statue on San Diego's waterfront.

"Ben Azmeh is an American citizen," he said. "Kalima Amin is a Syrian national in this country legally. They are armed and violent and should not be approached. Azmeh has pledged *bayat*—an oath of allegiance—to Islamic State. If you have any information on these suspects, call the number at the bottom of your screen immediately. If you're having trouble seeing it, the number is . . ."

I watched and drifted. Watched and drifted.

Tired as I'd ever been.

Willing to hit back but no target.

Taucher's desperate request for action gnawing inside.

I knew I wouldn't sleep, not with Blevins's blood under my nails and on my clothes and in my nostrils, my flesh held together by Burt's neat stitch, and the kaleidoscope of gore turning relentlessly in my mind's eye, with the threat of more upon the land.

This land.

Made for you and me.

42

JUST AFTER ONE in the morning I went to the barn and attacked the heavy bag with an anger I hadn't felt in years. Not since the day that Justine went down into the ocean in her pretty pink airplane. I was too tired to be sharp. Wondered what it would be like to step into the ring at thirty-nine. Foreman a champ at forty-five. When I couldn't throw any more good punches I jumped some rope and raised my heavy arms again to the speed bag.

Then shaved and showered and grabbed a handful of Oxley flyers.

I drove the dark curving streets of greater Fallbrook, stopping here and there to post a new one or replace a rain-faded original. It felt right to be doing something helpful. Something optimistic. *Something.* When I had covered miles and miles—trees and power poles and fences and the walls of buildings downtown—I drove to Los Jilgueros Nature Preserve, where Lindsey had twice met her son.

The preserve's gate was closed and locked, so I parked my truck out of the way and jumped it. The moon was up and the sky was clear and I walked the dirt trails under the sycamores and the young oaks, past the spindly flowerless stands of matilija poppies and the dying-back sage and the wild buckwheat gone brown and brittle with fall. I stopped and listened and looked. Tammy Bellamy had been quiet these last few days, and I sensed surrender. How good was my chance of finding Oxley here? *About as good as luring Caliphornia into the open again,* I thought.

Since when was hope foolish? Even just the hope of finding a cat?

It angered me that hope was foolish.

I wanted to knock out Caliphornia with an uppercut. Feel his jaw cave in and see his lights go out. Hate on an empty stomach. I wouldn't finish him off, though. I'd call Taucher. Or maybe just 911. Nation of laws. Roland Ford: model citizen.

I continued down the wide dirt road to the first pond, black and twinkling under the moon. Stopped and listened to a great horned owl hooting from the woods. Then heard the mate answer back—notes on the hunt, spoken in their own language. Something splashed near the close shore. Too cold for the frogs and birds. I wondered.

Sat on a bench donated in memory of a Fallbrook boy who'd died young. I knew nothing about him. I sat with my back to the water so I could oversee the central meadow.

What *was* this, looking for a lost cat while a terrorist stalks your city? The end of hope?

Then, the beginning of an idea.

Maybe just the idea of an idea.

You will know me again before forty-eight hours have passed . . .

Lindsey, and all the unclean infidels you mate with . . .

Lindsey. Forty-eight. My shy idea approached, brushed against me, then vanished.

What I really wanted to do was get *Hall Pass 2* into the sky at first light and fly her up to Mammoth, go fishing for a few days. Nothing like a rainbow trout dripping silver water in the sun of a Sierra day.

Maybe ski, too. On the slopes I'm graceless but fast. Size is your friend going downhill if velocity is what you're after. After that, dinner and wine in a good restaurant. Maybe get a farm-raised version of the trout I let go. Talk to a pretty waitress.

Or I could just go dancing in San Diego, right here close to home. I know the dance clubs and I have a calendar of the amateur ballroom competitions. I've done fairly well in some of them. Always content on a dance floor, so nice to be moved by music and to move with someone.

But instead, I sat on a boy's memorial bench and looked out at the pale meadow. Let my eyes relax and tried to dismiss the brutality of the day, to let something like light come to my mind, something good or promising or optimistic, something like Oxley luxuriating in the moonlight, studying me with his hypnotic green eyes. Anything. *Anything* but what I'd seen.

I thought of you, too, as you know I often do. I always start at the beginning. It's like getting to meet you all over again. The way you smiled at me when we met, at that awkward holiday party at the Grand Hyatt downtown. The big storm coming and you there with a friend and I alone. Of course, I liked the way you looked in the red party dress and your sleek red hair and your green eyes and the smile that gave up little and withheld much. And I said something male and witless, which you pointed out but seemed to forgive. *Justine Timmerman. I landed in the public defender's office about the time you ditched the sheriff's* . . . Right then, from the very beginning, we were Timmerman brains and Ford brawn and we were happy with that arrangement, weren't we?

And, as you know, after that first night together, life changed. Went in a fifth direction. How can something so surprising be so right? Love just mowed down the opposition, trampled everything in its way, left me panting but eager to keep up. Those two years we had—from the time we first laid eyes on each other until God and *Hall Pass* took you down, Justine—those were us. Young and passionate and fearless. Our own soap. Not everyone gets that.

I clearly remember what you said to me about death once: that you weren't afraid of dying, only of being forgotten. Rest assured—smart, funny, courageous, skeptical, sweet, lovely woman—you are not forgotten. I'll carry you as long as I live.

Want out? Sure you do. Here you come. There you are. I've missed you.

Later that morning, as I looked out my window to the first chill light of five o'clock, it came to me. Knocked right on my front door and introduced itself.

A way to Caliphornia. Not through Raqqa 9. Not through the Warrior of Allah. Rather, through someone who had recently done some work for Caliphornia. A licensed professional. A man who once told me he wanted to wake up and feel blameless for a day.

I found the contact and dialed.

"Ford," said Bayless. "Can you believe that shit?"

"This is important, Jason," I said. "I want you to Telegram Hector Padilla."

He chuckled sleepily. "I doubt he'll answer."

"I'm hoping his boss will," I said.

"Explain."

"Were your Telegrams with Hector group-messaged?"

Bayless was quiet for a few seconds. "Yeah. Someone calling himself Andrews was in the chain but he never participated. Why?"

"Hector wanted very specific information about Lindsey for his boss, right? Not just her address, but the layout of my place, which rooms were hers. Who the other tenants were. When she might come and go. Hector said she might not need a place to live for very much longer."

"That's when I pulled the plug," said Bayless.

"Plug back in," I said. "Because you have that information now. It took you some time and it will be expensive, but you've got it and it's for sale."

"To his boss. Andrews."

"Andrews wants it for something evil that we can prevent," I said. "Interested?"

"Is he part of the attack last night?" he asked.

My turn for a moment of consideration. Sometimes the most persuasive thing you can offer is trust. "You bet he is."

"Then I'm more than interested."

"Can you be in my Main Street office in two hours?"

Next I called the number that Frank Salvano, special director of the Western Region JTTF, had given out. Got put on hold for half an hour. Told Agent Camille Rodriguez that I had specific information about the San Diego terrorist Caliphornia that I would give only to Frank Salvano.

Salvano was on the line within half a minute.

Three hours later, Taucher, Salvano, Jason, and I were anxiously loitering in my Main Street office, each of us lost to the private thoughts and uneasy tedium that cops and PIs come to know so well.

It had taken us only minutes to compose and send Jason's Telegram solicitation to the deceased Hector Padilla. The Telegram had been received. Now we could do nothing but hope that Caliphornia, emboldened by a night of bloodshed and terror, would answer Bayless soon.

Another hour crept by. The manager of the Dublin Pub sent us up some breakfast, two plastic bags' worth, coffee and flatware, too. I always pay cash and tip heavily.

I was halfway through the egg-and-corned-beef scramble when Jason dropped his fork to his plate, stood up, phone in hand. "Ladies and gentlemen, we have a Telegram from Andrews."

Taucher pumped a fist.

Salvano raised an eyebrow.

I felt a wave of relief wash over me, followed by a wave of dread.

"'I am Hector's employer,'" said Jason, reading off of the screen. "'Need photos of property and house where Lindsey is staying. Not macro Google Earth but detailed close-up photos, TWO OF WHICH must contain Lindsey. Need view from road, entrance, gate, fences. Need gate code. How many residents/tenants? Landlord is still PI Roland Ford? Does he live there? What security company? Alarms? Neighbors near? Dogs? How much money for this? Need all by five thirty p.m. today or no deal.'"

Jason lowered the phone. "Son of a bitch," he said, as if baffled. "It worked. And he's in a hurry."

All eyes on me. Salvano and Taucher already on their phones.

"Tell him no problem," I said. "And charge him a lot."

Over the next hour we helped Jason photograph Rancho de los Robles on his phone. I kept the Irregulars out of the shots, causing them concern and curiosity. Told them I'd explain all of this later. Jason photographed Lindsey coming out of her casita and playing Ping-Pong against an unpictured opponent. She seemed anxious and uncertain. We left Zeno out of the frame. Jason shot the road and the gate and the keypad. I helped him write up a brief paragraph about the tenants and landlord, keeping us as vague and inconsequential as possible. No, landlord Roland Ford no longer lives on the property. No, the other four tenants have no firm schedules and are often gone. None are apparently employed. Lindsey Rakes almost never leaves the compound. No alarm system, no dog, neighbors not a factor. Charge: fifteen hundred dollars. Photos and gate code to come, will accept cash, credit card, or PayPal. Andrews said he would have cash delivered after receiving the images. Bayless accepted, based on Hector's record of prompt payments in the past.

Such a strange thing to be luring terror into your home, as if it was something you couldn't say no to.

It was just after three o'clock when Jason hit send.

43

I CALLED A MEETING of the Irregulars. Taucher, Salvano, Jason, and I waited at the picnic table under the palapa, overlooking the pond.

Burt sat right down and asked us what the plan was and how he could help.

"We won't be needing any help," said Salvano. "But you'll all need to be out of here in the next couple of hours."

Burt shook his head. "I'd reconsider that if I were you."

Salvano looked ready to say something, but Grandpa Dick and Grandma Liz arrived, each holding the other's hand and a large cordial glass filled to the salted brim with red liquid, sprouting a celery stick and a lemon wedge. Liz introduced herself and husband to my guests and offered to make them one of her "military-grade Bloody Marys."

No takers. So she and Dick sat down with us, Dick noting that he could spot federal employees "from miles downwind." No one had said anything about federal employees, so I had to take him at his word.

"What a gift that must be," noted Taucher.

Dick gave her a wry smile.

Next came Clevenger, recently awakened for the day. His hair was a mess and his face looked weighted. He plopped down across from Burt. "Another long night chasing coyotes," he explained. "Never even heard one."

"Any sign of Oxley?" asked Liz.

"No Oxley today," said Clevenger, rubbing his forehead. "The Oxster is a goner, Liz. We all know that."

"I choose hope over defeat," she said.

The agents and Jason looked at one another like this must be code for something, plainly puzzled by the Irregulars.

Lindsey came down last, Zeno plodding along big-footed beside her, ears up for all the new faces. She wore one of her cowgirl uniforms: Ariats and pressed jeans, a blue yoked satin blouse with white piping and mother-of-pearl snaps, a belt like a boxing champ would hold over his head.

Taucher stood and offered her hand. "I'm Joan Taucher. Nice to finally meet you."

Lindsey smiled apologetically. "Thanks for everything you've done for me."

"Thank you for trusting us," said Joan.

"I've been trying to hold up my end," said Lindsey. I knew she was talking about her son, and the unopened bottles of Stolichnaya still sitting in plain sight on her kitchen counter. This according to Burt.

"Nice dog," said Taucher. "We had Cane Corsos when I was a kid."

Lindsey sat at one end of the long table, Zeno beside her, facing the rest of us.

"Is this everybody?" Salvano asked me.

"Everybody who counts," said Dick.

Salvano stood. He looked taller than he did on TV, his face leaner and stronger. Exhaustion and anger still showing through.

"You need to move out for a few days," he said. "There's no safe way we can make this arrest with all of you fine citizens at risk and in the way. I assume this isn't a problem."

"Reconsider," said Burt. "Knowing that there are five total tenants here, what will our boy make of such emptiness? When you trap an animal, you scent the trap so it smells right. In this case, so it looks right."

Salvano looked sharply my way, displeased that Burt knew what was going on. "Nonsense," he said.

"I found Burt's logic convincing," said Dick. "Though I have no idea what you're all planning."

"We can't plan anything with you people in our way," said Salvano, sitting down. He seemed to sense he was in for a long fight. "But I can tell you that we'll be arresting a very dangerous individual. Perhaps two. They will certainly be armed and dangerous."

"The couple from the bombing last night?" asked Clevenger. "Here?"

"I did not say that," said Salvano.

"You wouldn't be here for anything less," said Dick. "Not after last night."

"The terrorists?" asked Liz. "I've got a sharp carving knife. I'll stay right here and *help*!" She raised her glass and drank.

"You're exactly what we're afraid of," said Salvano.

Lindsey looked at me questioningly. "Roland? Explain to them."

"There's no damned explanation necessary," said Salvano, "because I'm in—"

"Let me do this," I interrupted. I told them everything. From that day in April of 2015 when the Headhunters killed nine innocents to last night's terrorist attack in San Diego. From Caliphornia's threat against Lindsey to our plot to lure him here, literally straight into their backyard.

I'd never had such rapt attention from the Irregulars. Not a wise-crack to be heard. Dick looked grim, Liz affronted. Clevenger fixed a concerned eye on Lindsey. Burt sat still, hands on his lap and twiddling his thumbs.

"Y'all shouldn't be here for this," Lindsey said, looking at each in turn. "It's me he's after. I'm capable and I'm in good hands."

"Absolutely *not*," said Salvano, standing. "You can't be here, either, Ms. Rakes. We need this area secure and no civilians present. End of discussion."

She looked at me again.

My turn to stand, though I doubted it would have any impact on the outcome here. "He's right," I said. "All you can do here is get hurt or get killed."

"I disagree with that," said Dick. He took a big gulp of his cocktail. "I've got a perfectly good revolver under my bed. I haven't shot up any paper lately, but I'm actually pretty good with it."

"This is a nonstarter," said Salvano.

Clevenger leaned forward, rapped his knuckles on the wooden table. "Look—I can put a camera drone way up to where nobody can see or hear it. If you know his vehicle, we can pick it up before he even gets to the gate."

"We can get our own air surveillance and tactical backup," said Salvano. "But thank you, Mr. Clevenger."

"All of you," I said, "Lindsey included—you've got to clear out. You know what Caliphornia did last night. He's more than just dangerous. I'm asking you as friends, and telling you—as the owner of this property—that you have to leave this to us."

I caught Salvano's look.

Dick shook his head and looked down at the picnic table. Liz stared at me. Clevenger did likewise. Lindsey reached out and ran a hand over Zeno's immense head. Burt's thumbs kept on twiddling as he gazed out over the pond.

Liz took another drink, then stood and looked at Salvano. "Well, count me out," she said. "Or in. However you say it. This is my home and I'm not leaving. You can arrest me. Either way, nice meeting all of you, and have a pleasant evening."

She turned and limped toward her casita.

"You are endangering this operation," said Salvano.

Liz ignored him.

"I'm sticking with my wife," said Dick, standing. "She'll be the death of me, but I always knew she would."

He hustled across the patio to catch up with her, his aging frame bent forward at the waist and knees.

"I'm staying put," said Clevenger. "Let me know if you want me to get a camera ship up."

"Washington won't do it this way," said Salvano, his hard eyes trained on me. "They just absolutely flat-out won't."

"I'm not leaving, either," said Lindsey. "I wouldn't even consider it. Come on, Zeno. Let's get us a little walk by the pond while it's still light out." She stood and the dog led the way toward the water.

"I'm out of here," said Bayless. "I've got a wife and a little girl and I'm not going to die on this mountain. I won't bill you for my time, Ford. This one's on me." He nodded, then started down the path toward the barn and his black Mercedes SUV.

Salvano watched them. Put his hands on his hips and shook his head. Looked down at Burt, still sitting, his stubby strong hands now spread flat on the table in front of him.

"You?" asked Salvano.

"Wild horses couldn't drag me away," said Burt.

"Well, *shit*, Mr. Ford," said Salvano. "I think your renters have effectively shut down my operation."

"Your call, not theirs," I said.

"You really can't talk some sense into them?"

"They've already spoken," I said. "You're asking them to leave their homes on account of terrorists."

"I'm trying to defend the homeland," said Salvano.

"This is the damned homeland," said Burt. Salvano gave Burt a long stare. I thought he might say something about Burt Short's shortness, which, I've discovered, makes Burt retributory. Jason Bayless's SUV trundled from the barnyard toward the driveway and he gave us a thumbs-up through the open window.

"Let me see what I'm able to do," said Salvano.

"I knew you'd come around," said Burt, giving the agent his weird, bottom-toothed smile.

Salvano's craggy face creased deeper as he sat back down in front of his two phones—one white and one black—squared them perfectly, pondered them both, chose black, and started in.

"Joan?" he asked. "Can you get us a pot of coffee?"

"I'm not the waitress, Frank."

"I'll do that," I said. "You two try to get your team on the field."

Burt and I claimed two chaise longues by the barbecue, close enough to the feds to eavesdrop.

Salvano pled his case to his FBI superiors in Washington. *We have a chance to stop this terror, sir. The logistics are sound and he's given us a window. Don't make me waste it.* At times he had two conversations going at once, in parts, pleading with someone on the white line, bullying someone else on the black.

Taucher was busy, too—making her case and answering questions, her usually short temper dialed most of the way down to a softly urgent frequency.

I listened and looked out over the pond. The clouds flushed pink as the sun began to set and from the north the pale face of a storm looked down. It was being billed as an "atmospheric river" that the National Weather Service said could drop "copious amounts of rain" in San Diego County. And it was set to arrive approximately forty-eight hours from now.

Like Caliphornia, I thought, *if he was good to his word.*

When Salvano went silent, Burt and I wandered over. Salvano sat still, arranging his phones in front of him, squaring them minutely, as if their symmetry were mystical.

I saw him smile for the first time. "I'll be goddamned. They went for it. We've got two snipers and a bomb squad on their way. And seventy-two hours to make it happen."

Taucher jumped and threw a punch at the air. *"Yes!"*

By sundown we had the basics:

Dick and Liz in Liz's casita number six, farthest from the main house. Stay away from the windows and lock yourselves in the bathroom if you hear gunfire.

Burt and Lindsey in the barn watching the back road. Lights out after dark.

Bomb squad in casita one, closest to the patio—our hoped-for point of contact.

Sniper Reggie in my upstairs office, windows with good sightlines.

Sniper Daniel on the barn roof.

Clevenger hidden in the thicket of oleander near the gate, piloting his drone out of eyesight and earshot.

Zeno locked in Lindsey's casita three, well positioned on the long odds that Caliphornia even got near her front door.

Salvano, Taucher, and I, the welcoming committee, inside the main house.

Salvano to take down and cuff, Taucher and I to cover.

If Caliphornia ran, resisted arrest, or showed a weapon or cell phone, the snipers would shoot him dead, head-shots best in case of armor.

After all, with bombs, *hero* is another word for *dead*.

Loose or lumpy clothing, a backpack, bag, or any type of package meant explosives, so cover, cover, cover.

All agents wear their armor; the bomb team was bringing extras for the civilians.

Plan B is hit at the plate.

Fast but loose.

For Darrel and Patrick.

It all felt unreal. For a moment I let myself float up and look down on us, gathered under the palapa, making our plans. I hovered like one of Dale's drones. There we were, small humans at work. I liked my plan. I saw things that could go wrong. What worried me were the things I couldn't see at all.

44

LIFE IS WAITING.

Just before dusk, Burt and Lindsey brought back pizza from Vince's downtown. I watched on Clevenger's tablet as they made their first delivery to Clevenger himself, hunkered in the oleander down by the gate. Lindsey waved up at the drone she couldn't see, though she was very clear on the HD feed. So was Zeno in his armor, seemingly aware of the heightened threat level. Clevenger stepped from the bushes, zooming in on himself and Lindsey. The camera was so powerful you could see their expressions and the moving of their lips. Lindsey laughed. Clevenger moved the controller to one hand and accepted the white pizza box.

A minute later, Burt Short's relatively gigantic Cadillac Coupe deVille came up the drive and rolled to a stop. Out came Burt and Lindsey, bearing stacks of boxes, delivering them from casita to casita.

Later I lit a fire in the great room and sat well away from it, my FBI tactical vest on the back of a chair. The armor was lighter and covered a little more area than that issued by the San Diego sheriff's office just a few short years ago. Clevenger's tablet sat propped on a steamer trunk beside my chair, streaming his aerial surveillance of my home and property, eerily green in infrared.

The dark made everyone jumpy and fretful, except for Taucher, who hummed to herself contentedly as she carried Clevenger's tablet back and forth from Salvano in the kitchen to me in the living room, where she would look from the screen to me with her brown hawk eyes, fiercely beautiful within her heavily made-up face. She said that Lark and Smith had wanted to be a part of this, but they were running You Got It surveillance, which was Salvano's call, and Salvano knew this kind of business better than anyone. Said it a little loudly, so he could hear. Joan's nice-girl routine was sweet and funny if you knew her.

Back and forth with the tablet.

Forth and back.

For me it was coffee and memories of a woman I loved, snippets of dreams unlived. And a growing wonder at the things we human beings do to one another.

Barn lights out at eight. House lights out at ten.

The slow crawl of hours.

If there's a dead of night, why no dead of morning?

At 3:17 a.m., Taucher came across the room, looking down at the tablet screen. "I'd like you to come to my home and meet my people someday," she said.

"I'd be honored, Joan."

"Yes, I think you would be."

I saw a pair of headlights far down on the road. Then a glimmer in her eyes when she looked up at me.

"A white Taurus just went by the gate," she said.

Salvano came to the window beside me. We watched the car go past and disappear.

Five minutes later the Taurus approached from the opposite direction, slowed at the gate, and turned in. Pulled up to the keypad as the motion light came on and driver's-side window went down. The driver reached out to punch the numbers and I got my first clear, high-def look at Caliphornia. He resembled his father and his sister—the trim face, slender nose, and heavy eyebrows. Younger-looking than his twenty-two years, a mass of black hair, clean shaven. Eyes bright as he watched the gate swing open. Beside him the silhouette of a woman, shrouded in a darkness that even Clevenger's infrared camera could not fully penetrate.

Up the drive slowly, headlights off, running lights orange in the dark. I buckled on the tactical vest. We stood away from the windows and drew our weapons. I heard the creak of the floor in my upstairs office—Reggie the sniper settling in.

The car came up the drive between the house and the barn, setting off the motion lights, then continuing past their beams. In the semi-darkness farthest from the house, the driver half-circled the vehicle to face back down the drive, and parked.

No movement inside that I could see. Stillness, as the seconds slid into minutes and the motion lights went off. Then the car doors opened. Ben Azmeh emerged. Taller and heavier than I had imagined. Jeans and athletic shoes and a half-zipped U.S. Air Force sweatshirt over a dark T-shirt, the hood now pulled over his head. He shut the door softly with both hands and a nudge of his hip. In the faint light from the house I saw the glimmer of a gun just above his belt buckle—easy access, up front and in the open.

Kalima came around the passenger side. Tall, trailing layers of silky fabric—a caftan or a full-length duster—billowing pants and combat boots. Hair tied back, bunched at the top and flowing behind her.

And a bundle in her arms. She looked down at it, adjusted a blanket.

I saw what looked like a small face within the bundle.

Thought of Ben's letter to Marah: *Want to marry Kalima and have us a baby!*

"Oh, Christ no," whispered Taucher.

Salvano groaned softly.

Another little squeak from the floor upstairs.

I remembered Joan's description of the full Bakersfield video: *Someone walked past that security camera thirty seconds before Caliphornia . . . A woman . . . Carrying something against her side . . .*

Had Kenny Bryce opened his front door not only to a woman, but to a woman and her newborn?

Kalima led and Ben followed. Practiced and purposeful but not in a hurry. Silent on the concrete, touched by weak moonlight, Kalima cradling her infant, Caliphornia with his hoodie up. A young family. The future ahead. They came along the shadowed edge of the driveway, toward the house and the branching walkway that led to the patio. Caliphornia tall but swift, Kalima tall, too, striding more heavily with boots and infant.

Crouched and watching within the darkness of my living room, I saw Kalima lead the way around the house and toward the patio. When they'd gone past the window I sidled from the living room toward the kitchen. Salvano and Taucher massed behind me. Knowing my home and its dimensions, I saw that Ben and Kalima would be at our ground zero—on the patio, just under the palapa and directly in front of us—if we came through the mudroom adjacent to the kitchen approximately right . . .

Now.

Kalima triggered the motion lights.

I drew my weapon, pulled open the mudroom door, and followed Salvano and Taucher into the cold morning.

"*FBI!* Facedown on the ground!" boomed Salvano.

Salvano broke right and Taucher left. Beyond them stood Caliphornia and Kalima, frozen in the light. I dropped to a shooter's stance, both hands on the gun and the bright red dot of my laser sight dancing center-left on Caliphornia's chest.

Salvano again: "*On the ground now!*"

Kalima looked at Ben. I couldn't read her expression—an agreement or a confirmation, maybe—and at the same time she hugged the baby closer. It cooed softly.

Caliphornia had frozen. Kalima gave us a defiant glare.

"Put the infant on the ground and step away!" yelled Taucher.

Kalima seemed to consider, her expression changing from obstinate to hopeful. She nodded and knelt and snugged the bundled blue blanket. Again the infant cooed and warbled. Kalima then set it on the ground and arranged the blanket once more, raised a pistol at Taucher and fired.

The return volley was immediate and deafening, exploding from the guns of Taucher and Salvano on either side of me, and from Reggie above me in the house, sending a cloud of gun smoke into the damp cold air. I fired once and didn't miss. Kalima staggered back into the barbecue, but, apparently well armored, she scrambled over the blue-tiled counter and fell out-of-sight into the horseshoe-shaped island.

Bullets smacked after her, tossing blue tile and brick dust into the smoking air.

Ben grabbed the baby and threw himself over the barbecue, too, back first, like a high jumper. In the sudden silence I heard the infant cooing affectionately, oblivious. Caliphornia rose and fired and ducked down again. Daniel on the barn had a bad angle and couldn't risk bigbore fire in our direction. Then a frustrated cease-fire. In the eerie silence Caliphornia slammed home a fresh magazine and asked frantic questions in Arabic of Kalima.

"Enti kowais? Enti kowais?"

No answer.

Salvano ordered them to throw out their weapons and come out. The baby cried. Then, holding fire but brandishing the newborn at us, Caliphornia rose gracefully from behind the counter and began backing his way up the driveway toward the Taurus.

Taucher and Salvano sidled after him. I covered them from behind a palapa stanchion—a palm trunk as thick as my body. Good protection and a steady brace for shooting.

Caliphornia backpedaled hard and fast, but straight into Lindsey, charging him from the barnyard dark. She hit him at the knees and he went down, a *janbiya* clanging to the concrete. He rolled quickly upright, tucked the baby tight, and turned for his truck. Sniper Daniel took one shot, muzzle flashing orange from the dark.

Caliphornia's hips shuddered and he crashed to his back, another *janbiya* and his phone clattering to the concrete. Still he clutched his infant close. His gun spun to a stop inches from his outstretched right hand. The baby cooed.

Lindsey rose to one knee, steadying her handgun on Caliphornia, as Taucher and Salvano took aim from behind her.

Taucher: "Hold your fire!"

Glass shattered violently behind us, from the direction of the casitas, and I understood what was happening.

In the smoke and strange eardrum-pounding silence Caliphornia's blood snaked down the drive.

Then, as if charged by new life—or by Hector's Captagon fighting pills—he struggled to his feet. He swayed, a torn and bloody being, the infant still in his grip. He looked at the gun on the ground, then at us. I felt mass and energy behind me, as armored Zeno flew through the air, knocked down Caliphornia as if he were made of paper, then straddled him and took the man's head into his cavernous jaws. Held it still as the baby finally rolled free.

Lindsey screamed, *"Lasialo! Lasialo!"*

With a splat, Zeno dropped Caliphornia's head to the concrete. Then gazed at Lindsey expectantly, a red pendulum of drool swinging from one side of his mouth.

"Vieni, Zeno!" ordered Lindsey, backing away from the baby but her gun still trained on Caliphornia.

Zeno obeyed.

Caliphornia lifted his head, eyes wide open and his chest rising and falling rapidly, his gun in a pool of blood beside him, his child and phone just out of reach.

Zeno had almost made it to Lindsey when he suddenly stopped and hooked back to the baby, as if he'd caught a whiff of something new and important. Stopped and sniffed at the bundled infant, pawed it once like it was an uninteresting toy, then loped back toward his master.

"Bravo regazzo! Vieni!"

The good boy came.

I watched the infant roll free of the blanket, a rosy-cheeked, big-eyed plastic doll dressed in blue PJs.

"Get away from that thing!" Taucher ordered, wrenching Lindsey away from the doll.

Three rapid shots rang from within the barbecue. Taucher buckled and collapsed. Lindsey clambered toward me in seeming slow motion, Zeno at her side. Within the stout bunker of the barbecue, Kalima was swaying unsteadily when I shot her once in the forehead and put her down forever.

I was just starting my turn toward Joan when Ben weakly raised his head again, found Lindsey in retreat, then lifted something small and dark in a bloody hand. The doll exploded and the world shut down.

Heartbeat.
    Eyes
  burning: smoke
  palapa fronds
  dark and starless sky
  breath in breath out
  on my back
  alive.

Then: Salvano standing over the bloody rag of Caliphornia, gun still drawn and the bomb squad swarming in as bloodied Lindsey and Zeno shuffled toward me, Burt and sniper Daniel emerging from the barnyard dark, Clevenger entering the patio light with the drone control pad still in his hand and his mouth agape.

I crawled to Taucher. The bullet had caught her throat just over the top of her armor. Her blood gushed and her hawk's eyes stared up at me and there was a trembling hush upon her, the hush of life in flight. I put my hands on either side of the gaping wound and tried carefully and scientifically to keep her blood inside her though it was not possible but I kept my fingers and thumbs pressuring purposefully and I talked to her as I had talked to Avalos in that Fallujah doorway where he had lain. I don't remember what I said to my bleeding brother Avalos—probably something about hanging on and hanging in—and I don't now remember what I said to Joan, though it couldn't have been any more helpful, but I didn't have anything more to offer than pitiful, exhausted words.

I was aware of two bomb-squad personnel in their protective suits wheeling some kind of container toward Caliphornia's body while a third with a portable X-ray machine headed for Kalima.

Aware of Salvano on his feet.

Of casita six's open door, two faces staring out.

Of Lindsey kneeling beside me, Zeno down beside her.

I talked to Joan earnestly. More words, a battalion of them. Her eyes shifted and her pupils constricted and I believed she could see me. Then a jolt of strength that allowed her to lift her head. Followed by a sigh and a great shuddering release. I settled her head carefully to the concrete.

Lindsey wavered over to Burt, the backs of her arms riddled by shrapnel. Zeno shook his head once like his ears were full of water but followed her, otherwise unfazed. Lindsey tilted into Burt's outstretched arms, she a head taller than Burt but Burt bull-like and strong, his arms closing around her.

I stood. Leaned against the palapa palm trunk for balance.

Saw Salvano limping toward Kalima and the bomb-squad tech, phone to his ear.

Liz pulling gently on Lindsey's sleeve.

Dick on his way over to me with some unreadable expression, revolver jammed in his belt, trying to step around the empty brass and bits of doll rubber and shards of blue tile scattered in the blood.

45

CHRISTMAS DAY, Tuesday, bright and blustery. Our reign of terror over. The atmospheric river had hit us just a few hours after Caliphornia and Kalima, bringing four inches of cold, hard rain to rinse off our bloody world.

Everyone on the patio had been hit with mini-bomb shrapnel— carpet tacks again. Salvano had caught shrapnel near his left eye, but no ocular damage. I'd caught my share—one high up on my thick skull, two in my left shoulder, two in the butt, and two in the thigh. First came the delight of having the jagged pieces pulled out, then nine stitches. A haze of painkillers. For three days after the blast I felt like I'd fought a bear. Then the healing itch took over.

All of us had still been turned toward Kalima when the bomb exploded, and our back-side armor had done its job. In some cosmically inscrutable way, Kalima—in killing Joan—had saved us others from worse damage or death. And left Caliphornia to bear the brunt of their own creation.

Then, suddenly and almost surreally, there were no more hospitals, doctors, needles, or stitches. No more detectives, reporters, well-wishers. Nothing but our wounds and our freedom.

And inside me, silence.

Now Lindsey was packing, with help from her son, John, and ex-husband, Brandon. She had caught shrapnel in her arms and legs, including one tack that had gone through the middle of her left hand and would probably leave some "minor" nerve damage. The hand was still thickly wrapped, though she was already deploying it for light duty. Her front door was open and her car pulled up close, trunk open.

Zeno lay smack in the middle of her living room, considering me from within his white plastic cone. It was tied at his neck by a strip of gauze. A monster in a bonnet. He'd cut his leg jumping through the casita window and taken his share of shrapnel, too. No worries, by his expression. I helped Lindsey load up the Mustang, not a roomy car to begin with, and I saw that she had tucked a serape over the backseat, most of which would be claimed by Zeno.

Lindsey took Johnny and Brandon down to the dock. She'd gotten her son a remote-controlled sailboat that he was eager to launch. He was a slender boy, and not tall yet, given his parents' height. Brandon was well over six feet, and Lindsey just under. In the mother's and son's postures, I saw affection and reserve, hope and wariness. I was proud of Lindsey for taking on her demons, one by one. She was beating them back. I saw in Johnny a gentleness that would let him forgive his mother for whatever excesses she'd shown him. Brandon? Hard to say. He looked angry, while Lindsey appeared to be on the humble. They both had plenty to let go.

I sat in one of the Adirondack chairs on her front porch, in the sun, which felt good on this brisk day. Heard a grunt, then the slap of paws on floor tile inside. Zeno came from the casita and dropped his brindled gray bulk down in front of me. Head up and alert. He watched Lindsey for a moment, then threw down his head, cone be damned, and rolled onto his back. There he lay, at my feet, legs spread to reveal his shaved inner thigh where the window had cut him, his stitches and balls. Upside down, he looked at me from within the drool-smeared cone, his tongue lolling and cropped tail wagging. Something like love in his eyes. Something like, *We are now together forever.* I thought of him straddling Caliphornia with the man's head locked in his jaws. It's easy to overestimate the nobility of dogs. Other beasts come to mind, too. Everywhere I look.

Lindsey and I loaded the last of her things. The two bottles of Stoli still stood unopened on her counter, temptation overcome. "All yours if you want them," she said.

"I'll put them in the community stash," I said.

"Do you have another tenant in mind?"

"No," I said. "You know I like to have one casita open."

She smiled. "For emergencies, like me."

"Emergencies like you."

Brandon started up his Jeep and Johnny climbed in. Lindsey opened the door of the Mustang and flipped the driver's seat forward. Zeno lumbered to the threshold and jumped in, bashing his cone into the seat back. The car rocked. He climbed onto the seat and turned around with some difficulty, then looked at us hopefully as Lindsey threw the seat back into place.

She gave me a light hug. Too many wounds between the two of us for anything more than that. The breeze threw her hair against my face and I felt the warmth of her tears on my cheek.

"I cry when I'm happy," she said, stepping away. "You're a friend, Roland. You must know that."

"You're my queen."

"I don't want to be a queen." She looked at me with an odd defiance, wiped both cheeks with her bandaged hand, then gingerly touched my face.

"You and I are alike, Roland," she said. "We think that if we give up on even one small thing, everything will cave in. So we try to hold the whole world together."

"Some truth in that," I said.

"I'm sorry to have brought so much death and destruction to your home," said Lindsey. "I can't stop thinking I should have found a way to stop him. After all, I made him."

"We all made him."

"It's generous of you to share the blame."

A moment later the black Mustang was heading down the drive toward the gate. I'd watched a red Porsche Boxster head toward that gate one fateful day, never to return with its precious driver. I could see the outline of Zeno's shoulders and cone as he sat up in the back, facing forward, looking out for his queen.

The next day I knocked on the front door of Joan Taucher's home in the Uptown area of San Diego. Uptown is just that—up. I looked down at the Pacific and Interstate 5 and Lindbergh Field and the downtown buildings.

I waited on Taucher's porch. The house itself surprised me. From the outside, it didn't look anything like a place where Special Agent Joan Taucher would have lived. It was old and easygoing and needed paint.

I'd like you to come to my home and meet my people someday.

But if life is waiting, it is also a series of surprises. Such as the call from Special Agent Mike Lark early that morning. And the sight of Lark himself now opening the door. "Glad you could come, Mr. Ford."

He led me through a narrow foyer that had a coatrack with two FBI windbreakers hanging side by side. Plenty of hats and umbrellas this time of year. Then into a living room. Hardwood floors, dark and scarred. Floral wallpaper, white paint, bookcases, and a dartboard bristling with darts. Mullioned windows with the curtains half drawn across views to the ocean. A fireplace with a tidy orange fire.

In the middle of the room was a well-used leather seating group— sofa, loveseat, and an armchair that looked roughly as old as the man sitting in it. White hair, light brown eyes. Dressed in a dark suit, white shirt, and blue tie. A wheelchair to one side of him.

"Mr. Ford," said Lark. "Please meet Max Taucher. Sir, this is the private investigator that Joan spoke so highly of."

He turned his gaze from an ocean-view window to me, brought a gnarled hand to his brow and back down in a slow salute. "You're not as old and ugly as she said you were."

"Neither are you, sir."

"Sit," he said. "You're just in time to see the atmospheric river slam the coast."

"It hit two days ago, Max," said Lark.

"There will be another," said the old man. "Just who *are* you, Ford?"

I sat. "A licensed private investigator. Locally sourced and hopefully sustainable."

"Done anything interesting in your life?"

I tried to sum up the interesting things in my life in less than five minutes. Which is hard if you're not prepared. What is mundane and what is telling? One man's highlights are another man's edits. Max Taucher stared out one of the windows as I talked.

A hefty young man came into the room, a tablet in his hand and a stethoscope hanging around his neck. Langdon Bissett, RN. Big hands, polite shake. He motioned Mike to a far corner, where they had a brief, hushed talk.

"They talk behind my back all the time," said Max. "I don't really care."

The nurse excused himself. Mike brought coffee and we talked shop. An address found in Hector's home had led San Diego JTTF to a Chula Vista storage unit containing bomb-making materials and instructions. And ten formerly dummy U.S. Army hand grenades repacked with gunpowder. And one still-in-the box Baby Coo at You doll that could make five different baby sounds at the squeeze of any hand, foot, or its tummy, and came with four ready-to-wear outfits.

"We're burying Joan here in San Diego on Friday," said Lark. "She would have liked you to come."

Max watched us with a stoic, faraway look that I guessed wasn't faraway at all.

"You're invited," he said without looking at me. "Joan has literally thousands of admirers, but she admired you."

A beat then, as we all no doubt thought of Joan Annabelle Taucher and how she had lived and died. A few years ago I took part in a Gold Star Families memorial ceremony on Pendleton, staged for the families and buddies of Marines recently killed in action. Young guys, brave guys, the 3/5 Dark Horse Battalion. That day on a hill overlooking the base and the ocean, I looked around me at the battle crosses—the boots and tags and rifles of the dead Marines—then at the heartbroken and the scarred and the blind and the amputated and the paralyzed, all remembering someone they had lost. It was the most wrenching and wretched experience I've ever gone through. Mountains of grief, unclimbable.

"Are your tenants traumatized?" asked Lark. "Joan told me a little bit about them while you were waiting for Caliphornia. The Ping-Pong guy, and the drone operator, and the funny old couple. And of course Lindsey Rakes. Joan was worried about them. With all of the . . . possible danger involved. Something about them affected her."

"They're a tough old crew," I said.

And that they are. Christmas Eve day they had all pitched in to help me scrub the blood and related matter off the pavers, patch and paint the bullet holes in the walls and the palapa uprights, and replace some of the barbecue bricks and tiles. Clevenger, who had apparently apprenticed as a mason before turning filmmaker, got that barbecue looking good again in less than a day. Burt replaced the window that Zeno had blasted through on his quest to defend Lindsey. The Ping-Pong table, which had been folded in half, covered, and rolled far under the palapa against the next round of rain, had taken ricochets that tore six ragged holes about a foot inside each baseline. I ordered a new one—Merry Christmas from your landlord—and it had arrived just this morning, before I'd come to Taucher's home. Liz made Moscow Mules for the work party. Dick wandered from project to project with advice and direction.

"Mike? I'm tired," said Max.

"You've been up since sunrise."

"Wake me up as soon as that storm hits," he said.

Bissett and Lark got Max into his wheelchair. He was a tall man and it took the two of them to do it. His legs were wrapped in a Pendleton Indian-patterned blanket. The nurse backed him around to face me and the old man nodded and gave me another slow salute. His pale brown eyes caught the muted light coming through the curtains and I saw that they were the raptor eyes of his daughter, clear and intent as they studied me.

"It's the love you make," he said.

"I'll bear that in mind," I said.

"That's how I got Joanie. She wasn't like anyone else in the world. I should know. Now they took her away from me."

"Come on, Mr. Taucher," said Bissett.

Lark walked me to my car. America's Finest City stood proudly before us, scrubbed clean and bright by the storm. A bright orange and blue passenger jet came in from the southeast and seemed to thread the buildings. A vigil for the agents and visitors killed in last week's attacks in San Diego, and for Joan Taucher, was set for this evening on the *Midway*. Already the streets were jammed with motorists trying to park. Sidewalks filled with people bundled in heavy coats, toting folding chairs and blankets. Cops in cars and on foot and on horseback. Hundreds, it seemed. The police and media choppers dipping low, coming and going like bees.

"Joan liked working with you," said Lark. "She knew you could do things that our hands were tied on at the federal level. You saved a lot of lives when you broke into that storage unit and found the guns and the attack plans. We wouldn't do that. Joan said thank God for good outlaws."

For a brief moment I pictured the *Glorietta* dinner ship gliding across the bay while hundreds of the unsuspecting partied and two men down in the little hold got their balaclavas on and their weapons ready.

"She always kicked herself for not telling the people she liked that she liked them," said Lark.

"I didn't understand you were close to her," I said. "Until now."

"We're private people."

I studied Lark, his hair tossed by the wind, his twenty-four-year-old face, his hard brown eyes, not unlike Joan's.

"I loved her. Very much," he said. "Still do and always will. She was so intense. So vivid. So absolutely funny sometimes. Seventeen years between us. But I knew that woman. And I actually made her happy, occasionally. Max and I connected right off, though sometimes he thinks I'm the son he never had. Joan was afraid I'd find someone younger, and she told me she would never let me get my eyes checked or buy a pair of glasses. That was one of our standing jokes."

I felt a great relief that Joan had more than her job and her demons. Much more.

"It crushed her when the SAC showed her the door," Lark said, an edge to his voice I hadn't heard before.

"Will you stay on here with Max?" I asked.

"Sure," said Lark. "We've got our routines, and twenty-four-hour care. Max inherited this house from his parents. And lots of money. It's his world. Joan grew up in it. She loved her mother, who died young. Leaving her a daddy's girl, all the way."

"I'm glad she had you."

"Please come to the service," said Lark. "Joan would have liked that."

"I'll see you there."

Lark nodded, let his eyes wander my face for an unhurried moment, then turned and walked back toward his house.

Later that day I decided to get that beautiful red sports car out of the barn and say hello again. I keep her clean and covered and the battery charged and the tires full. Fuss over her quite a bit sometimes. But I hadn't driven her since the day I brought her home from Fallbrook Airpark.

By now it was afternoon and the wind had come up, bending the cat-tails near the pond and swaying the big oaks and sycamores. So when I steered her outside into the daylight she shined as she always had—red, beautiful red—the color of passion and desire.

When is the time right and when is it wrong?

I let her idle while I cleaned the windshield. Got back in and set the mirrors right and chose a CD from Justine's wallet, still on the passen-ger seat.

Took Old 395 fast to I-15, tore south a few clicks, spun off the free-way, and gunned her back up the country roads, the Porsche flat through the turns and the engine screaming for more, shot under the freeway, back over it, then scorched Lilac to Old 395 again, all the way up to Reche to Live Oak Park, always Justine's favorite, hugging those curves while the oaks high-five above you, the asphalt coming fast but the car true, then south again on the back roads to home and the final roar up the drive and into the barnyard, where stood Burt and Clevenger, poised to jump for their lives as I slid the Porsche across the grass at them and drifted long to a stop, neatly lined up with the open door.

L ater I poured a provocative bourbon with a splash of water, put on a heavy coat, and took the drink down by the pond. Daylight was fad-ing on this brisk winter afternoon. I watched the big sycamore leaves zigzagging down.

I dug the business card from my wallet, given to me by the elegant woman with diamonds in her ears and a green dress and a faux-mink stole at the Treasures of Araby who claimed to love the scar on my face. Who had recognized me from news coverage the year before and almost blown my cover.

WYNN RENNER AGENCY

Talent, Media, and Performing Arts

I turned the card over: "Sorry. Do call."

So I called.

She seemed genuinely surprised and happy. Her voice sounded practiced. Formal. I pictured her face and her cinnamon hair and blue eyes. We had one of those highly energetic, free-range conversations only interested strangers have.

"You certainly have a flair for getting yourself into the news," she said.

"I'm hoping to stay out of it for a while."

"But seriously," she said. "What terrible things are landing on us. On our city. Our republic. I haven't been sleeping well at all. Looking over my shoulder. Afraid of things I was never concerned about before. Wondering just how fair I am. How brave I am. Or am not."

"But do you dance?"

A long pause from Wynn Renner. A soft clearing of throat. "I love to dance."

We made a date for Saturday. When I rang off I felt as if I was back in high school, getting my first brief green light from Trudy Yates. Which was like jumping off the edge of the Grand Canyon and discovering you really could fly.

As the sun set I closed my eyes and thought a short prayer. There is a god to believe in, though I don't know much more than that. Not sure I need to. You chart by your beliefs and fly accordingly.

I gave thanks and was concise and clear and not demanding. Finished, then listened for the voice of God and heard what I always hear.

God's silence.

And it was good.

When I opened my eyes, the western hills were plated orange on top and purple below and the pond was spangled with gold.

Oxley lay in a shaft of sun a few yards in front of me, licking a gracefully extended hind leg. Toes splayed as cats do. He paused and stared at me, his eyes hypnotic green in the falling light.

ACKNOWLEDGMENTS

With true thanks to the San Diego division of the FBI for their help and patience, and the Islamic Center of San Diego for their graciousness.